Dance of the Broken

Dance of the Broken

Jacob Grovey

Global Genius Society, LLC

Copyright © 2016 by Jacob Grovey

All rights reserved. No part of this publication may be reproduced, distributed, or transmitted in any form or by any means, including photocopying, recording, or other electronic or mechanical methods, without the prior written permission of the publisher, except in the case of brief quotations embodied in critical reviews and certain other noncommercial uses permitted by copyright law. For permission requests, write to the publisher, addressed "Attention: Permissions Coordinator," at the address below.

Global Genius Society
www.GlobalGeniusSociety.com
info@globalgeniussociety.com

Ordering Information:
Quantity sales. Special discounts are available on quantity purchases by corporations, associations, and others. For details, contact the publisher at the address above.
Orders by U.S. trade bookstores and wholesalers. For orders: www.globalgeniussociety.com
Published by: Global Genius Society

Cover Photography: Korenn Grovey, Kokovisions Photography

Cover Design by: Mike Madden, Mike Madden Design

Editing by: Chris O'Toole

Library of Congress Control Number: 2016908377

ISBN-13: 978-0-9910633-6-9

First Edition Printed in the United States

This book is dedicated to everyone who understands the value of hard work. It is for those who have found the strength to move towards their goals even when it seemed pointless.

2 Chronicles 15:7
But as for you, be strong and do not give up, for your work will be rewarded.

Table of Contents

Part I (Age 6, "And so, it Begins")..1

Part II (Age 15, "Growing Pains")..47

Part III (Age 18, "The Anger of 18")..124

Part IV (Age 22, "California Love")...264

Part V (Age 25, "Life's Next Chapter")..307

Part I

     We all have a moment that seems to start a series of changes in our lives. My moment happened during my 6th birthday: our house was filled with my friends from school, my relatives, and even some of the families who went to church with us. It was awesome! I remember my mom bringing out the cake she spent all night trying to get perfect. It was shaped like one of my favorite cartoon characters. It was colorful, filled with sprinkles, and it made all of my friends go crazy!

     Everyone liked the way the cake looked, but there was no denying we all loved how it tasted even more. After what seemed like only a few seconds, the cake was completely gone. We all were dancing around with leftover frosting on our faces (including some of the adults). My mom just sat back and smiled while my dad tried to capture every second he could with his camera.

     With the cake gone, I stared at the huge pan that had been completely full only moments before. I had convinced myself I would be able to use one of my birthday wishes to make some more cake appear, but that obviously that didn't happen.

     "Since the cake's gone, do you think it's time to open your presents?" my mom asked.

Her question somehow made me forget about the dessert I wanted. It was as though I had no choice but to think about all of the possibilities of what I was about to get from everybody.

     I remember looking at the huge pile of gifts stacked in our living room. It seemed like I was staring at a mountain of greatness! I'll be honest: as excited as I was at that point, I can't even remember what most people gave me that day. Looking back, most of what was given to me is now just a blur, but there were some stand-out gifts given to me by my family. One of the things I actually remember getting was a beautiful dollhouse. It had bedrooms, bathrooms, televisions, garages, and it even came with two sport cars. Normally, something like that would have easily been my favorite gift, but that year was different. That year my little sister (who was four years old at the time) spent her entire life's savings (about $15) to buy me something.

The smile she had on her face was huge, but she was so tiny, she struggled to get her gift over to me.

"Here, sister."

My sister and I hardly ever called each other by our names. Normally, we simply said "sister" and I loved it. I had no idea what my sister had gotten for me. All I knew was, whatever she had for me, she seemed to be very proud of it.

When I took the box out of her hands, she started getting so excited; people could have easily thought she was the one getting the gift. At first, I took my time opening the box just because of how anxious she was.

"Hurry! Hurry!" she yelled.

Her little four year old voice went up even higher than normal, and it was super cute! By that point, I was just as excited as she was, so I quit playing around. I tore off the remaining wrapping paper as quickly as I could. When the box was opened, I immediately started crying. Even though my sister was only four years old, the gift she gave me showed she had been paying very close attention to me.

She knew I loved watching all of the shows that had anything to do with dancing. I never said anything to anyone about wanting to be a dancer, but she knew. So, she spent all of her money to buy me a ballerina's tutu.

"Why are you crying?" she asked.

"I'm crying because I'm happy."

The face she made when I said that was priceless. She seemed to be very confused to see someone crying when they were happy.

"You're happy?"

"Yes, sister, I'm happy!"

I heard everyone jokingly say "awww" in the background. They were obviously trying to make me feel embarrassed, or ashamed, but it didn't bother me at all. I gave my sister a hug and told her I loved her.

"Love you, sister. Now you can be a lallalina."
Hearing her try to say "ballerina" made that moment even more special.

A few days after my birthday, I found myself carrying around that tutu as if it were glued to my hands.

"Elise, are you ever going to use that thing, or are you just going to hold it forever?"

My mom would ask me some version of that question almost everyday. I usually said nothing. I would just give her a nervous smile and a slight giggle. I did that because it usually would stop the questioning for the day. It usually bought me some time to actually come up with a reason (other than pure fear) why I was not actually trying to do anything with the tutu other than hold it. I knew my mother would not really accept my saying I was afraid to follow my dreams, so I couldn't force myself to say it.

One day, the smile and giggle routine became unacceptable to her. She decided to take it upon herself to finally move things forward.

"Guess what, baby?"

"What's going on, mom?"
She was quiet for a moment as she handed me a small piece of paper. She broke her silence only to tell me to read it. I did what I was told and I read what was handed to me. My heart sank in my chest as I looked over the brief amount of information. I was both excited and scared out of my mind.

"So, what do you think, Elise?"

My mom had a smile on her face as she asked me. I knew any type of negative response would not go over very well. So, I tried my best to match her level of glee as I responded.

"I think it's awesome, mommy!"

"Good. Well, I've already called to make sure there's still an available spot for you, and thankfully there is! We have to meet with your instructor before the classes start for all of the new students."

I immediately became more anxious. I couldn't believe my mother had actually forced me to take a major step towards me becoming a dancer. I'm pretty sure I would have never done anything to learn the art of ballet alone (besides watching it on TV). I guess my mother recognized that. She knew my shyness sometimes held me back from doing things I wanted to. She obviously knew I was the type of person who sometimes needed a little push to get things accomplished, so that's what she did.

In what seemed like the blink of an eye, a few days had passed. I didn't even have time to mentally prepare myself to get ready to jump into something new. Before I knew it, my mother was walking me into the dance studio (along with my sister). Jasmine was way more excited than I was. People would have sworn she was the one ready to start her first class, not me. My mother smiled because she had been waiting on that moment for a while. I, on the other hand, was not really in a smiling mood.

When we walked through the door, everything started to hit me. The studio, while small, was still much larger than I thought it would be. I could tell it had been there for a while because parts of the floor creaked as we walked on it. The lights were so bright they almost scared me. I was literally frozen for a few seconds. Once I was able to move again, I looked around at all of the other girls in the class. Even though it was supposed to be a class for new students, it seemed like everybody was far more prepared than I was. They were doing stretches and moves that made me feel lost even before we officially got started. If that weren't enough, I noticed that, outside of my family, I was the only person of color. That had never been the case for me and it made me feel very strange.

I looked everyone in the room up and down. I noticed their hair and their rosy cheeks. I expected the members of the class to be a little bit different than me because I had never seen a black girl doing ballet on TV, but their appearances got to me for some reason. I had never thought of myself as being a big girl. I thought I was an average build, but seeing everyone else made me feel very different about myself. They all looked like models and I didn't fit that mold.

Also, I think things really hit me when I looked down at their feet. Before that moment, I thought ballerinas only wore pink because it was pretty, but I was wrong. From what I could see, the color was chosen because it closely matched their skin. I almost wanted to cry. I felt myself beginning to shake very nervously. For a moment, I actually had to tell myself to breathe.

"Sister, you're better than them!"

My sister Jasmine was always so great at helping my confidence and her whispering that to me was just one example. She always had the uncanny ability to say the perfect things at the right moments.

"She's right. I'm sure once you get used to being around everyone, you'll be the best dancer," my mom said.

My family was so great! As soon as my mother said what she did, she (and my little sister) gave me a hug. Just like that, my nervousness started to disappear and the shaking stopped.

Even though I wasn't as nervous, I was still a bit caught up in the bright lights as one of the instructors introduced herself and took all of us into the actual room where the lessons would be taking place.

"So, are you ready?"

I was so intrigued by my new environment. I heard the question, but I didn't really realize anyone was specifically talking to me. So I said nothing until the question was repeated.

"Young lady, I asked you a question. Are you ready?"

I was silent for just a moment longer before I said anything, and then, all of a sudden...

"Yes! I'm ready!"

Once again, I found myself watching my sister jump up and down. My mother smiled, but didn't say anything.

"This will be your home away from home," the instructor, Mrs. Mears said.

"Now, I'm not gonna lie to you. If you are here because you think this is just gonna be something fun and easy, you need to go ahead and tell your mothers to take you home right now!"

I couldn't believe this was the first impression this lady wanted to make. Some of the same girls who seemed so confident only a few minutes before, started crying. I could tell my nervousness wanted to come back stronger than ever, but I wouldn't allow it. For some reason, at that moment, the desire to actually become a dancer took over.

"Nope! I don't need to go home. I wanna dance!"

At that moment, at that very young age, I officially requested what I wanted for my future. I said it loudly because I not only wanted my mom, Jasmine, Mrs. Mears, and the other girls to hear me, I wanted to make sure God heard me. Even though I knew He sees and hears all, I felt the need to repeat my statement just to make sure.

"I wanna be a dancer!"

My mother, now smiling even harder, looked at Mrs. Mears. She moved away from where she was and closer to my new instructor.

"You heard my daughter. Now, are you going to be able to help her?"

My mother was no longer in the viewing area the parents normally stood in, but it didn't seem to bother Mrs. Mears at all. With a look that straddled the line of arrogance and confidence, Mrs. Mears smirked.

"There is absolutely no doubt I can."

By that time, every pair of eyes seemed to be focused on me. I wasn't the one who normally enjoyed being the center of attention, even when I was the reason why everyone was focused on me. I immediately started to second guess myself. I began to regret what I had just said.

My heart started pounding so hard that I felt like everyone could hear it. Mom stopped smiling. She knew something had started to steal my joy and she was not having that. With a serious look on her face, she kneeled down and whispered in my ear.

"Do not let their stares shake you. Even before you have learned how to dance, they can feel your greatness. They can feel you are special. They don't know why you're special, but you know what?"

"What, mommy?"

"They don't have to know. As a matter of fact, you don't even have to fully understand it yourself. All you have to know is, God made you special. He has given talents to all of us and we will all see that dancing is your God-given gift!"

"But how do you know?"

"Well, baby, sometimes a mother just knows what she knows."

That was more than a good enough answer for me.

The rest of my first class was amazing! Granted, I didn't really do much dancing. Instead, I started to learn about dancing positions. I learned about why my teacher danced and the dedication it would take. I started to hear some of the things I would need to actually have the future I wanted. The whole time my mother and sister were cheering me on like I was performing a solo in front of the entire world. I didn't know it then, but that day changed my life.

During the following classes, I saw my skills starting to grow exponentially. I also noticed the disdain the other girls had for me growing as well. I got along with some of the other girls with no issues, but Paula was definitely not one of those girls. It was obvious from day one she was the alpha female, at least in her mind.

My family had raised me not to just blindly follow anyone and classmates were no exception. I totally understood she supposedly had more experience than me and I respected that, but somehow we were in the same class. So, regardless of what she had done before, we were both classified as beginners. My goal was not to anger anyone, though. I simply wanted to learn all I could so I could become the best dancer possible. My goal was not to just blend in like normal; my goal was to become number one.

As time continued to pass, I kept feeling as though I was genuinely making progress. The positions and moves I found to be incredibly difficult at first were becoming almost second-nature. First position through fifth position were no longer feeling as uncomfortable as they were at first. Sautés, pirouettes and almost everything else were becoming as easy as doing simple pliés. I had to thank my family for my quick improvement. Every time I had class, my mother or father (sometimes both) were there with my sister loudly expressing how proud of me they were (even though they weren't supposed to). My instructor never really told any of us how good (or bad) we were doing. She just wanted us to continue to work harder.

"Work as hard as you think you can work, and then work harder!"

That's something we heard at some point during almost every class. Many of the girls hated when she said that, but for some reason I appreciated it. Sure, I would sometimes sigh heavily when she spoke (just like everyone else), but I understood the importance of the message. Even at a young age, my parents taught us hard work would always pay off, so thanks to that, I was already very familiar with the concept.

Every day I went to dance class, I was extremely focused. On the days I did not have class, I made myself focus even more. Before my mother enrolled me in the class, I thought I liked dance. After I got started, I found out I loved dance. After a few more classes, Mrs. Mears asked us a question.

"So, who's ready to show their families what we have learned so far?"

Some of my peers were excited about the idea of having some sort of dance demonstration, while others seemed to be scared out of their minds. I, surprisingly enough, was more towards the former. The thought of having my family see how far I had come in such a relatively small amount of time seemed great to me.

When the announcement of the date and time were initially made, I had no idea what role I would have in it all. As a matter of fact, I had no idea what the demonstration would really even be about. None of that seemed to matter, though. Mrs. Mears could have told me I would be a tree who didn't actually dance at the very back of the stage where I wouldn't even be seen, and I still would have been excited. I knew if I really wanted to advance as a dancer, I would have to take advantage of every single opportunity that was presented to me.

Now, I smile whenever I think back to that first performance. The evening it happened, I remember having butterflies in my stomach. I was nervous, but it was not because of a lack of preparation. I think that day I grew increasingly more nervous every time I peeked out from behind the curtains and looked out at my family. Jasmine was sitting in her chair swinging her legs while she was trying to be on her best "big girl" behavior. My mom was reading over the few pieces of stapled paper that was serving as the program of the events. My dad, well, he was hilarious. My mom convinced him to wear a tie and he was constantly adjusting it. He made it obvious to everyone around him that ties were not a part of his everyday routine.

"Elise! Will you please quit looking through that curtain? I promise you will be able to see all of the people very soon," Mrs. Mears said firmly, but with a smile on her face.

Somewhat reluctantly, I did what I was told. Once I finally quit looking out of the curtains, I went over to visit with a few of my friends. While we were mostly being encouraging to one another, Paula wanted to make sure she was not. When I first met her, I thought she didn't like me, but as we all had more classes together I discovered she didn't really seem to like anyone. I thought maybe nobody ever approached her or tried to become her friend, so that evening I tried to change that.

"You've done this stuff like a million times already. You're not even scared, right?"

I thought she would have understood I was just trying to start a conversation. Common decency should have made her at least respond, but none of what I thought were common seemed to be present at that moment. Paula looked at me as if I were crazy or something. My parents taught me I always had to try my best to not allow the words, actions, and emotions of others dictate how I was, so at that moment I had to put that into practice.

"Well, I know you're probably in the zone, so I won't bother you. I just wanted to tell you to have a good show!"

Again, I got no response; at least I know I tried. After trying to have the conversation with Paula, I went back to the group. Before I knew it, Mrs. Mears (and almost our entire class) were all holding hands in a circle.

"I don't know if any of you girls pray or not, but I would like to say a prayer before we get started. Is that okay?"

Some of the girls nodded silently while others yelled out our affirmations.

"On second thought, I take that back. It would be great if one of you would say something. Don't worry, you don't have to be a professional. Just speak from your heart and God will help you through it."

For some reason, many of us had our heads down at that point. We looked up only to find ourselves looking at each other waiting for a brave soul to volunteer. Nobody did, so I slowly raised my hand.

"Thank you for volunteering, Elise. Go ahead."

I almost immediately regretted my decision, but I was not going to shy away from it. So, without knowing what I was going to say or how I was going to say it, I got started.

"Dear God. Ummm... today is very, very, veeerrrryyy important to us. We all worked really hard in practice and we just want to have a good show. My dad and mom...wait, I mean...our moms and dads are all out there and we just want to make them really happy with huge smiles. And uh… please God, I know this is not for everyone, but please let my little sister be proud of me. She used her money to buy my first tutu and I don't want to let her down. Thank you for listening, God. Hope you enjoy the show!"

By no means was I the person who generally prayed for everyone, especially publicly. I couldn't even say I was the type of person who really prayed for myself privately when being told to--- at least not at that point. But for some reason, something made me want to try. After I said what I felt I had to say, I felt better. It was like God either calmed me down or He distracted me enough to forget I was even nervous in the first place. Whatever it was, it not only seemed to work for me, but for everyone else as well. I remember everyone smiling and giggling like they had absolutely no fears, nor any worries. Well, everyone except for Paula. She just stared at us very intensely. I remember thinking, "If she had lasers for eyes, we would all be burning."

I didn't know if she didn't believe in God, us, or all of the above, but I believed in her. There was no denying how good she was and I knew if she didn't do well, the performance wouldn't go over very well. So, I felt the need to speak to God again.

"God, please help Paula. I don't know why she's mad, but please help her be happy."

It seemed like as soon as I finished the rest of my prayer, Mrs. Mears was telling us it was time for the show.
We heard the sound of the lights being turned off in the auditorium. A few seconds later, we were all out on stage dancing our little hearts out. Paula was up front. As much as I didn't want to admit it, she was the best dancer and that was where she was supposed to

be. The crowd was going crazy with every little basic move any of us pulled off without falling down. We were enjoying each and every moment of it, too. The applause made us feel like we were Baryshnikov (even though at that point I seriously doubt any of us even knew who that was).

I looked at the crowd to see my family's reaction as the show came to a close. I chuckled a little when I saw my parents jumping up and down as they pointed at me. I felt like I had made them proud, and by doing that, I was proud. Then I saw my sister. I was expecting her to be doing even more than my parents were. I expected her to loudly proclaim I was her sister and how great she thought I was. I admit, I was possibly thinking too highly of myself, but normally when either of us did anything positive, the other one normally went crazy over it.

It didn't happen that time, though. She wasn't jumping, she wasn't standing, she wasn't yelling. In fact, she wasn't even smiling. Instead, she was just sleeping. My father quickly told me she had worn herself out by cheering for me. That made sense, but as much as I wanted to think about how my family viewed my performance, I didn't really have much time to think about it at that moment because something else caught my attention.

I noticed how sad Paula looked. In my mind, she had no reason to be anything other than ecstatic. I mean, she was the star. She was the girl most of the other girls in our group would have traded places with in a heartbeat, but she just stood there after the show by herself. I don't know why I felt I had to be the one to try and help everyone be happy, but it had always been a part of my personality. So, even though I was not friends with her by any stretch of the imagination, I felt compelled to once again go and speak to her.

"I know we've only been in class together for a little while, but..."

I didn't really know what I was supposed to say, or even if I was supposed to say anything at all, but I continued.

"My name is Elise. Umm… you did really good! I hope I can be as good as you one day! I'm gonna keep practicin'!"

"Thanks."

I couldn't believe all she gave me was a one word response. She didn't even crack a smile. It was okay, though. I didn't allow the feelings of whatever was going on with her spread to me. I also felt whatever was bothering her could not be "cured" in one day, so I told myself I would continue to extend the branch of friendship out to her.

"Girls, I know you all want to go to your families so you can go home, but could I speak with you for a moment?"
We all gathered together.

"I will make this very short. The show you all put on today was great! I am so proud of you girls and the work you have put in, but you need to know we can always get better. We will worry about improving during class, though. For now, you all are free to go ahead and enjoy your families and the rest of the night."

We all ran as if we hadn't seen our parents and siblings for years. I did so mainly because I really wanted to see what everyone thought of my performance. I'm sure everyone else's reasons were fairly similar.

"Sister, daddy, mommy, did you see me? How did I do? I know I can get better, but this was my first time on stage. But I'm going to work and work and work some more! I'm gonna get so good and I'm gonna make everyone proud and one day, I'm gonna buy you a huge house and you will never, ever, ever have to work again!"

By this point, my sister was still fully asleep and my parents stood silently as they let me run a ton of words together, almost completely disregarding actual sentence structure.

"Baby, you did a wonderful job! We are very proud of you, we always are. As for buying us a house and all of that, it sounds like a wonderful idea, but there is no need for you to worry about things like that. We just want you to keep dancing as long as it keeps you happy."

"Yeah, Elise, we just want you to be happy. When you grow up, we want you to love what you do for a living. If you love to dance, just work hard at it and become the very best you can be," my father said.

My parents were awesome! I knew the level of support they showed was not something everyone had and I was very grateful for it.

"Well, I really like to dance and I really like the idea of being able to take care of you one day. You are the best parents anybody could ever have and I just you to know it!"

As my dad held my sleeping little sister, he and my mother gave me a huge hug. They were squeezing me so hard I could barely breathe.

"Sorry about that, Elise. I know you don't like it when we squeeze you like that, but we are just so very proud of you and everything you do."

"Thank you, Mom! Thank you, Dad!"

We all were smiling from ear to ear. I looked at my sister.

"I can't believe Jazz is sleeping, though. She usually is running around all night tryin' to stay up as long as she can."

"Yeah, you're right. Today, I guess she was just so excited she got to see her big sister dance, it just wore her out. Tomorrow your sister will be back to normal," my mother said confidently while still smiling.

I grabbed her hand.

"Can we go home?" I asked.

"Yes, baby. We sure can. Do you need to go and tell your friends bye first?"

"No ma'am. I'm okay."

And with that, my first performance experience was over. It was so much better than I could have ever imagined, but I immediately wanted to experience it again. It was at that moment I no longer wanted to be a ballerina. That was the moment I knew I had to be a ballerina.

The next day, things started to change for me. I always loved school, but for some reason it seemed different. I continued to do my work to the best of my abilities and I listened to everything my teacher had to say, but I found myself constantly thinking about dance. I was either replaying the performance in my head, or I was practicing my dance positions (even while sitting). All of my classmates started to look at me strangely. At first, it didn't bother me, but when the people I thought were my friends questioned me, I began to feel very hurt.

"What are you doin'? Why have you started to do all of those weird moves?"

"I'm just practicin'"

"Practicin' what?"

"My dance."

I remember seeing frowns take over people's faces.

"Your dance? What do you mean? That ain't like no dancin' they do on TV!"

I felt bad for my peers. They really thought the only type of dancing was what they saw in music videos. They thought if it wasn't something that was popular or trendy, then it wasn't "real dancing". I remember putting my head down on my desk because I quickly found myself regretting even mentioning what I was doing. Then, things got exponentially worse when a few words were yelled out by someone I thought was my best friend.

"You're stupid and so is that dance!"

I was so confused. I didn't understand why my friend would say something like that. Did she really mean what she said? Did I do something to upset her? Was she just trying to impress the new group of girls who had started hanging around her?

It seemed like I had a million questions in my mind and I didn't have answers to any of them. The week before, Tracy and I were best friends and almost like sisters to each other. The week before, we would have never even thought about speaking a negative word about each other. Well, at least that was what I thought. I found out my thoughts and reality were sometimes very different. It was during that time I started to beat myself up internally because I felt so bad. I mean, how could someone who was like your sister turn into someone who would loudly talk badly about you, just to get a few laughs from some girls she hardly even knew?

My negative feelings towards myself at that moment started to impact me physically. I felt like my stomach started to attack me. I put my head down on my desk hoping that would help, but it didn't. Things only started to get worse. My head started to get jealous of my stomach and soon it started to attack me as well. Then I heard a strong and powerful voice speak out to me:

"Get up!"

I tried to ignore the voice, but then it spoke to me again:

"Get up and wipe your face! Do not give them the satisfaction of breaking you!"

I didn't know who or what I was hearing, I just knew I couldn't ignore it any longer. I sat up very quickly and wiped the tears from my cheeks.

"Yes, Tracy, I was dancing."

She looked at me as if she didn't expect me to speak, but I continued.

"It may not be the dancing you like, but you know what? You don't have to like it, because I do!"

The easily impressed girls who stood by Tracy's side tried to hide their desire to giggle, but they didn't do a very good job of it. I looked at the clock hanging on the wall and noticed I had wasted five minutes of my recess time.

"Well, I'm about to go play. Y'all should come, too!"

Looking back, I'm sure my offer to everyone may have come across as anything but genuine, but I didn't mean for it to. My offer was very real, but it wasn't received well at all.

"We don't need you!" Tracy yelled out.

It was amazing to see how the other girls allowed Tracy to be their voice. It didn't really matter, though because it was during those few moments I learned more about followers and leaders. I learned those who are weak will follow behind anyone who will give them the time of day. I also learned leaders, contrary to what I thought at first, do not have to be strong. Weak leaders exist to lead even weaker followers.

I also realized when you're not even ten years old, for the most part, you don't really have a reason not to like those around you. At least, not in my opinion. The reason why we tend not to get along with people is because we end up creating controversy for no reason, or doing what others are doing (even if they don't have a reason for doing it). This realization helped me to quickly move beyond my friendship with Tracy.

"Ok, thank you."

I made my three word statement and stopped to see how confused all of them looked.

"Thank you for what?" one of the other girls asked.

I giggled before saying, "Thank you to everyone for helping me see Tracy is not really like my sister and she is not my best friend."

I second-guessed myself and wondered why Tracy and I were ever friends in the first place. I felt as though something had to be wrong with me, but I tried my best to throw away those negative feelings. I decided to quit wasting time and energy dealing with those who didn't want to deal with me in the first place. I decided simply to go about the rest of my day, week and month almost as if they didn't exist.

It would have been much easier if the girls just ignored me the same way I was trying to ignore them, but it didn't quite happen like that. Instead, I had to deal with at least one member of the group trying to verbally attack me in some way every single day. Each time it hurt, but the amount that it hurt dropped tremendously as time passed. Soon their little attacks became so insignificant that they finally realized it was a waste of time for them to continue.

I would go to school every day and try to maintain a positive attitude like I had always been taught to do. I was doing well for a while, but one day I just lost it. We were in the art portion of our day, so everyone was drawing and coloring. It seemed like there were no problems with anyone, but then Tracy had to ruin it all. She started pointing and laughing at me and I had no idea why. Of course, her friends soon started doing the same thing.

"What is wrong with you?" I asked very loudly as I stood up.

Mrs. Pauley, my teacher at the time, motioned for me to both calm down and sit down. I normally was a very respectful and obedient person, but at that moment I felt like I couldn't be myself. I was at a point where I just needed some type of answer.

"Why do you keep messin' with me? What did I do to you?" I didn't actually think she would respond, nor did I think my teacher would allow her to. I was wrong.

"We just don't like you! You think you're better than us 'cause you started dancin'! Well, you're not! You are ugly and stupid!"

I wanted to be as strong as I had been during the days and weeks prior to that moment, but I was unable to. Mrs. Pauley yelled out for everyone to be quiet. We all listened to her as the room became eerily quiet.

"This makes no sense. Tracy, you and Elise were once friends. Even if that is no longer the case, you both need to respect each other."

She was right. The entire situation really didn't make any sense. It was clear I had no idea why our friendship had changed, but I didn't know if Tracy knew, either. I said nothing as our teacher continued to speak directly to us. The rest of the class just sat there, listening and observing the reactions of everyone else.

For a moment, I just began to think. I thought about how things were. During the early years of our lives, we think when we tell each other we'll be friends forever that that will be the case. The truth of the matter is, when you're that age, you haven't started to live long enough to begin to understand the concept of what forever truly is.

Our teacher continued to speak and I continued to remain silent. I accepted the seemingly harsh words she was dishing out, at least for a moment. Then, all of a sudden, I lost it again. That time, I didn't stand up and yell. Instead, I just cried as if someone had hit me. The more I tried to stop, the harder I cried. It felt like the eyes of everyone in my class were glued to me. The rest of my school day was a blur, so I can't really recall what happened. When I got home, my dad (who was at home early for some reason) could immediately tell something was wrong.

"What's bothering my Lisey-poo?"

He would mainly only call me Lisey-poo if he felt we needed to have one of those heartfelt "daddy-daughter moments". It was true we needed to have a talk, but for some reason I wanted to pretend we didn't. I guess I wanted to be strong even thought I was having a moment of weakness.

"I'm okay, daddy!"

My eyes couldn't make contact with his. I hated lying, especially to my family. I didn't want to add some trivial little girl problems to whatever adult issues he had going on.

"Elise, are you telling me the truth?"

His question was the most simple, yet difficult question I had ever heard.

"Umm...no. I'm sorry, daddy!" I'm not tellin' the truth! I'm sorry! I'm sorry!"

"Calm down. Take a deep breath."

I did as I was told. He soon picked me up and carried me to the living room. Jazz was sitting on the couch, swinging her legs happily as she watched one of her very silly cartoons. We both sat next to her.

"I want you girls to know something."

My sister and I both looked at each other, not really having an idea of what our father was about to say. I was a bit fearful I was going to get yelled at, and for some reason, it seemed like Jazz was too.

"I want you to know I love you very much. Did you know that?"

We both giggled, but we didn't say anything.

"Yeah, it's true. I love you... aaaaaannnnddd... I love you!"

He pointed at us as he smiled, which quickly put me at ease.

"And I know you haven't learned this yet, but when you love someone, you sometimes have to help them out when things are not-so-good. Do you know what I mean?"

I knew he was talking to me. It was time to just come clean and let him know I was hurting.

"Daddy, why don't people like me anymore?"

I wish I knew what my father was thinking at that exact moment, the moment before he had a chance to get his thoughts together, but I didn't. I just knew his smile disappeared very quickly. His face showed the pain I was feeling that day and I hated to see it.

"What do you mean?" he asked.

"Well, since I started dancin', I have less friends. Tracy doesn't like me anymore and she says I'm weird and she says I'm ugly! And she has all of the other girls follow her around and talk bad about me, too! Today, I started cryin' in class and all of the other kids were looking at me funny."

He hugged me and then Jasmine did the same thing.

"Do you know the difference between ordinary and extraordinary?" my father asked.

I had heard the word before, but I wasn't quite sure of its actual definition.

"Umm, no, not really."

"Well, ordinary is regular. It's the type of stuff you see everyday. It's common and not unique."

"Okay..."

"And extraordinary is what you two are. Extraordinary means you are unique."

I still didn't quite understand the word was a positive one.

"So that means we are weird!"

I was ready to cry again, but I didn't because my father wouldn't really let me. He continued to explain.

"I don't know about you, but I don't want to be like everyone else. I want people to be see I'm different and ask how they can be like me."

I knew he was trying to make me feel better, but I didn't know if I was ready to embrace the positivity.

"But how come my friends don't like me?"

Jazz had been surprisingly quiet until that question was asked. She then felt it was necessary for her voice to be heard.

"All of my friends like me and we always play together!"

I don't know what type of intent my sister had by saying that, but it was actually quite insightful.

"And that's along the lines of what I was going to say to you, Elise. If that girl Tracy or any of those other girls were actually your friends, they wouldn't be treating you the way they do. That's not how friends treat one another. To Jazz's point, friends like each other. They also accept the difference of others," my father said.

"But daddy, it was like that at first. What happened? Did I do something wrong?"

He leaned over and gave us both hugs and kisses on our foreheads.

"Let me explain something to you: everyone in this family is different. I am different, you two are different and your mother… now she is very different!"

We all laughed for a moment, but then I remember saying something that quickly changed the mood of the room:

"Daddy, if being different makes my friends not like me, then I just want to be the same."

My father shook his head.

"That's the wrong way to look at things. If your friends don't accept you for being who you are, then they shouldn't even be given the title of a friend because they don 't deserve it. "

That moment was like an epiphany. I initially didn't agree with the concept of accepting your own differences. I thought we were supposed to pretty much be the same, but then I realized how boring the world would be if we were. It was like the light switch was turned on at that moment.

"So... it's good that I'm not like them?"

My father looked around as if he heard a strange noise. Crazy enough, because he did it, my sister and I did the same thing. We had absolutely no idea what we were looking for, but my sister and I laughed uncontrollably for some reason.

"Can I tell you a secret?"

I had almost forgotten I had asked my father a question and now he was asking me about a secret. I didn't know what he was about to tell us, but he was great at distracting me from my issue.

"Sure! I love secrets! I'm the best secret keeper!" I yelled out very excitedly.

"Well, not only is it good that you're not like Tracy and the rest of those girls, it's great! Don't tell anybody, but I don't think anybody wants all of the little girls in the world to act like a bunch of Tracy copies. That would be....well, that would be just so... ewww!"

He started to laugh and once again, we did too.

"Yeah, Tracy is a yucky, stinky, doodie-head!" Jazz said.

"You're right, sister. She's a doodie-head!"

Without saying anything more about the matter, I felt 100% better. Having the power to make my problems seem non-existent was one of the many reasons I absolutely adored my family.

"Thanks, dad. Thanks, sister."

"No, thank you for not being a doodie-head!" my father jokingly said.

As we laughed, the phone rang. My father, still with a smile on his face, got up to answer it in the other room. I could no longer see him, nor could I hear him, but I could feel something wasn't right. Hesitating for a moment, I finally told my sister to stay seated as I went to go check on our father. I expected her to want to follow me, but surprisingly she seemed to have no desire to do so. She was battling sleep and she did not seem to be winning.

I got up and slowly went into the other room. My father's face was so blank that when I saw it, it almost scared me.

"What's wrong, Dad?"

He didn't actually answer my question. Instead, he just told me to get my sister so we could go. I became very concerned, but I didn't express anything. I did as I was told, and before I had time to think, we were in the car headed to a destination that was unknown to me.

During the time we were in the car, my father was breathing differently. It was as though the task was difficult for him.

"Daddy, why are you breathin' funny?" Jasmine asked as she tried to keep from falling asleep.

"No reason, Jazz. Please, just sit back. We're almost there." He didn't tell us what was going on or where we were going. I decided not to bother him because I saw questions were getting us nowhere. A few minutes later, we stopped.

I was still strapped into my car seat, so I couldn't see where we were at first. My father said nothing as he got my sister out of her seat and then did the same for me. Once we got outside of the car, I stood still and looked at our new environment. My heart felt like it left my body when I realized we were at the hospital.

"Daddy, I don't wanna be here! I wanna go home!" Jasmine screamed as she started to cry. It was amazing how she so easily expressed the sentiments I couldn't find the words for.

"I know you don't want to be here. Trust me, I don't, either." He took a deep breath and reached out for both of our hands as we started to walk inside.

We walked quickly and stopped at the information desk. I have always been a little bit on the short side, but I remember thinking that desk must have been made for giants. I wanted to try and climb up just so I could try to see more of what was going on, but I figured that wouldn't have been the right thing to do. So I just held my sister's hand as my father tried to gather information.

"Excuse me, could you tell me where Adeline Morgan is?"

Whoever he was talking to went through some papers and typed something on her computer before she said, "119."

My father still hadn't told us what was going on, but when we reached room 119, I found out why. As we entered the dimly lit room, I saw a tall cop speaking to someone. At first, I honestly couldn't recognize who the cop was talking to.

"Adeline! Adeline, baby, what happened?"

I remember being frozen. Adeline was my mother's name, but there was no way the person I was looking at was my mom. I tried to step in closer, but my father wouldn't really let me.

"What happened?"

My father was frantically pacing back and forth.

"Sir, are you Ian?"

My father ignored the cop and continued pacing. The cop was very patient and simply asked the question again. The second time, my father stopped and told him he was. They started to get into a conversation and I decided not to pay attention to what was being said. Instead, I tried again to move closer to the woman in the bed.

I stared at her in silence. She turned towards me and my sister. Then she silently gazed at both of us. Her eyes seemed to tell me everything while actually telling me nothing. After a few seconds, she started to cry. Although she didn't look the same, at that moment I knew who I was looking at.

"Mom, I love you!"

Of course I wanted to know what happened to her. I certainly wanted to know how throughout the course of the day she had gone from the beautiful woman we all were used to seeing to someone whose face had been disfigured and very close to being unrecognizable. Even with that being the case, I wanted my mother to know, no matter what she looked like on the outside, I would always love who she was on the inside.

She didn't say anything. I looked around the room and found a box of tissues. After grabbing a few of them, I gently wiped the tears from her face. She still hadn't made a sound, but a very slight smile appeared. I remember that smile was one of the most wonderful things I had ever seen. I rubbed her hand to comfort her, just as she had always done to me. I prayed for her, but I didn't know if I did it correctly. I wasn't sure what I was supposed to say or how I was supposed to say it, but I hoped God understood me regardless.

"Mommy, you're sick, but it's okay. We'll take care of you."

My little sister always said and did the most caring things. She was so nurturing and her sweetness was so infectious.

"Baby, are you okay?" my father asked as he stood very close to my mom.

His questions were rhetorical. They were also so stupid that they were almost upsetting. I guess he was so shocked at whatever had happened to his wife, he didn't really know what to say. I can understand that now, but back then it didn't make any sense to me at all.

With the exception of Jasmine, it seemed like none of us in that room could get our thoughts together. I found out how easily shock can create chaos out of your thoughts.

"Adeline, we will be okay. I promise! I promise you we will!" What my dad verbalized at that moment was not really what I felt he wanted to say. I didn't know much, especially at that age, but my father's eyes showed several different emotions. They showed concern, but they also showed a desire for revenge. He always talked about how my mom was the love of his life and it was easy for everyone to see when she was in pain, the way she was in that hospital… it really bothered him.

The police officer, who was still in the room for some reason, walked over towards my father.

"Look, man to man, I can only imagine what type of thoughts are running through your mind. I know this is your wife and as a husband, I know it's our job to protect our wives. With that being said, I advise you to not act on anything you're thinking about right now. Let the law and the Lord take care of whoever did this. You just worry about taking care of your wife and those wonderful little girls."

Those words stuck in my head. For the first time, I actually witnessed a cop show that he cared for someone in the community. I know he had the best of intentions, but I also believed he was lying to my father.

The job of an officer is to ensure the safety of the people. Better yet, their job is to make the people feel like they're safe. At that moment, he did what he was supposed to. My father, sister, and I felt justice would eventually be served in some way. Perhaps it was naive, but optimism will sometimes bring that out in all of us.

After a little while, the cop left the room. My dad said nothing. He looked like he was holding back tears while trying to control his rage.

"Dad, did he tell you what happened to mom?" I asked.
He put his head down.

"Somebody robbed her. She tried her best to fight back and this happened."

I was so confused. I didn't understand why she would do that. Why wouldn't she just let the thief take whatever materialistic item he or she wanted?
I looked over at my mom. I moved a little bit.

"Mom, can I ask you something?"
She still didn't say anything. She just looked back at me and nodded.

"Why?"

The one word was all that was necessary. My question baffled my mother. She was beaten so badly we didn't even really know if she could speak, but we all waited patiently to find out. She cleared her throat. If nothing else, we knew she was about to at least try to speak her mind.

In a very difficult to hear voice, she said, "I wanted y'all to know a woman can be strong."
I didn't understand exactly what she meant, so I knew Jasmine didn't either. I hoped someone would keep the conversation going so we could get some clarity about her words and her actions.

"Babe, you have to be one of the strongest women I have ever seen in my life! You don't have to prove anything to anyone! These girls know who their mother is. Your strength and character has never been, and will never be in question by anyone! I know you're an adult and you will do whatever you want to do, but I'm begging you to never intentionally put yourself in danger again, especially just to prove something. We need you too much for this sort of thing to ever happen. What are we going to do if we don't have you? Please Adeline, please never do anything like this again! Please!"

My father wasn't one to completely run away from his emotions, but he got more emotional during that speech to my mother than I had ever seen before. I guess it was to be expected, though. Nothing like that had ever happened to our family, so he didn't really have time to rehearse his actions.

"Daddy, sooo when is Mommy coming home? Is it today? Or will it be tomorrow? Ok, ok, so when is it, daddy? We have to make sure she's okay. Right, daddy? We're gonna make sure she gets better, right?"

My sister was very inquisitive, but her questions (as usual) were very valid.

"Jazz, I don't have any answers for you, but I wish I did." He walked away from us seconds after saying that. He immediately started mumbling as he once again started pacing around the room.

"God, please keep me from going out there and doing something stupid. Please God, don't let me find out who hurt my wife! Please don't let me find who robbed her of her materials and her peace. Lord, right now I want to kill whoever did this to her! Please forgive me for my thoughts, but your word says we can come to you at any time, with any emotions. Please cleanse me of this negativity and give me strength for my wife and our daughters. In Jesus' name, Amen!"

I know he thought he had moved far enough and was speaking low enough we wouldn't be able to hear him, but his plan didn't work.

"Dad, would you really hurt someone? Did you mean that?" He was disappointed, not in my question, but in himself. He couldn't hide it, either.

"Could you two please come over here next to me?" Jasmine was starting to get sleepy again, so we slowly walked over to Dad. He had just sat down in a chair that was stationed in the corner of the room. He sat still for a few seconds before he pointed at my mother.

"How do you feel about her?"

I didn't know how I was supposed to respond, so I just spoke honestly.

"Mom is awesome! She's the coolest, and whenever we need her, she's always there!"

"That's exactly how I feel. Today, someone tried to hurt that awesome woman and I didn't like that at all. Now, it is completely wrong to talk about hurting anyone. I don't really want anyone in this world to be hurt or be a victim of violence. So, when I said that I wanted to hurt the person who did this, I didn't really mean it. Sometimes, as a man, I'll say things that are not right when someone has harmed my family. I apologize for you two hearing those things and I apologize for saying and even thinking them. I ask that you forgive me. I made a mistake."

    I felt compelled to speak for both my sister and myself.

    "We forgive you! Just make sure you ask God to forgive you. If you really mean it from your heart, He will!"
My parents took us to church all of the time, so God was very important in every aspect of our lives.

    When I was Jazz's age (around 4), I never really understood why we went to church so much. Truthfully, I mainly liked going because the music I heard while we were there made me feel good. Many times I didn't even understand what the preacher was talking about. I just knew whatever bad feelings I had, they always left whenever the choir sang. So I figured if the songs about God made me feel better, then maybe talking to others about God would make them feel better. That quickly proved to be true when I talked to my father about forgiveness. It was as though a very heavy weight had been lifted off of his shoulders.

    "I'm proud of you, dad!"

    He couldn't hide his confusion. It was easy to see he didn't understand why, at that moment, I would tell him I was proud of him. I really didn't know why, either, but something in my spirit said that was what was needed to be done.

    "Thank you, Elise. I needed to hear that. You really just helped your father out."
I smiled. My parents always did so much to help out everyone around them; it was great to return that sort of thing to him.

    My moment quickly passed when I looked over at my mother. Right then, she was watching everything we were doing, but she wasn't really saying anything. I wanted to know what was on her mind and what had actually happened, but at the same time I was somewhat afraid to try to find out anything. I was afraid to hear if my mother was having the same type of vengeful thoughts my father had. I also was afraid to get further confirmation that there were people in this world who valued things more than they valued the lives of other people. I actually got so afraid that I had to stop looking at my mother. I know that probably saddened her, but I had to.

Seconds after putting my head down because I couldn't face my mother, a nurse entered the room.

"I'm sorry, everybody, I just need to check on Mrs. Morgan." Everyone nodded, but none of us said anything. We stayed out of the way as she did her job. I kept hoping she was going to tell us my mother could go home that day, but it didn't happen. What would have been even better would have been waking up and finding out the entire incident was just a very bad nightmare. Sadly that didn't happen, either.

"I know you want to get out of here and go home with your family, Mrs. Morgan. Trust me, we want to get you outta here as quickly as we can."

She adjusted the machines connected to my mother. Then she took some type of tests. None of us knew what she was actually doing. We just wanted her to help my mom.

"Excuse me. May I ask you something?"
The nurse's face and reaction showed she wasn't expecting any questions. She also seemed a little annoyed by my father. Perhaps she was having a bad day. Who knew what was going on her?

"Yes, go ahead."
Sure, her words were positive, but her tone was not. My father needed information, so he was able to ignore her sarcastic way of speaking.

"Does she have any internal damage? Will my wife ever fully recover from whatever happened to her?"
She rolled her eyes very slightly.

"She will be okay. She possibly has some internal bleeding and some bruising. Fortunately, she doesn't have anything broken, though. Although that is great news, she's still been through a lot. Mainly she just needs to get plenty of rest."

Following my father's questions and the nurse's response, Jasmine decided she needed some more information.

"So, Mommy needs to go night-night?"
She was so sincere and serious about her question. She really wanted to know the best course of action to get my mother well.

"Yes, ma'am. If she gets her rest, she should be fine."
When the nurse respectfully answered my little sister, it made me forget about how horrible her body language was when she answered my father.

"So, when does she eat dinner and her snack and get to watch her favorite shows? Mommy can't sleep without her shows and snacks. She likes funny stuff and choc'late chip cookies!"

Up until this moment, the nurse had a serious look on her face, but Jasmine's words gave her no choice but to smile.

"Okay, we'll take care of everything. Don't you worry your pretty little head about anything. We'll make sure to take very good care of your mother."

"Okay, that's good, 'cause Mommy needs to get better real fast!"
I smiled and chuckled a little as I remained still, silent and just listened to Jasmine. Her heart was huge and it was amazing to be around her. At six years old, even I could tell how special she was. She was destined for greatness, and even before any of the greatness actually happened, I was very proud of her.

After all of the conversations, exhaustion had defeated my mother. She looked so peaceful as she slept. She had gone through a lot and even though we all wanted to talk to her, we were grateful she was able to get her rest. The nurse quietly walked out of the room as my father started pondering what we were going to do for the rest of the night.

My father put his head into his hands and said nothing. I wanted to talk to him, but I didn't know what to say. Jasmine, as always, wanted to talk, but I whispered to her to be quiet until dad talked to us. So, we were all quiet. The machines inside of the room competed with the sounds of nature that we heard from outside. It was as if the noises were competing for our attention as we acted like captivated members of an audience.

For a while, it felt like my father wasn't going to talk again. Then he broke his silence:

"You cannot spend the entire night here. I'm about to call your cousin to see if you two can stay with her and your aunt for the night."
It was not at all what I was expecting to hear.

"But daddy...."

He put his finger to his mouth to tell me to be quiet without actually having to tell me. It wasn't what I wanted, but I wasn't about to voice my disapproval for his decision. About thirty minutes later, Jasmine and I were being picked up by my favorite cousin, Laura.

Normally my sister and I would have jumped for joy at the opportunity to visit with her, my aunt, uncle, and their puppy, Tiger Rabbit Punch. Things were different that time, though. We didn't want to leave, but as my father moved his chair closer to my mom, we were reminded there was very little we had control over. He waived to us as we stepped out of the room. I don't think he said anything to us as we left because I don't think he was able to. It was yet another sad moment that I couldn't do anything about.

I couldn't enjoy myself while we were staying at my relatives' home. I just kept thinking about my mother and praying she would get better. Then, I pictured my father. I'm sure he spent the night holding my mom's hand as he sat in that uncomfortable hospital chair. My parents really cared about each other, so they were always willing to make sacrifices. It was a wonderful thing to be around. Even in those days they were teaching me about love without even trying to. So, that night I went to sleep happy that dad was there to watch mom, but I was sad because Jasmine and I weren't there with them.

Since Jasmine and I visited our family so frequently, we had clothes over their house already. As Jasmine and I were getting ready to go to school, the next morning, I heard my cousin's phone ring.

"Hello. No, everyone is already up."

I didn't want to eavesdrop, but I felt like I was being talked about in the conversation.

"No, they weren't any trouble at all. They were sleeping by the time we made it to the house..."

The conversation continued and I started to listed for any information regarding my mother, but I didn't hear anything. After a few minutes, I started to think my prior feelings on what would be discussed were wrong. I soon quit listening and just finished preparing for the day. I knew we would be leaving for school a little earlier than normal because our cousin had to take us by our house to pick up our backpacks.

"Laura, I have a question for you." Jasmine said as our cousin ended her phone conversation.

"Okay. What's up Jazzy-Jazz?"

"Umm... I just wanted to know why morning always has to get up so early? Why can't it ever sleep longer?"

We laughed very loudly at my sister's brilliant question.

"You know what? That's a very good question. I have no idea why it gets up so early."

Laura paused for a moment.

"Hey, Jazz..."

"Yes," she replied.

"Can I ask you a question?"

"Yep!"

"Why do you want the morning to show up later?"

She put her finger on her head as if she were deep in thought.

"Well, I just want more sleep 'cause a sista be tired!"

Talk about being surprised! Laura and I looked at each other and laughed even harder than we did at the question she asked a few minutes before.

"Where did you get that from?" I asked.

"I dunno. I think it was one of those TV shows where the girls use those words mommy and daddy won't let me say."

"But we aren't allowed to watch those shows."

"Yeah, I know, but sometimes when I'm sitting with mom, she goes night-night and then I'm still up and the shows come on TV. They are crazy and they say crazy stuff and sometimes they fight and they throw those red drinks and those weird glasses at each other and they take their shoes off and they throw them, too!"

The mind of a four-year-old is amazing, but the mind of the four-year-old version of Jasmine Morgan was so far beyond that. She was so comical when she wasn't trying to be and so wise beyond her years, no matter what the situation was.

The conversation continued as we left. We briefly visited our home and only ended our talk when we were dropped off at school. When I was alone with my sister, the happy Jasmine slowly faded.

"Sister, is mommy gonna be okay?"

I didn't know how to answer her. When I looked into her eyes, I saw a scared little girl. It made me nervous because I hardly ever saw her that way. I knew she wouldn't accept silence, so I had to say something. As the big sister, part of my job was to try to make my little sister understand things would get better— not only because we had our family, but because we had faith in God.

"Gimme your hands, Jazz."

She was confused. She had no idea what I was about to do, but she trusted me, so she placed her hands into mine.

"God, please help us. Mom is hurt, so please, please, please make her feel better so she can come back home. We need her and love her ver much..."
"In Jesus' name... amen!"

I continued to hold my sister's hand as we skipped into the school. For a very brief moment, I felt very guilty about not being able to do more for Jasmine, but then I thought about something my parents always told us: they said, "When things are difficult, you have to understand we can't change everything. We don't control everything, but God does! When we need help, we just need to ask Him. He will help us through any situation if we believe."

When we made it to Jasmine's classroom, she stopped and stared at me for a little while.

"Sister, I love you!"
I don't know why I started to cry, but I did.

"I love you too, sister!"
Then I gave her a hug. She acted like she wanted to break free, but I knew better. I held her with one hand and wiped the tears from my face with the other. I closed my eyes and silently thanked God for Jasmine, my father, and for the recovery of my mother. I didn't let go of my sibling until the warning bell rang.

"Sister, I have to go now. I'll see ya later!"
She just hugged me and smiled before we finally let go of each other and she went into her class.

We went our separate ways and went about our days. I don't know how Jasmine dealt with everything in her class, but I had a difficult time. I pretended to be focused as I answered the teacher's questions. I tried my best not to get upset as Tracy and her friends continued to verbally attack me for no reason.

Of course, they had no idea what I was going through. Even if they did, they probably wouldn't even have cared. Since understanding what was going on in my life at that point wouldn't have mattered to them, I didn't tell them anything. I also didn't want to give them the satisfaction of letting their words and actions get under my skin. So I tried to act as though nothing was bothering me, but that didn't work out at all. By the end of the school day, I found myself not wanting to speak to anyone. The hope I had at the start of the day was gone.

Despite how I actually felt, I knew when I saw Jasmine again, I would have to pretend I was not upset. Doing so could have made her lose whatever happiness she had as well. I could not be responsible for that. I kept that in mind as school ended and I walked towards the door. I had no idea who was going to be outside to pick me up, but I made sure I had a smile on my face (even if it was a bit disingenuous). My walk to the door was a very slow one that seemed to take longer than forever, but that was what I was going for. I was preparing myself for not only who I saw outside of the doors, but whatever news they had to tell me. As I walked, all I knew was that I wanted to see my father. If I saw him, it would lead me to believe my mother was better. If he was not there, it would make me think my mother was more injured than people said.

Crowds of people passed by me as I stopped at the door and just looked at it. Why couldn't I just face reality, whatever it was? Why was I being so stupid? The current (adult) version of me had questions the younger version had no possible way of answering.

Before I walked out of the school doors, I went over to the nearest set of lockers and sat down against them. I held onto my backpack very tightly. I was fighting tears with every passing second. I was probably being too emotional at that moment, but I didn't really have any control over it. Eventually the tears started flowing very freely.

"Are you okay, young lady?"
Some older, well-dressed lady (whom I didn't know) reached her hand out to me. She seemed so genuine and so caring, even though I was absolutely sure she had no idea who I was.

"Yes, ma'am. I'm okay."

A slight smile appeared on her face.

"Well, I'm just old and maybe I don't understand kids and your emotions, but you appear to be crying some of those 'sadness' tears. Back in my day, when we had those type of tears, it wasn't because we were feeling good. I guess things are very different these days."

Maybe I didn't know the word sarcasm at that time, but I understood the concept of it. Normally sarcastic comments are used to make someone feel bad, or maybe even stupid. This lady's comments didn't seem to be coming from a negative place at all. Her smile made me smile and since I stared smiling, I stopped crying.

"I'm really okay."

I grabbed ahold of her hand that she still had stretched out in my direction so she could help me up.

"Well, I'm glad you're okay."

"Yes ma'am."

"Very good. If you ever need me, my name is Mrs. Henderson. What's your name?"

"Elise."

"It was very nice to meet you, Elise. Try to keep those sad tears off of your face and go ahead and go home to your family." I hoped she didn't find it weird, but I gave her a hug before I finally walked outside of the door.

When I got outside, I stood still for a moment. I looked around for our car as I listened for my father's voice. Sadly, I didn't see or hear what I was looking for. Instead, I heard jazz music playing nearby. When I looked to see where it was coming from, I saw it was my aunt. As with my cousin, I was happy to see her, but my response wasn't the same as it normally was.

My walk, once again, became very slow. My aunt got out of the car and met me halfway.

"Hey, baby! How are you?"

"I'm good."

"You wouldn't lie to your auntie would you?"

Aunt Katie was like a human lie detector test. If anyone around was telling anything other than the truth, she would know it. That time, I'm sure, was much easier to detect than others.

"Sorry, Aunt Katie. I'm not good, but I'm not bad."

"I know, I know. You were hoping to see your mother, weren't you?"

I didn't want to lie to her again, so I didn't. I said nothing. I put my head down, as if in shame.

"You don't have to say anything, Elise. I can only imagine what type of thoughts have been running around in your head all day. I'm sure you were hoping you would end your day by coming outside and seeing your mother, healed and home from the hospital. Does that sound about right?"

I remained silent, but I nodded my head to confirm her theory.

"I'm sorry, baby. Sometimes life doesn't always play out the way we want it to, but we can never give up on it. Does that make sense?"

"Yes ma'am. I just want mommy to be okay."

She put her arm around me and walked me to the car. She fastened me into the backseat and we started to head toward her house.

"She'll be okay. Do you think your mother would let some stupid robber stop her?"

Without hesitation, I answered: "NO!"

"Well, if you know she won't let a robber stop her, why are you so sad?"

"Because maybe mommy..."

"Maybe your mother what?"

"Maybe she won't be the same. Maybe she... I don't know. I just don't know, Aunt Katie."

My aunt didn't say anything else. I couldn't really understand why, but she didn't. She turned up her music a little bit. It seemed like I had upset her, but I certainly wasn't trying to. Maybe with her being my mom's big sister, she couldn't think of her little sister being hurt. Maybe I made her think negatively about something when she was trying to force herself into only having positive thoughts about. Maybe I just messed things up.

I was sad when I got into the car, but I became increasingly so the further we went without speaking. I had upset my aunt and she was one of the few people in the world I never wanted to do that to.

"Auntie..."

Admittedly, I used my "cutesy little kid voice" hoping if Aunt Katie was actually mad at me, she would stop feeling that way.

"Yes?"

"I'm sorry."

I saw her looking at me in the mirror.

"What exactly are you sorry for?"

That was another one of those moments when I wasn't exactly sure if there was something I was supposed to say.

"Umm....I'm sorry for saying that about mom. I didn't mean anything bad. I know mom will be back, so I don't know why I said that. Please don't be mad."

I thought she would tell me it was okay, or that she forgave me for what was said, but she didn't say anything like that. In fact, she didn't say anything. I was surprised, disappointed, and hurt. And although those emotions were present, I also could understand any anger or frustration my aunt had in her heart and mind at that moment, especially if I caused it.

For a little while, I wanted to say something else. I wanted to redeem myself, but I didn't follow through. I looked into the mirror to catch a glimpse of my aunt's eyes and when I saw them, I was frightened. The joy I saw in her eyes a few moments before were gone. I knew it was because of me. That hurt even more. I didn't want to deal with the pain I had caused, so I tried to make myself go to sleep until we reached her home. I guess I was trying to avoid any negative looks or comments. Sadly, the more I tried to go to sleep, the more awake I seemed to be.

Soon, I just gave up on it. Instead, I just stared out of the window. I tried to imagine how life was for all of the people I saw as we drove past them. I wondered why the homeless man on the corner was homeless. I wondered why the lady walking her dog seemed so happy. I wondered how the kids doing all of the tricks on their skateboards were brave enough to ever try the things they were doing. After looking at so many random people, I ended up looking back at my aunt.

I started wondering what life was like for her, my mom, and their three brothers while they were growing up. Mom always said they didn't have a lot of money, but they still had a great time because their house was so full of energy and love. Ours was just like that.

Just when my thoughts were happy enough to temporarily make me forget how mad I had seem to make my aunt, we reached her house. She got me out of my seat without saying a single word to me. The silence frightened me. I kept my thoughts to myself and I tried to do the same with my emotions. I put my head down and walked very quietly into the home.

When I walked in, my cousin spoke to me but something felt different. She smiled as she started a conversation, which made me feel better. Then my little sister ran over to me.

"Hey, sister! Guess what? Guess what? Guess what happened today?"

Jasmine always had so much going on in her head, so I had no idea what she was so anxious to tell me. I was very excited to hear the breaking news, though.

"Are you gonna guess?"

It was funny how quickly she was getting upset that I hadn't taken a guess about why she was so happy. So I finally started saying random things just to please her.

"Did you get a pony?"

"Noooooooo!"

"Did you win free toys?"

"Nooooo!"

"Okay, okay. I got it. Today, they made you the queen of the earth and they gave you a crown and a billion, trillion, zillion dollars. And with some of the money, you want to buy your big sister her own space to practice dancing!"

She slapped me on my hand as she continued to giggle.

"No! You're wrong, sister! Follow me, follow me!"

She grabbed the hand she had just slapped and made me follow her towards the living room. I was sure she was going to show me some new cartoon or something, but I was glad I was wrong.

What she had to show me was that our parents were there. I mean, it would have been a huge surprise to just see dad, but to see mom there as well was amazing! I certainly didn't expect it and the fact that I seemed to be frozen made that apparent to everyone. All of the eyes in the room were on me. I knew everyone wanted to see me run to my parents, but I couldn't. It was as if my feet were glued to the ground.

"I'm sorry I had to pretend I was mad at you," my aunt said, "but pretending to be upset was the only way I could be quiet and keep this wonderful reunion a surprise! Now, go over there and hug your parents!"

As soon as those words were said, I felt like I was released. I was finally able to move and I quickly ran to my parents and hug them as I was "instructed" to do.

"Mommy, daddy, I'm so glad to see you!"

"And we're glad to see you, too!" my father replied.

Then, I stood back and looked at my mother.

"How are you doing, mommy? Are you feeling better?"

She looked at me and I started to tremble and cry. I didn't know if she would really be able to talk, and if she were able to, I didn't know if what she had to say would be positive.

I waited for her to speak. Then, after seconds of nothing, she smiled.

"I'm much better, Elise. Thank you."

Even though we had only gone about a day without being able to hear her speak, it felt like it had been forever. Hearing her was like listening to an angel talk.

"Can I ask you something, Elise?"

"Yes, ma'am."

She beckoned for me to move closer to her.

"While I was in the hospital, did you pray for me?"

"Yes! And we prayed for you today while we were at school! We asked God to make you feel better!"

My mother was obviously was touched by what was said. She immediately started crying even more than I was.

"I thank God for my beautiful, wonderful little girls. Thank you! Do you two see what happened? You prayed to God and believed in your heart He could help me and here I am!"

I couldn't say anything after that. She was absolutely right. God was great, just like He always was. Everyone got together as shared a family hug. At first it was just the four of us, but soon, Katie walked over and joined in. Aunt Katie expressed how great she thought the family was as we all hugged. Nobody could disagree because she was right. I took a moment to look at everyone. Even at that young age, I realized things could have turned out much worse than they actually did. In spite of what had happened to my mother, we were blessed.

Soon my father found it necessary to address everyone in the room.

"This is a wonderful moment and all, but I think Miss Elise still has a dance class she needs to go to!"

We laughed, but he was right. I never wanted to miss dance class, but at that time, I didn't know if it was right for me to leave my mother so soon after she had gotten home.

Mom, always being the observant one, could see something was on my mind.

"What's wrong, Elise?"

Her question made a million questions start to cross my mind. Should I speak? Should I say nothing? I tried to process the various reactions to the different things that could be said, or the reactions to me saying nothing.

"Nothing's really wrong, mom."

"I know better than that. Let me guess what's really on your mind. You're probably wondering if I will be okay with you going to class because I just got back. Am I close?"

She was exactly right and I felt incredibly guilty.

"Yes, ma'am. You're right! Maybe I shouldn't go today."

She shook her head in disappointment, almost synced with everyone else in the room as if they had practiced it or something.

"One of my greatest joys is seeing my girls do things they love to do. When Jasmine is drawing and coloring, she is so happy. And when you are dancing, it's a thing of beauty!"

"So it's really okay for me to go?"

My mother not only told me she wanted me to go, she pretty much insisted that I did. Then she pulled me in even closer to her and she whispered in my ear. She tole me as I went through life and pursued my dreams that there would be plenty of things that would try to distract me. She made me promise her, no matter what life tried to throw at me, I would never let anyone or anything make me give up on what I wanted to accomplish. She made sure to emphasize nobody should be allowed to throw me off course.

I agreed, but in my heart I really didn't know if I could live up to what was said. Who was I to think I would be strong enough to turn away from distractions? And if I couldn't, would I be able to handle letting my family down? It was actually amazing how the state of confusion I was in at that moment brought forth a level of focus. That focus told me (once again) I didn't just desire to dance, I was destined to.

Later, while I was in class, I had an extreme level of enjoyment. The work was difficult, but it didn't matter. I felt like things already had a greater purpose. There were moments we were stretching and we were all getting yelled at. It didn't even bother me. Of course the words stung a little, but I was more encouraged to keep going when I looked and saw my father smiling. If that weren't enough, seeing my mother holding my sister encouraged me even more. Having them there as my personal cheerleaders reminded me how great life really was. It was funny that I got to a point where I almost wanted to hear my dance teacher yell at us more. I know that sounds strange, but I knew (for the most part) when a person had that much passion in what they were trying to tell you, it meant they cared about what you were doing.

The yelling and constant work made the two hour class pass by very quickly. All of my peers were exhausted and most of them just were just anticipating the end of the day. My family waited for me as we were dismissed. Through my gestures, I silently asked them if I could have a moment to speak to my instructor. My father nodded his head and granted me permission. I walked away from the practice area and towards Mrs. Mears.

"Excuse me, Mrs. Mears."
I couldn't tell if she was just ignoring me or if she just didn't hear me. So, I tried again, but the second time I decided to pull the ever-so-annoying "pull on the clothes of an adult, so they can pay attention to you" trick.

"Excuse me."

She turned around. The look on her face was so stoic it was scary. It didn't matter, though. I had questions and I really was hoping she would be able to answer them honestly.

"Yes, Elise. How can I help you?"

"I wanna know a few things and when I ask, please don't just be nice to me because I'm a little kid."

I could tell she didn't really want to be bothered with me (or anyone else from class) at that moment. I fully expected her to tell me to leave her alone, but she didn't.

"Okay. So you're asking for honesty in my response?"

"Yes, ma'am."

A slight smirk appeared.

"Okay young lady, go ahead."

I was nervous, but I continued.

"I just wanna know... do you think I'm a good ballerina? Do you think one day I can be on a stage and dance with a lot of people and have everybody watching?"

The smirk turned into a full smile.

"So you want to be a professional? Don't you think that will take years and years of hard work? Are you sure that's what you want?"

I didn't understand why she had to ask me a bunch of questions before she answered mine, but I guess the motives didn't really matter. I answered what was asked in hopes she would simply do the same.

"I know it's gonna take lots and lots of hard work, but that's okay. My heart tells me I want to be a dancer forever and my mommy and daddy and sister are all proud of me."

You would expect that to be enough of an answer, but it wasn't. So Mrs. Mears found it necessary to ask me even more.

"That's good, but what if you did all of that work and you were not able to get paid? What if you still have to have a regular job when you're an adult? Will you still have the desire to be a dancer then?"

I was confused. It was almost as though she was trying to convince me not to continue with ballet. I found that to be incredibly strange, but it also made me feel like she didn't think I was good enough. Once again I was presented with questions I didn't really know how to respond to.

I went from being confused, to sad, to almost being upset within a matter of seconds. I didn't know if I wanted to hear anything else she had to say. I almost wanted to cry, turn around, and just run to the arms of my family, but I didn't do any of that. My family hadn't raised me to be the "run away from your issues" type, so I would not allow negative words (or even the possibility of hearing negative words) make me want to give up. So I fought my feelings and made myself stand still and not only listen to what she had to say, but also force myself to answer the difficult questions she was asking.

"If I had to dance for free, I would, because I love ballet! I love how it makes me feel and I really love to see my family smile because of my dancing."

My comments stunned her. I didn't know what she was expecting me to say, but my words were seemingly different than what she was prepared for.

"How old are you, Elise?"

"I'm seven!"

If there were an age limit for the "hold your fingers up to show your age" thing, it probably had to be around six or seven. It was funny how I was acting like a kid at the same time I was trying to verbally respond as if I was an adult.

Mrs. Mears pointed to my parents.

"Those two have done a great job with you."

"Thank you!"

"You're very welcome, but that's not all I have to say. You said you want to know if you should keep dancing, right?"

I nodded.

"The short answer is you absolutely should! There's more to it than that, though. I've seen very few starting students catch on to things as quickly as you have. It's quite astonishing."

"Thanks!"

Admittedly I didn't really know what astonishing meant, but all of the other words were positive, so I could only assume that one was too.

"I want you to know something. You have a gift, as we all do. The man upstairs will one day allow you to do great things in this world with ballet. So I have to ask you to promise your teacher something."

"Okay."

"Promise me no matter what happens while you're growing up that you will never give up on your dreams. There will be times when you will want to throw it all away, but make sure you always find your way back. Don't let go of your goals, okay?"

"I won't let go of them. I promise!"

I was very surprised her words were not condescending, disparaging, or sarcastic. She spoke to me like I was a person, not a kid. Not as her student, but as a person. I appreciated that.

"Now go to your family and I will see you next class."
I had all of the answers I needed, but I also had more confidence in myself. I ran over to my folks. As soon as I got there, I found Jasmine had some questions of her own.

"Why did you stay and talk to your teacher? Did you do something wrong and get in trouble and you had to see if you were gonna be grounded from dancin'?"

"Nope! I just had to find out if I was good at ballet."
My mother, still a bit swollen and obviously sore, sat up and smiled as she started to talk.

"Of course she said you were great, right?"
My father joined in.

"You know he did, babe. Elise is an excellent dancer."
After my father spoke, I continued.

"Yes, she said I was good and no matter what, I should never give up on my dreams!"

Being humble and having a sense of humility was something that was instilled in me, so I didn't feel it was necessary to speak as highly about myself as Mrs. Mears did.

"That's wonderful, Elise! We are all so proud of you!"
I put my head down. I guess even though my conversation with Mrs. Mears helped me gain confidence, I wasn't really comfortable with all of the nice words directed at me. I certainly appreciated it, but I wasn't comfortable.

"I have dreams!" Jasmine yelled out as we walked out of the studio doors.

"What are your dreams, sister?"

"Well, sometimes I dream I'm a fish. I'm a pretty little pink fish with sparkles on me. And sometimes, when I'm swimming, I'll jump out of the water really, really high and people who see me are

like 'Oooh, look at that pretty fish. She's so beautiful!' And then I'm like 'Thank you!' And then they get scared 'cause fishies can't talk, but I can!"
She giggled.

"You keep that dream alive, Jazzy! That's wonderful!" Mom said.
We could always count on my sister to entertain us and keep the mood light, no matter what.

Judging by the smiles on everyone's faces at that point, I think we were all feeling pretty good. The feel good moments vacated very quickly, though. It was crazy that, even though my parents were always very vocal about how they felt about my abilities and although Mrs. Mears basically echoed their statements, I didn't know if I actually believed them. Perhaps I was actually so insecure that I couldn't even really hear when people told me I was good. Maybe I was just so humble, I could hear only enough positivity to keep me going, but not enough to make me think I was better than anyone else. I didn't know which was actually the case, but I figured when it was time for me to understand, God would help me do so.

What was actually concerning me was the fact that I knew how people felt about my abilities, and because of that, I knew what they expected from me. If they had expectations, then I would have to live up to (or surpass) those expectations, or I would be disappointing everyone who believed in me. To this day, I still don't know why I am never really able to allow myself to be in the moment. I am always thinking how one part of my life will impact another (or other people). I guess that's just how I'm wired, but I digress.

Later that evening, I tried to go outside of my character and just enjoy the moment as my family sat down to eat dinner. Of course, I wasn't able to. I couldn't just share stories and laugh like everyone else. That would have been too 'normal,' I guess. Instead I sat at the table and stared at them for a moment. I looked at my sister and wished I had her enthusiasm and zest for life. When I looked at my father, I saw a leader. Dad was the type to allow himself to be open to emotions. He wasn't really a fan of keeping things bottled up (at least not for too long) because he knew that would end up doing more harm than good. He didn't fear appearing weak because he knew he wasn't. When it was all said and done, his main concern was to simply follow God and do what was best for us. He was amazing! And my mother...wow! My mom had so much strength, it was just unbelievable. My family's unique characteristics made me feel inadequate and almost out of place. They never tried to make me feel that way. They only spoke positive words to me, so I honestly don't know why I ever felt like that, but I did (and quite often).

"Can I please be excused?" I asked.

Family dinners were very important, so it was considered very rude to leave the table without everyone else being finished, or at least asking to be excused.

"Sure you can, baby, but could you come here first?"
I didn't know what my mom wanted. I was actually kind of nervous, but I went over to her any way. She leaned over to me as she started to whisper:

"I love you, Elise, and there's nothing you can do about it!"
A grin took over her still swollen face, and just like that, I felt better.

"I love you too, mom."
I tried to whisper so only she could hear, but that didn't work. It should have been expected, though. I had been told on several occasions I was absolutely horrible at whispering.

I started to walk away from the table, but my sister felt the urge to say something to me. She waved for me to come over to her. Her face had an expression that a mix of many different expressions. It was like a combination of excitement and anxiousness with just a bit of a sneaky undertone thrown in.

"Yes?"

"Sister, I just want you to know..."
She paused. She wanted to make me wait on her words (once again). So, I did.

"I just wanted you to know...olive juice!"
We both laughed very loudly as our parents looked at us as if we were crazy. They didn't understand what "olive juice" was. To them, it was just nonsense between two sisters. To us, it was one of our very silly ways to say "I love you" to each other without actually saying it.

"Yeah, olive juice, sister." I replied.
We laughed even more as I finally walked away and into my room.

As the seconds passed, the smile on my face slowly faded away. I sat down in the corner of my room between my desk and my window. I did this whenever I wasn't felling well (emotionally or physically). I liked that spot because it was far enough away from the door to make me feel alone. It also put me in a position to see a small amount of sun or moonlight, even if the blinds were closed. That natural light would somehow always make me feel better. I didn't know why. I take that back; I knew it made me feel better simply because the Creator was responsible for it.

I sat in my place of solitude and I cried. I went into my room with a smile on my face (because of the words from my sister and mother), but I was actually still upset. My tears, however, were not born from that emotion. They instead were born from the sense of freedom the light provided for me. They were born because I stopped feeling inadequate and unworthy to be part of my own family. They happened because I started feeling thankful. They were because my family was awesome, and even though I sometimes didn't believe it, I was awesome too.

I soon became drowsy, so I wiped the remaining tears from my face and stepped outside of my room to say goodnight to my parents. When I went into the living room, my mom and dad were watching some funny-looking television show. Jazz rested comfortably on my mother's lap.

"Mom, dad..."
I startled them. I guess they thought I was asleep already.

"Yes, baby? Are you feeling better?" my father asked.

"Yes, sir. I'm feeling much better! I just wanted to say goodnight to everybody."

As if they had rehearsed their movements, they both motioned for me to come to the couch. It seemed like I was getting motioned to come over a lot, but it was okay. Once I moved, they hugged me as if I had been gone for years. I had no complaints. I enjoyed the fact my family had no problem expressing the love we had for one another. It was nearly impossible for a person to feel bad for themselves when the people around only said and did things to make you feel good.

My sister woke up.

"But how come nobody told me it was family hug time?" she asked, slurring her words as she tried to wake up.

Her ability to make everyone laugh at any given moment was uncanny and expectedly unexpected. We all exchanged our words of love and I went to sleep feeling great. God allowed me to rest with no worries, care-free and hopeful for what the immediate and long-term future held for me.

Part II

  I was fifteen. As expected, I was a very different person than I was when I was six or seven. My life no longer swung so freely from the peaks to the valleys based strictly on my emotions. It did, however, still swing based on my reality. I had a much better understanding of how life worked. At least, I thought I did. As much as I wanted to think nothing but good things happened to those who were "good people," I knew better than that. I knew life didn't exactly follow the rules we thought it should. I had already been given a real life example of that when my mother was robbed and attacked.

  It was bad enough that happened, but it was even worse that our local police department never found out who did it. I used to always ask my mom if that bothered her. She always told me she found it unsettling her attacker was never found, but she was not angry because she knew whoever that person was, God would be sure to take care of them. She said that thought always comforted her. Her faith was amazing and I don't know why, but even though I had faith, mine never seemed to be as strong as hers.

  My mother's attack wasn't the only thing that seemed to test my beliefs. By the time I was 15, I didn't know if the life-long decision I made when I was six was right for me anymore. My body was sore most days because of ballet. My muscles didn't just ache, they often times felt like they were on fire. It was more than uncomfortable, but I was still willing to make the sacrifice because of my love for dance. I was conflicted, though. Although I was still willing to give up a lot of things for dance, I still didn't fully believe in myself. Sometimes I even questioned the plan God had for my life.

I would envision myself being the center of attention as I performed a beautifully choreographed show, but then parts of my mind would tell me those thoughts were crazy. I found myself saying there was no way I could become a world-famous dancer because I wasn't good enough. I would also hear voices constantly tell me nobody from my city has "made it big" doing what I was trying to do, so why did I think I would be able to?

No matter what people are trying to do with their lives, we all deal with doubt. I understood that, but this was a time when I just started to question the legitimacy of everything I hoped and dreamed for. I felt the time and effort I was giving were not worth what I was getting in return.

One day, after a very difficult class, I found myself walking home very slowly. Something didn't feel right, but I didn't know why, at least not initially. Logically, I could have been moving the way I was because of class, but that didn't seem to be it. It didn't take long for me to find out what was going on. I got a call on my cell phone (which was still a big deal during those days).

Usually whenever I got a call, I ended up either just having an enjoyable, but pretty pointless conversation with one of my friends, or I ended up having to check-in with my parents. I didn't really like that, though. I was a responsible teenager and I didn't like them smothering me, but I had to realize them checking on me was the main reason I even had the phone in the first place. So, somewhat reluctantly, I looked at my phone as it rang.

The important phone numbers were stored in my phone. So, when I saw the word "Home" appear on the caller ID, I thought I knew the type of conversation I was in for. I quickly found out how wrong it was to make assumptions.

"Elise, where are you?"
My mother seemed very frantic for some reason.
"I'm on my way home. What's going on?"
She asked me another question without answering mine.
"How much longer do you think it will take you to get here?"
"It should be something like ten more minutes. Why? What's going on?"

She still didn't answer my question, which both annoyed me and made me very worried. Something was going on and I knew it was bad because she didn't want to tell me over the phone.
At that moment, it was as if all of my aches, pains, and soreness decided to vacate my body. I began running home so I could find out what had my mother acting the way she was. When I arrived, she was sitting in front of the television pretending things were normal. Her legs and hands were shaking. She didn't seem to notice I was even home until I was almost right next to her.

"I made it!"

She started crying, without saying a single word, as she hugged me very tightly.

"Where's Jazz? Where's Dad?"

Just as she did over the phone, she refused to answer me. It was getting increasingly frustrating. She just grabbed my hand as we left the house, got in the car, and started going towards a destination I had no idea where it was. The ride was silent. My mother said nothing to me and I had grown afraid to say anything to her. I looked out of my window and just sat quietly as the trees seemed to fly by.

My heart was beating so fast, my chest began to hurt. Honestly I didn't know if the pain was psychological or if it was real. I could feel the discomfort showing on my face. I knew my mother had to see it when she looked at me briefly during a stop at a red light. She acted as though she was going to speak, but she didn't. I decided I had enough.

"What did I do, Mom? Why aren't you talking to me? Where are we going?"

Seemingly with no regard to safety, she pulled the car over to the side of the road.

"I am so sorry, Elise. And no, you didn't do anything wrong. I'm very sorry for making you feel like I've been acting this way because of something you did."

She reached out and hugged me very tightly as she cried.

I still had no idea what was going on, but at least I knew nothing was my fault. I became more nervous, though. My mother's tears caused me to have some of my own.

"Mom, can you please tell me what's up?"

She wiped the tears from my face and then from her own.

"I wish I could, but I don't really know everything myself. And I don't know where to start with the information I have. So, let's just find out everything together."

She took a deep breath, fixed her mirrors, kissed me on my forehead and carefully got us back onto the road.

She smiled, but it wasn't a "real" smile. It was one of those smiles I had seen her and my father put on when they were being brave for us. Right then I knew she may not have had all of the answers to whatever was going on, but she sure knew a lot more than she tried to lead me to believe. I closed my eyes and sat back in my seat. I tried to allow my mind to go blank, but it wasn't happening. My thoughts were running all over the place, yet they weren't really focused on anything in particular.

I opened my eyes only when I felt the car had been still for too long for us to be at a light or a stop sign. My mom put her arms around me about the same time I saw we had reached the hospital. I hated hospitals, especially this one. This was the same place that not only diagnosed my aunt Katie with cancer, but the one that had people tell us they would do everything the could for her. They told us she would have the best care, but even with all of their promises, we still lost her. We lost the woman who helped our family so much when my mother was there. I absolutely hated that place! I tried to tell myself when that happened that I never wanted to see that place again, but as I sat in the parking lot, I saw I had very little control over what life would bring our way.

"Come on, Elise. I can't do this without you."

If I hadn't just heard her speak those words, I don't know if I would have believed her. Not because my mother was a liar, but because sometimes parents will say things to their kids to build up confidence, or to show they feel the child is important. The look in my mother's eyes showed she was being totally sincere. Whatever was going on inside of that building was already draining my mother. At that moment, she really did need me.

I jumped out of the car and ran to where she was. I grabbed her hand and helped her out.

"I got your back, Mom."

She wiped her face once again and smiled very slightly. Hand-in-hand, we walked into the hospital. We soon saw the information desk. My mother immediately asked the nurse behind the desk where Ian Morgan was. That was the first bit of information I had. Even though nobody was speaking to me directly, I knew something happened to my father. It would have done me no good to act like I suddenly understood what had actually happened, so I acted as if I knew nothing as I followed behind my mother.

We made our way to Room 209. I looked on the door before we entered. My father's name was on there along with some medical terms I really didn't understand. I felt terrible, but things got even worse when I saw the second chart.

"This is a mistake, right?" I asked.

My mom looked at the chart. She was unable to respond verbally. She just tightly held my hand and we opened the door together. I walked in with my eyes closed, not really having any idea of what was going on in the room. I remained silent and still for a few seconds. I heard machines alternating noises. Hearing everything frightened me even more than I already was. I quit putting off the inevitable and opened my eyes.

Slowly, I focused on two of the most important people in my life. It felt as though my world was moving in slow motion as I tried to comprehend what I was looking at.

"What is this?" I yelled out.

Everyone who was anywhere near the room heard me, but I wasn't actually speaking to any of them. My mother looked at me. It seemed like she was trying to come up with some soothing, comforting, "everything will be okay" type of word to tell, but she didn't do that. Instead, she just spoke what was on her mind.

"Elise, this is our reality. This is not some nightmare we will just be able to wake up from. This is life."

She was very calm with her delivery.

"Do you have any idea how this happened?"

I didn't know if she would answer. I didn't even know if she had an answer, but I waited.

"From what I was told, your father picked up Jazz from school. They were heading home when someone decided to not only go faster than the school zone limit, but also to run a red light. When they did, they did the whole "t-bone" thing to them."

I knew what I heard, but I didn't really know how to take it all in. It didn't make sense to me.

"You mean this is the result of someone's stupidity and arrogance? You mean this happened because someone chose not to follow the rules? Are you kidding me?"

I was very angry, but I knew my anger wasn't going to change what had already happened. So I calmed down.

"Mom, do they know who did it?"

"Yeah, I think they know, but I wouldn't be surprised if nothing happened to her."

Two things really stood out about what she said. First, I found it to be very surprising that even though someone knew who was responsible, my mother felt they wouldn't be punished. Secondly, I was surprised the person who did it was a woman. It was shocking, not because I didn't think women were capable of such things— the proof of that was literally right in front of me— but normally we are thought to be more caring. And since this happened near a school, I would have thought a woman would have been more likely to be extra careful because she didn't want to do anything that could possibly harm a child. Obviously my thought process was wrong.

"Why do you think nothing will happen to her? Look at what she did to our family!"

We stopped our conversation to take a good look at Jazz and Daddy. They both had those wrapping bandages covering most of their bodies. What wasn't wrapped up was covered with cuts, scars, and bruises. It was sad, and seeing them made me question my mother's statement even more. So I simply had to ask my question again.

"Why don't you think anything will happen?"

She didn't hesitate to give me a response.

"Elise, we live in a word that is far from being fair. Look at us. Look at our family. We are just a hard working family and we all are just trying to live the right way. Yeah, we're chasing after our dreams, but in the grand scheme of things, the world doesn't think there's anything special about us."

Was she right? Maybe, but I still didn't quite understand what she was telling me. So I kept my mouth closed and my thoughts to myself just long enough so I could hear the rest of her explanation.

"...and not only that, we're black! Now, your father and I try our best to raise you girls with an understanding that racism does still exist, but we never try to use it as an excuse, or a reason why things turn out the way they do. This is a very different situation, though. See, I don't know for sure, but I heard the woman who did this is a very wealthy white woman."

My mother's monologue had gotten to a point where I felt I had to interject.

"But Mom, what does us being black and not rich have to do with anything?"

"Elise, simply put, in most cases when it come to rich white people versus not-so-rich black people, the white people will normally come out on top."

I can't lie, when she said that, the anger I had for the woman who caused the accident began to spread out to include my mother. How could she think this would end up being an issue of race? It was easy to see this was just a matter of right and wrong. The woman responsible for everything would have to suffer some type of consequences for what she did. I didn't want to think about her too much, though. I cleared my head of what my mother said and the thoughts of the woman I didn't know.

I had been in the room for a few minutes and hadn't even actually went to see my sister or my dad. So, I had to change that. My mother had moved closer to my father, so I did the same. I stood next to my mother (even though I was still very upset with her) and I looked at my dad before I leaned over and kissed him on his cheek. Honestly I expected him to open his eyes and try to talk to me right at that moment. It hurt very badly when he didn't.

"Ian, baby, we're here," my mom said.

It was easy to see she was expecting a reaction similar to what I was hoping for. I also was able to see she had some things she want to say privately to him, so I went over to my sister.

It was crazy. Jazz was just barely a teenager, yet there she was in a hospital bed.

"Sister, I am so sorry this happened to you. I wish it would have been me instead."

My mother heard what I said. She moved over to me and once again, she grabbed my hand.

"Why would you say something like that, Elise?"

My answer was given very quickly. It was almost as though I had practiced it.

"I said it because it's really how I feel. Look at her, Mom! She's thirteen! She doesn't deserve this."

"You're right, she doesn't deserve this, but who does? And think about this: I'm in the same hospital where my sister died. I'm looking at my husband and my youngest daughter fight for their lives while my oldest daughter says she wished it happened to her. How do you think that makes me feel?"

I thought her question was totally selfish, but I could also completely understand why she asked it. While the intent of my statement was for me to show I would do anything to make my sister get better, including taking on her injury, my mother didn't hear it that way. She just heard me say I would take on my sister's pain, which would have still left her with an injured daughter alongside her husband.

"My bad, Mom. I'm sorry. I just don't want my family to be hurt. Dad is like a superhero to me and I never thought I would see him like this. And Jazzy, that's my little sister. I'm supposed to be able to protect her! I failed! I failed you! I failed dad and I failed Jazz! I'm so sorry!"

That wasn't the first time I felt I was not only supposed to protect Jasmine, but my entire family. I don't know why, but I felt like I was responsible for everybody. In my mind, this was my second major failure. The first was not being able to stop my mom from being robbed and attacked. When I thought logically, I knew these things were beyond my control, but when it came to thoughts about my family, sometimes logic was nowhere to be found.

My mother hugged me as if I were still 5 years old. I didn't push her away, or act as if I didn't need it because I did. At that moment, I was not a teenager who was too cool to want to share an emotional moment with my mother. Right then, I was simply a sad little girl who needed her.

"Elise, you have never failed at anything. The things that have happened to our family have nothing to do with you. Bad things happen. That's life. I know you probably don't want to hear it, but some more things will probably happen in the future, just like they do for everyone else. You know what, though?"

"What?" I asked, anxiously awaiting her response.

"As a family, we will deal with whatever comes our way. We will not allow ourselves to get too high when we have our great moments, or get too low when the opposite happens."

Her words were comforting, but I couldn't tell if she even believed what she had just said.

We stopped talking. We just looked and Jazzy and my dad. The sounds of the machines monitoring their heartbeats mixed in with some machine that was helping my little sister breathe. A few more seconds passed and then it hit me: I didn't pray enough. I didn't speak to God enough and, well, perhaps this was punishment for that. I started to cry again. I was trying to hold them back, but I was losing the battle badly. Despite what my mother tried to tell me, she couldn't convince me our situation wasn't my fault and that I couldn't have done something to prevent it.

"I know you want me to be positive, Mom, but look at them. Do you realize our family will probably never be the same? When we all left the house today, that was it! It's all different now!"

"I can't disagree with you, because you're right. Our lives and our family will probably never be the same again, but however we turn out, that's just how we'll turn out. "

"But are we gonna be okay? I mean, are they gonna be okay?"

She stared at them. She didn't know what to say and how to say it. I didn't even know what I wanted to hear.

I may not have understood the words I saw on the charts that fully described my family's condition, but I didn't have to. My eyes showed me beyond the shadow of a doubt how they were. I really didn't know if I wanted my mother to lie to me, or just confirm what I already felt I knew.

"Baby, I would love to tell you I am sure they will both fully recover, but I don't want to say that because it just may not be true.

Now, don't confuse what I'm saying as me losing hope because that's not the case at all.
Right then, a doctor walked into the room.

"Are you Mrs. Morgan?"

"Yes, I am."

"Mrs. Morgan, do you mind if I speak to you alone for just a few minutes?"

If I didn't already know things were bad, that question would have let me know. I knew the doctor was probably asking to speak to my mother alone to guard me from the news, which was considerate, but it was not necessary. It actually was just another thing that made me upset.

"You want to speak to her alone? Maybe you don't understand that's my family, too! I'm not leaving this room! I need to know what's going on!"

My mother looked directly at the doctor and apologized for my rudeness.

"No, it is I who should apologize. I'm sorry, young lady. You should absolutely be informed about what's going on with your family if that's okay with your mother."

I looked at her. Neither of us set free a single word. She just nodded to give the doctor her approval.

"Would either of you ladies like to have a seat?"

That was yet another question indicating how bad things really were.

My mother sat down, but I chose not to.

"I won't disrespect you ladies by sugarcoating the truth, nor will I beat around the bush."

My mother put her head into her hands. With her face covered, she asked the doctor to continue, which she did.

"As you can see, your family is in critical condition. Mr. Morgan had cracked ribs and a punctured lung, but there could be more to it than that."

With her face still partially covered, my mother asked, "What about Jasmine?"

The doctor looked at the clipboard full of papers she had in her hands. She flipped through the pages a few times as if she were trying to change the information into something different.

"Mrs. Morgan, your daughter's condition is... well, her condition is more severe."

"More severe?"

She went on to explain in greater details what all was wrong with Jasmine. Every additional word she said about my sister or my father made me feel worse. I felt helpless. No, I was helpless. There was nothing I could do to make them feel better, to make them get up and walk out of the hospital, to allow us to go back in time and make it so the accident never happened.

I looked at my mom. Her eyes were a well of negative emotions. The tears flowed continuously. At first I questioned who was worse off between the two of us, but I think that was only because I didn't want to admit to myself I was in a better situation than she was. Sure, the people were extremely important to both of us, but her relationship was much different.

My father was the person my mother had been around the majority of her adult life. He was her first true love and, according to what she had told me on more than one occasion, he was the first man (besides my grandfather) who always showed her how valuable she was as a person. So, for her, seeing him helpless was different than it was for me seeing my father there. She said he had always been strong when she was weak and now, when he was weak, there was no way she could be strong for him. That hurt her a great deal.

And my sister, well, that was different as well. I loved Jazz. She was the coolest sister anyone could ever wish for. She inspired everyone around her, even without saying anything. Her smile always made me believe anything was possible, but seeing her in that bed, with her face not having a trace of her smile, made me doubt if that was true. I just felt she had to get better, though.

My mother was battling with keeping her faith and losing hope. Each second that passed made things worse. Looking at her youngest daughter forced her to realize something. She was facing losing the love of her life, her youngest child, or maybe even both. How would she handle that? How could she move forward in her life? And then, selfishly, I thought how her relationship with me would change. How would we act towards one another if we suffered a loss? How would things be different if we didn't?

I went to the corner. I briefly needed to be away from everyone. I needed a few more minutes to speak with God... alone.

"God, can you hear me?" I whispered very, very lowly.
I wanted to hear an answer, but I knew I wouldn't, at least not in the "regular conversation" sense of it all.

"Okay, I just need to speak with you. I know as much as we want things to be perfect, they're not. I just need to know: what are we supposed to do with this?"

I pointed at my mother first, and then to my father and sister. I wanted an answer and I knew God was the only one capable of providing that. I asked the questions verbally, so I was trying to hear God respond the same way. I waited, as if the response were actually going to happen the way I wanted. But again, I already knew any response I got would be non-verbal (if I got a response at all).

The doctor provided as much info as she could before she was called away. She excused herself from the room and once again it was just my mom and I, staring at my father and my sister as we wondered what was going to happen.

"Elise, I have a question for you."
I was shocked my mom broke the momentary silence of the room. I had no idea what she wanted to ask me, but I still pushed the conversation along by responding.

"Yes, ma'am. What's up?"
She wiped some of the leftover tears from her face.

"Do you remember that year we had your father's birthday party at that skating rink?"
A smile snuck onto my face as I started to recall that day.

"Yes, ma'am! That was a pretty awesome day! We all were just being so silly!"

"Do you remember when your dad swore he was the best skater ever?"
I started laughing.

"Yep, I remember that!"
"One minute he was skating backwards..."
"…and the next minute, he was on the ground, in the middle of everyone else with his hands and legs in the air asking for someone to help him up. Everyone laughed at that for days."

"Well, everyone except for your father. He didn't find that moment funny at all!"

For a few minutes, it almost felt like nothing was wrong. I prepared for my sister to jump into the conversation and say something to make us laugh even harder than we already were. That, of course, didn't happen. We also didn't hear the voice of my father asking us not to tell the story of his embarrassing birthday. We heard none of that. Instead, we heard our laughter fade slowly back into silence. Fond family memories of the past were soon replaced by the bleakness of our present.

My mother's lack of shock and devastation returned.

"Life is so crazy, mom. We always take it for granted until we come face-to-face with losing it," I said

I had no idea where the statement came from or why I said it. My mother agreed, though.

"You're right, Elise. We know tomorrow is never promised, but for some reason we always act like it is. If nothing else, this will certainly serve as a wake-up call."

"I don't know how to deal with this, mom. Are we supposed to still go to work and school like they are not fighting for their lives? Or are we supposed to stay here and let everything else we have going fall apart?"

"Elise, do you think those two would want us to stop everything and use them as an excuse for why we let our hard work crumble? How do you think Jazzy would feel if she knew you weren't going to ballet practice because you were here in this hospital?"

At first I couldn't really understand why my mother would ask me those sort of questions. Was she trying to make me feel guilty about caring? Was she already forcing me to think about life with my father and sister?

"You look confused, Elise."

My mother, like many mothers, could always look at their kids and tell what was going on inside of their heads, even if there was no facial expression to go along with it.

"I am confused! I don't know what you want me to say. I don't know what you want me to do."

"What do you mean?" mom asked.

I felt myself getting more tense, so I took a deep breath before I continued with our conversation. I didn't want possible misunderstandings lead to our talk getting off track.

"Well, it almost feels like you want me to act like I don't care. I can't do that! Maybe you can, but I can't!"

She stepped back a little. She looked at me, my father, and my sister.

"I'm sorry if my questions made you feel like that, Elise. That was not my intent at all. You three are the most important people in the world to me. So, there is no way I could ever even pretend like I don't care about any of you. That also means I would never want you to act like you don't care about any of us. Does that make sense?"

"Yeah, I guess."

During those moments, my mother caused my emotions to run all over the place. I was obviously sad because of the condition of my family, but at the same time, I was annoyed with my mother. Even if her questions had a purpose, it didn't matter to me. She was upsetting me. I didn't want to argue or cause any type of commotion in the hospital, so for the most part, I just started nodding my head, cutting my answers very short and agreed with what she was saying to me.

"Do you remember when I was robbed? Do you remember how everyone came to visit me? Even when I couldn't speak to you, I could hear you. When I couldn't open my eyes, I could feel your presence."

I wanted to leave the room because her words were confusing me. I didn't know if there was actually a point to what she was saying.

"If all that's true, why are you acting like you want us to leave?"

"I was just about to answer that for you. Although I appreciated every second you all were here, I didn't want you to put your lives on hold for me. I wanted you to continue doing the things that made you happy because, in turn, that made me happy. Elise, we will have many tragic moments in our lives. It is during those times the devil watches us very closely. He wants us to be angry, he wants us to be sad, he wants us to be emotional wrecks without having any trace of hope left in us. He loves it when we're like that. That makes him happy. So when I say we need to continue with our lives, it's not because I don't love my family. That couldn't be further from the truth. Nope! It's because I don't like the devil and I refuse to let him get joy from my family. I refuse to completely give up my hope. "

That's when things started to make sense to me. I was once again reminded of the unparalleled spiritual strength my mother had. Of course she was hurting because of the situation, but she would not let it all deviate her away from the positivity God wanted us all to be a part of.

"Mom, how can I be more like that? How can I not be mad at the person who did this? How can I keep hope?"

"Do you believe once it starts raining that it'll keep raining forever?" mom asked.
I wasn't sure of what she was getting at, but I answered anyway.
"No."

"I don't know if you realize it or not, but that's hope! So, we can be upset when that rain comes into our lives, but we can't think it will stick around forever. We pray for those sunny days, even if the forecast doesn't show it. In fact, we're supposed to give praise and thanks for those better days even before we get them."

"So we're supposed to be thankful right now?"

"Actually, we are. Elise, when that man robbed me, I felt broken, both spiritually and physically. While I was on the ground, waiting for someone to help me, a rejuvenated spirit seem to come out of nowhere. When it did, I realized that person may have hurt me and took some things away from me, but he couldn't take away my love, my joy or my faith. It may sound silly, but even while I felt broken, my spirit was dancing because I had so much joy. And that's what's going on now: our entire family is hurting, but what we all have to do is dance while we're broken."

I don't know why my mother chose to use the word dance, but I'm really glad she did. She was right: spiritually, emotionally, and physically, I had to find a way to dance while I was broken. That day was the very first time I ever heard that phrase, but I knew I would carry it with me for the rest of my life.

"Thank you, mom. I really needed that!"

"You're welcome, baby. I love you, Elise. We're gonna make it through this."

"I love you, too, mom."

I'm sure my mother didn't plan on giving such a long speech when she began to speak, but I was certainly glad it happened. Although I was spiritually lifted at that moment, I still understood the severity of our circumstance. My mother did too.

"Elise, will you pray with me?"

There was no hesitation before I answered, "Yes, ma'am."

Mom positioned us so we were both between Jasmine and my dad. I used one hand to touch Jazz, while the other hand was being used to tightly hold onto my mother. Her free hand was holding onto daddy. We bowed our heads and closed our eyes.

"Lord, we thank you for everything. We know the situation and we thank you in advance for getting us through it. We are not able to get past this without you and we won't even try. Guide us, God. Lead us. Give us strength during this time because we are very weak."

I didn't know if it was proper for me to add in a few words, but I had some things I needed to say.

"And God, we ask that you heal them. We know you can do things we can't even dream of. Please God, let us be able to dance while we're broken."

My mother didn't seem to mind that I interrupted her. She let me speak what was on my heart, then she continued.

"In the mighty name of Jesus, amen!"

My mother and I stood silently after our prayer ended. Our hands were still together and I kept my eyes closed. It felt like our prayer was the start of a conversation God wasn't quite ready to let end. So, even thought I wasn't actually hearing any words from Him, I was feeling them. My heart seemed to start overflowing with love and hope. My spirit felt lighter. I felt better, even though nothing had really changed.

Once I opened my eyes, it seemed like I was able to view everything differently. I no longer saw my family as steps away from dying; I saw them fighting for their lives. That change of perspective made a huge difference. I still knew the severity of everything, but I felt a little more at peace right then.

I inhaled and exhaled very deeply.

"You don't have to say it, Elise, but I know you feel better even though the situation hasn't changed. That shows the power of prayer."

I wanted to say something, but I had no idea what that was. Since I feared messing up the moment and taking away from the positivity that was now floating around in the room, I said nothing. In lieu of words, I just hugged my mother. It's crazy that there had been so many times I almost resented my parents and didn't really want to be around them, but whenever it came to the serious moments (like in the hospital), I quickly found out how much I still needed them. They were like my security.

"Elise, we need to figure out what we're going to do today," my mother said.

Her statement was confusing and it seemed to come out of nowhere.

"What do you mean?"

"Well, you can't stay here, baby. You have school and dance practice tomorrow."

I was disappointed in what she was telling me, but in a way, it was expected. Plus, whether I liked it or not, I knew she was right.

"Can I stay just a little bit longer?" I asked.
Reluctantly she said yes. After about an hour or so, we found ourselves headed back home. It was a very quiet ride, and for most of the ride, I just looked out of the window. It seemed like every building and every street reminded me of my family. Contrary to what I thought would have happened, the sights didn't make me sad. They actually made me happy.

"It's amazing, right?"
My mom had no idea what I was talking about.

"What?"

"It's just funny that all of these streets are reminding me of some great times we've had all around this city."
Mom agreed and for the remainder of the car ride we talked about what we called "The Adventures of the Morgans." Talking about the good times helped me get an even better understanding of what my mother meant by finding joy in the bad times.

When we got home, Mom let me know she was going back to the hospital; it was expected.

"Mom, I don't know if you should go back out there by yourself."

"I appreciate your concern, Elise, but I have to go back."

"Are you okay, though?"

"That's a good question. I don't actually know if I'm okay now, but I know I will be."

Although she was uncertain about how she felt at that moment, I was glad she expressed that honestly. It let me know I was not alone in my feelings. I was happy one second and miserable the next.

"Mom, why did this have to happen? Why don't I know how to feel?"

Niagara Falls couldn't compare to the waterfall my eyes produced. I wanted to stop the tears, but my eyes didn't seem to care about my desires.

"This whole thing is worse than a nightmare, Elise, but it's real. We can't wake up from our reality. And you know why this happened?"

"Well, I don't really know why. The 'why' doesn't even matter, though. If you knew exactly why all of this happened, how much would that actually change?"

I was at a loss for words. I think my mother said (and asked) what she did just to get me to that point. It didn't matter if I knew why everything happened because I don't think it would have changed anything at all.

My mother fixed a quick dinner and gave me my overnight instructions, as well as what she expected from me the next day, I started to focus on how I was going to handle myself throughout the whole ordeal.

Before I went to sleep that night, I prayed harder that I ever had before. With no one else in the house, I felt a freedom to talk to God like I had never experienced before. So I took advantage of that. The Creator and I had a very long conversation. He allowed me to yell without getting upset or resenting me for it. He allowed me to express the full range of my emotions without shaming me for it.

During the conversation, one of the things I remembered most vividly was when I begged God to help me make it through that situation. As if I were having a discussion with someone right next to me, I heard him say, "I'll help you through, but don't think it's going to be easy." Admittedly, I was almost disappointed in what I heard. I almost tried to convince myself I wasn't hearing the voice of God (even though I knew I was).

Then He provided me with a moment of clarity: if the situation I was asking God to help me make it through was incredibly difficult, how could the journey beyond it be easy? Once that was made clear, I once again felt a different energy. I was reminded that watching two of my family members fight for their lives meant I had to fight right alongside them. While my mother was showing strength, I had to do the same. Granted, each one of us was dealing with different battles, but we were a team. So their fight was mine and I knew that's the way it had to be.

When I woke up the next day, I still was on a natural high from the night before. I felt I was not only prepared for my normal everyday routine, but I was also ready for hearing news about my dad and sister (good or bad). It didn't take long at all for my positivity to be tested. When I got to school, Tracy saw me in the hallway. You would think whatever problems one child had with another when they were five or six would fade away as the years passed; such was not the case. Tracy's maturity didn't seem to grow as we did.

Just like when we were younger. I was able to handle her insignificant combination of cruel words (most days), but sometimes we all lose control.

"What's up, Elise?"

"Nothing, Tracy."

"I heard what happened to your family."

Her face had a look of what appeared to be genuine concern. I thought not even Tracy would use my family's situation against me.

"Yes, we are going through a really tough time."

She moved over to me and hugged me. For a moment, I thought the girl who used to be my best friend was returning. She held onto me. Then she decided she released her true character.

65

"I'm sorry your folks got into an accident. And I'm sorry whoever did it wasn't able to finish the job."
She said some horrible things over the years, but I didn't think she was capable of reaching that level.

"Wait! What did you say?"
I pushed her off me.

"You heard me. They would've been better off if it would've ended already. I feel sorry for your sister. She doesn't deserve to be stuck with you! I hope they both die because that would be sooo much better for them."

Those last few words crossed the line. She caused me to momentarily disregard my better judgement. For a few moments, I didn't know who I was.

I remember hearing the bell ring for first period and that was when I started swinging at Tracy. I was not a fighter, but without knowing it, Tracy instantly turned me into one. Her insensitive and totally inappropriate words made me go outside of the type of person I thought I was. She tried to fight back, but it was useless.

I heard my peers yell out in excitement over the unexpected violence. I heard adults scream for me to stop as a few of them tried to unsuccessfully pull me off of her. The only thing that was able to bring the fight to a halt was when I imagined my family in the hospital. Some of the words Tracy said only minutes before jumped to the forefront of my mind. "I hope they both die…" played over and over like a broken record.

I stopped swinging. The people around me were still yelling. I saw their overly animated motions. I saw their mouths moving, but I heard nothing. I had beaten Tracy down to the ground and I stood motionless over her. She was injured, but it didn't appear to be anything serious. Mainly she just had some scrapes and bruises on her face which would serve as a reminder that even words can have consequences.

I was soon escorted to the principal's office. I had been there a few times before, but it had never been for anything bad. Normally my visits were for academic achievements or to do the morning announcements. It felt very different to be in there under those circumstances. I was ashamed of myself.

When I sat down, I lowered my head and slumped down in my chair. I knew better than what my actions had just shown. I was not brought up in an environment of violence, so why did I resort to it? I silently begged God to forgive me. I learned (and read) God was forgiving, but I would have understood if He didn't forgive those actions.

"Miss Morgan, please follow me," Principal Thomas said. I did what I was told. I went from the lobby of his office to his actual office. I didn't want to be there, but I knew I deserved to be. The room was quiet. Mr. Thomas didn't say anything, at least not until I was sitting down in one of the chairs right in front of his desk.

Since I hadn't been in there for anything bad, I wasn't 100% sure what I was in for, but I expected there would a lot of finger pointing, judgement, and scolding.

"Miss Morgan, please explain why you're in here."

It was a simple request, but it was very difficult at the same time. I didn't know if there was something he wanted me to say, something he expected to hear, or just the truth. I thought about it for a moment, then I just spoke from the heart.

"She hurt me, so I wanted to hurt her."

"I understand the logic, but could you explain a little more in detail?"

The rage finally started to leave as I actually heard and processed what I said. It made me feel even worse than I already did.

"My dad and sister are in the hospital in terrible condition. Somehow, she found out. She pretended to care before she told me she hoped they'd die."

It was obvious that he not only believed what I told him but was appalled by what he heard.

"Please tell me you're exaggerating."

"Sir, I wish I could, but that's honestly what she said. I have been taking a lot of abuse from her over the years. Most of the time I'm able to control my emotions, but I just couldn't handle that. She went way too far. Mr. Thomas, you have to believe I'm not a bad person. I always try to behave myself, but she shouldn't have done that. I don't know why she hates me, but she does. Nobody should wish death on another person's family!"

"You're right, nobody should wish death upon anyone, but let me ask you something: since you fought Tracy, did that take back the fact that she said what she did?"

"No but…"

I tried to plead my case, but Mr. Thomas didn't really seem interested in allowing me to do so.

"All you did, Miss Morgan, is give her another reason to dislike you. And her negative energy attached itself to you. Her anger created a companion, and that companion is your anger. If you allow the energy of the others to control your emotions, then you become nothing more than a glorified puppet. Do you understand what I'm trying to tell you?"

He paused. He quietly awaited my response to all he had said. My still-clenched fists opened up and fell loosely on the armrests of the chair I was sitting in. While I may have won the fight, Mr. Thomas helped me realize Tracy had actually defeated me that day.

"I'm sorry. I wish this never happened!"

"I know you regret your actions, I can see that in your eyes. Don't get too down on yourself, though. We're all human and none of us are perfect. We will go our entire lives trying not to make mistakes, but part of the irony is we're making a mistake by thinking we can go with out making them."

"What does all of this mean for me, Mr. Thomas? Am I getting suspended? Please don't tell me that's going to happen. I don't want to miss class. I have projects and assignments that I have to turn in. I can't get zeroes and bring my class averages down."

"Take a breath and calm down. I'm not the only one who has a say in this decision. I will present what happened to a few other people and that decision should be finalized before the end of the day. For now, I need for you to stay here as I try to contract your mother."

Somehow I had almost forgotten mom was going to be called. That stressed me out. I hated letting down my family and I knew what I did would certainly accomplish that unwanted goal. I sat restlessly as I watched each digit of my mother's phone number get dialed.

"Hello, may I speak with Mrs. Morgan?"

I closed my eyes and imaged my mother's expressions as she heard and responded to what Mr. Thomas was telling her. The conversation seemed longer than it needed to be, but somehow it was also over before I expected.

"Well, Miss Morgan, your mother kept wanting to know what was said to push you over the edge. I didn't feel it would have been appropriate for me to actually tell her. I think if she hears that information, it should probably come directly from you."

"Yes, sir. Mr Thomas, do you think I can go to class for the rest of the day— I mean, until you make the final decision?"

I guess he hadn't heard of a student wanting to go to class after they had gotten into a fight. In that regard, I was a little different. I really liked school (at least at that age) and I didn't want to miss any of it. I had worked hard to maintain my high grade point average and I didn't want that to be in jeopardy.

"I don't think that will be the best idea, Miss Morgan"
He was right, even though I tried to convince myself otherwise.

"Okay, I understand. Can I ask a favor of you?"

"Go ahead."

"Do you think it would be possible for me to apologize to Tracy?"

As soon as I asked that question, I wondered where it came from.

"Are you seriously asking?" Mr. Thomas wondered.
Then it hit me. God must have been speaking through me.

"Yes, sir. You were right. I can't let other people be in control of my emotions. So apologizing would help out with that a lot. She shouldn't have said what she did, but I absolutely shouldn't have reacted the way I did."

"Well, that's very mature of you. If you're truly serious, we can make this happen. You do understand I will have to be in the room with you two, right?"

"Yes, sir."

"It also needs to be perfectly clear that just because you apologize to her doesn't mean she'll accept it. That sort of thing can hurt your pride and your feelings. I do not, and I repeat, I do not want another incident to occur."

I silently acknowledged his statement as he got on the PA system and called for Tracy to come to his office. I started to regret my request as soon as she actually walked into the office.

"Why is she here?" Tracy asked loudly.

I remained in my chair. I fought the urge to stand up, yell, clench my fists or even look at her in an angry manner.

"She's here because you two need to talk."

Tracy was expectedly upset.

"I don't wanna talk to her. Look what she did to me!"

She held a tissue stuck in her still-bloody nose. She had a bandage on her arm, but again, she didn't have any major injuries.

Mr. Thomas moved the chair that was near me.

"Please have a seat, Miss Campbell."

She hesitated before doing what was requested of her. When she did, that was when I stood up and moved a few steps closer.

"Tracy, I really want to apologize for what happened this morning. I went way too far and it was totally uncalled for. I was wrong and I hope you can forgive me."

It was easy to see how shocked she was.

"What?" she asked.

"Will you please forgive me?"

It was amazing how God humbled me in the midst of my anger.

Mr. Thomas spoke.

"Miss Campbell, how do you feel about what you've heard from Miss Morgan?"

She stood up quickly and started pointing at me.

"I think she's just sayin' all of that stuff so she won't get in trouble. You probably made her apologize."

"I assure you she will have to pay for her actions. I also want you to know apologizing was her idea, not mine."

It was then I felt I had to speak again, instead of allowing a conversation to continue about me as if I weren't actually in the room.

"Tracy, I know I'll get in trouble for what I did and I deserve that, but this isn't really about that. I'm truly asking that you forgive me for what I did."

She wiped her nose again before turning more towards me.

"This is stupid! You keep talkin' about what I didn't deserve. You know what? You are wrong! I deserved everything you did to me and probably even more. Girl, I don't even really know why I said what I did. I remember when I used to go over your house when we were little. Your dad always made sure we had snacks and we used to always play with your little sister because she would not stay away from us!"

We both laughed. Sharing happy moments with Tracy was something that hadn't been done in a long time. It felt like old times.

"Yeah, my sister was always persistent and she never gives up on anything. So, I know…"

Reality hit me again. My little sister was not only in the hospital, but her condition was really bad. And the man who provided us snacks while we were playing was in the same situation. I didn't want to cry again, but I did.

Then, out of the blue, Tracy hugged me.

"I'm sorry I've been so stupid all of these years. My jealously made me lose my friend. I forgive you and I hope you can forgive me, too!"

And just like that, years of animosity between us were gone. Not only did I get my friend back, but somehow it felt like she was never gone.

"How do you two feel?" Mr. Thomas asked.

We both giggled like we used to do all of the time.

"I feel relieved, Mr. Thomas. I feel relieved." Tracy said.

"That's great to hear, but you girls do know you are both going to suffer the consequences from your earlier actions, right?"

We both said yes, almost in unison.

That was another one of those times when I witnessed God perform a miracle. Sure that situation probably wouldn't have come to mind when people thought about what a miracle is, but I knew it was. Having a fight actually bring together people who were basically enemies for almost nine years was nothing short of miraculous. I was extremely happy about how things seemed to be, but I was still cautious.

"What do you girls think should happen? I want to hear your honest thoughts."

Once again, the shame and embarrassment became present; I didn't know how to respond to Mr. Thomas, so I didn't. I looked at Tracy to see if she had anything she needed to say.

"Sir, this may sound crazy, but you should just let her go. I said some stuff I shouldn't have said. I've been saying disrespectful things to Elise since we were in elementary school. She has done nothing to me. She should have beat me up a long time ago— I know I would have if the roles were reversed. She's a better person than I am, though. She makes good grades and everything. She's not a bad person at all. Please let her go, Mr. Thomas."

As I stood there, I wasn't just thinking about my punishment because whatever happened was beyond my control. I was thinking about how quickly life can change. I though about how one minute your friend can become your enemy, and in the blink of an eye, it can go back to how it was. I thought about how one minute you could be in your way home, continuing with what you do everyday, and then life decides to teach you a lesson to show you how little you control.

"Did you hear all of that Miss Morgan?"
I nodded my head. I wanted to talk, but the lump of emotions that was stuck in my throat wouldn't allow it.

Mr. Thomas' phone rang. Whoever was on the line must have been important because he wrote passes for us to go to class and told us, "I'll be speaking with you later on." Tracy and I walked out of the office, grinning from ear to ear.

"Elise, I really do want to apologize to you. I'm so very, very, very sorry for everything I have said and done to you, especially today. Like I said, I was just jealous of you and I wanted you to feel bad about yourself."

"Why, though? Why were you jealous?"

"Well, since you started talking those ballet classes, you've been different. You've had so much confidence. You walked with your head high and I, for some reason, took that as you thinking you were better than everybody else. I didn't like that."

"But I never said or did anything to make anyone feel like that."

"You're right, you didn't, but it's still how I felt."

"Well, you have no reason to be jealous. You are so pretty and your fashion game is bananas."
She laughed.
"Yeah, you have a point! I am an all-around awesome chick! But normally my fashion is better than it is today."
"I like your outfit! What's wrong with it?"
"Well, some girl decided to beat me up today and made me get my own blood all over me."
I had somewhat of an uneasy feeling when she said that, but she quickly let me know she was joking.
We laughed and talked until it was time for us to go to our separate classes. I was hoping I wouldn't be a distraction when I walked, but I was. Most of the class couldn't wait to ask me about the fight and how I felt.
"I don't want to talk about it. It was dumb and I just want to learn and forget that it ever happened."
It was not what the room full of teenagers wanted to hear, but I didn't care. I truly just wanted the rest of the school day to be as close to normal as possible.
My hopes were granted because after my first class, I was able to focus on school. Nobody wanted to know why I fought Tracy; in fact, as the day passed, it seemed like they had forgotten about it completely. It's a good thing teenagers can sometimes only focus on some things for a short amount of time.
Things changed after lunch, though. I was called back into the office. When I got in there, my mother was in there waiting on me. Her legs were moving as she rapidly tapped her left foot. I had seen that action before. When she did that, it meant she was very angry and was trying to control herself.
"Hello, mom."
There was no exchange of pleasantries. She gave me a laser-focused glare that cut me right to my core.
"Miss Morgan, we now know what your punishment will be."
"Oh, okay."
"Come have a seat next to your mother."
After the look she had just given me, I wanted to stay as far as I could, but I knew that wasn't an option. So I sat down.

"We have a zero-tolerance policy here for violence of any kind. Your display of aggression this morning was not befitting of one of our students. It's also obvious that this is not the behavior your mother expects, either."

He stopped speaking just long enough for me to look over at my mother. The anger had not left her face; it seemed like it had actually gotten more comfortable there. With a very meek tone, I told her I was sorry, but nothing changed. For a moment, I gave up trying to make her happy. I still hadn't heard what my punishment would be; then, Mr. Thomas continued.

"I do want to say I appreciate you wanting to speak to Tracy and apologize for what was done. In spite of your brief moments of immaturity, that action shows what a mature person you really are. You showed remorse for what you did and the fact that you and Tracy seemed to have already move past everything was a wonderfully rare thing to see. Those things were discussed and factored into your punishment."

That's when the nervousness really began to kick in. I almost wanted to try and plead my case again, but that could've done more harm than good. So I didn't.

"I know you all have a lot going on, so let me just get right to it. Elise, after careful consideration, it has been decided that you are being suspended for three days, effective immediately. In addition to the three days, you will also not be allowed to attend the next school dance."

I didn't say anything for a few seconds. I hoped he was joking but he wasn't. I hated the entire punishment and I felt it was unfair. Why did I have to miss so many days of school? I hated to miss class and being forced to miss three days was going to be miserable, and as someone who considered herself to be a dancer, hearing that I had to miss a school dance was the absolute worst! I hated it, but I could do nothing about it.

"Forgive me for being blunt, Mr. Thomas, but are we done?" My mother's tone and demeanor were scary. I feared the type of words she would throw at me once we left the office.

"Yes, ma'am. We're done, Mrs. Morgan," Mr. Thomas said.

We left the office in silence and it stayed that way for a long time. It was nerve-wracking. The silence was far worse than if she had just went off and yelled at me. I think I would have been able to handle the much better. As we traveled, it got to a point where I just couldn't take it anymore.

"I'm sorry, mom! I know I let you down because I let myself down. I didn't want to fight, but it was almost like I had to."
I was trying to justify my actions, but my mother was not having it. I thought everything would be better if she just talked to me; that's what I kept wishing and praying for. They always say be careful what you wish for because you just may get it. I learned that lesson first-hand when Mom started to talk.

"Are you proud of yourself? Do you think you were protecting your family's honor by fighting? We are literally going through the worst time in our lives and you, for some reason, want to make it worse! What is wrong with you? You must have lost your mind!"

Her barrage of harsh questions and statements were not something I was prepared for. They were something I had a hard time dealing with, but I guess that was the point of it. I wanted to try to stop the pain she was dishing out, so I tried to speak.

"I'm sorry, I just..."

"Be quiet, Elise! I don't really want to hear what you have to say."
I quickly found out my attempt was an absolute failure. At that moment, I felt less like a teenager and more like a little girl while my mother was scolding me.

"Why, why, why did you do what you did? Do you understand what we're going through? Do you understand what I'm going through? How much am I supposed to be able to take? What do you want from me?"

I was very confused. I couldn't tell if she wanted me to actually answer her sound set of questions or remain quiet. Then I realized at some point, she went from asking me questions to asking God. Once I understood that, I knew nothing I could say would help her out, at least not at then.

My mother hadn't told me where we were going, but once I saw we were not headed in the direction of our home, there was only one logical destination. I hadn't been given any type of update on anyone's condition. That didn't allow me to have any peace as my mother drove.

As expected, we soon reached the hospital. When we stopped, I wanted my mother to talk to me again. I prayed if she did, the conversation would have a different tone. She didn't say anything, though. She just got out of the car, slammed the door, and briefly looked back to make sure I was behind her. When she saw I was, she just kept walking.

Once we made it inside, I almost had chills. Something was different. My gut was telling me I needed to prepare to receive some bad news. I didn't know who it would be about or who would be delivering the news, but I felt I would be finding out soon. I tried to convince myself I was wrong, but when we got to the room, I found out how right the feeling was.

"Are you Mrs. Morgan?" the nurse asked my mother as she stood in front of the door.

"Yes, I am. Will you please move out of the way so I can see my family?"

"Before doing that, I need to tell you something."
I heard this sort of thing before and it just confirmed my premonition.

"Whatever you need to tell me, please just hurry up."

It hadn't yet hit my mother that we were about to hear some sort of bad news. I stepped back a little. I didn't know if I was trying to get myself far enough away so I couldn't actually hear what was going on, or if I just didn't want to be near mom at that point. Whatever the actual reason was, it didn't even really matter. It was selfish of me.

"Alright, Mrs. Morgan, the injuries your husband and daughter sustained are very significant. We thought both were progressing fairly well, but it seems we may have had a bit of false hope."

"False hope? False hope? What do you mean? What are you trying to tell me right now?"

I assumed the worst. I assumed she was about to tell me one of the most important people in my life had passed away. With that thought in mind, I ran over to my mother and grabbed her hand. We both tried to brace ourselves for what we were about to hear.

"Mrs. Morgan, not too long ago, Jasmine fell into a coma. We are still running tests to try and figure out what happened, but as of right now, she is non-responsive. To be honest with you, she is no longer breathing on her own and we don't know if these things will change."

"This has to be a mistake. She's just a kid!" I said.

Mom hadn't said anything about what she heard. In fact, she had no reaction. She not only didn't say anything, she had no facial expression, no physical changes. There was nothing, at least for a few seconds; then everything changed.

"You did this! This is your fault! If I didn't have to go to that school to pick you up, I would have been here with my baby! This wouldn't have happened If I would have been here! I hope you're happy, Elise!"

She let go of my hand and moved the nurse out of the way so she could enter the room.

I was devastated for so many reasons. Not only had I just heard some terrible news about Jazzy, but my mom was blaming me for it. I wanted to go in the room, but at that time, I couldn't. I was frozen. I looked around and it was like there was no one around (even though I knew they were). Time felt like it had stopped, even though I knew it hadn't. Worst of all, I felt like God had left me, even though I knew He never would. I soon felt the nurse place her hand on my shoulder.

"I'm sorry for everything. I"m sure she didn't mean any of that. She's in shock right now."

I looked at her while she was talking to me. It was like I could see the thoughts forming in her head as she tried to figure out what to say to me. I wanted to respond because I knew she meant well, but I couldn't. My mind had shut down and my mouth wouldn't work. I stared at her blankly until she removed her hand and decided to move on. I saw her shaking her head negatively as she walked away. Did she agree with my mother? Did she also think everything was my fault?

It was like my tears were stuck in my eyes and wouldn't fall. Because of that, my vision was getting more and more blurry with each passing second. I couldn't really see anything. I still didn't have the ability to move, so I just stood there. I was hoping a doctor or nurse would pass by and tell me they had made a mistake. That would wake me up, but it didn't happen.

After a little while, I heard a voice say, "Move!" There was still nobody around, so maybe I hadn't really heard anything. There was silence for a few more seconds, then I heard it again. "Move!"

I felt like I was released. I wiped my eyes and I went into the room to see what was going on. I was hoping the nurse was lying, but she wasn't. I had never seen a person in a coma before, but somehow it seemed familiar when I saw Jazzy.

"Are you okay, mom?"

I knew she was still upset with me, but I also knew she needed me.

"No. I'm not, Elise. I- I'm not okay at all."
She didn't scream hysterically like I thought she would. Instead, she was calm and almost whispering.

"Elise, I didn't mean what I said earlier. I apologize for that."

"It's okay, mom. None of that even matters now."

"Thank you for that. Look at her, Elise. Look at her."

We both looked at Jazz. Even though we knew she could no longer breathe on her own, we expected her to all of a sudden be okay.

"What do you want me to do, mom?"

"There's very little we can do. Look at Jazzy! She's not supposed to go out like this. Come on baby, fight!"
My mom's voice grew far beyond a whisper as she tried to encourage Jasmine to continue fighting to survive.

"Jazzy, what are you doing? You have to wake up, sister. We have a lot of things we have to do."
I joined my mother and we begged Jazz to open her eyes. Even though we didn't know if our words were actually reaching her, we kept speaking anyway.

After about thirty minutes of hoping for a miracle, my mom asked me to leave the room for a little while.

"I know you don't want to leave, but please give me just a few minutes. Then you can come back. Agreed?"
I didn't understand the reasoning behind the request, but I did what she wanted me to do anyway.

I walked to the nearest waiting room. It was empty and it seemed like it may have been that way for quite some time. There were a bunch of magazines all over the table, but nothing that would have served as a diversion to my thoughts. Silence filled the room, and as much as I wanted to hear something, it was probably good there was nothing there.

I sat down in a chair, but I was restless. Every 30 seconds or so, I would find myself moving to another chair that was exactly like the last one. I was trying to make myself be comfortable in an uncomfortable situation. I couldn't focus on anything, then an alert from my phone seemed to echo as it went off. It was a text message from Tracy.

"Hey girl! So, they suspended me too! My folks were not happy at all! How are you?"

"Not good." I responded.
I expected an immediate response asking me what was wrong, but for the next few minutes, I got nothing.

I stood up and began to pace back and forth. My mother didn't really tell me how long she needed, so I was trying to decide if I should go back or not. At the moment, the phone rang. It was from a number I didn't recognize. I didn't even want to answer it at first, but I did.

"Hello."

"What's up? It's me, Tracy! My mom took my phone as part of my punishment, so I had to call you from the house phone."

"Oh, okay."

"So, what's goin' on? Was your mom trippin'?"

"Yeah, she was."

"She shouldn't have been. Did you tell her why you did it? Did you tell her what I said to make you go off?"

"Nope! She didn't want to hear any of it. She was just saying I should have known better."

"Dang, that's messed up!"

I don't know why, but I started to question if she truly wanted to be my friend again or if she had some type of ulterior motive. I wanted to tell her the news about Jasmine, but I also didn't want to give her more ammunition she could use against me later. I didn't say anything for a little while.

"Are you there, Elise?"

"Yeah, I'm here."

"Oh, okay. I didn't hear anything, so I thought this cheap phone hung up on you or something."

"Nope! I'm still here."

"Cool! So, what's up? How do you feel about your suspension? What do you think you're gonna do?"

"I hate it! I like going to class and trying to make good grades and this is gonna ruin a lot of what I've worked hard for."

"Yeah, you always have worked hard on your grades and perfect attendance. I really do apologize for messing things up. I was an idiot! And I'm not just talkin' about today, either."

Just like with the first time she apologized, the second one also sounded incredibly honest and genuine.

"It's all good, Tracy. In my heart, I don't believe you meant what you said about my family."

"I'm glad you said that because I really didn't mean that. How's your family doing, for real?"

Her question made me come face-to-face with the decision to trust her or not. If I ever wanted our friendship to get anywhere near where it was before, I would have to trust her at some point.

"If you don't wanna talk about that, I'll understand," she continued.

"Well, it's not that I don't want to talk about it, it's just..."

"It's just what? Somethings definitely on your mind. Let it out."

I knew if I didn't actually speak to someone about what was going on. The bottled-up emotions wouldn't do anything except cause me more paint at some point. So, I decided to give her more insight on what I was dealing with.

"We got some not-so-great news about my little sister today."

"Really? What?"

I took in a few breaths very slowly and released them even slower.

"We... they... they told us that she went into a coma and she's no longer able to breathe on her own."

She was shocked. She almost didn't believe what I told her, which was understandable because I couldn't really believe it either.

"Are you serious?" she asked.

"Yeah, I am. I wouldn't joke about anything like that."
"That's crazy! She's just a little kid."
"I agree with you, but obviously that doesn't matter."

I wondered if she realized she wished for my little sister's death and we seemed to be headed towards seeing her wish come true.

When I thought about that, I wanted to go to her house so I could fight her all over again. I knew if I were to do that, it would've been very hard for anyone to get me to stop. I simply had to stop thinking about that. That was much easier said than done.

"Do you need anything from me? Is there anything I can do?" she asked.

For a moment, I remember getting more and more upset with every word she said. I found myself thinking, "Yeah, there's something you can do: you can just shut up!" I didn't say it, though.

I maintained my composure long enough for us to finish our conversation. When I was left alone with my thoughts, I started to hyperventilate. It was as though I had almost forgotten how to breathe. I had to consciously make an effort to take in air. I started to have flashes of Jasmine before she went into the coma, before she needed a machine to breathe for her.

My heart was beating rapidly as the effort to make myself inhale and exhale became harder and harder. I remembered my vision getting a little blurry. Then, as if I were looking at the night sky on a clear night, I started to see stars. Those stars soon faded to black as I fell to the ground. I'm not sure how long I was there before someone found me, but when I woke up I was alone in a hospital room of my own.

"Hello?" I called out.

Nobody responded. I sat up and looked around the tiny space I was occupying. There were no pictures on the wall. There was no television showing mindless entertainment. The only thing in the room for my eyes to gravitate towards was an older version of the Bible. It was a "New American Standard" version and it had obviously seen better days. I took that as a very clear sign that I needed to read.

I had no idea what I was supposed to take a look at, so I just flipped through the pages until I felt I needed to stop. Once I did, I saw had reached John 14. My eyes focused on the first verse, so that's where I started.

"Do not let your heart be troubled; believe in God, believe also in Me. In My Father's house are many dwelling places; if it were not so, I would have told you; for I go to prepare a place for you. If I go and prepare a place for you, I will come again and receive you to Myself, that where I am, there you may be also. And you know the way where I am going."

As much as I had prayed and as many times we intently listened while we were in church or Bible study, I didn't recall hearing or seeing those verses before.

The anxiety I was feeling started to vacate. The weight I was feeling on me started to lift. Even though the overall situation hadn't changed, I was a little more at ease. There was an obvious reason why I just happened to turn to those verses. God was giving me peace in spite of being in the middle of tragic circumstances. I needed to take advantage of that, so I re-read verses 1-4 over and over again. Every sentence spoke to me.

"Do not let your heart be troubled" and "In my Father's house are many dwelling places; if it were not so, I would have told you; for I go to prepare a place for you." were both parts that seemed to stick out to me even more than the rest.

My understanding of those words said I shouldn't worry because there was still room in Heaven. Jesus even let me know there was a promise made and it wouldn't be broken. My mind started to create images of an angelic version of my little sister as she rested in her home in the sky. It was beautiful seeing her so happy and free. She was able to see Aunt Katie and everyone else we lost over the years. As wonderful as it was, it dawned on me the only way Jasmine could see this was for her to pass away.

Selfishness kicked in. In essence, we live our lives so we can try to make it to heaven. For reasons that were far beyond my comprehension, Jasmine was moving closer to that goal. She was getting ready to go "home" before anyone ever would have imagined she would. Yeah, they were beautiful thoughts of a glorious place, but I didn't want that for her. At least not at that age. Again, it was pure selfishness and I didn't want to be without my sister. I didn't want her to go, but so what! It didn't matter what I wanted. Her life was not in my hands, it was not in the hands of our parents or the doctors. It was simply up to God.

"Jaaaazzzyyyy!" I yelled, as if I thought she would not only hear me, but get up and tell everyone she was okay and she was ready to leave. None of that occurred. Instead, members of the hospital's staff ran in the room with my mother.

"What happened, Elise? Are you okay?"

"Yes, I'm okay. I think I just passed out. I don't know how I got in here, though."

Some of the staff explained how they saw me in the waiting room, found the first empty room, and made sure I got there safely. I thanked them and asked my mother how she found me.

"I heard you yelling out for Jazzy and I tried my best to find where it was coming from."

"I'm sorry, I'm sorry, I'm sorry! Please forgive me for everything! I don't want to be here! I don't want daddy to be here and Jasmine... she... I don't..."
Whatever statement I was trying to make, I was unable to complete it.

"Stop, Elise. Please, baby, just stop."
She hugged me tightly. The staff didn't want to intrude, so they quietly excited the room as I shared the moment with my mother.

"This shouldn't be our life! We shouldn't be dealing with this! Why is this even happening?"

"All I can say is it's happening because it's supposed to."

My emotions had a habit of going from one extreme to the other, but never had I gone from sad to angry as quickly as I did when I heard her say that.

"It's supposed to? What does that mean? We're supposed to be here while my dad is struggling to live— while the doctors say my sister has already lost her battle? Is that what you're saying?"

"Yes, it is. I'm not going to act like I understand why. I'm not even going to pretend I like it, but everything will play out the way it's supposed to. It always has, it always will."

The Bible that had just allowed me to be comforted by God's words was something (at that moment) I no longer wanted to deal with. I knew the words she was speaking were somewhere in that book, but I couldn't accept it. I knew it was a conflict to agree and disagree at the same time. Not only that, in my heart I knew it was both wrong and idiotic.

"I don't want to accept my little sister dying! I don't want to be without daddy! I'm tired of this! I want us all to go home!"

"I know, Elise. I feel the same way, but these are the times when we're supposed to rely on our faith and our hope. It's easy to believe when everything's going well. Anybody can do that. We have to show how much we believe in God, His will, and His promises to us when we are going through the absolutely worst times imaginable."

She was right, but I couldn't force myself to vocally admit it.

"Am I able to leave out of this room?"

I needed to switch subjects a little bit and asking that question was the only thing I could think of. I was glad my mother decided to respond to what I had just asked instead of the previous subjects of my sister and dad.

"Yeah, I think you're free to get out of here if you want. From my understanding, you had a panic attack, but you're okay."

"Well, let's go."

Hospitals are not the greatest places to have to visit. When you have to be inside of a hospital room for any amount of time, it feels as though every second is drawn out. If you're there for something bad, each tick of the clock seems more depressing than the last. And when you're in your own room, you're almost forced to look at life differently. That's what happened while my mother walked with me as we headed back to Jasmine and daddy's room.

"I'm glad you're okay, Elise. When you didn't come back, I didn't know what to do. I started having all type of thoughts that I shouldn't have."

"My bad, mom. I'm cool. No worries!"

I was lying— not only to my mom, but to myself as well. My emotions were going back and forth like a tennis volley. Honestly I was very confused how I really felt. All I knew was that I wasn't happy, but maybe if I pretended to be long enough, it would have changed how I was (at that time). So, for a little while, that's what I tried.

When we made it back to the other room, neither of us seemingly wanted to go in. We looked at each other before making a move.

"As a mother, you never think you'll see something like this. I never prayed that you two girls would outlive me because I just assumed that's how it would be. I guess you shouldn't make assumptions, huh?"

She did one of those fake smile things people do when they want to keep from crying. I recognized she was doing this only because I was doing the same thing.

"Did you get to speak to them like you wanted to while I was away?"

"Yeah, I did. Do you need some time to do the same?"

"No, thank you. I don't really have anything to say."

That was another lie. I had plenty to say to both of them, I was just very afraid.

"Are you sure, Elise?"

She saw right through me, but I stuck with the lie.

"I'm sure."

And with that, we finally walked into the room.

"Dad, here's what we need. We need for you to get better. This isn't what we want, this is what we need!"

"Jazz, let me tell you something. Sister, you are the best! The doctors gave us some bad news about you. In case you didn't know, we are praying for you. You may not be able to hear us in the flesh, but we know when we talk, your spirit hears us. Nothing that ever happens in this world can stop the love we all have for each other. The love we share will be with us longer than the rest of our lives. It will be there forever!"

"That was beautiful. Where did those words come from?" Mom asked.

I shrugged my shoulders as if I didn't know, but we both understood I was again being used as a megaphone for God's words. Neither of us had the fake smiles on our faces anymore. We also weren't frowning or crying. We were simply in the moment.

The alarm soon went off on my phone. It was a reminder for my dance class.

"Is that for ballet?" Mom wondered.

"Yes, ma'am," I answered with my head down as if I were ashamed.

"Are you ready for me to take you?"

"What do you mean?"

She looked at me as if my question wasn't one that really needed to be asked.

"I mean do you want me to take you or did you still plan on walking?"

"Ummm, I hadn't even thought about it."

She didn't waste any time getting to her next question.

"Do you still want to be a dancer?"

"Of course I do!"

"Well, don't you think if you want to do something professionally, you have to practice at it as much as you can?"

I knew she was right. I heard many different variations of the same talk over the years, especially when life didn't seem like it cared about cooperating with our agenda. Each time I questioned going to practice, it was only because it felt like the questioning was actually necessary.

"But they need us!" I said.

"Yep, they do, but all you have to do is make sure you keep sending prayers and positive thoughts their way. I know we both want to be here 24 hours a day, but we can't. So, do you want me to take you?"

"No ma'am. I'll walk."

Parents seemed to be masters of pretending to give their kids choices that usually will make the kids do what they want them to do.

There was no point of me worrying about that. I just needed to get ready to go. After I got my backpack that had my dance clothes, I started to make my way towards the dance studio. During most of the walk, I was second-guessing myself and my decision. A part of me was loudly telling me I was being obnoxiously selfish. The other part of me agreed with my mother. That side of me kept saying I'd be doing everyone a disservice by not doing what I knew I was supposed to. Was dancing even that important to me? Was I still doing it because I had just gotten accustomed to doing so, or did I still have that burning desire to be the best ballet dancer the world had ever seen? Did I want to be another girl to start something and not finish or did I want to show my peers and everyone else in the world that a woman of color was able to do things some people thought were impossible?

The more I thought, the more my questions actually made things clear for me. At first, my questions were along the lines of "Should I or shouldn't I?" They ended up being more like, "How could I not?"

I made it to dance class very early. None of the other girls had made it, so it was just me and Mrs. Mears. She acknowledged my arrival, but she continued with her own personal workout in front of the mirrors. Her movements were majestic. Every bit of body articulation seemed to be calculated and purposeful. None of the people in her classes got to witness her brilliance in action. She stopped performing individually a long time ago to focus on all of her students; at least that was part of the reason. The other part was that she had sacrificed her body to dance for so long that every part of her body hurt, and although her movements were beautiful, they were limited.

Being in various classes with her over the years, she always explained being a dancer was more than just pretty outfits and performances. It was a lot of time, dedication, practice, and sacrifice. She never complained about it, even though we often would. At any given time, one of us would complain about how difficult practice was. She would always say, "We practice hard so our performances look easy." We would always breathe heavily whenever she said it, but every time we did any sort of routine in front of an audience, we would see how right she was.

It was funny that after our shows, we'd always see someone from the crowd try to emulate something we did. Most of the time they would land awkwardly and quickly learned there was a huge difference between making something look easy and it actually being easy. Because of that lesson, Mrs. Mears would almost always see an increase in the amount of people enrolled in her classes. It always made me think back to how I felt my first day of class. It always refueled my desire to press on, in spite of what may have been going on in my life.

As I watched Mrs. Mears that day, I didn't just flash back to my first day of class; I thought about that birthday party when Jasmine gave me my first tutu. Then I started to feel absolutely horrible! I refused to cry. I bit my lip and tried my best to hide how I was feeling. I turned around so she couldn't see me. I foolishly thought those things would work, but they didn't.

"Elise, what's wrong?" she asked as she stopped her movements.

I turned back around to answer.

"I'm just goin' through a lot."

I expected her to immediately talk about dancing and somehow find a way to relate what was happening around me to ballet, but that's not what she did.

"Do you want to talk about it?"

I didn't really want to talk, but I knew I should. So, I pushed my feelings somewhat to the side as I stepped a little outside of my character.

"My life is not very good right now. I am trying to be positive, but it's hard. I keep praying and praying, but it seems like everything is getting worse!"

Almost as soon as I spoke, other girls started to walk through the door.

"Never mind! I'll just deal with it!" I said as I convinced myself she would quickly focus on the class and not just the one girl with the problems.

She looked towards the back of the room where Natalie was; she was one of the older girls in the school.

"Could you come here for a minute?" she asked from across the room.

Natalie came over to where we were almost immediately.

"Do you think you could get the other girls started? I need to talk to Elise for a little bit."

"No problem! I got it!" she said in a very bubbly tone.

She started to play the music we all warmed up to as Mrs. Mears walked me into her office.

"Have a seat."

I did and my foot began to tap rapidly. I, once again, had a lot of nervous energy that I had to do something about.

"I don't know if we need to talk while class is supposed to be going on."
I was trying to avoid talking even though I was practically ready to spill my guts just a few minutes before.

"That's nonsense, Elise. Natalie is out there and she's more than capable of handling the class. Now, let's get back to what's going on in your world. I don't like to see my girls emotionally stressed out and you obviously are. So, what's up?"

I didn't know what I needed to say. Should I be long-winded and give her all of the details or should I put my ugly situation in a nice little package? I thought about it briefly.

"Well, the short version of it all is that my dad and sister are in the hospital. They're both in terrible condition and they just told us my sister's not gonna make it."
I was interested to see how she'd respond and she didn't make me wait long at all to hear her reaction.

"I'm not going to smile and pretend this is not bad, because it is. I'm also not going to act like you won't be able to make it through this because you will. Do you know how I know?"

"No, ma'am. How?"

"I know because you are just like me. Our lives are more similar than you may believe.

"When I was younger, one of my family members had a heart attack and died very suddenly. As far as we knew, she wasn't even sick. So it wasn't something we were prepared for at all. This was my cousin and it hurt when she died and it made me want to quit everything! Her death, for some reason, made me hate ballet. It felt like it had taken me away from her."

"But you kept dancing, so what happened?"

"Actually, for a few days I quit, but every day I didn't practice, I regretted it. I still didn't get back into practicing the way I had been for a while, though."

"What happened?"

"Well, this part may seem strange, but I promise it's true."
"What?"

"One night, I was struggling as I tried to go to sleep. I was tossing and turning. I kept sweating even though it was cold in our home. I knew I wasn't sick because for the most part, I felt fine physically. When I finally was able to go to sleep, I had a dream about my cousin that vividly replays in my mind whenever I want to give up on anything, even to this day. In it, she never yelled at me, but she clearly expressed her disappointment not in me, but in my actions. She kept asking me if she had wasting her time watching my performances and supporting my dreams. That really got to me. Yeah, I had some people say it was only my imagination, or you can't really take dreams too seriously, but those type of words went in one ear and vanished before they could even go out of the other. To me, her speaking to me in that dream was as real as any of the conversations we had in the physical world. And I think when you hear a loved one tell you something after they've passed away, you have to listen."

    She stopped speaking for a moment. I was so interested in what she was saying, I was just staring at her in hopes she would continue with her story.

    "Yes, ma'am. You're right."

    "I said all that to say, I understand the pain you're dealing with. I also understand if you have thoughts of just wanting to stop everything and cry all the time, but that won't do you any good. Correct me if I'm wrong, but when you first go started here, didn't you have a little tutu that your sister had given to you?"

    "Yes. She gave it to me for my birthday."

    "How did she feel after you started?"

    "She felt good. She always made sure I practiced and was ready to go to class. Even before I stepped into this studio for the first time, she was telling me I was the greatest and that she was happy she helped me get started."

    "See, she was genuinely happy because her big sister was doing something she liked. That is an amazing feeling and sometimes one of the things that can keep our family smiling is when we pursue or passions. They love to see us progress in our lives to the point where everything we want to accomplish is right in front of us and we can just reach out and grab it."

    "Yeah, you're right, but what if they're not actually here to see that happen?"

    I thought that would have been the type of question that would have made her at least stop and think for a moment before she answered, but it wasn't. Instead, she answered as if she already knew what I was going to ask.

"Being here physically is one thing, but if a person's spirit is with you and you're honoring their wishes, their lives and their legacies by doing something positive, the rewards are far greater."

"Did those sort of thoughts make it easier when you lost your cousin?"

Within seconds of asking, I felt terrible about doing so. Although I had absolutely no negative intentions in my mind or heart as the words were leaving my mouth, I could understand if she took them in a negative manner. Surprisingly, she seemed to understand what I meant and she didn't get upset at all.

"Did the thoughts make it easier when I lost my cousin? Well, at first they didn't. I think that was because when she died, I wouldn't allow myself to have any positive thoughts. I didn't listen to anything anybody was telling me because I only wanted to see things from my perspective. I had convinced myself there was nobody in the world who could understand my pain. So, for a while, I felt like I was alone. It took me some time to understand I felt alone because I let the sadness I had because of my cousin turned into anger. I directed that anger towards the people who loved me, which isolated me. I will never pretend dealing with that sort of thing is easy because it never is, but what I learned is when you put yourself on an emotional island, the results usually won't be good. I also must stress to you life will continue to be difficult, especially when you have to deal with something as serious as what you're dealing with."

I could tell by the way she was speaking, she was consciously trying to avoid saying words like "death" and "dying". We both knew that was the main point of what we were talking about, but I really appreciated the fact she didn't want to harp on that. We continued our conversation for a few more minutes before she asked me what I wanted to do. I wasn't sure if she meant for that day or if it was more of a long-term question. Either way, the answer was the same: I wanted to dance. So that was what I did.

For the rest of the class, I was able to focus more than I thought would be possible. My movements were nearly flawless and as we explored new choreography, everything felt strangely familiar. For those few hours, I didn't really think about how different life would be for me when I left the safety of the dance studio. The other girls had the luxury of going home to their comfortable lives where they would continue their evenings without a care in the world. I, on the other hand, literally had to deal with life and death. For that reason, I didn't want to leave class that day. It served as a distraction for what was happening outside of the studio.

    Even then I felt like a horrible person for wanting to be distracted from what was going on. Sure, Mrs. Mears gave me some great words of inspiration, but I wanted to have some time to not have to be in a hospital room looking at my sister and father come face-to-face with their own immortality. I wanted some time to be a teenage girl who was free to mess up without feeling like mistakes were beyond repair. I didn't want to be strong, no matter what the circumstance was. I didn't want to do any of that. In fact, I didn't even know if I was comfortable being Elise Morgan. I almost wish I had the ability to step outside of myself, but I couldn't, so I knew it would be both foolish and a waste of time to continue thinking that way. So that thinking stopped.

    My mother called me shortly after I left class. Her voice sounded different. She didn't sound happy, angry or sad, she just sounded different. I asked her if she was okay and she never answered. Instead, she asked me a lot of questions that seemed to have no purpose and she only answered my questions with short (sometimes cryptic) responses.

    My mind created several scenarios that would cause her to act the way she did; none of them were good. She asked me if I was going home or if I was going back to the hospital. I didn't want to do either. Going home would mean seeing the huge leather recliner we had gotten not too long before. It was where my father liked to sit in when he got home as he let go of the stress from the work day and focused on his family. Going home meant seeing Jasmine's room with a combination of both comic book heroes and pop stars. Going home meant seeing what used to be knowing none of it would ever be the same.

    What was the alternative? Well, the hospital was a place I had seen more than enough of. It was supposed to be a place where health was given back to the sick and the hurt, but I had only seen one case of that. In spite of what it was supposed to be, I saw the hospital not as a place where life was restored, but where it faded away.

    I didn't want to deal with anything. So, for a long time, I didn't. I knew my mother was worried about me as I walked around that evening, but I didn't care. When I didn't show up at the hospital, I was sure she assumed I just went home, so that was what I let her believe. As I walked, I had no idea where I was going or why I wanted to get there. I soon passed by a diner that my family had stopped by on many occasions. I didn't remember there being anything particularly special about the place, but evidently that didn't matter. I was soon sitting down looking over the menu.

    "What'll it be, hon?" the waitress asked.

    She was an older lady. Her hair was in a bun similar to how I had to wear my hair for dance class. She seemed like she had been working for quite a few hours that day, but she had a smile on her face that seemed permanently fixated there. I wanted to smile right along with her, but I was unable to conjure one up.

    "Can I get a medium-rare cheeseburger with no onions and extra pickles?"

    "You certainly can. Let me ask you something, though."

    "Yes, ma'am."

    "What's a young girl like you doing here this time of the evening all by yourself?"

    Other than the name badge she had on that read "Gladys," I really had no idea who that woman was; but I felt like I not only knew her, but could trust her.

    "I just needed to go somewhere for a while. My family and I used to come here when I was a little bit younger, but we haven't had much time for that recently."

    "Well, where are they now?"

Why did she have to ask me that? I was doing okay until then, but once that question hit the air, I once again was unable to control my emotions.

    I tried to explain why I suddenly went from ordering a burger to crying, but I couldn't get my thoughts together. I stumbled over words I had said a thousand times before. I put my head down on the table. Within seconds, my tears were almost flooding the area around me. I was forced to sit back up. When I did, I saw Gladys had sat down beside me and put her arm around me as she let me know I could cry on her shoulder if I needed to. With her free hand, she was wiping up the collection of tears that had made a home on the table. I still was unable to say anything as I looked over at Gladys.

"Don't try to talk before you finish lettin' your emotions out," she said.

It was sound advice, so I listened. I silently sat and waited for my tears to stop.

"Thank you," I said, once my emotions had given me the clearance to speak.

"Well, aren't you sweet? You are more than welcome, young lady," she said with her smile planted firmly on her face.
She gave me a hug and went back to work almost as if she hadn't even done anything.

As she went back to her normal work routine, I saw her checking on me every once and a while. When she brought my order, she stopped momentarily.

"If you need to talk some more, you just let me know. I know you didn't expect a waitress to care, especially since I don't know you, but I care about everybody. And I think we should all be like that."
As she walked away again, I thought about that statement. It was simple in concept, but could be very difficult to put into practice.

I continued to think as I ate my burger. Soon I looked down at what I was feeding my face. Burgers weren't exactly on the list of foods I was supposed to be eating to stay in tip-top shape, but that was not why I stopped. I stopped because as I was about to take another bite, I realized I didn't even like medium-rare burgers. I didn't, but my father did.

I chuckled out loud as I thought back to one of the times my family was in the same restaurant. When we got our meals, Jasmine saw the little bit of pink in my father's burger and she was very vocal with how grossed out she was.

"Eww, daddy! They didn't even finish cooking your food. That's gross! I think you should send it back because if you eat that, you might turn into a cow or something!"

My father looked all around the restaurant. Then, he looked at my mother, me, and then he stared at Jasmine.

"Well, you know what?" he asked.

"What?"

"I just loooooovvvvee cows! Mooooooooo!"

He took the most gigantic bite of food I had ever seen before in my life. It was hilarious. Jasmine laughed so hard everyone in the building started looking at us. It was one of countless great memories our family had made together and I was very grateful for it.

As the memory temporarily faded, I found myself still holding a greasy burger in my hand. It was dripping with calories and awesomeness! I almost wanted to put it down, but that would have been a tremendous waste. So I thought for a moment. "What would daddy do?" Then it become blatantly obvious what needed to be done. I took a look around and took the largest bite I possibly could. After that, I loudly yelled out, "Moooooooo!"

I laughed just as I had when we were all in the restaurant together. As I continued, I "moo'd" with almost every single bite I took. Gladys soon came by and let me know how contagious my laughter was.

"It's good to see you smilin'. Laughter looks much better on you than those tears did!"

"Yes, ma'am!" I said, as I continued to smile.

"What turned everything around for you?"

"Miss Gladys, I just thought about good times my family had here. I couldn't help but laugh."

"That's good to hear."

She looked at my plate and saw it was just about empty.

"So, do you think you'll need anything else?"

I looked at my plate and then briefly at the menu.

"Yes, ma'am. Can I get a double scoop sundae with whipped cream, sprinkles, pecans, caramel and a cherry....no, no, two cherries?"

"That sounds amazing! I'll get that out to you as soon as I can."

As I waited, I got a call from my mom. I didn't want to answer it, for some reason, but I did anyway. I think my hesitation was mainly because I feared she was going to deliver some bad news and I didn't think I could handle that. Luckily there were no words of negativity in the conversation. She said she simply wanted to make sure I was okay.

"Yeah, Mom, I'm good. I'm not at home, though."

"Okay, where are you?"

"I'm just at the diner we all used to go to."

She sounded both surprised and delighted.

"That's cool! What made you go there?"

"Umm, I don't really know. I think my mind just made me go somewhere we already made memories."

"Well, there haven't been any changes here, so just enjoy yourself. Please, please don't stay out too much longer. I want you to make it home safely."

I agreed and we ended our conversation around the same time my ice cream sundae arrived at the table. It was yet another thing I wasn't "supposed" to be eating, but just like the burger, I wasn't really having it for myself. The sundae, yeah, that was for Jasmine. I enjoyed pigging out just as an eight- or nine-year-old Jazzy did when we visited after she had an art show at school. She dove face-first into it. She came up every once and a while only to get air. Then she dove right back in. She had no shame, and according to her, she had the most fun ever!

I'm sure if anyone was watching, they had to think something was wrong with me. (I know I would have.) Not only had I been impersonating a cow as I was destroying a burger, but I decided to follow that up by not only eating a large sundae with numerous toppings, but doing so without even thinking about touching the spoon that was still partially wrapped up in the napkin on the table. I didn't really care about what the other people around me may have thought. For those few minutes, in spite of what I was going through, I was happy. For a brief moment, I wasn't gasping for air while the tragedy tried its best to suffocate me. For a moment, my hope had been restored.

I didn't want that moment to end, but eventually it had to. When it did, I thanked Gladys for her service, time, and advice. I tried to just quietly walked out of the door after that, but she wouldn't allow it.

"Remember, if you ever need anything, you can always stop back by here. Again, I don't know you, but I can sense what type of young lady you are, who you are spiritually, and that you really need to gain some extra spiritual strength. Just know I care about you and I'll be praying for your well-being."

"Thank you, Miss Gladys. That really, really means a lot."

"You're welcome."

I walked out of there feeling much different than I did when I walked in. Although things had not improved, my perspective was a little different. I didn't know if it would last, but it felt good to have my emotions ruled by happy memories of the past instead of the harsh reality of what was happening at that time. The walk home was a quiet one. It seemed like everything was on mute. The moon, which appeared to be shining brighter than it ever had, helped me get home safely. When I arrived, I tried to call my mother to let her know I was safe, but she didn't answer. She had been spending the majority of her days (and nights) in the hospital, so I figured she was finally able to get a little bit of rest.

Rest was something I needed as well, so I prepared to go to sleep for the night. Before I actually went to bed, I felt a strong urge to pray. So that was what I did.

"God, I thank you for allowing me to see the day. Thank you for letting me get reacquainted with some of the happy times we've had as a family. God, I'm scared, though. I really don't know what I'm supposed to pray for. The doctors said my sister doesn't have any chance at survival, but that hasn't stopped mom from being there everyday, watching Jazz and dad while she hopes for some sort of miracle. My dad hasn't been given the same death sentence from the doctors that Jazz has, but he's only opened his eyes a few times since the accident and he has yet to say a single word. We don't know if it's because he can't or because he just doesn't want to. It's all confusing and I pray we can just understand this. If it is your will for us to lose a part of our family, I ask that you make us strong enough to handle it. I pray you give Daddy and Jasmine peace, no matter what. They both deserve to have peace, and if it takes them to leave this earth for them to get that, then I pray your will be done. I pray this in the name of Jesus. Amen."

I got in the bed thinking I was about to fall asleep very quickly, but that didn't happen. I was restless all night. I tossed and turned, but I didn't know why. My thoughts were all over the place one second and totally nonexistent the next. My mind wore me out enough to finally put me to sleep after what seemed like hours. As tired as I was, I found myself waking up every so often. I was having various nightmares that seemed so important I had to wake up, but after I woke up, I couldn't even remember what happened. It was upsetting that I was so tired after the night was over, but I couldn't do anything about it.

After I thanked God for the day, one of the first things I did when I got up the next morning was check my phone to see if my mother tried to contact me. I was disappointed and worried to see she hadn't. I called and again hoping she would answer.

"Hello."

"Hey, Elise."

She seemed like she was somehow able to get a decent night's rest and that made me happy.

"How are you, mom?"

"I'm okay. Last night, I had a very long conversation with God and I asked Him to help me to be able to deal with what is going on."

"I was doing the same thing, mom."

"That's good..."

She stopped speaking, even though I could easily tell she had much more she wanted to say.

"Mom, be real with me. What's up?"

We sat in awkward silence for what seemed like days before she finally responded.

"I've prayed and prayed and I've been able to make a decision."

I didn't know exactly what she made a decision on, but I had an idea and I got nervous.

"Okay. what are you talking about, though?"

"I've made a decision about Jasmine."

My mother spoke as though she had to choose her words very carefully and I didn't like that.

"Okay. What decision?"

"Elise, we can't keep Jasmine around like this. This is not her. She should not be breathing only because she is hooked up to a machine. That's not life! Baby, we are being selfish with her. God is trying to get her to go home and we are holding her back. Why are we being so selfish? Why are we trying to do this to her? What's wrong with us?"

I couldn't tell if she honestly felt letting go was best for Jasmine, if she heard that was what she needed to do from God, or if she had simply given up hope of things getting better. Whatever the reason was, she had her mind made up and I didn't feel it would be in the best interest of anyone involved to try and convince her to go against what she decided.

"Nothing's wrong with us, mom. We just don't wanna see Jasmine go."

"Would we rather deal with the pain of letting her go or deal with more pain while we watch her suffer in a hospital bed?"

I knew we were being selfish, but I hadn't realized to what extent until my mother asked what she did.

"I don't want my sister to..."

"You don't have to say it, but trust me, I don't want that either. Sometimes, what we want is actually God's least concern."

That was a hard dose of realism my mother made me swallow.

"Mom, is it okay for me to come out there?"

"Yeah, I think that would be good."

About an hour and a half later, I was back at the hospital. I had grown very tired of being there, but I never said that to anyone. The silver-lining of still having to go was that Jasmine and daddy were both still alive.

"Hi, mom."

I tried to have a happy tone in spite of my actual feelings.

"Hey, Elise."

My mother and I hugged each other. We were both fighting our tears (again). I was scared to look over at Jazz. I couldn't even comprehend why, but I was.

"I'm sorry, Mom."

I didn't even know what I was apologizing for, but it felt like that was what I was supposed to do.

"You don't need to apologize for something you had no part in. You had no control over this, Elise."

She was pointing towards Jasmine and Dad while she was talking, but my focus stayed on her.

"Elise, I'm glad you made it because I was just about to let the doctors know they can pull the plug."

Hearing her say that took the air out of my body. I had to constantly think about trying to remain calm so I wouldn't have another panic attack. The crazy thing was, I went to the hospital knowing what my mother was going to do, but being in there and hearing her say it was much different than talking about it on the phone.

"Are you really ready to do that?" I asked.

"Ready? No, I'm not ready to tell the people here they can quit trying to save my little girl. I'm not ready to tell them I give up. I'm not ready to tell them I've pretty much lost hope in witnessing a miracle. I'm not ready for any of that, but I'm gonna move forward with it anyway. It's what's best for her."

Without saying anything else to me, she broke away from our hug and went into the hallway. The further she got, the worse I felt. While I was in the room without Mom, I finally forced myself to look at my little sister. I walked over to her and stared at her. Maybe she just hadn't heard our requests for her to open her eyes and feel better. Maybe the accident took a lot out of her and she just needed time to rest and recover. Or maybe I was just being delusional.

After a little while, my mother walked into the room only to tell me she had to fill out some paperwork.

"Dad, did you hear that?" I asked.

I had the urge to speak to my father. I wanted him to know what was about to happen.

"Mom has decided that we can't force Jasmine to keep living. She has decided today will be the last day machines will breathe for her. She said it's time we let her go."

I felt like I was telling on my mother, and in a way I was, but I wasn't quite ready to fully accept the same things that she was. I wanted my father to wake up and do something about it, but he didn't. He just continued to lie there with his eyes closed, barely able to breathe for himself.

My mother came back into the room with her head down, almost as if she had committed a crime. Any doubts I had about her actually going through with what she said she was going to do were gone. Her face had the look of guilt written all over it. I knew she probably wanted me to say something to her to help ease her mind, but I didn't have it in me. We were about to suffer together (in a way), but we were going to still be doing it separately.

More people gathered into the room. They took turns explaining what was about to happen. I couldn't listen to them. It seemed like they were okay with having a hand in basically letting my sister die. I could only focus on Jasmine and although there was a sea of people around her, I made my way over to Jasmine and held her hand. My focus broke away from my sister for a moment when I heard one of the doctors say at the most, she would only last a few minutes after she was "disconnected".

My mother stayed back. I guess she couldn't bear being that close to Jazz at that point. The doctors and nurses did what they had to do and soon Jasmine's little body was gasping for air, but she wasn't able to pull any in. She really didn't have much time left, so I had to speak to her quickly before she "went home".

"So, sister, it seems like God needs you back. I guess it makes sense because you didn't belong on earth anyway. It's time for you to get your wings so you can fly around heaven with Aunt Katie. We didn't deserve you. Sister, I'm sorry I didn't take care of you! Please forgive me! Please! And don't think for a moment that I will ever forget you. You are my best friend and nobody will ever be able to replace you! I love you, Jazzy! I love you, I love you, I love you. God, please take care of her better than we were able to do!"

What happened after that was either a miracle or my mind playing a very cruel trick on me. For a few seconds, Jasmine opened her eyes and looked at me as her famous smile made its final appearance. She then closed her eyes and finally was able to take her last breath. The vitals on the machine went to zero as it showed a flatline just like on those hospital television shows. One of the people in the room looked at their watch and the clock on the wall.

"Official time of death, 11:20 am."

I didn't want to believe what I heard, but the cold temperature of Jasmine's hand forced me to. My sister, in the physical sense, was no more. Her spirit had been set free and that thought gave me some level of comfort. That didn't seem to be the case for my mother, though.

As I still held onto the lifeless hand of my sister, I watched mom as she fell to the ground. She had her mouth open as if she were yelling, but there was no sound. One of the doctors sat on the ground next to her to try and comfort her. It didn't seem to be working. I wasn't close enough to hear exactly what was being said, but I could imagine what the conversation was generally about, so I quickly stopped paying them any attention.

I went back to looking at my little sister. It was amazing (and incredibly daunting) that her body was there, but she wasn't really there anymore. I was both fascinated and fearful at the same time. I wondered if my sister's spirit was still in her body as she waited for it to be fully lifted by God or was it set free as soon as her body shut down?

Whatever the timing of everything was, I figured her spirit was on its way to doing some important things. I wasn't sure what those important things were, but I figured they had to be very important or else she wouldn't have been taken away from us so soon.

"Sister, I know you're not here anymore, but I hope it's okay for me to talk to you anyway."

Nobody in the room was paying any attention to me and that was exactly what I needed. With them not focused on me, I was able to keep having a conversation with my sister.

"I miss you already, sister. I never was able to tell you how important you were... I mean how important you are to me. And now..."

My words stopped flowing mid-sentence. I didn't know what else I wanted to say or how it was supposed to be said. So, right then, I had to stop trying. I wanted to speak with God, but the words to Him didn't flow either. So with my sister's hand still in mine, I just closed my eyes, bowed my head, and tried to clear all of my pre-existing thoughts.

While my eyes were closed, what I saw was beautiful, inspiring, and sad all at the same time. My sister and I were playing together, but I couldn't tell where we were. The sun was shining brightly and I had to squint my eyes a little. Jasmine was talking to me, but I couldn't hear what she was saying. Then an angel flew near us and stuck out her hand. It looked like Aunt Katie, but I couldn't really tell. Jasmine looked at me and touched me on my shoulder. She kept talking and it seemed like the more she said, the louder she got. I wasn't able to hear most of her words, but she grabbed the hands of the angel. I heard her say, "It's okay, sister. I'm much better now. Don't worry, I love you forever!"

I opened my eyes and found I had unknowingly let go of my sister. The imagery I saw when my eyes were closed comforted me. If my sister had to go, I was glad to see an angel was escorting her and helping with her transition. Even though I was comforted by what I saw, I was still in pain. I cried in silence as the pain poured from my eyes. I felt bad about wanting to leave my sister's side, but I knew no matter how long I stayed there, the outcome would not change. I leaned over and kissed her on her forehead.

"See ya later, sister. Have fun up there. I already miss you like crazy Jazzy, but I guess the folks in heaven needed you." Those were the last words I said to my baby sister.

I passed by my mother, who was still sitting on the floor, and walked just outside of the room. I faced the wall as if I were on punishment. I didn't want anyone to see me, nor did I want to see anyone. I was there for only about a minute or so before I heard more people headed towards the room. I didn't know what was going on, but I turned around to try and find out. Soon I had my answer. The people were there simply to "collect my sister's body".

My mother was yelling and running alongside them as they started to transport her away.

"Don't take her away, please! Just give me a few more minutes!"

"We're sorry, ma'am. We can't."

The words came across as if the person who said it didn't care about our family's situation, even though I didn't think that was the case. More than likely, he had seen death so much he had almost become completely unattached to the emotions that generally come along with it.

    My mother absolutely hated his response and she let him know it, especially when they had to cover up Jasmine's body. She started pounding on the man's shoulders as if she believed he were the one that caused Jazzy's death. Although I wasn't really in the best position to do so, I felt it was necessary for me to calm mom down.

    "Mom, it's not his fault. Please, stop doing that," I whispered as I tightly wrapped my arms around her.

    It was easy to see how baffled she was by my actions. Quite frankly, I was too. She just looked at me. She didn't say another word as the "empty" body of my sister faded further and further into the distance.

    "I was worried, too, mom. Now I know she's okay because I saw Aunt Katie come to get her. We don't have to worry anymore. Jazzy's good, trust me."

    Hearing her sister's and youngest daughter's name together in that context hit her like a punch to the stomach. Her breathing slowed down dramatically. In between her breaths, she cried out in ways that hurt me all the way to the center of my very existence.

    "We're in this together, mom. And it's not gonna be easy, but we'll make it."

    After that, we were both quiet. For a moment we were no longer needed. We both had similar feelings and we didn't need to really say anything for us to understand that.

    We walked back into the room. Our movements were slow. With each step, it seemed we needed each other's strength to even remain upright. We staggered clumsily until we reached a seat so my mother could sit down. Once she was comfortable, we surveyed the room. It was very different than it had been just moments before.

    All of the people who were in the room seemed to be distant memories. There was no more commotion and chaos in the room. There was nobody from the hospital making sure my mother was okay. Obviously the biggest difference was that Jasmine was no longer there.

    "It's gonna be different," mom said.

"Yeah."

Once again, I didn't know what to say, but it should've been more than that. I should've been able to be more helpful, but I was in need of help myself. We didn't say much else and it was absolutely terrible. The silence pounded in my head like a jackhammer against concrete. My mother, on the other hand, needed it. I left her alone as she stared at the spot where her youngest daughter put up a good fight but ultimately lost her battle.

She put her head down. I left her alone for a little while longer before I walked towards her. She heard me approaching, and she put her arm out to let me know she wanted me to keep my distance, so I did.

"Are you gonna leave us too, Ian? Jazzy left us already, so are you trying to do it, too?"

She asked her questions to my father while keeping her head facing the ground. My father, of course, said nothing. My mother was basically venting out of sadness, anger, and maybe a hint of emptiness. And even though my father wasn't in a position to respond, I felt like I was eavesdropping on what was supposed to be a private discussion between my parents. So once again, I decided it would be best for me to leave the room for a moment.

"Mom, I'm about to take a walk. I won't go too far and I'll have my phone in case you need me."

She didn't say anything. It wasn't surprising because I didn't really expect her to.

When I left, I had no clue where I was going. All I knew was that I needed time away from the hospital. So I walked until I felt my feet starting to hurt. It was almost as though I wanted myself to experience a small amount of physical pain so that I could be distracted from the emotional pain. I stopped to rest, but I soon found out I was restless. I kept pacing up and down the sidewalk. It felt like people were staring at me, but I didn't bother checking to see if they were.

"God, did we do something wrong?"

I unexpectedly started talking to God, but we didn't converse very long. Actually, that question was the only thing I asked. I not only wanted God to have time to answer, but I needed time to prepare for whatever it was He ended up telling me.

I thought my family all were good people who behaved the way God wanted us to, but of course I would think that way. My biased opinion of who I thought we were could have clouded my mind about who we actually were. Maybe one of us did something so bad, Jasmine had to be taken away from us. Maybe we had not paid attention to the warnings we had been given and my sister was our wake up call. Or maybe none of that was true. Perhaps we were not being punished or taught a lesson at all. Maybe the explanation was simply that life happened, as it does with everybody.

I would have loved to have been able to convince myself one of this things were true, but I couldn't. I didn't know what to believe and that was dangerous. Suddenly the amount of walking I had done was not enough to get me away from the thoughts I was having because of Jasmine's death. I decided I didn't need to be distracted; I actually need something to focus on. One of the few things I could always focus on, no matter what, was dance.

I needed to practice my craft, but I had never attempted to go to the studio during "regular business hours." I had no idea if going there would even possible, but I prayed that it was. I called the studio and Mrs. Mears answered the phone. I can't say I was surprised, because she seemed to live at the studio. Her love and dedication to dance were unequaled.

She was surprised to hear from me and even more surprised when I asked if I could practice.

"I have never really been one to stop one of my girls from dancing, but don't you have other things you should be worried about?"

I questioned whether I should tell her what had already happened.

"Elise, are you still there?"

"Yes, ma'am, I was just thinking."

"If you don't mind me asking, what are you thinking about?"

There were about fifteen seconds when the only sounds that could be heard were not words from our conversation, but the music playing in the background in the studio. After I had a little time to ponder, I interrupted the music to speak.

"I was thinking about how different things have already become and how much more they're going to change."

"Why? Have you heard more news?"

"No ma'am, I didn't hear anything that would make things be different, but I did witness something."

"What did you witness?"

"Well, Mrs. Mears, today… today I saw my little sister pass away."

It sounded like she began to cry immediately. It was as if she truly were feeling the same pain I was.

Jasmine wasn't her sister, daughter, cousin or related to her in any way, yet she was sobbing as if she were.

"I am so sorry, Elise. Are you okay? Is there anything I can do for you?"

She asked a lot of questions in a very short amount of time, but it was not overwhelming and I knew she was asking things because she cared about me.

"Thank you. I can't really say I'm okay, at least not now, but I know at some point I will be."

"I know you will. You're a very strong young woman, and as difficult as this is, it will not break you."

Each word she said stuck out to me, especially when she said the word "break." It stuck out the most because it reminded me of when my mother said you have to dance, even when you are broken.

"Mrs. Mears, can I please come and practice?"

"Absolutely!"

That particular conversation ended there. I tried to get my mother's permission to go, but she didn't answer. So, I proceeded and hoped she wouldn't get upset with me later on. The thought of my mother's possible anger vacated my mind quickly as I walked towards my destination. Every few steps, I seemed to either notice something I never had before or I was able to see things from a new point of view.

What once was just seen as graffiti on many of the buildings (and a waste of time) suddenly became a creative artistic expression that showcased the artist's passion for his/her work. The old library, a few blocks away, was no longer viewed as a run-down building I thought needed to be torn down. Instead, I saw it as a historic place of education and entertainment. This sort of "re-imagining" of everything continued all the way to the studio. Part of me thought it was dumb to think the way I was, while another part of me thought it was refreshing. Either way, I didn't even really know why I just couldn't see things like normal.

Perhaps the new perspective of life was because I saw my sister lose hers. Maybe seeing how fragile life was made me quit focusing on how ugly I thought everything was and actually made me find the beauty in things instead. Then, the magic and enchantment that had "clouded my judgment" left as quickly as it appeared

"Why is my sister dead? Jazzy! Why?"

I couldn't understand why feelings took over, but they did. One second I was appreciating the beauty of the world; the next second, the ugliness of the world had me on the ground, crying loudly in front of the dance studio.

It was another one of those times when I noticed people watching me. I don't recall any of them walking over to me to see what was wrong, though I don't really blame them if I saw something similar. I doubt I would have approached that person and said anything either. It was actually sad to think how little we care about one another.

"Elise, please get up. Let's get inside," Mrs. Mears said as she ran outside.

Just as I was questioning humanity, Mrs. Mears grabbed ahold of me while she helped me get back onto my feet.

"I think I'm okay, but I'm not even sure anymore."
It was strange to me that I was so emotional around my dance instructor because of Jasmine's death, but I wasn't like that around my mother. I had learned that emotions many times didn't make sense and weren't usually controllable. How I felt after Jasmine's death was proof of those things.

I was helped into the building by Mrs. Mears and one of the first things I noticed when I got inside were all of the mirrors. It wasn't like they had just been installed or anything, but they stuck out to me that day. That day they were not just there to make sure I had the correct forms as I went though my positions or practiced my choreography. It seemed their primary purpose was for me to see how I looked when life had me down. So, I looked.

I let the tears continue on their journey. I watched many of them as they traveled to their resting place. I finally had the chance to see what my sadness looked like and I wasn't fond of it at all. I made myself stare at my reflection in spite of the fact I hated what I was seeing.

"I don't know if you're ready." Mrs. Mears said.

What did she mean, she didn't know if I was ready? Ready for what? Did she question if I was prepared to dance or continue with my life? Either way, I didn't like it. Without warning, the girl I was staring at in the mirror, the one who couldn't stop crying, started to change.

"Yeah, I'm ready."

I wiped my face and stared into the mirror so I could look into my own eyes. I saw myself change from a scared and sad little girl to a determined woman who had something to prove to herself and everyone around.

"Well, the studio is yours for a little while. I won't have a class coming in for a few hours. Don't force yourself to do anything, Elise. You don't have to try to distract yourself from your life. It's okay to feel."

I knew she had a point, but I didn't acknowledge it at all.

"Umm, I don't have the proper dance attire. Is that okay?"

"Normally, you know how I feel about that, but I am willing to make an exception for you. But I do have some extra clothes in the back if you need them."

Mrs. Mears told me it was "okay to feel" and right then, the only thing I felt was the desire to dance. We had a performance coming up, but with everything that was going on, I hadn't put in the time to practice like I normally did. So I used that time to change that. I danced until my feet and all of the muscles and joints in my body were hurting so much that I felt like I was unable to continue. Then I eliminated those thoughts of pain and made myself keep going. I kept dancing until any traces of tears had been replaced by the sweat that served as proof of my hard work.

I almost didn't pay attention to how much time had passed, but the incoming class of younger girls reminded me. Seeing all of the five-year-olds took me back to when I was their age. They all had such hope in their eyes and joy in their movements. They all had huge smiles on their faces, and even though I wasn't feeling that great, their happiness spread to me. They were all so cute and friendly. Almost every one of them waived at me as they took their places around the mirrors to stretch and warm-up.

"Hi, Miss Lady. You're pretty. Are you gonna be in the class today?" one of the girls asked.

She was very small and adorable.

"I might stay around for a little bit and just watch you and the rest of your class, if that's okay."

"Ooooohhh! You wanna stay and watch me? I like that! I like dancin' and one day I want to dance in front of a lot of people and theeeennnnn, I wanna help little girls like me be dancers, too!"

"Well, that sounds like a great plan! If you're gonna do all of that, of course I want to watch you. I don't want to wait until you're famous and I have to ask somebody, 'Who's that talented ballerina? She's awesome!' I want to tell people that I've been knowing you'd be a famous dancer since you were a little girl."

"Yaaaaayyy!"

She was so happy that I promised to watch her. She giggled as she ran over to "her spot." Mrs. Mears came out from her office and turned on the music to let everyone know their class was officially about to start. Everyone immediately got in line, but my new little friend ran away from the spot she had just gotten to.

"I forgot to tell you my name," she whispered.

"Yeah, you sure did, but I was just gonna call you Pretty Awesome Little Ballerina Who's Gonna Be Famous."
She loudly giggled again.

"That's not my name, Miss Lady."

"Okay, what's your name, then?"
With a huge smile on her face, she replied.

"Jasmine, but my mommy calls me Mini because she said I'm like a Mini her."

"Nice to meet you. My name is Elise."

"Okay, Miss Elise, I have to practice 'cause I don't wanna get in trouble!"

I kept a smile on my face as the little girl ran to where she was supposed to be. She turned around and waived. I waived back still in shock from what I had just heard. Out of all of the little girls in the room, why did she have to be the one to talk to me? Out of all of the names in the world, why did she have to have that one?

I wanted to walk out right then, but I didn't. I made a promise to that little girl and I couldn't go back on my word. It was strange that even though I didn't know her, her name alone made me feel like I did.

"How crazy is that, sister?" I whispered as I looked up towards the sky.

As I watched the girls in the class, every once and a while I would look over at the seat next to me. I imagined my sister with a sketch pad in her hand as we watched the class together. She would smile as she drew pictures of what she saw.

"Little Jazzy is good, isn't she?"
She was referring to the five-year-old she shared a name with.

"Yeah, she is. She reminds me of me when I was around her age. No, actually I think she's better than I was."
Then reality set back in. I looked over in the same chair only to see nobody there.

Their class was soon over. I didn't think I was going to stay until they were finished, but I had. All of the families of the girls were there picking up their children. A few of the girls were sitting down, though. It seemed like they were used to being there longer than everyone else, which was sad. I felt bad for them. I especially felt bad when I saw Little Jazzy sitting down alone in the corner. I felt obligated to go check on her.

"Hey. You did great today!"
I couldn't make myself say her name while I spoke to her.

"Thank you, Miss Elise, but I wish my mommy wasn't late."
"Do you know if she's on her way to come get you?"
"Umm, I think so. If not, somebody will be here... I hope."
"What do you mean, you hope?"
"Well, sometimes mommy is late and sometimes somebody else comes to get me and sometimes I have to get on the bus."
"Sometimes you have to ride the bus? By yourself?"

"Yeah, but only sometimes. It's not far. I just get on the one bus when it gets close to us outside. And then, when I get on, I wait until the bus driver says, 'Next stop, Blaylock.' When he does that, I know I can get off and I'll almost be home."

When I heard her explain how she sometimes had to get home, I felt even worse than I did before. Sure, it was good that she had knowledge of how to get home if nobody came to pick her up, but I thought it was terrible that a kid so young would ever have to travel alone. I didn't really know her or her family, so I was not in a position to judge anything they did. I just knew I couldn't leave her there.

"Well, I think I'm going to wait with you. Is that okay?"
That huge smile returned. Sadly, that beautiful smile of hers reminded me of my sister.

I tried to conceal my true emotions again, but I was unable to. Even Little Jazzy picked up on it.

"What's wrong, Miss Elise?"
"Nothing. You just have a very pretty smile."
She was confused by what I said, but she didn't want to upset me, so she tried to cover her smile up with her hands.

"I'm sorry," she said with her face still covered.
"It's okay," I told her.
She put her hands down.

"Miss Elise, why were you sad when I was smiling? I didn't mean to do anything bad. I promise I didn't."

"I know you didn't. And you didn't do anything bad, your smile just reminded me of someone."

"Who, Miss Elise? Who did it remind you of?"
I wanted to ignore the little girl's questions, but that wouldn't have been right. I took a deep breath.

"You reminded me of my little sister."
Her smile made a return, which tore me up inside.

"Oooh! Miss Elise, I bet your little sister is pretty like you. Does that mean I'm pretty, too?"

"My sister was even prettier than me. She was the best!"
Although Little Jazzy was young, I could tell she was very smart. She picked up on the fact that I talked about my sister in the past tense.

"She was?" she asked innocently.

"Yeah, she... she passed away today."

I thought I would have to explain what passed away meant, but I didn't. She probably had heard the words before because her actions were ones to try and comfort me. It was clear she understood exactly what I meant.

"I'm sorry, Miss Elise. I'm sorry" she said as she hugged me.

The true nature of that little girl was showcased right then. Instead of her feeling bad (or mad) about her mother not being there to get her like everyone else's was, she showed that she felt bad for me. She showed how we don't have to necessarily know each other to show compassion.

"Thank you," I said.

"Hey, Miss Elise, you wanna see a cool move?"

The clever little girl knew she could at least temporarily stop me from thinking about my sadness by making me do something dance related.

"Yes, ma'am! What kind of fancy moves do you have to show me?"

She grabbed my hand and took me to the center of the floor.

"Mrs. Mears didn't show us this, but look!"

She twirled around in excitement several times. It was an unorthodox combination of moves our dance instructor would probably never teach anyone, but she was having fun with it.

"That looks like a hard move!" I said.

"No, it's not too hard. I bet you can do it, Miss Elise!"

Normally, when it came to dance, I took everything very seriously. Her special moves made me change that for a while.

"Okay, show me what you did again."

She jumped and twirled in a fun, complex, but different combination that she put together the first time. To entertain her, I tried to match what she did.

"That's good, Miss Elise! You're almost as good as me!"

"Almost? Are you sure I'm just almost as good?"

"Well, okay, you're good!"

I laughed just as hard as she did while we continued to do crazy moves for a few minutes before I saw Mrs. Mears came back out from her office.

I was almost certain I would hear her tell us both to quit being so foolish. I expected her to tell us ballet was to be taken seriously, and if we were going to play around, then we would need to find something else to do. She didn't do any of that. Instead she let us have our moments of craziness before she told us she received a call from Little Jazzy's mother.

"She said she wouldn't be in to get you today?"
She stopped in the middle of one of her spins. Her smile changed only slightly.

"It's okay. I know how to get home."

I looked at Mrs. Mears and it was clear neither of us were too fond of the idea of Little Jazzy traveling alone. Mrs. Mears was in a different position than I was. As an instructor, she wasn't really allowed to be very involved in the lives of her students. She could get in all sorts of legal trouble if she did. Fortunately, the same was not true for me.

I remembered the route the little girl said she took when there wasn't anyone there to get her. It wasn't too far away from my house, so I decided I would take the trip with her. Mrs. Mears understood why I was trying to do that, but she didn't necessarily agree that I should.

"Jasmine, could you go back to dancing? I need to speak with Elise for a moment."

"Yes, ma'am."

She did what Mrs. Mears wanted her to do and I was pulled over to the side to be a part of a different conversation.

"I understand what you're trying to do, and it's a wonderful thing, but I need for you to know what comes along with it."

"I'm not sure I'm following you."

"It's like this: you want to help her. Like I said, that's wonderful, but did you see how happy she was just because you were paying attention to her?"

"Yeah."

"She got very excited because many of the people in her life don't really care."

"I understand, but I don't really even know her. I just met her today and I doubt it'll mean anything to her if I make sure she made it home this one time."

"That's what you'd like to believe, but you're be wrong. She's five and she easily gets attached to people who seemed like they may care about her, especially since her mother doesn't seem to. If you go with her today, she might just expect that later on. And if you don't do it the next time, if it ever happens again, she may just view you as another person who let her down."

Her explanation cleared things up, but at the same time, she could have just been putting a little extra drama on her words. Whether she was telling the truth or being overly dramatic, she had never steered me wrong before and I didn't believe she was trying to do it then.

"Thank you for telling me all of that. You know, today has been very rough for me and that little girl has helped me out a lot. To me, it's more than a coincidence that her name is Jasmine. It may sound stupid, but I think God and my sister worked out a deal for me to meet her in your class today. If they did, I don't believe it was just for me to see her once and that's it. Mrs. Mears, today I lost my job of being a big sister. I feel like meeting her, in some kind of way, will give me that opportunity again."

I could almost see the light bulb go off in her head as she processed everything I said until it made sense to her.

"Elise, just don't hurt that little girl because she's already been hurt enough. And remember, even though her name is Jasmine, she's not your little sister. Please don't use her as a replacement for who you lost. She doesn't deserve that and neither does your sister. Whatever type of bond you form with her, be careful. I don't just mean that for her sake, but for yours as well."

"Yes, ma'am."

With our thoughts released out into the atmosphere, Mrs. Mears left the dance floor.

The things she said made perfect sense, but I couldn't let that little girl make the journey home by herself, even if she had done it several times before.

"Hey! Are you ready to go home?"

I felt ashamed of myself almost immediately. I didn't feel ashamed because I decided to go against what Mrs. Mears suggested I do, but because I had yet to say the little girl's name aloud. In my mind, I called her Little Jazzy, but I couldn't dare actually say that, especially not on the same day I lost Jasmine. I hoped Little Jazzy didn't catch on to it because I didn't know if I would ever be able to actually say my sister's name again.

"You're gonna take me home?" the little girl asked as she looked up at me.

"Well, sort of. I'm going to ride with you on the bus to make sure you make it home."

I could tell she got excited, even though it took her a little while to say anything.

"Miss Elise, you don't have to go with me. Mommy told me I was a big girl and I can do this stuff when it's just me."

Her words saddened me. Of course I could understand why parents normally tell their kids they are big boy or a big girl. It makes the child feel like they accomplished something, encourages them to be able to do some things independently; but it also could be used so parents would have an excuse to neglect their kids or have them do things they really shouldn't have to. That's what I felt was the case with her.

"I know you're a big girl, that's why I want to go with you. Can I tell you something?"

"What?"

I kneeled down so that we were both just about the same level. I looked around as if I had a secret that I didn't want anyone other than her to hear.

"Maybe I need to go with you because I'm scared."

I stood up and waited for her reaction.

"Miss Elise, you can come with me. I don't want you to be scared," she said.

"Thank you very much."

After that, we let Mrs. Mears know we were leaving and then we waited at the nearby bus stop.

"How often do you have to do this?" I asked.

"What do you mean, Miss Elise?"

"Do you have to take this trip by yourself a lot?"

Before she could answer, the bus showed up. She tried to dig through her bag to find her money to pay the fare, but she was having a difficult time, so I just paid for both of us.

"Thank you!" she said as she found us both a seat.

Once we were comfortable in our seats, I started speaking to her about her life. She told me her mother hardly ever stayed to watch her practice, but it didn't bother her anymore. I can only imagine how I would have felt if my mother wouldn't have been around to watch me when I first got started.

"How does that make you feel?"
I shouldn't have asked her that question, but I only realized it after it was done.

"Sometimes it makes me sad because I like to dance and I want my mommy to see me so maybe she'll be proud of me, but most of the time she says she's too tired."

How could a mother do that? How could she make that little girl think she wasn't proud of what she was doing? How could she not support what Little Jazzy obviously loved to do?

"I'm sorry about that. I'd like to make a deal with you, if I can."

"Okay, what kind of deal?" she asked as she hopped up and down in her seat.

"I just want to know if I can come and watch you in class a few times a week?"

"Are you for real? 'Cause if you are, that would be great and you can dance with me after class and you can show me new moves and I can show you new stuff! Then, you can help me with the hard moves and then I can be the best and then I can be the star of the shows!"

I don't know if she even took a breath as she ran multiple sentences into only a few seconds.

"So, I guess it's okay?"

"Yeah, It's okay! You can come to the classes, that would make me happy!"
After that, the rest of the ride was pretty quiet.

Little Jazzy just looked out of the window, watching the cars and people go by as we moved closer to her destination. Her little legs swung excitedly. I was glad I was able to make her happy, but I kept what Mrs. Mears said in my mind. I told myself no matter what, I couldn't be a person who set her up with high expectations only to let her down.

"Next stop, Blaylock. Get ready, young lady," the bus driver said as he looked at Little Jazzy in the huge mirror inside of the bus. That let me know she had taken the ride way too often.

"Miss Elise, I'm almost home but don't worry, you'll be okay. Mr. Bus Driver will make sure you are safe. He's really good!"

"But what about you? Are you gonna to be able to get inside your home?"

"Yep! I always keep my key with me."

I had no doubt she knew how to get inside of her home, but I didn't feel comfortable letting her exit the bus without me accompanying her.

"You live where I live, Miss Elise?" She asked.

"No, but I need to make sure you get all the way home safely."

"Okay, but mommy said I'm not ever supposed to let anyone get close to my door when I'm walking or when I'm going inside of my house. So, I'm sorry Miss Elise, but you can't go all the way to my house 'cause my mommy will be mad, okay?"

"Okay. Those are some very good rules. I won't go too close. Neither one of us want your mom to get upset."

I walked her close to her building, made sure she had her key, and sent her on her way. When I did, the feeling of loneliness returned almost immediately. I realized I hadn't heard from my mother since I left the hospital. In the priority list of what was going on at the time, I understood being at the bottom, but I thought my mother would have at least called to see where I was. I wasn't really even sure she knew I was gone, though. And it's not that I really cared about that, but it is cool to know your parents think about you, no matter what is going on. Being alone right then made me question if that was how my mother felt. Then I thought, "How could I question how much she cared about me when I hadn't called to check on her, either?" I needed to change that as quickly as I could. So, as I tried to find my way back home from Little Jazzy's apartments, I called my mom and prayed she would answer.

"Hi, Mom!" I said.

I tried to have a positive tone, even though I knew how terrible we both actually felt.

"Hey, Elise."

"How are you? And I mean for real, how are you?"

"I'm not good. I'm actually terrible. Jazzy's really gone, Elise. How could I let something like that happen? What kind of mother am I? How could I not protect my baby?"

Surprisingly, she was not crying as she spoke. It almost seemed as though she was beyond crying, like she had no more tears to give. It was strange, but I understood it. I also understood how she blamed herself for Jasmine's death, even though she had nothing to do with it. I blamed myself when she was attacked, when I first heard about the car accident, and I just about convicted myself of a crime when Jasmine passed away.

We needed each other to get past blaming ourselves for something we had no control over and there was no way we could do that alone.

"Mom, this didn't happen because of you and there's nothing either of us could have done to change it. If it's time for any of us to go, it's just our time. God has a plan, mom. I know He does."

Did I even believe what I was saying? Who knows? Whether I believed it or not was one thing, but it was more important for both us to first hear the message.

"I don't think any one understands..."
Whatever I was going to say, I wasn't able to finish. As soon as my mother heard me say understands, she interrupted me with a Bible verse that seemed like it was written for our situation.

"Trust in the LORD with all your heart and lean not on your own understanding."
She repeated it a few times. Even when she stopped saying it, it was almost as thought it remained on a loop for a few more seconds. The more I heard it, the more it seemed I needed to hear it.

We were not following the words that had been put out for us. Our instructions were clear, yet we were acting like we didn't know what we were supposed to do.

"Are we actually doing that, mom?"

My question wasn't complete, so I knew she wouldn't quite get what I was really asking.

"Doing what?"

"Are we actually trusting Him, even though we don't understand why things happened the way they did?"

I didn't have to be next to her to picture her facial expression after that question was asked. There had been many times our conversations made each other have those "light bulb" moments that shed light on whatever situation was keeping us in the dark.

"You know what, Elise? I don't think I have truly trusted Him. I think going through this has caused my faith to flip-flop and I'm sorry. That's not setting the best example for you."

"It's okay, mom. We're human."

"And humans are flawed, but I pray God doesn't give up on me."

"He will never give up on us, mom."

"You're right. By the way, I apologize for not calling to check on you and see where you were and how you've been coping with all of this."

"I'm fine. I'm headed home right now. I just spent the day practicing."

"I'm so glad ballet is a part of your life. It has been such a blessing to see you start something as a little girl and continue to be even more dedicated to it the older you get. I've been so fortunate to witness the passion for your craft grow."

"Yep! And I don't even know if I would have ever gotten started if..."

I had to stop myself form saying my sister's name because I couldn't predict how either of us would have reacted.

"Well, even if Jazzy hadn't given you that tutu, I think you would have eventually gotten started. Dancing is your destiny and no matter how you got started, nobody will ever be able to take that from you."

While I appreciated my mom's nice words of encouragement, I felt almost uncomfortable being the focus of the conversation. I felt like we should have only been talking about my father or Jasmine. The conflict with that was I couldn't even make myself constantly say my sister's name aloud whenever I was talking about her. I had to switch the subject.

"Are you gonna come home tonight?" I asked

"Yeah, probably in a few hours. I just need to talk to your father for a little while longer before I leave."

Hearing her say she needed to talk to dad gave me hope of a sudden improvement with his condition.

"Is dad better? I need to come back then! Is he talking?"

"Calm down, Elise. Nothing's different with your father. We just have to keep praying and remain optimistic."

"Oh."

I couldn't hide my disappointment. My mother had to know what she said would make me think my father was doing better. If she didn't, she should have.

We kept the conversation going for a little while before I could no longer talk. As I continued to try to find my way home, every once and a while I would just stop. The sky was beautiful over the city. The light from the sky forced me to look up. When I did, I started to have another talk with The Creator.

"God, right now I can't pretend. I can't pretend I get why you would make something so beautiful and also make some things so ugly. I thought I felt better when I heard my mother say we are not supposed to lean on our understanding. I know we are supposed to trust in you, but I'm scared to. I'm scared that the more I trust you, the more people you will take away from me."

God had to be upset with me because I certainly was. How could I go from accepting life to not believing what I was going through was real? I was tired of all of my emotions. I just wanted them all to just go away, but I didn't know how that could possibly happen.

I prayed for God to make me numb, no matter how temporary. And for a few days, that's how I was. From that night until the day of Jasmine's funeral, I didn't feel anything. I was not sad, but I was far from happy. I couldn't even keep track of time or what was going on around me. I would almost black out with my eyes open. Before I had the chance to comprehend what was happening, I was being called to speak.

"And now, we'd like to hear a few words from Jasmine's big sister, Elise."

I trembled as I got up from my seat and slowly went to the podium that was only a few feet away from my sister's body.

I looked at her without saying anything. Then I looked out at the crowd of people there to celebrate the life of my sister. That's when the numbness left and all of my feelings returned.

"She... was like nobody else. That girl, in some kinda way, changed all of our lives."

I looked out as I was speaking and locked eyes with my mother. She was wearing an all-black dress and the only bit of color she had was a blue scarf she had in her lap. It previously belonged to Jasmine and she absolutely loved that thing. She called it her "super fancy scarf" and whenever she wore it, she said she had to act more dignified than normal. Seeing it made me smile a little and helped me be able to continue.

"Let me tell you about..."

I felt pains in my stomach that wanted to make their presence known just as I was about to say my sister's name. I couldn't let the pains ruin any of my sister's time, so I pushed forward.

"Let me tell you all about Jasmine Emilia Morgan, the girl I mainly just called 'sister'. I know we've all heard stories about how much sisters can end up hating each other and how much they fight. Well, that never really happened with us. Don't get me wrong, sister could annoy the heck out of anybody, but at the end of the day, that little girl had more love in her heart than everybody else here combined. She cared about everybody and she could always find a way to make you smile, even when you were miserable."

As if everything I said had been practiced, for no reason, a huge smile appeared on my face.

"You see this smile? That's what my little sister did! Way to show out, Jazzy!"

Almost everyone who could hear my voice seemingly had no choice but to laugh, even my mother. I pointed out towards everyone.

"Look around. Do y'all see that? Do you see how we're smiling even thought we are here for this occasion? Only a person of God, a person with a wonderful spirit, a person of love can make that happen. We ask that y'all pray for us, yourselves, and each other. We are all going through this, not just my family. I gotta hurry up and finish before my brain remembers how sad I am and I get all choked up. I just want to say that almost everybody here has said Jazzy was too young. We all have, including me, but we said that because we're looking at things from our point of view and on our timeline. Our time really means nothing because we're on God's time. He can take a little girl named Jasmine and put such an overwhelming amount of love in her that before she was even a teenager, she was able to share love with people of all races, ages and all walks of life. She was able to do things some of us will never be able to recreate. I guess because she was called home, whatever mission God had for her has been completed. Thank you, Jazzy, for letting me be an angel's big sister. Thank you for helping me get over my fears. Thank you for helping all of us smile a bit more than we ever would have without you. Thank you and I love you, sister. Now, please... go home and get your wings. Aunt Katie is waiting on you."

    I wanted to say more, but I couldn't. I stepped from behind the podium and walked over to my sister's casket. She looked like she was asleep. Perhaps, even as she went further into her eternal slumber, she could hear all of us talking positively about her and know what a great job she did while she was on earth. I kissed her forehead and grabbled a small, folded-up note out of my purse. I put the note in her hand and hoped when she got a chance, she would read the message. It simple said, "I'll see ya later, sister! Luv U!" And then, 30 minutes later, Jasmine Emilia Morgan was officially laid to rest as her body was returned to the earth.

    The sadness I felt at the finality of it all was beyond what any words could ever describe. My mother was a wreck. For the remainder of the day, she didn't say anything. She gestured with her hands or nodded her head, but that was about it. Her youngest daughter had just been buried, and her husband wasn't able to stay awake or talk consistently, so he was in no shape for us to even consider trying to get him to the funeral, and then there was me. I was nothing more than a 15 year old kid who grew up a little that day. Contrary to what I used to believe (prior to that time), my sister's death taught me life is going to come at you and it's going to be difficult, no matter how old you are. Finding the ability to keep your faith and pray that God gives you the strength is crucial. Life will be difficult, especially in bad times. And as bad as it may sound, I was reminded when someone else's life ends, you have to make sure you actually continue to live.

Part III

    Three years passed by very quickly after my sister's death. I don't even remember grieving the loss. It seemed like one day we were at the funeral, and the next day was almost like business as usual. I expected things to be different with our family, but I didn't expect us all to adjust so quickly. There were some differences, though. The first thing I noticed was my mom's personality. It was not the same and it started at the funeral. Short responses became the norm for her. The smiles and laughter she used to bring with her wherever she went all but disappeared.

    I could understand. Not only did she have to move beyond losing Jasmine, she also had to learn how to take care of my father. After the accident, the doctors told us he was severely injured, but we thought it would just take him a long time to recover. We thought at some point, my dad would be back to normal. We were wrong. It turned out, my father was paralyzed from the waist down. The man I had once looked at as unbreakable, was no longer that.

    It was very sad, but for some reason, the whole thing made me angry. I was upset at my father for not being able to get better. I was mad at the lady who caused the accident and ruined my family. I was mad at my mother for not being able to get back to being who she used to be. I was even mad at myself for stupidly being so mad at things I knew none of us had any control over.

    Every day I would pray for the anger to just go away, but even on the days I felt good, I discovered the anger was still there. It was just laying dormant until it had the right opportunity to make its presence known. I didn't like the fact it seemed like I was becoming a stereotypical angry black female. I didn't want to become that at all, but it was almost like the world was giving me no option. How could I stay happy when I thought about the influx of negativity I was constantly dealing with?

    I battled with myself almost everyday about magnifying the bad instead of glorifying the good. It was not what I was supposed to do and I knew that, but I had a difficult time doing otherwise. When I woke up in the mornings, I normally started off with a talk with God as I looked outside of the window towards the sun. God would tell me I had a purpose and a destiny that I had yet to fulfill. It gave me hope and then I would walk out of the room.

    I would pass by the room that used to be inhabited by my sister. It was mostly unchanged and looked pretty much like it did when she was there. The posters of the pop stars and comic book heroes from three years prior were still hanging on the wall. I could always feel her vibe when I went in there. Sometimes that vibe of hers made me super happy, other times it made me miss her even more. On one of the days when the sadness was overwhelming, it would birth the anger again.

    Then that feeling would get worse as I went into the kitchen and saw my parents. My father would normally have his wheelchair pulled up to the table as he ate his breakfast. Unlike my mother and I, he didn't even seem to be upset. Out of everyone, he had it the worst, but he never complained about anything. Many days his sunny disposition of life was inspiring, but on the days when I convinced myself to be mad, he was just one of the things that usually got me upset.

"Good morning, Elise. How are you?"

"I'm okay, dad. How are you?"

He smiled and took a deep breath.

"I'm wonderful. I'm looking at two of the prettiest women to walk the face of the earth and I have the spirit of our little angel watching over us. Life is good, God is good!"

"That sounds good, dad, but do you really mean what you're saying?"

"Yep! I sure do!"

"Are you living in some type of fantasy world? I'm sorry, but I don't understand."

"I get why you feel upset about how everything has turned out, but what good does that do you?"

He waited for me to answer his question.

"I guess it doesn't do me any good, but it's hard not to be mad. Look at us! Look at you!"

I didn't really expect him to actually look around, but he did. I also wanted to take back what I said, but I couldn't.

"Elise, we can absolutely look at our lives and say that it sucks. I heard you two praying when Jasmine and I were in the hospital. I know exactly how you wanted everything to turn out. You want things to be perfect and I saw how upset you were when you saw it wasn't going to be your reality. I know the sadness and disappointment that came from that realization caused you to hate many aspects of life, but you know what? It's easy to show hatred and disapproval for all of the things you don't like, but the rewards of life don't come from doing what's easy. You are rewarded for doing what everybody finds difficult. And what's difficult for me is to be positive everyday in spite of how things are. I mean, how do you think it made me feel to wake up to find out Jasmine was gone? That was, and still is, more difficult to be positive about than anything, but focusing on the negative will kill you inside. Negativity can stop you from living, even while you're alive."

"But how do you not be mad?"

"The simple answer is God. When I couldn't keep my eyes open, when I couldn't talk to you, I wanted to die. But right before Jasmine died, I talked to God. I begged for our lives to be spared, but God told me it wasn't a part of His plan. He told me Jasmine's time on earth was over. He also told me He would not allow me to wake up until I not only accepted her death, but I was at peace with it. So when I was about to wake up, tears poured out of my eyes before anyone told me anything. I knew what happened because God told me it would. I was at peace because it was necessary for me to be so I could continue living. This is not without challenges, though. I would be lying if I said I wasn't hurt by the fact that I dream almost every night about me walking only to wake up and see I still can't. Those dreams, as much as they hurt, they give me hope. So whenever I go to therapy, or the doctor's office, I will always give more than I thought I could because the dreams have given me hope for the future. When you get married, I don't want to roll down the aisle to give you away. I want to walk and unless God says something different, that's what I'm working towards doing."

His words, under most circumstances, would have been inspirational. They could have made people re-evaluate their perspective of life. The same was true for me on most days, but sometimes anger and aggression clouded my judgement and wouldn't let me actually hear what was being said. On days like that, even if I couldn't fully "hear" what was being said, the words still sunk into my mind. The words always seemed to be resurrected at a time when I needed to hear it.

"Okay, dad. You're right."

I knew he was right, even during the times I didn't want to admit it. I stored what he said and took it with me as I said goodbye to everyone. My mother didn't say anything, but she hugged me. Her emotions were conveyed by her touch instead of her words. Her touch told me she wanted both of us to get better; it told me we were not being who we really were; but most of all, it told me, regardless of what was going on with either of us, she loved me. And the love from my parents (and God) was what I knew would eat away at the unwanted buffet of negativity I carried around with me.

"I'll see y'all later," I said as I grabbed my bags and left for the day.

Since it was the summer after my senior year, my day no longer consisted of going to school. I no longer had to deal with classes with teachers who didn't really care while I sat with kids I didn't like and who certainly didn't like me. Instead, the majority of my days were spent in the dance studio, but unlike three years prior, I wasn't just going there to practice. I was also going there to teach and it was so exciting!

When I was about 16 or 17, I was still going to practice, no matter how I felt. The majority of the girls I started with had all given up on ballet, including Paula. They found it wasn't the type of art that could help you get rich quick. So, they decided it was no longer worth their time. I was different. Like my long time teacher, Mrs. Mears, I didn't dance for the money I hoped would come along with it. I did it because I loved the art of it. I liked the beauty of the movements, the enjoyment I got when I was watching, or when I was dancing myself; and most of all, I liked how every time I prepared to dance, I was reminded of my little sister when she gave me my first tutu. Dancing made me happy, and because of that, Mrs. Mears wanted me to be more involved.

One day after class, she asked if she could speak with me.

"Would you mind staying after class for a little while? I need to talk to you."

"Okay."

"How do you like ballet?"

"I don't like it, I live for it. I can't really imagine my life without it."

She smiled.

"I thought you would say something like that. That's why I want to ask if you'd like to help me teach my classes."

"Yes! Yes! Absolutely!"

I didn't give her the time to finish her sentence, nor change her mind. And from that moment on, I not only helped teach, but helped a little with the day-to-day operations. At first it was done for free as somewhat of an internship, but by the time I had graduated from high school, it had officially become my job.

I mainly handled the beginner classes and I enjoyed every minute of it. The little girls all looked up to me and the combination of that and the dancing itself made me temporarily forget about any problems I was having outside of the studio walls. When our classes started, it was all about those girls, and what impacted me greatly was when something was bothering one of them.

One day, as I prepared to start class, one of my students came through the doors, threw her bag down, sat on the floor, and started to cry.

"What's wrong?"

"I don't wanna dance no more! I don't wanna!"

"Why not? Don't you like it?"

"Yes, ma'am, but the girls make fun of me 'cause I don't look like them. They are little! I don't wanna dance with them!"

She was four and she was a little bigger than the other girls.

"Don't you let anybody stop you from doing what you like to do. Do you like being a ballerina?"

"Yeah!"

"Do you want the other girls to be able to practice and put on shows for their parents, but not you?"

"No!"

"Oh! Well, I guess you want to quit because everybody is better than you are, right?"

"Nuh-uh! They're not better than me!"

"So why do you want to quit?"

"Because one of the girls is white and skinny and she made fun of me and said people on TV looked like her and not me."

"The people on TV don't look like me either, but that doesn't matter. When I first started, I had people telling me I couldn't do it, but you know what helped me keep going?"

"No, ma'am. What?"

"When some people told me I couldn't do it, I had people who loved me tell me that I could. When they did, I felt like nothing could stop me and look, I'm still dancing!"

"But do you think I should still dance?"

"Yep, I sure do!"

She stood up straight and wiped her face.

"Okay! I'm gonna dance!"

And for the moment, I helped a little girl regain her confidence and hope. I just had to find a way for me to do the same thing for myself.

I was happy the little girl was feeling better, but I couldn't allow the bullying to continue. So I patiently stood at the front of the class and waited for the rest of the girls to get in. Once everyone was there, I had to speak my mind.

"Girls, it has come to my attention that we haven't been treating each other fairly. It seems some of you have been bullying others because they look different than you do. Do you think that's fair?"

"Noooooo!" they said.

"So if you don't think it's fair, then why would you do it?"

Nobody said anything. They all were just staring at me as if they were being scolded by their parents.

"I guess since nobody has an answer, that means we don't have a reason. If we don't have a reason, then that means we shouldn't be doing it. When we're inside of here, we're not only dancers, but sisters. I don't want anybody talking bad about their sisters. Is that understood?"

"Yeeesss," they answered.

After that, we didn't really have a need to talk about them bullying or disrespecting each other because it didn't really happen. We continued throughout the remainder of class with everyone focused on the dance and it was amazing to see the results. I was so proud of them. After class, the little girl who was sad before class started made sure to talk to me before she left.

"Thank you very much for talking. They were nice and it was fun today."

"You're welcome, and thank you for not giving up. That took a lot of courage."

"Cour-age? What's that?"

"Well, that just means you were brave."

"I was brave?"

"Yep, you sure were!"

She put her hands on her hip for a few seconds. Then she smiled as she playfully ran around in a circle, saying, "Brave, brave, I was brave. I was so happy I was brave! Yaaaayyy!"

It was beautiful to see such a quick turnaround for her. She went from crying and wanting to give up to shouting while she celebrated her success. Her ability to move on after a bad experience was more than amazing. I tried to keep the thought of what I saw that day with me. I figured if I did, perhaps it could help me turn things around as well.

The end of my work day arrived, so I headed home. I had a car, but most of the time I preferred to just walk to and from class. I usually needed that time to try and clear my head of things I shouldn't have been thinking about. I also used the time to talk to God. The conversations with Him were difficult— not because I never heard anything, but because often times I would hear more than I was ready to.

Unlike people, God constantly showed grace and mercy with His actions. He also never lied when it came to His words and that's what was tough. People sometimes stretched the truth or danced their way around it, but this wasn't an option for God. His truth didn't have any levels like ours did; it just was the Truth.

"Father, why can't I ever just fully release these bad feelings?"

I couldn't even fathom why I was even having any bad feelings after such a great class, but I was. I continued speaking to God as I walked.

"Why am I the way I am, and will I ever change? Why can I be in a building full of people and feel like I'm alone? Why is there nobody here on earth who I can talk to who just cares about me?"

No sooner than I finished asking my last question, my phone rang.

"Hi, what's up?"

It was my friend, Hamilton. I met him about a year before when I was at the mall with one of my friends. One of them dared me to go over and talk to him and so I did. By the way he was dressed, I was sure he'd be a jerk, but he turned out to be one of the nicest people I had ever met.

"Some friends and I were going to the game at the university. Since one of my friends canceled, I was hoping you would want to go. I know you probably just got out of practice or something, but if you're not too tired, I think you'll have fun. Plus I'll come and pick you up!"

"I don't know. I did just get out of class and I'm a little sweaty."

I was trying to use any excuse not to go. It's not that I didn't want to, it's just that Hamilton and his friends were from a more "well-to-do" part of town. Whenever I hung out with them, I always felt out of place, like I didn't belong. They usually never said or did anything to make me feel this way. More than likely, it was just my self-esteem issues.

"Maybe you didn't hear me, Elise. We're just going to the game. Who cares if you're sweaty? After cheering on the team all game, we'll all probably be that way. So just think of it as you getting a head start on us. Don't worry, you'll be in the car with me, you'll sit next to me, and if anybody says anything, just blame it on me. I don't care."

He laughed and I did too.

"So, it's a date, right?"

"Sure."

"Great! I'll pick you up in about an hour."
Just like that, I went from talking to God about being alone to having plans with a group of people in a matter of only a few minutes.

I sped up my walking pace a little bit. Even though Hamilton said he would be at my house to pick me up in an hour, I had to try and freshen up. I couldn't go out smelling like the dance studio and sweat. Even though the scent came from working and was almost like a badge of honor showcasing my hard work, I couldn't carry it with me to the game.

"Hey mom! Hey dad!" I said when I made it home.

My dad rolled closer to where I was.

"Hey, Professor Elise. How was class today?"

Since I started teaching, every once and a while, my dad would call me Professor Elise. I tried to fight the name at first, but my dad's use of the name eventually wore me down.

"It was good. I had to have a talk with my girls about bullying, but I think we all have an understanding now."

"Well, that's good. It looks like you're in a hurry. Are you about to go somewhere?"

"Yeah, I'm just going to the game."

"At the university? For real? I used to be unstoppable, you know that, right? Ask your mom, I schooled everybody!"

According to my dad, he was the greatest basketball player that never made it. When I was a kid, I used to kind of dismiss his stories because we all go back and exaggerate how good we used to be at something. Then, as I got older, he started to show me proof. I saw all of the trophies, ribbons, medals, and newspaper clippings. So, I started to believe that if nothing else, he wasn't lying. I always wondered if he was so good, why didn't he get an opportunity to play somewhere professionally, but I figured he neglected to tell us that for one reason or another, so I never asked.

"Oh, I believe you, dad! I know how good you were!"
He kept a child-like grin on his face. I could see him reliving some of his basketball moments in his mind.

"Yes, ma'am. I was pretty good. That's enough about me. You go ahead and get ready to go to the game."

I did exactly what he said I should and soon, Hamilton was ringing the doorbell. My father answered the door while I finished getting ready in my room.

"How are you, sir?"

I could hear the conversation while I was in my room. I hoped they would get along until I was ready.

"I'm doing well, young man. You know what, I'm glad you had enough respect for my daughter to actually come to the door. Most guys your age would have kept blowing the horn until it annoyed everyone in the neighborhood."

"Yeah, I'm a little different. Plus, I just don't like doing things like that."

"Well, that's good to hear. So I hear you are going to the game tonight."

"Yes, sir. We're going to meet up with a group of friends. Our team is playing well and we just want to cheer them on. Hopefully we can make the summer tournament this year. I know it's not like the actual tournament, but it's still something fun to be a part of. Plus, that always gets us ready for the next season."

"Yeah, I don't see why you wouldn't. Your point guard is averaging fifteen points and nine assists a game. And your center, that dude is a beast! How in the world is he getting almost four blocks a game? Oh yeah, the way y'all are destroying schools, it would be a crime if you weren't be able to play in any of these tournaments, including the ones from the summer leagues."

"Oh, snap! You really follow basketball, for real!"

I thought for sure my father would start talking about his glory days, but surprisingly, he didn't.

"Yeah, I follow basketball on all levels! Don't let this wheelchair fool you, I know the game!"

They were both very hyped up about the game. I was certain they could have kept talking. In fact they were getting along so well, I almost expected Hamilton to tell me he was going to take my father instead. So, I hurried up and went out of the room.

"Wow! You know we're just going to the game, right?" Hamilton asked when he saw me.

"Yeah, this isn't anything fancy. I just threw this on." Okay, it wasn't fully the truth, but I said it anyway.

"Well, you look wonderful. I don't know if I'll be able to focus on the game with you looking like that."
I appreciated the compliment and I knew he only said it to be nice, but I think, for a moment, he forgot my father was in the room.

"Thank you," I told him.

"Mr. Morgan, I'm sorry. I wasn't trying to be disrespectful at all."

"I know you weren't. She's a beautiful young woman and you were just acknowledging that."

"Yes, sir. That's true."

"I know. Now you two have a good time, but not too good. And I don't want my daughter to get back here too late. Is that understood, young man?"

"Yes, sir. Absolutely."

We finally left the house after that. I felt good because it seemed like Hamilton and my father really got along. Even though we had no official title to our relationship, I was happy dad and Hamilton were able to have more than just a cordial conversation without me being around.

"I appreciate that," I said as we drove towards the arena.

"What?"

"The conversation you had with my father, for not looking down on our home or making sly remarks about my dad being in a wheelchair."

"Your dad genuinely seems like a cool guy. He certainly knows basketball and that's awesome! As for that other stuff, I have no right to look down on anybody. I have nothing."
I knew what type of car he drove and where he grew up, so his comment needed some explaining.

"What are you talking about?"

"Well, I grew up a certain way because of my parents. I'm still living a certain kind of lifestyle because of them. I know how blessed I am, but I also know I have nothing on my own because I haven't earned anything yet. I know you've seen many of my friends and you think that I must be friends with them because we have similar personalities, but it's not like that. My friends and I are cool almost in spite of our personalities, not because of them."

"So you don't think you have some sort of sense of entitlement because of your name, your zip code, or who your parents are?"

"Entitlement? Nope! I don't believe in that. I am super proud of all of my family's accomplishments, but I want to accomplish some things on my own. I want to get to a point when people won't question if the things I have, the people I'm around, or anything I have earned has anything to do with my last name. I want them to know only about what I have worked hard for and earned."

"That's really cool, Hamilton. I really like that."

The conversation continued until we reached the arena. I wasn't one who frequently went to basketball games, so I wanted to really take in all of the sights and sounds. All of the cars, all of the people... it was amazing. It was so hard to believe everyone was there to support two teams.

"Is it like this every week?" I asked as we parked the car and went towards the entrance.

"Not quite. We're playing against our rivals tonight, so the atmosphere is just a little bit crazier than it normally is."

As soon as we walked in, I was almost in shock over everything I was seeing. Sure, I had seen plenty of games on television before, but it was completely different when you were actually there. Everywhere you went, there were people and whenever you looked in a different direction, there seemed to be even more. You almost had to choreograph your steps with the person in front of you to avoid being bumped by the person behind you.

"Hammy-hamm! What's up, buddy? It's about time you made it! " Zach, one of Hamilton's friends, called out as we reached the section where our seats were.

I didn't really know Zach, but I didn't like what I had seen. Zach was not like Hamilton. He had no problems exploiting his family's name. He had no problem trying to get everything he could for free because he, for some reason, felt like he deserved it.

"Is this the same chick we saw the other day or is this somebody else? We know how you do it, lady killer!"
He also had no problem being a jerk!

Hamilton apologized for Zach's behavior as we greeted the rest of the group. If I would have purchased tickets to the game, we would have been in the nosebleed section, but I was in a different world with them. Our seats were so close, I felt like I could stick my feet out and trip the players.

"These are amazing seats, Hamilton. I never would have thought I would ever be in seats like these!"

"Well, hopefully we'll be able to hang out a lot more. That way, you'll be able to experience other things you never thought you would."

I wasn't one who blushed, at least not normally, but I did then.

We got comfortable in our seats. We yelled out our hatred for the visiting team and cheered for the home team. I didn't know any members of either team, but I got caught up in the excitement of it all very quickly. As the first quarter drew closer to a conclusion, the different foods that were available in the arena started hitting me at one time. I must have unknowingly had a look of hunger on my face because Hamilton soon asked me if I was ready to eat.

"Elise, do you want something to eat?"

"Yeah, well... kinda."

"Okay. I know you probably are used to only eating all of that healthy stuff so you can stay looking so good, but they don't really have a lot of that stuff here. But don't worry, you are in the land of almost limitless hotdogs, burgers, nachos, and pizza. And any of it can be yours!

I looked around at what had to be over 20,000 people. Most of them seemed to be thoroughly enjoying at least one of the foods that was just mentioned to me. I wasn't the kind of girl who counted calories, but I couldn't help but imagine how many calories were in each bite. There was no way I could even begin to convince myself any of that food would be okay to eat.

"No, thank you. None of this food will help me out when I'm in dance practice tomorrow. I want to, but I won't."

"Your decision is commendable. Even when nobody's watching, you remain disciplined."

When situations arose before that time, the people around me would try to pressure me to do like the were doing. Sure, most people wouldn't think eating certain foods is a big deal; but when you want to be a dancer, that kind of stuff could ruin you. I had worked way too hard to let some arena nachos knock me off course.

"It's nothing special. I just have to do what I have to do. A lot of work goes into being a ballerina, both in and out of the studio," I said.

"Yeah, I can only imagine being so passionate about something that you're willingly ready to give up things and make sacrifices for what you love."

"Thank you."

"You know what? I want to make a little sacrifice, too. As good as the pizza is looking, I'm gonna pass on it. It would be rude to be scarfing down a greasy slice of pepperoni pizza while you just sit there."

"I'm okay, really."

"Nope! I'm not gonna do it. I'll tell you what: if you're hungry after the game, we'll grab something quick and healthy. Is that okay?"

I agreed and we went right back to watching the game. Every once and a while, we'd glance over at each other and make eye contact. We would smile and then look away as if we hadn't noticed each other. It was cute and innocent and I enjoyed every second of it. Over the years, I (for whatever reason) wasn't the girl people seemed to be attracted to, so getting attention from someone was new. Quite frankly, I didn't know how I was supposed to handle it.

As the game went on, I caught myself giving high fives and having a good time with just about every one of Hamilton's friends. Zach was not included in that. Obviously, in his mind, he was "better than me". Since he felt this way, it seemed like he thought associating with me was beneath him. He didn't just come out and say it, but that's how it seemed to be.

I understood everyone can't get alone with everyone else, but the way he acted towards me actually hurt. I tried my best to hide it. I didn't want it to show that how someone felt about me was almost ruining an otherwise very cool night. I fought very hard not to let it happen. I just enjoyed my time, and by the end of the game, I didn't even realize he was still there.

"So did everyone have a good time?" Hamilton asked as we talked outside after the game.

"This, by far, was the best game of the year!" multiple friends of his said.

"Yeah, it was cool except..." Zach started.

"Except, what?" asked Hamilton.

He didn't say anything for a little while. Instead, he chose to just look at me. We all got the point of what he was trying to get across.

I had enough. I had to speak my mind.

"What is your problem with me? What did I ever do to you?"

With one of the most evil grins I had ever seen, he replied, "Don't flatter yourself, hon. Contrary to what you may believe, the world doesn't revolve around you. Yeah, I heard about you from around town. I heard you like to call yourself a ballerina. Do you think that makes you special? 'Cause if you do, you're wrong!"

I didn't know where any of that was coming from, but he seemed jealous of me for some reason.

I could see Hamilton was getting upset with all of the words Zach was spewing. He clenched his fists and he seemed ready to shut Zach up one way or another. It wasn't necessary, though. I leaned over and told him not to worry about it because I could handle it.

"Zach, I'm sorry. I didn't know it would be a problem."

"What are you talking about?"

People were watching us like school-aged kids watched after school fights. It amped me up and almost forced me to continue.

"Well, I didn't know my being a dancer would be a problem for you. Maybe if you would have practiced more and put in more work on your legs, you may have at least been a little bit better at it. I hate you stopped, though. I'm pretty sure I could have helped you make it."

He was getting more and more upset by the second.

"Hamilton, get your girlfriend before she talks her way into something she won't be able to talk her way out of!"

His anger was funny to me. I should have stopped, but I didn't.

"Are you threatening, Elise? Is that really what you're doing right now?" Hamilton asked.

I let him know I didn't fear Zach. Without saying it, I basically told him I was okay and he could just enjoy the show.

"Now I get it! Not only are you jealous of me being a dancer, but I think you may be a little upset Hamilton is spending time with me, instead of you. I'm not saying anything, but..."

I left it there. It was not necessary for me to say anything else. People were laughing hysterically at him and he wasn't used to it. His ego wouldn't allow him to be embarrassed and his lack of intelligence wouldn't allow him to understand that his inability to be humbled caused me to tell him exactly how I felt. I will never try to force anyone to like me, but I try my best not to disrespect people or have them disrespect me.

As Zach left the group, I instantly felt bad for going outside of my normal character. Did he deserve what I said? I wasn't really sure, but I hoped the things that were said would cause some type of change in him. Since everyone in their group of friends seemed to be pretty good people, I figured somewhere deep down inside, Zach was too. I just hoped my words would push him more to being cool than to being a bigger jerk.

"Daaaaang, Elise! I've never seen Zach run away so quickly! You really made him shut his mouth. I have to say; it was pretty awesome!" one of the girls in the group said.

I laughed, but it was more of an awkward reaction than anything else.

"I didn't really want to talk to him like that, though," I said.

"Well, we sure couldn't tell. It seemed like you were waiting to tell him off."

"No. I promise you it wasn't planned and I hope that side of me doesn't come around again."

The appearance of the "non-civilized" version of Elise was entertaining to the group, but the more they talked, the more ashamed of myself I became.

"That's not me," I said to Hamilton.
He chuckled and tried to cover his face as if he hadn't laughed.

"No apologies needed, Elise. Sometimes that guy's ego gets a bit inflated. Usually, we just let his sly comments go, but it's a good change to see him get put in his place. I'm happy with how you handled him."

We talked about what had happened for a little while longer before that subject faded away. We told everyone bye for the night and then tried to figure out where we were going for food.

"Do you know of any good places to go, Elise?"

"Not really, but I'm just looking to get something light, maybe a salad or something."

And so we simply got a healthy meal and then he dropped me off. He said he promised my father he wouldn't keep me out late, so he wanted to stay true to his word. My father appreciated that.

The night of the game changed some things for me; even though nothing actually happened, I started to feel different. I had been carrying around the feelings of being "weird" since I first started dancing. I thought I had long moved past feeling bad about myself because of what I was called when I was six, but it wasn't until that night that I learned it wasn't actually true. I realized even those who accept their quirks and weirdness still get happy when they're recognized by the cool kids.

I stayed up light that night just reflecting. Just like when I was a kid, I found it comfortable to just sit in the corner of my room. I smiled and laughed when I thought about all of the events of that happened that night. I gained a lot of hope. Since I was younger, my family helped me believe I could make it as a ballerina, so I always had hopes for my career, but because of what I had seen— because of my interactions that night— I had hopes for my personal life.

I could imagine myself dancing on stages all around the world, but when doing so, I couldn't say for sure I ever imagined myself smiling and enjoying those moments. Why was that? My mother was robbed and attacked, yet nothing happened to the person who did it. My father was paralyzed and my little sister was killed by a woman who walked away from it all as if it had never happened. So, I don't know if it was that I didn't have hope in what I could do or if I just felt eventually something bad was going to happen to me, in the way things happened to my family. Those thoughts made me question my morality, my loyalty to my family, and my belief in what was destined for me (according to God's plan). My hope, or lack of it at times came from all of those things.

That night gave me some of my hope back because I wasn't necessarily worrying about avoiding the bad, but expecting something good. Spending time with Hamilton let me find peace in our possible futures, even if we ended up as nothing more than friends. Just as I was becoming a little more comfortable in my feelings, my mind showed me it wouldn't allow me to stay there for long.

As I thought about Hamilton, for some reason I started to hear my little sister's voice.

"Oooh, sister!!"

I cried while I smiled. I knew she wasn't there, but it didn't stop me from talking to her as if she was.

"What are you oooing about, Jasmine?"
That's when I went from just hearing her voice to seeing her as she spoke.

"I'm talking about you and your new boyfriend. I'm happy that you're happy, sister."

"How do you know I'm happy? What makes you say that?"

"It just seems like you've been a little bit happier since you met him. Don't be embarrassed. I'm glad to see you like that."

In life and in death, she still was able to be happy for others, but the fact that she really wasn't there quickly eliminated the joy I was feeling. Once again I became angry. I screamed out. My pain was felt in every corner of the house and soon my mother came rushing into my room.

She knew where I sat when I needed to have a moment, so she walked over to the corner as soon as she stepped into the room. As expected, she had no words for me. She sat with me and tightly held my hand. It felt like she was almost trying to squeeze the negative emotions away, but it was impossible. There was no doubt she had the best of intentions, but I couldn't handle her non-verbal communication. Again, I was sick of it.

"I can't take this! I'm tired of you being quiet. Don't you understand what has happened to all of us? Have you grieved for Jasmine? Have you ever talked to daddy about how things are different for him?"

She stood up. I expected her to leave, like she often did, but she didn't do that. For the first time in what seemed like forever, she gave her emotions freedom as she expressed herself. She sighed very heavily.

"How do you think all of this has affected me? Do you think I'm happy I lost one of my daughters? Do you think I feel good about attending her funeral instead her going to mine? Is that what you think?"

"I don't know! You never talk to us anymore!"

By this time, I was standing up, almost as if it were my defense against her questions.

"Okay, you want to hear how I feel? If you want to hear, I'll tell you! Life is way beyond terrible! I don't have a lot of good things to say, so I wasn't going to say much of anything at all. You asked me if I've grieved for Jasmine. Elise, that's almost all I've done for the past three years! I cry every single day. At work, I'm not even there, even when I am. And then, when I get home...."

She went from being very loud, to speaking at a low whisper.

"... when I get home, I see your father. It hurts me so much to see him like that. It's even worse knowing I can't do anything about it. And don't think I don't know what you're doing."

"What do you mean?"
I was perplexed, but at the same time, I was curious to hear her continue.

"I mean, do you think I haven't noticed how you've steadily increased the time you've been at that dance studio since Jazzy died?"

"I practice a lot because I want that as my career. You know how long I've been saying I want to be a ballerina."

"Yeah, that may be true, but it now seems like you're also practicing so you can always have an excuse to leave the house. It seems like you're using it to run away from your reality."

"Run away from reality? Ballet is my reality! The fact that I'm even doing it is because of the little sister who's no longer here. If I stop, it'll be like disrespecting her memory. Didn't you tell me something like that? Didn't you tell me I had to find a way to dance when I'm broken? Weren't those the words you told me? Did you hope I'd forget you said that because it seems like you want me to stop dancing because of how broken we all feel right now. Well, I'm sorry, mom. You may have lost your ability to follow your own advice, but I haven't! I'm hurt every day, too, but I'm expressing it because I don't want it to eat way at me like it seems to be doing with you. I pray about strength and emotional growth everyday because I still believe God is working on me. You are acting like He just gave up on you and that's not cool! He hasn't give up on any of us, and no matter how hard it is, we're never supposed to forget that."

My mother was obviously upset by what I said. She was no longer concerned with consoling me. My words hurt her feelings. That's now what I was trying to do, but at least she showed she was still capable of having feelings.

"I'm glad you have it all figured out, Elise," she said as she left the room.

Usually, I couldn't stand to see my mother upset. Normally, I would have chased her down and apologize over and over until she forgave me. That night wasn't a normal one in the Morgan household. Sadly that night was when I felt a dramatic shift in the relationship I had with my mother.

The next morning, I hoped things would just go back to how they were, but they didn't.

"Good morning, everybody!" I said

"Well hello, Elise," my father said happily.

"Hey daddy!"

My mother just cut her eyes at me as she gathered up enough "love" to make herself say hello. It didn't feel good at all, but I didn't know what to do about it, so I didn't do anything at all.

When I sat down to eat my breakfast of oatmeal with organic strawberries, bananas, and honey, I received a call.

"Good morning, Miss Elise."

It was Little Jazzy. She and I had become very close over the years and I had almost become like a mentor to her, especially when it came to dancing. We spoke to each other almost on a daily basis and I was able to pick up on even the slightest of variations in her tone. Her "hello" felt like it was accompanied by some nervous energy.

"Good morning! How are you?"

I didn't want to be rude, so I excused myself from the kitchen so my parents could try to enjoy their meals while I continued on with my phone call.

"I'm good... well, kinda good."

"Kinda good? I don't know if I like the sound of that. Be honest with me. What's going on?"

"Umm... since our dance class is going against other ballet schools, I've been scared."

"Why have you been scared?" I asked.

"I'm scared 'cause they may be better than me and if they are, I may make our class lose and then everybody will be mad at me!"

"Nobody's perfect and I think we all know that. And it's a team competition. So, it's about everyone, not just you. The judges will want to see how the team works together. If you mess up, so what? You'll just practice and get better!"

"But you don't ever mess up, Miss Elise!"

"Oh, that's is so not true! I mess up all of the time. That's why I always have to practice."

"Miss Elise, do you think you can help me practice?"

"I will absolutely help you! When do you want to go to the studio?"

"Whenever you can!"

"Okay. Have you already gotten permission from your mother?"

"No. She already left for the day. Plus, she doesn't care anyway. She never cares about me!"

She always said things like that and it always saddened me. Hearing them then, only a night's sleep removed from arguing with my own mother, helped me see kids (no matter their age) are deeply affected when they feel their parent doesn't care. At that moment, she and I were almost like emotional twins, sharing each other's pain.

"I know she cares about you."

"I dunno. If she did, how come she doesn't do all the stuff you do?"

"Moms are very busy. I'm sure she's just making sure she is able to take care of you. That's called making a sacrifice."

"A sacrifice?"

"Yeah, your mother probably wants to spend a lot more time with you every day, but she gives up some of that time to go to work. When she does that, she's able to get money to pay for where you live, your food, your ballet class, and even the phone you're talking on. She sacrifices some things so you can have what you need. That's what sacrificing is."

"Oh, I get it now! And you sacrifice for me and for ballet, too!"

"Yeah, I guess I do, but so do you."

We discussed the sacrifices we all made, and then I went to go get Little Jazzy. While we were in the car, we just had random conversations. It was almost scary because sometimes it felt like I was talking to a younger version of myself and other times it felt like I was actually talking to my sister.

"Do you realize how special you are?" I asked her when we made it to the studio.

She looked at me like I had just said the most outrageous thing she had ever heard.

"I'm not special, Miss Elise. I'm just me!"

"You being you is why you're special. Do you remember when I first met you?" She thought about it for a few seconds.

"Yeah, I remember. I was just a little kid, then."

"Yep! It was a long time ago, but something happened that day."

"Oh yeah! Wait, what happened?"

"I saw kids tell you your dance moves were cool and ask you how you did them. Do you know why they did that?"

"Nope! I don't know."

"It's easy. It's because you're special. Your differences make you stand out. Now, some of those girls who were in your class want to be like you. You're a great dancer!"

"Thank you, Miss Elise! Thank you! You're a great dancer, too and you know what else?"

"You're like my big sister or something. No, you're almost like a second mother!"

That statement was one of the nicest things anyone could say, but at the same time, it was also a very hard thing to hear. For some reason, my mind made me believe having another little girl say I was like a big sister was disrespecting the memory of my actual little sister. Once again, I didn't want to cry, but it was like I had no choice.

    We had stopped, but we hadn't yet gotten outside of the car. I put my head on the steering wheel and just started sobbing uncontrollably.

    "I'm sorry, Miss Elise. I didn't mean anything bad. I'm sorry. I didn't want you to feel bad. I take it back, you're not my sister. I'm sorry!"

I had to let the last tears leave my eyes before I could raise my head and wipe my face.

    "Don't take it back. It was a very nice thing to hear and it made me feel very good. It just made me miss my sister."

    "Can I ask you something?" she wondered.

    "Sure. What's up?"

    "I know you're not my big sister or a second mom in real life and I know I never met your sister, but you always say I remind you of her. So would it be okay if I call her Auntie Jazz? If not, it's okay."

    Moments like that served as a reminder (at least to me) how close kids are to God. Only somebody close to God could not only know the words that need to be said at a particular moment, but they also seem to understand and be able to handle emotions that are a result of something they said.

    "Auntie Jazz?" I asked.

    It felt weird for me to say it, but it felt good. I imagined how life would be in the future if we hadn't lost her. I could see myself married with a child and Jasmine would be the best aunt ever! She was such a good person that this little girl, who had never seen my sister (let alone build any type of relationship with her), wanted to refer to her as Auntie Jazz. I was shocked, but then again, I wasn't. My sister was always able to make a positive impact on everyone; it was as though that was one of the main jobs God assigned to her and she wasn't going to let anything (not even death) stand in the way of her assignment.

    "Yes, ma'am! The way you talk about her, she had to be a really, really cool girl aaaaannnnd if that's my aunt, that means I'm part of your family! That would be sooo awesome!"

All I could do was smile after I heard her say that.

"Well, consider yourself a part of the family."

"Yaaaayyy!"

Her reaction to becoming an honorary member of the Morgan family was absolutely priceless. We both smiled and laughed with each other.

"Now that we're family, we need to get in there and do what our family does best."

"Yes, ma'am! Let's go!"

We both seemed extremely excited to simply go in the studio and dance. Granted I got excited every single time I danced (whether it was at home, in the studio, or in front of an audience), but the energy level seemed higher then than it had been in a little while. I felt almost like I did the day I went to my first class. I had a nervous energy, but I didn't understand why. Perhaps the energy came from a feeling of something new about to start in my life. I prayed that if that were the case, I would at least have a little bit more of the good than the bad that had been plaguing my life's story.

Jasmine and I went into the dance studio. Whatever was causing the new feelings within me had seemingly spread to her as well. We looked around as if we had never been there before.

"How does this place make you feel?" I asked.

She turned around in full circles, multiple times, just trying to take it all in.

"Miss Elise, I love this place!"

"Why do you love it? We don't have any video games here. We don't have any TVs or anything like that. Most kids would think this place is boring and they wouldn't want to stay here. So why do you like being here?"

"We don't need to have games and all of that other stuff here because it's perfect just how it is. When I'm in here, sometimes I forget about all of the fights and stuff that happen around where we live. Miss Elise, when I'm in here, you and Mrs. Mears make me feel good about myself and I feel like I can do important stuff with my life. I think I will be able to be great at dancing and do this forever!"

"Do you mean that?"

"Yes ma'am. If I couldn't do ballet here, I wouldn't like it at all. I wouldn't know what I would do. I just wanna dance!"

"I really like to hear that. So let's finally get started."

Little Jazzy moved a little closer to where I was.

"Miss Elise, before we start, can I tell you something?"

"Sure, go for it."

"I just wanna say thank you very much!"

"You're welcome."

"Can I tell you something else?"

"Yes, you can."

"I don't wanna sound weird or anything, but I love you, Miss Elise."

"That's not weird at all. I love you too, Little Jazzy."

As soon as those words hit the atmosphere, I realized what I had done. I didn't feel bad about saying what I did because I truly loved her as if she really were a part of my family. The strange part of it was that, for the first time, I was able to feel fully comfortable when I said her name. I thought for sure hearing myself say her name would cause me to have yet another breakdown, but it didn't. It felt as though my sister had given me the go-ahead to move on.

I closed my eyes for a few seconds and had a very brief conversation with my sister. Once my eyes opened, Little Jazzy had her arms wrapped around me very tightly.

"Thank you, Miss Elise! Thank you, thank you, thank you. And I love my nickname! I think Auntie Jazz would have liked it, too. I feel so good!"

"Yeah, I agree. I think she would have liked the name, but she would have absolutely loved you."

After hearing that, she had a huge smile on her face as she let me know she was ready to get to work.

"Being the best is not going to be easy. We are going to spend a lot of time practicing, exercising, and praying." I said.

"Praying?"

"Yep. Praying. You have to have God in your life to truly be successful. Praying is how we communicate with Him."

"Mama talks to God sometimes, but not a lot."

"What about you? Do you talk to God?"

She stopped so she could really prepare her response.

"Miss Elise, I try to talk to God, but I don't really know how. Every time I try to speak, I always think I'm doing something wrong. I don't wanna say anything wrong...'cause that's God. He is super important!"

"You're right! He's super important, but that doesn't mean you can't talk to Him the way you would talk to anybody else."

"But what if I'm really, really mad or really, really sad? Can I talk to Him then?"

So many of the moments of my life played back to me when she asked me those questions. I remembered times when I prayed to thank God for my happiness and when I wanted to yell at Him for making me go through everything that was bad. I also recalled times when I was so devastatingly sad (like when Jasmine passed) that I wanted to give up on everything. Then I snapped out of thinking about the past so that I could speak with Little Jazzy at that moment.

"There is no time or any emotion that God can't handle. In fact, He wants you to speak to Him, no matter what. In Proverbs Chapter 3, verse 6, it says to acknowledge Him in all your ways and He will make your paths straight."

"Huh? What does that mean?"

"To me, it simply means talk to Him, no matter what, and He'll help you figure things out."

"For real?"

"Yep! Trust me, I talk to God all the time, even when I don't think He's listening to me. He always helps me and that's really all there is."

"Oh, okay! Cool! I like that a lot! Now can we start dancing?" she asked.

"Yes, now we can finally get to work."

From there, that was what we did; we worked. We stretched, practiced, and exercised for quite a while. I thought she would give up and want to stop for the day, but I was wrong. She worked harder than I thought was possible, especially for a person as young as she was. Again we seemed like we were the same person. I was the older version of her and she was the younger version of me. We both had no problems working hard and asking for help from God and people around us. We also were both given the passion for dance and maybe she didn't know, but I felt our God-given talents and work ethic would be used to open people's eyes. We would be used to show what people of God can do, what women and people of color can do. I believed we would be in the forefront to show the world what could be accomplished when you don't have limitations on who you are and your potential.

    We were in the dance studio on a day when there wasn't supposed to be much activity. So, during much of the day, it was just the music, the dance, Little Jazzy and me. The space allowed us both to focus on what we were there for without being distracted, but soon that changed. Our practice session was interrupted by a phone call in the office. I answered the phone in the professional manner Mrs. Mears had instructed me to do so. When I did, I was surprised to find out it was actually Mrs. Mears who was calling.

    "I knew I was more likely to be able to reach you there than on your personal line," she said.

    "Yes, ma'am. I can't take any days off. I want to accomplish my goals way too much to rest."

    "I love to hear that! Your dedication to ballet is ultimately why I was hoping I'd be able to work with you today."

    I momentarily paused the conversation to check on Little Jazzy. She was still practicing as if I had never left. I shouldn't have been surprised, though. It was what I would have done if I were in the same situation.

    Once I made sure she was okay, I excused myself and went back into the other room to continue the conversation.

    "What's going on, Mrs. Mears?" I asked.

    "Elise, what have you been telling me your ultimate goal is? What have you been telling me you wanted to do since you were a little girl?"

    "I've always said I want to be a professional dancer. That's all I've ever wanted to do."

    "Is that still true?"

    "It's true now more than it ever has been!"

    "When do you think you'll be ready to take the next step towards your goal?"

    "I'm not really sure I understand what you mean?"

"Don't overthink the question. Just hear what I'm asking and respond to that."

"Okay," I said.

At that point in the conversation, I was confused, but I also didn't want to hear more of what was starting to sound like annoying stall tactics.

"When do you think you'll be ready to take the next step towards your goal?"

She asked the exact same question without any additional information. So I did what she said and simply answered the question.

"I'm ready now!"

"Are you sure?"

"Yes, I'm very sure!"

The nerves started to kick in a little bit because I had agreed to something, even though I wasn't yet sure what it was. I listened more intently to gather all of the details I could about what she had to tell me.

"I'm glad you said that, Elise. Just a few minutes ago, I received a phone call. During this call, I got some really great news…"

"The suspense is killing me! Please tell me what's going on."

"You're right. Let me just get to the point. Whenever you dance, someone is made aware of it. Whenever we all perform, there are always people watching to see who the standout stars are. Over the years, people have been talking about you, without you even knowing about it."

"And what does that mean?"

"It means it's time for you to take the next step."

"Okay, but what are you saying?"

"Elise, one of the largest and most prestigious dance troupes in the country has been watching you for years. They feel you would be the perfect candidate to audition for them."

In the world of dancing, I knew I was far from being a professional, or well-known ballerina, but I didn't think I was still at a point where I would have to prove that I deserved to be a part of their group. To put it lightly, I was upset and any trace of an ego I had was deflated. Mrs. Mears was telling me something she thought was great news, but it didn't feel that way. It felt like she was telling me something to make me question myself and doubt if I had wasted almost my entire life.

"Great! I get to audition!" I said with my teeth clenched together.

I tried not to sound disappointed, but I'm sure my attempt failed miserable.

"You aren't auditioning to be a part of their dance group, though. You're beyond that. You are one of the only four girls in the United States they want to audition to become a principal dancer."

"Wait, are you kidding me right now?!"

"Nope! I wouldn't joke about something like that."

"How? Why? I don't understand."

I was in shock, so I wasn't quite able to put together the most eloquent sentences.

"Well, last week, they started to practice for one of their biggest shows of the year. When they did, their principal went down with an injury."

"When do they think she'll be back?"

"That's the problem. The doctors estimate it'll take at least 6-8 months for her to be back to one hundred percent and you know the show must go on."

"But don't they have understudies? What about them?"

I was so nervous and scared of the possible opportunity, I continued to ask Mrs. Mears questions simply because I was questioning myself.

"Yeah, they have understudies, but the 'higher-ups' don't feel any of them are ready for the spotlight. Since their reputation is on the line and tickets have already started to go on sale for the next show, they are stepping way outside of the box with these auditions."

"Oh. Okay."

"You just told me you were ready to take the next step, Elise, but you sure don't sound like it."

She was right. I said I was ready, but just the thought of what could possibly happen scared me. God was trying to open up a door for me, but I didn't know if I would be brave enough to walk through it.

"I'm ready, but then... I'm not ready."

"I understand where you're coming from, Elise. Your mind may temporarily force your mouth to release statements of doubt, but you're ready. You are more prepared to move to the next level than I ever was. Your work ethic far surpasses mine!"

Her words were incredibly encouraging, but also very surprising. Growing up, there had never been a time when Mrs. Mears wasn't working to not only make all of her students better, but to improve her own skills as well. Whenever I wanted to practice, she was already working. So, to hear her say my work ethic surpassed hers made me feel as if I had really accomplished something.

"Thank you, that means a lot to me."

"You're welcome. I never have had a problem speaking the truth."

I quickly went back to what we were speaking about.

"So, how long do I have to save up for a plane ticket and stuff?"

"Well, here's the thing. They need for all four of you to audition as soon as possible, so they are prepared to fly you out as soon as tomorrow, but no later than Friday."

"Are you telling me they are willing to fly me out to Los Angeles just so they can see if I'm good enough?"

"Yeah, that's pretty much what I'm telling you. See, when you work hard, people will notice and things will start to happen for you."

"Is this really happening? Am I dreaming or are you playing a joke on me?"

"I assure you, this is very real and the tears I'm already crying for you should let you know this is definitely not a joke."

I don't know why, but that's when the "realness" of the situation hit me.

I screamed very loudly! My excitement echoed throughout the dance studio. It startled both Mrs. Mears and Little Jazzy, who stopped dancing to see what was going on.

"Are you okay, Miss Elise?" she asked.

"Yep, I'm doing great! Sorry to scare you, but Mrs. Mears is on the phone and she just gave me some really great news!"

"Oooh, I like to hear great news! Can you tell me what it is, or is it a secret?"

"It's not a secret. I'll tell you as soon as I get off the phone, okay?"

"Okay! I'm gonna go back and practice until you get finished, then."

She left the room and my phone conversation continued.

"Was that Jasmine I heard?"

"Yes, ma'am. She called me earlier today and told me she was nervous about the upcoming performance. She wanted to get some extra practice in, so we've pretty much been here all day."

She laughed.

"You two are definitely cut from the same cloth. She, without question, is following along the path you're clearing out for her. The things you will do will impact the things she does in the future. Not only her, but so many of the other girls you teach don't just learn from you, but are inspired by you. They look up to you. You show them how great you can be when you work hard. You serve as proof that the desire to chase a dream can overpower the obstacles that will undoubtedly try to block your path. That's why you have to go to Los Angeles. Regardless of what happens when you go, you just have to go."

"Is that really how you feel?"

"Yes, it really is."

"That's a lot of pressure, Mrs. Mears."

"Yeah, it is, but they say, 'Heavy is the head that wears the crown.' And that's how you need to start looking at things. You are the best dancer I've ever been blessed to work with. You are the best here. In other words, you are the queen!"

She had told me before how good she thought I could be, but never to that extent. Her words seemed to instantly add more weight to me. For a moment, I had difficulty breathing. I was excited, but once again, I was very scared. I didn't want to be, but I was and I didn't feel like I could really do anything about it.

"I appreciate you saying all of that, but if I'm the queen, shouldn't I stay here? Wouldn't it be wrong for me to leave everybody?"

"I know you're asking these things out of fear and I understand that. I also understand I have added a lot of pressure to you, a lot of extra weight, but I know you can handle it. If you couldn't, I wouldn't have said anything."

"But what about me leaving?"

"Elise, there are times when kings, queens, presidents and even leaders of companies must leave home for the benefit of the people. Sometimes, there are things that have to be done and they can't always be done where you're from. If we could all accomplish everything we wanted to do without leaving the comfort of our home, I'm sure that's what most of us would do. That's not reality, though. Picture this, Elise: there's a student in one of your classes who has not only never been out of this state, but they've never been out of the city. No, they've never even been able to venture outside of their neighborhood. To them, the world is very small, but only because they don't even know how much of it exists. It would change their world to know you have the chance to go out to California, especially if they know you're going because of ballet. Believe it or not, some of the kids don't even know Los Angeles is a real place. They think it's a place that only exists on television. You can change their entire perspective on life."

"I think I get it now."

"Good. I'm glad you do. So does that mean you're going to go?"

I wanted to give her an answer right then, but I couldn't. Saying yes or no at that point would have felt a bit selfish.

"I don't know if I will or won't. I will say I'm leaning more towards going than not going. I have to speak with my family about it all. I can't make a major decision like that without them."

"I understand, and I respect that. Please speak with them and let me know what your decision will be as soon as possible."

"I will."

"And please don't work all day. You and Jasmine need to take a break at some point. Relax, have a meal, and talk about the decision you have to make. Believe it or not, whatever you decide will impact her a great deal."

"Yeah, you're right. I'll talk about it with her, I promise!"

The conversation with my mentor ended there. I went back into the main room of the studio and Jasmine was still dancing. Her little feet were obviously hurting, but it didn't stop her.

"Hey! Don't you think it's time to take a break?" I asked her.

"I dunno. I want to make sure I get everything right."

"Part of getting everything right is making sure your body gets enough rest. You've been working all day, you deserve to come and get a meal with me. Plus I have something I have to discuss with you."

She went along with my request. We turned off the music Little Jazzy was dancing to and we soon were in one those family-friendly restaurants. I wanted her to feel comfortable, so she was able to order whatever she wanted to. Doing that actually made her anxious to find out what was going on.

"Miss Elise, I'm glad I can get some free food and stuff, but I wanna know why we're here."

She was young, but she was very straightforward with most of her conversations. Unlike many kids her age, she didn't really like people making their conversation feel like it was geared towards kids. She didn't like "sugar-coated" talks, so I didn't give her one.

"I needed to talk to you about something."

"Okay."

"I need to talk to you about the phone call I had with Mrs. Mears."

"Yeah, that seemed weird."

"It was, but it was important and I need your help with making a very important decision."

"You want my help?"

"Yes. You're very important to me and you're one of the people I have to speak to about it."

She sat up straight. She showed she didn't want to take the rest of what I had to say lightly.

"Dreams are very important. Sometimes you'll get the things you wish for quickly and other times you'll have to wait so long for your dreams, you almost think they'll never come true." I explained.

"Do you mean dreams like when you go to sleep, or dreams like the stuff you want to happen?"

"For me, they both are the same thing, but I'm talking about the stuff you want to happen in the future. I'm talking about the things you work hard to try and get."

"Oh, okay! You're talking about like us both wanting to dance in front of lots of people and make being a ballerina our job?"

"Yep! That's exactly what I'm talking about. I was just told about an opportunity that could help me reach my goal, but I'm scared. I don't really know what I should do."

Yes, I understood I was speaking to an eight-year-old about a decision that could change the trajectory of my life, but it didn't stop me from talking to her about it because I knew she would give me honesty. That's all I needed.

"Miss Elise, you don't have to be scared of anything. You're very, very good at ballet, so you shouldn't be scared!"

"Normally, I'm not, but..."

"You practice all the time. You got so good, Mrs. Mears lets you teach the classes and whenever there's a performance, you are the one who gets to dance by yourself. That has to mean you're pretty good, right?"

"Maybe, but that's not why I'm scared. I'm scared because Mrs. Mears told me about doing something, but I'll have to go far away."

"How far? Like the other side of town? It's okay if that's where it is. I know you wouldn't be able to pick me up for practice. I'll be sad, but if that's what it is, we'll be okay!"

I wished it were that simple. That would have made things much easier, especially when it came to telling Little Jazzy the truth.

"It's not really like that. I don't know if I'll be moving at all, but I will probably be visiting another city."

"Where?"

"Los Angeles."

"Whoa! Are you for real? You mean, in California, like on TV?"

"Yeah. There's a major studio there and Mrs. Mears said they've been watching me and they want me to go out there and audition?"

"But why?" she asked.

"One of their main dancers got hurt and I'm one of the few girls they want to go and try-out to be a part of their dance troupe. If I succeed, I could have a chance to perform with them. If that happens, my life can change, for sure. It could help me reach my dream."

She no longer wanted to talk to me and she didn't try to hide it. She started picking at the food that was in front of her. She turned her body away from me and acted as though I wasn't even there.

I felt the pain I assumed she was feeling because of me. I understood her emotions even without her acknowledging they existed. I gave her some time to herself so she could not only cool down a little, but also so she could process the information I had just given her. I tended to my food and every once and a while I would look up at my meal companion. In a five minute span, she didn't look in my direction at all.

Then she suddenly decided it was time to resume our conversation.

"So are you gonna go?" she asked very directly.

"I don't know. I really need to know what you think."

"Miss Elise, you don't care what I think because I'm just a kid. Grown-ups always pretend we're important, but we're not. We just have to do whatever y'all tell us to do. You don't care. I thought you were different!"

"Of course I care. That's why I brought you here. I needed to talk to you about what's going on. Good or bad, I wanted to know what you thought."

She put down her fork down and pushed her remaining food away from her.

"I don't think you should go! It's stupid! Why do you have to go dance with them? Why can't they just use their own ballerinas? Why do they want to make you leave here and go there? Why?"

"They just... I... whenever other people..."

I tried my best to answer her, but I couldn't. The words I started to say didn't seem like they would lead me in the right direction. Everything I thought seemed to be inappropriate as well.

I was already regretting a decision that hadn't even been made. If it was affecting someone who wasn't really related to me, how would it affect my parents? How would it impact the other girls that I taught? What about the girls I danced with? Even if I only left long enough for the audition, I would still be letting people down. If I didn't, I would be letting Mrs. Mears down. Not only that, not trying is the type of thing people end up regretting later on in life. Disappointment or regret? The longer I thought about everything, those seemed to be my only actual choices and I didn't really like either of them.

"I don't car what you do, Miss Elise! You can just leave and go to your fancy studio in California! We don't need you here! I don't need you! You don't care about me! You're just like my momma! She doesn't care, either! That's why she's always gone and now you're gonna go, too!"

For the first time (at least in a while), she wasn't acting like someone who was mature beyond her years. She wasn't handling the situation as if it were something she had gone through before. At that moment, she was simply a hurt little girl and I had to deal with the fact that I was the one who hurt her.

"I'm sorry."

Those were the only words I could say. They were the only ones that felt right, so they were the ones I kept saying over and over again. I got up from my seat and hugged that little girl, not just because I knew she needed it, but because I needed it more than she did.

"Why are you gonna leave? Why don't you care? Please don't leave us! Please don't leave me! Please!"

As we held on to each other, we both cried intensely. Initially our conversation was just between us, but as it went along, Little Jazzy got louder and louder. By the time she started begging me not to go, we seemed to be the center of everyone's attention. I couldn't stop the tears from Jasmine and it was tearing me up inside.

I had no idea that simply talking about leaving would get to her (or me) the way it did. For the first time, Little Jazzy wasn't the overly mature young woman who was able to control her emotions. Instead, she was simply a hurt little girl in a lot of pain.

"Calm down," I said, hoping she would listen.
She wiped her eyes and looked up at me.
"Did I do something wrong?"

That question made me hurt even more than I was already hurting.

"No. You absolutely didn't do anything wrong at all. What would make you think that?"

"Sometimes when people in my family get mad at me, they'll leave. That's how I'll know I did something bad. Sometimes they'll only be away for a little while, but sometimes I never see them again. I know you said I didn't do anything, but if I did and you leave, will you please come back? I would miss you every day if you don't."

I couldn't tell if she said that because she meant it or because she knew it would make me feel bad.

"There's no way I could ever leave you forever. If you think you would miss me, how do you think I would feel? It would be crazy!"

Admittedly my words were chosen because they had the potential to make her be okay with me leaving (if I chose to go out for the audition), but they were also said because I really wanted her to think about them.

We both knew we were not actually related, but being bonded by the same bloodline couldn't have made us any closer than we were. Since I met her, people were far more likely to see us together than they were to see us apart. There was no way I would ever not be a part of her life. I had already lost my sister Jasmine, I couldn't lose another Jasmine (especially if I had a choice in the matter).

"Miss Elise, I don't really get how leaving here can help you get closer to your dreams," she stated.

"When you go to different cities, more people get to see what you do. When more people see you, the more opportunities you'll have to continue doing what you love to do."

"And you can get more money, right?" she asked as she finally started to smile again.

"Yeah, it may help me get some more money, but that's not what it's about. Don't get me wrong, getting a lot of money would be cool, but if you're only going after the money, you won't really be happy."

"Huh? I don't know about that. If I had a lot of money, I think I would be super-duper happy! If I had money, I would buy stuff for everybody and everybody would be happy."

I was happy we had moved beyond the extremely sad portion of our talk. I wanted to keep the positivity going, but I also felt obligated to pass along a little bit of knowledge.

"So you think money will make you happy, right?" I asked.
"Yep!"
"Okay, let me ask you something: what is something you really hate to do?"
She thought about it for a few seconds before I saw the light bulb go off in her head.

"I hate washing dishes! Whenever my mom makes me do it, I'd rather be doing anything else, even extra homework!"
I laughed.

"I know what you mean. I used to hate washing dishes, too. So, what if somebody told you they'll pay you to wash all of their dishes. Would you want to do that over and over?"

"Ewwww! No! I wouldn't want to do that!"

"But they're gonna pay you!"

"Even if somebody gave me money, I wouldn't want to keep doing that."

"See, money's not everything. It won't always make you happy. That's why we all have to try to find that job that you really like to do. For us, it would be dancing."

"Oh, okay. Now I get it!"

"Cool. That reminds me about something I talked about with Mrs. Mears when I first got started when I first told her I wanted to be a professional dancer. She asked me if I would still want to do it if I didn't get paid."

"I know I would. Dancing is so fun! Sometimes I can't go to sleep because I want to dance. I may wake up early, even before school, so I can dance." Little Jazzy said.

"Exactly! That's because dancing is our dream. We enjoy doing it and if I left, it may give me more chances to dance."

"And then one day you might give me a chance to dance, right?" she asked.
I hugged her again.

"You don't even have to question that. We're bonded for life and if I can help in any way, if it's a year or 20 years from now, I got you!"

"That's good, Miss Elise. I love you!"

"I love you, too."

"And Miss Elise, I think I wanna change my mind. If you need to go out to California, you can go. I just don't want you to forget about me AND I want to make sure when you go out there and get famous one day you'll let me come out there and dance with you."

"I promise you that will happen. If I go out there and stay out there, we will dance on stage together for sure!"

During our meal, we laughed, cried and had a bit of a "falling-out" with each other. For a moment, I felt a small bit of what it must be like when a parent says something that unintentionally hurts their child. I saw what it was like to disappoint someone who looks up to you. That moment took my maturity levels up a few notches. It also helped with my decision.

Little Jazzy and I completed our meal and we went back to practice for a little while longer before I took her home and I went home myself. I wanted to have the conversation with my parents that I had at the restaurant. I wasn't sure how they would respond, but I was just hoping they wouldn't take the news quite as harshly as Little Jazzy.

"Hey, y'all. Could I speak to you for a few minutes? There's something really important I need to get both of your opinions on."

I wasted no time explaining the situation and they knew how important it was to me.

"So what do you want to do?" my father asked.

"I don't really know," I replied.

"Yeah... I don't believe that for one second. This can't be the same person who has always wanted to dance, can it? Excuse me miss, I'm not sure who you are, but I'd like to speak to my daughter please."

He was right. Being a ballerina was my lifelong dream. I was obviously letting fear make a fool of me.

"Yeah, I want to do it, but I don't want to leave y'all."

"Why? What is holding you back? Why don't you want to leave?" my mother asked.

Other than being scared, I didn't know what else I could tell them. They were silent as they waited for me to answer. As I tried to come up with answers, the silence made me feel worse with every second that passed by. I finally grew tired of making them wait. I quit trying to think of an answer and I just answered without thinking.

"Yes, I want to go, but I kinda also want an excuse not to. This is all I know. What would I do in LA? I don't know anyone."

"Are you going there to be popular?" dad asked.

"No, sir."

"Then, why would you be going?"

It seemed like a trick question, but I didn't treat it that way.

"I would be going to audition."

"And what do you want to accomplish with the audition?"

"Hopefully it can help me become a professional."

"So, if you have something to gain by going to Los Angeles, your decision has been made. The only thing that should stop you is if when you pray about your trip, you hear God tell you not to go. If that's not it, nothing should stop you!"

"But what about Jasmine?"

"Your sister, or that girl at the studio you've been looking after for the past few years?"

"Both, but mainly I'm talking about Sister."

Speaking about her to my parents allowed me to say the name, Sister. It felt strange because I hadn't used that word as her nickname in a while.

"Baby, your sister is gone. Staying here is not going to bring her back. If you deprive yourself a chance to make it and find a way to use your sister as an excuse, at some point in your life you'll regret it," mom said.

Their words were on my mind for the rest of the night. I tried to think of something they said I disagreed with, but I wasn't able to. Whether I liked it or not, I agreed with them. The more I thought about everything, the closer I was to finding a reason why I was apprehensive. When I seemed to have no thoughts in my head, my reason became clear. I was afraid, but not afraid of trying. I was simply afraid I would let everybody down.

Since I first got into ballet, I had been hearing how good I was. It seemed that people's expectations of what I would be able to do with every practice couldn't compare to what I ended up doing whenever we had a performance. How would everyone feel if I went to a city full of great dancers and they told me I wasn't good enough?

Would Mrs. Mears feel like she had wasted her time with me? Would my parents feel like they had wasted not only their time, but their money as well? And what about my sister? If I went to Los Angeles and failed, how would that affect her spirit? And would Little Jazzy really resent me if I left, or if I failed? Would I find certain people were only in my life because they thought I had a small chance of making it in a world most didn't think a little black girl could make it in? Would they leave me? If they did, would I be able to handle that?

Just when I thought my head was clear, it became more clouded than ever. I couldn't prolong prayer any longer. One way or another, I had to figure things out for good, but I needed to get God's help. I went to my room, closed my door, turned the lights off and I sat in my corner so I could be comfortable during my discussion with God.

"Father in heaven, I thank you in advance for the opportunity you have given to me. I know there are dancers all over the world who would have already jumped at the chance to audition without giving it a second thought. I know they feel they would be ready for something like this, but I don't know if I am."

I continued to voice my concerns to God for quite some time. After hearing what I was saying to Him, I had just about convinced myself not to go. Then I heard His voice speak to me very clearly.

"If you're not ready to go, why would I give you the chance to go?"

That was all He said because that was all He needed to say. His words finalized my decision. I didn't allow myself to think about it anymore because I knew I would just try to convince myself to do the opposite of what God wanted me to do. Almost as soon as He spoke to me, I went to tell my parents. They were excited, but I could also tell they were both sad at the same time. It was strange to see them celebrate a major step while almost wishing it wasn't happening. I could understand the conflict.

That night, I had to force myself to try to go to sleep. I sat in my bed just thinking about the possibilities of what could happen. The fear that had control of me turned into excitement very quickly. Soon I was asleep with visuals to go along with what I was imagining when I was awake.

I saw myself on a plane, listening to music that mentally prepared me to dance. And once I got off of the plane, I ended up in a magnificent dance studio. The studio was filled with brilliant dancers from all over the world. Each was very different, but they were all very accepting of each other. It was beautiful.

When I woke up, I felt better than I had in a while. I felt like I was ready to conquer the world. I didn't have anything to do until my class later on in the day; but I had so much energy, I just had to get up and move around. I also found it necessary to thank God for refreshing my spirit and giving me life, love, a passion for the arts and the ability to pursue a dream.

Before I went to prepare for the day, I had to call Mrs. Mears and let her know a decision had been made. Once she heard the news, she sounded as excited about the opportunity to audition as I was. She provided me with as many details as she could before finally asking me when I would be able to leave.

"I want to make sure I have the chance to at least teach my classes today. I really need to explain to my girls what I have to do."

"That's a very good idea! Elise, I'm so glad you care so much about the girls."

"Yes, ma'am."

"Well, how about if I see if you'll be able to finish out the week and fly out to Los Angeles after that. Will that be okay?"

"If that happens, that'll be great!"

"Okay, so that's what I'll work on. You go ahead and get ready for the rest of the day. I'll see you later on, but if I get any updates before that, I'll give you a call."

"Yes, ma'am. Thank you!"

After the brief talk with Mrs. Mears, I went to see if my parents were up.

"Good morning, mom. Good morning, dad."
Mom was finishing breakfast while also helping my father get situated at the kitchen table.

"Hey, Elise! How did you sleep?"

"I had the best sleep I've had in a while. What about you two?"

"Pretty good," my mom said.

"I wish I could say that's how it was for me!" dad yelled out.

"What happened, Ian?" mom asked with a very concerned look on her face.

Dad looked at both of us very seriously. Neither of us knew what he was going to say, but we were very interested to find out.

"Babe, you were snoring so loud, I had a nightmare that a grizzly bear had broken into the room. I truly feared for my life! I kept telling him I didn't have any fish. I begged him to leave us alone. I woke up in a cold sweat. It was terrible!"

"Boy, shut up! You had me thinking something was really wrong."

"Something was wrong! I would have gotten up and ran out of the room, but for some reason, my legs wouldn't let me!"

We all laughed very loudly while we looked at each other. There hadn't been that much laughter in the house since the accident. I was already feeling good that day, but that moment was beyond words. Even though my sister wasn't there, the positivity in the room made it feel like she was. It was a wonderful feeling.

"I love y'all!" I told my parents.

"Well, how could you not love us? I mean, we are kinda awesome. Not only that, our daughter has a chance to go to LA to be a part of one of the most famous ballet troupes in the country... no, in the world!" mom said.

Hearing her sound happy, like the old her, made me feel so good I couldn't contain my emotions. My parents were proud of me, not because I had already earned my spot in Los Angeles, because I hadn't. They were proud simply because I had been given a chance to go to the next level.

"Hey, I made a decision," I said as we were all still smiling.

"You're gonna go, right?" dad asked.
I put my head down as if I was about to say something that would disappoint them.

"I thought about it for a long time last night and I have to let you know..."
As I looked up briefly, I saw they were hanging on each word. They were waiting with anticipation and were almost becoming annoyed with every second they had to wait.

"You have to let us know, what?"
I kept my head down for a few more seconds before I continued.

"...I have to let you know... I... have... decided to go!"
Everyone immediately began to yell like crazy, including me. I jumped up and down like a kid who had been given an extra ten minutes of recess time.

"That's amazing, Lisey-Pooh! I'm glad to hear that!" dad told me.

"Me too, Elise. So do you know when you'll be leaving and for how long?" mom wondered.

"Not for sure, but Mrs. Mears is supposed to be finalizing all of the details and she's supposed to let me know at some point today."

"I'm glad to hear that! We are so grateful to have raised such a wonderful young lady. You let us know we actually did alright," my father added with a huge smile on his face.

"Thank you for saying that and I'm grateful y'all believed in me enough over the years to not only pay for my classes, but to take the time to go with me to so many of them. I owe you so much!"

"Owe us? No, ma'am, we just played our positions. All glory and thanks go to God."

We once again thought about how Jasmine got me started in ballet.

"Mom, can you imagine how it would have been if Jasmine didn't get that birthday gift?"

"Elise, even if things hadn't happened exactly the way they did, they still would have happened. We told you, this is your destiny. Regardless of what we did, at some point, you would have made your way to ballet. God made you a dancer, no human can stop that, nor take credit for it."

Both of my parents (and Mrs. Mears) had said similar things on a few different occasions, but it was always good to hear. It reminded me that no matter how I felt, I truly had a God-given purpose. I was not worthy of such high praises, but I was so glad people kept bestowing those types of words on me.

"Have you already told your friends about what's going on?"

I hadn't even thought about my friends. It wasn't because of anything bad; I was just so excited about everything that they hadn't crossed my mind. I was focused on actually trying to make a decision, talking to my family, and making sure I had a conversation with Little Jazzy.

"No, I haven't really talked to too many people about it because I had no idea what I was going to do. I'll talk to them within the next few days."

"That's good because I know your little boyfriend would be very upset if you just went out to Los Angeles and he didn't know about it," dad said.

"You're right. He's not my boyfriend, though," I said as I started to laugh.

"Well, why not? He seems like he's an alright guy, much better than some of the other guys who have called or tried to come around here because they were trying to date you."

"Dad, nobody really came around here trying to date me like that."

"I don't know how true that is, Elise. I remember that one time that super tall, skinny guy came over here looking for you," my mom said.

"Who are you talking about, mom?"

"That one dude, you know...that one that looked like he would get full from one eating one rice!"

"One rice? Mom, what are you talking about? Do you mean like a bowl of rice?"

"No. I don't think you heard what I said. I mean one, single, solitary grain of rice would have filled up that skinny little guy."

As she talked, I was honestly trying to think of who she was talking about, but the name escaped me.

"Elise, you know who your mom's talking about! Don't act like you're embarrassed. Plus the dude didn't make it to dating status because if he did, you wouldn't have such a hard time remembering who we're talking about," dad said as he laughed right along with us.

Then the name hit me.

"You mean Corey?"

"Yeah, that's it! Corey! That guy Corey had more craters on his face than the moon and he had the nerve to always be looking at himself in the mirror!"

"Mom, you're funny!"

"You know I wouldn't normally talk about people, but Corey thought he was the world's gift to women. And I don't know how he ever thought that! To this day, I don't understand how someone who had a face that looked like pepperoni pizza could have the audacity to be so arrogant."

"I didn't know he was like that. What did he do?"

"One time he came over here to try to take you out. Yeah, the first time he came over here, he didn't even pretend to be a good guy. I remember him saying something like, 'Hey, what's up? I'm your future son-in-law and it's a pleasure for you to meet me.' I was so shocked. I couldn't believe he actually said that."

"I don't ever remember that happening, mom."

My mother looked at me directly in my eyes.

"Of course you don't. When he said that, for some reason, the doorknob slipped out of my hand and the door slammed shut in his face. Once that happened, I just tried to erase that memory immediately! I guess I must have forgotten to tell you he stopped by. Ooops!"

I couldn't even be upset with my mother. That guy really was a jerk, and if the story she told had any truth to it (which I'm sure it did), she helped me get rid of someone who wasn't worth my time.

"I think you need to thank your mother," dad said.

"Yeah, you're right. Thanks, mom."

"No problem. You know neither one of us want any knuckle-headed, arrogant little boys around you, Elise."

"Yeah, that's why you need to make that call to Hamilton. He seems like the exact opposite of that other guy. He seems very respectful and you two look good together. Plus you seem to be happy when you're with him," dad said.

"Yeah, but it's not like we're a couple or anything," I said as I walked away smiling.

The conversation ended there. My parents were acting like they were ready to start preparing for my wedding to Hamilton while I acted like we weren't into each other like that. It was just a fun little game none of us seemed to mind playing. When we were done talking, I actually was happier than I was when I got up.

I decided to do what my parents wanted me to do and make a call to Hamilton. I knew the message I needed to convey, but I wasn't really sure how I was going to say it. So, I quit thinking about things so much and dialed the number. It was so early, I almost hoped he wasn't up yet. That wasn't the case, though. He answered the phone before it even made it to the second ring.

"Hello there, Elise! And what makes me fortunate enough to get such an early morning call?"

Sometimes Hamilton annoyed me when he spoke as if he were reading poetry, but it was still kinda cute.

"I have something very important I need to talk to you about."

"Okay, you got me interested. What's up?"

"I'll make this quick. You know how much I love ballet, right?"

"Come on, Elise. I think everybody knows how much you love it. Dancing isn't just what you do, it's who you are."

"That's true! Well, I just found out I have the opportunity of a lifetime…"

"Cool! Don't keep me in suspense, what's going on?"

"Well, my ballet mentor told me they want me to fly out to Los Angeles to audition to be a part of one of the best ballet groups in the country, if not the world!"

"What? Are you serious? How did they find out about you? When do you you have to go? What does this even mean?"

For the first time ever, Hamilton wasn't the calm and collected person he normally was. No, right then, he was someone who couldn't contain his excitement because his "friend" shared some good news.

"Hamilton, you just asked me about a thousand questions. I won't even pretend to remember everything, so I'll summarize what I know so far. Mrs. Mears said a total of four people have been asked to audition for a spot that only opened up because someone was injured. She said they basically had scouts checking out ballerinas everywhere and I am one they want to see more of."

"Wow! That is beyond awesome! So do you know when you're supposed to go out there?"

"Well, they're actually flying me out, but Mrs. Mears is supposed to let me know when at some point today."

"Elise, I am in awe of you and your accomplishments."

"But I haven't really accomplished very much."

"Well, I hate to tell you this, but that's a straight up lie! No disrespect, but it is. In case you don't know who Elise Morgan is, let me tell you about her. Even though she is only eighteen years old, her lifelong dance instructor and mentor has pretty much entrusted the entire dance studio over to her. Not only is she one of the main dancers, but she's also now one of the main instructors. If that weren't enough, now some of the big shots out in Cali want to fly her out there just so she can audition! What? If that's not accomplishing anything, I don't know what is!"

"Wow! I guess when you name everything, it does sound like quite a bit. Plus I don't like to brag, especially about myself."

"I understand that, but you're so great at what you do, you won't even have to brag about yourself because other people will do it for you."

I had never thought about it like that, but he was right. You hear discussions among different people all the time about who's the greatest at something. It doesn't matter if it's about who's the best athlete, singer, rapper, writer, dancer or whatever... if people think you do a good job at something, your work will speak for itself.

"Well, I appreciate it," I said.

"No problem. So what are your plans for today?"

"I don't really know. More than likely, I'll end up going to practice."

"That sounds about right. I don't even know why I asked. If you're ever looking for Elise, she's in practice!"

We both laughed a little, but it was true.

"Yep! I always have something I need to work on, something I need to improve and practice is the only way to get better. I can't have a goal of wanting to be the best if I'm not willing to work for it."

"I keep saying it, but the level of dedication you have is almost incomprehensible. If I wasn't around, and somebody told me about you, I don't know if I would actually believe a person your age would actually be capable of constantly being so dedicated."

"I get where you're coming from, but when God allows you to find what you've been put on this earth to do, no amount of work seems to be too much. In fact, you become so focused on doing what you're supposed to do, no amount of work seems to be enough. You may not believe it, but it's been put in my heart that I can help change the world through dance. I don't understand how this is even possible, but this is what God has told me, so this is what I believe. Somewhere in the world, there may be a little girl who doesn't even know what an arabesque or first position is. She's never heard the word plié. She may not know how long ballet has been around, but she knows she wants to dance. She probably doesn't even want to become a professional ballerina. She may want to be a teacher, judge, politician, or a surgeon, but she will gain the confidence needed to do those things through dance. I want to be a part of her gaining that confidence. She may see me dance, or someone who I taught or influenced. Either way, I want to do whatever's necessary to not only see my own dreams come true, but hers as well."

I didn't realize how much I had been talking, but it soon hit me that I had probably been talking longer than I should have. It always seemed to happen like that when ballet was a topic in the conversation.

"Elise, you know I have no idea what those dance terms you just said mean, right?" he asked.

"Yeah, sorry about that. I didn't mean to talk so much. I actually thought I'd be able to call, tell you the news, and be off of the phone in a matter of minutes. Wait, I actually was kinda hoping you wouldn't even pick up the phone."

"Why? You didn't really want me to share in the moment with you?"

"No, no, no! It's not like that at all! I was just a little nervous about how you'd react."

"As you can see, there was no need to be concerned about that. I'm with you, no matter what! If you wanna go, I support that. If you wanted to stay, I would support that too. Wait... no I wouldn't! I take that back!"

He interrupted himself. He suddenly had a different train of thought and it made me nervous.

"I would not support any decision you made!" he said. When he said that, I was both confused and hurt. How could he say he would support either decision and then act like he wanted to take his words back?

"Why would you say that to me? Were you trying to hurt me? If you were, congratulations!"

"Babe, I'm sorry! I didn't mean it the way it sounded. I love you and I wasn't trying to hurt your feelings at all. Please, let me explain."

Prior to starting that conversation, I told my parents I wasn't in a relationship. I didn't say it because I was lying or even because I was trying to hide anything from them. I said it because prior to the start of that conversation, Hamilton and I never had that conversation to establish what our status was.

Hearing those words together was another one of those important moments that served as a turning point in my life. I wanted to be mad, but those words disarmed me.

"Okay, explain yourself, please."

I didn't acknowledge the fact that I had just been called "babe" and that he just said he loved me. I acted as though those things didn't even happen.

"Elise, what I was trying to say is that I just wouldn't agree with you if you had decided not to go out to Los Angeles to audition."

"Why not?"

"Because your talent is too large to be confined to Austin. Going to Los Angeles is exactly the step you need to take to help make those dreams you talked about come true. If you stayed here,

I'm sure you'd eventually reach your goals, but I think you'd be making things more difficult for yourself than they would actually have to be."

I not only thought about what was being said to me, but also the manner in which they were being said. It didn't feel like what he was saying was just a defense mechanism for what he said before. It all felt honest.

"Maybe you're right, but how do you think leaving will affect our relationship?"

Relationship. I used the word on purpose to see how Hamilton would react.

"It will most certainly have some kind of impact on our relationship, but that's not necessarily a bad thing."

"But what if my audition goes well?"

"Elise, I totally expect it to go well. I also expect them to immediately ask you to stay. I mean, how will they be able to turn you down? That'll be crazy."

"Will you be okay with that?"

"Will I be okay with you staying in LA? Will I mind you showing the world what you're capable of? I will absolutely be okay with that. Don't get me wrong, every day that I'm not able to see you or talk to you will drive me crazy, but I think our relationship and friendship is strong enough to last, in spite of the distance."

"That is really cool! I think we can make it, too, but people say long-distance relationships are hard. I've even heard people say if you have a choice between a long-distance relationship and being single, you'd be much better off being by yourself."

"Wow! That's really harsh, but I think there are always exceptions. We can be one of the exceptions instead of being a part of the negative statistics."

We continued to talk for over an hour. I had no intention of being on the phone longer than a few minutes, but I was glad it was a long conversation. Every once and a while, I'd find myself giggling for absolutely no reason. At times, I felt like I was in junior high again. I had to fight myself from saying "you hang up first". It was a very nice feeling, but once we finally hung up, I needed some time to think about my future. Unlike other times when I reflected or thought about my life, I actually felt good. It seemed the hope and faith I kept losing over the years had made its way back to me.

For some reason, I was expecting to get a call from Mrs. Mears right then. In my mind, I was prepared to hear that my ticket had already been taken care of and I could leave whenever I wanted to. That moment would have to wait, unfortunately.

"Elise, your father and I have to go out and take care of some things. Do you want to come with us?"

The question was surprising because my mother just seemed to appear out of nowhere to ask it. Also, I hadn't really gone out with my parents in a few years. I walked out of my room for the first time since I got off the phone with Hamilton to get a little more info from them.

"Where are y'all going?"

"We just have to take care of some errands. Nothing crazy," my dad said.

They were being weird and secretive. They obviously had something planned and I was interested to know what it was, but I had already spent time at home that I should have spent practicing. I couldn't let myself lose focus just as I was moving closer to my goals.

"I kinda want to see what you two have up your sleeves, but I can't. I have to make sure when I get that call from Mrs. Mears, I'll be mentally and physically prepared."

"We understand that. Do your thing! We'll see you later, then," dad said.

"Please don't stay out too late, Elise. I would really like us all to have dinner together tonight. Since you'll be leaving soon, you never know how many chances we'll have for us all to be together and enjoy each other's company."

"That sounds good, mom. What time do you want me to try to make it back?"

"That's very nice of you to ask. If you can make it back home by 7:00, that would be great!"

"Well, 7 it is."

With our dinner time confirmed, my parents left. I almost convinced myself I needed to stay home and relax, maybe catch up on some reading or some of the many television shows I never seemed to have time to watch. The key word was almost. I did a little bit of back and forth with myself. I thought about the pros and cons of having a proper work-life balance and how you're supposed to be able to waste some time every now and again, but that argument with myself ended fairly quickly. I kept hearing words like "failure" and "disappointment" and I just couldn't let them end up being associated with me. My decision had been made: I needed to work!

Shortly after finalizing my decision to spend another day practicing, I was parking my car at the studio. Surprisingly Mrs. Mears' car was already there. I wasn't quite sure what she was doing there, but it was her studio, so she didn't really have to have a reason.

"I expected you to be here at some point," she said as soon as I walked into the main rehearsal hall.

"Yes, ma'am. You know this is like my second home."

"Well, I'm sorry... but... well, never mind. You just go ahead and do what you were about to do."

What she said (and how she stopped saying more) disturbed me. She looked like she was about to go into her office or one of the smaller practice rooms, either way, I didn't want her to leave without finishing what she had to say.

"Please don't go anywhere without letting me know what's going on."

Her face showed sadness and I didn't like that at all.

"I'm sorry I even started to bring it up, but when you said this place is like a second home to you, that's when it hit me."

"That's when what hit you?"

Her facial expression didn't change as she sat down in a nearby chair. There was a seat to the left of where she was and she asked me to have a seat.

"Elise, I know you like to come here to teach, practice, and maybe still learn some new things about ballet, but soon you won't be able to."

"Why not?"

I had no idea what she was talking about, but I didn't like how it was sounding. I was quickly getting very nervous.

"I don't know if you've really paid attention to it or not, but it's pretty difficult to constantly raise awareness about ballet. It's even more difficult to use ballet as a platform to make people be more open-minded and less judgmental about what people of color are able to do. It's crazy how people still judge us based on stereotypes."

"Of course! I've been almost forced to pay attention to all of that since I started. I mean little things like having pink shoes. Most people still think they're pink only because that's a pretty color. They have no idea that they have that tone because it's flesh-colored for most of the dancers."

"Yeah and I'm almost to a point where I can't continue to take on so many things like I used to. I can't even promote the art like I'd really like. That's one of the many reasons why I'd always get so excited when you or anyone else wanted to practice more, wanted to learn more, or just genuinely show some level of curiosity about what ballet is. But this paperwork I have received not too long ago is going to change pretty much everything, especially around here. The sad thing is, I won't be able to do anything about it. I don't even have a chance of stopping it. Plus, at this point, I don't know if I would even if I could.

I still didn't know what she was talking about, but Mrs. Mears had grown to be like family to me. Whatever she was dealing with, she wouldn't have to go through it alone.

"I'm here, Mrs. Mears. Whatever the problem is, whatever I can do, I'll do it. I'm here for you!"
She sunk down a little in her seat.

"Elise, I appreciate it, but you won't be able to be here for this one. This is something I'm going to have to handle without you."

She reached into her pocket as she stood up. She pulled out a folded piece of paper. She didn't say anything, she just handed the paper over to me. She stood by silently as I read over the contents of the page. I read what was on the paper several times and I still didn't believe what I was looking at.

"Is this real?" I asked.
Mrs. Mears, my teacher, my mentor and my friend hugged me.

"Yes, Elise, this is real. This paper is your boarding pass for your flight to Los Angeles. It's officially your time to shine, Elise. I want you to prepare your mind for what's in store, because when it comes to ballet, you're more than prepared. You have been for a long time and I am so proud of you!"

My happiness was overwhelming, but at the same time, my heart sank with sadness.

"I'm sorry I have to leave you, Mrs. Mears."

I cried and hugged her. I felt like I was six years old again. I knew I really had no reason to be sad or apologize for anything, but I really felt bad. The trip meant I would literally be disregarding all of my responsibilities. It meant I would also be leaving Mrs. Mears alone and I wouldn't be there to help.

"There's no reason for you to apologize. Don't feel bad for being great. Don't feel bad for getting what you deserve for working hard. Everything you get from this point on will come your way because of God and your hard work. Everything else… the stuff that comes from other people exists because sometimes people know the most beneficial thing they can do in someone else's life is play their position. For example, I just played the role of your teacher. I just helped you to get started, but I will never be the person to say I was the main one to start what Elise Morgan is doing in ballet."

"Thank you so much! Thank you for everything you've done for me. I know you just said you can't and won't take credit for what I've done or what I will do, but I have to say, I truly owe you! No matter where my audition takes me, I will never be able to deny your importance in my life. You are my family, Mrs. Mears. You may not agree with me, but there's no way I would have made it to this point in if it weren't for you. You made me work when I didn't want to. You taught me about the importance of ballet. You made sure all of us were serious about our craft no matter how old we were. You saw enough in me to allow me to teach others."

As I named some of the many things she had done for me over the years, her body language and facial expression were almost as though she was in disbelief over what I was saying about her. She was the complete opposite of the demanding, egotistical caricature people normally think of when they imagine how a ballet dancer would act. Her awards and accolades gave her the right to have a bit of an ego (if she wanted to), but that was not who she was. She remained humble because she didn't even feel her own accomplishments happened because of her. She said she simply played a role in her own success, and what she was able to do was because of God (and in spite of her).

Over the years, she briefly touched on some of the many times she wanted to quit because the work was getting too hard, but God made her continue because the work she was doing wasn't just for her, but for all of the lives of the people she would impact in her future (including myself and all of the other girls who ever stepped foot in the studio to take a class). Mrs. Mears' ability to keep the "it's not about me" mindset when most people would have certainly thought it was was truly admirable.

"This is what faith, obedience, and hard work will do for you. It will show God you believe in His plan. When you do that, He will show you opportunities and possibilities far greater than anything you can think of."

"Yes ma'am. I'm starting to see that now."

I was still holding the printed proof of my flight in my hand. I still didn't believe it. My heart was pounding like a jackhammer on cement. I couldn't understand why out of all of the girls who had danced with me in classes and performed with me on stage, I was being looked at by people I had no idea were watching. Why me? Why not them? What made me different? What made me worthy? Why was I getting an opportunity that most never knew existed?

I was questioning myself, yet again. The fear always found a way to creep back into my head. I tried to dismiss all of the questions I was suddenly having again by not vocalizing them, but it's as if they were stuck on repeat in my mind.

"How do you feel, Elise? How do you feel seeing this is real?" Mrs. Mears asked.
I was just going to tell her it made me feel good, but it wasn't the truth. Well, it wasn't the full truth.

"I feel wonderful, but..."

"But what?" she asked.

I was forced to make a decision right then. Either I was going to tell her how I really felt, or I was going to keep my questions to myself. I thought about it briefly before saying anything.

"Umm... I don't know if I should actually say anything."

"Whatever it is, you know you have the freedom to say whatever you need to."

"Okay. Honestly, I'm just really scared that I may not be good enough."

"Not good enough for what?" she asked.

"What if I'm not good enough to be accepted by the people in Los Angeles? What if they don't think I'm a good dancer? What if they feel they made a mistake by saying I could go out there? What if..."

"Stop! Take a moment to breathe."

She waited as I inhaled and exhaled a few times.

"I'm just concerned," I finally said.

"I understand the questions and I understand the concern, but I won't accept the fear. Elise, you can't allow yourself to get so worked up over this stuff. They think you're a great dancer, that's why they've been watching your performances for so long. It's why they have called me on several different occasions about what kind of person you are. And if you weren't good enough, they certainly wouldn't be taking a chance to fly you out just so they can watch you dance in person."

Mrs. Mears' perspective on things was much different than mine, especially when it came to the potential of her students. Many times, we were only able to see what we were doing wrong. She was not only able to tell us how to improve, but she also made sure we were aware of the things we did well. Doing that made us stronger and kept us going instead of just tearing us down, which would have pretty much ensured the majority of us would have not only quit ballet, but also loathe it.

"I just really don't want to let anybody down," I said.

"Elise, there are pretty much only two ways you'll let anybody down: first, if you didn't go at all, people would be upset with you. The other way would be if you went, but you didn't give it your all. That's really about it."

"But what if I don't make it?"

"Do you mean what happens if the ignorance takes over their minds and they decide to not make you a part of what they have going on?"

"Yes, ma'am."

"If that happens, we'll know they don't have the brightest people making decisions for them, but we won't be disappointed. Everyone loves you here and all the girls would be excited to have you back. I'm sure they'll all be ready to ask you about your trip and if you saw any movie stars and what their studio was like. I can almost guarantee you nobody will say they are upset with you or that you let them down. There's no way that will happen."

That was yet another example of Mrs. Mears' uncanny ability to give affirmations in times when people lacked any sort of confidence in themselves.

"Thank you. You always know the exact thing to say at the exact time it needs to be heard."

"You're very welcome, Elise. Now that we've kicked out that doubt you were holding onto, what are you gonna do now? Do you want to celebrate?" she asked.

"No, ma'am. I'm very happy right now, but I just want to do what I came here to do."

"I figured you'd say something like that. I will say, you are very consistent and dedicated. The world needs more people like you and I'm extremely happy God allowed our paths to cross. You don't even realize how much you're going to impact this world. It has already started with all of the girls you teach and it started with me on the very first day you and your family walked through those doors. I could talk about how you impact the people around you all day, but I won't because I don't want to distract you anymore. Go ahead and practice, and allow me to make a suggestion to you."

"Ok. What is it?"

"I strongly recommend you practice a portion of your favorite routine from the show you like the most. Learn everything you can about it. Learn who performed the dance, learn when it was written, and know the routine backwards and forwards. Make sure you stand out from the others. Make sure they remember you without making it seem too obvious that you're trying to stand out."

"Yes, ma'am."

When she gave me those words of wisdom, she left me so I could focus.

Normally when I practiced, I turned on some music. That day, I didn't want or need it. After I stretched and warmed-up, it was as thought the music that accompanied my favorite routine started playing in my head. I couldn't even watch myself practice in the mirrors. Instead I closed my eyes and imagined I was on stage with my favorite dancers of all time. Although many of them were famous for being ballerinas, some were not. It was wonderful my mind momentarily made believe I was on stage with Kayla Radomski, Debbie Allen, Darcey Bussell, Michaela DePrince, Galina Ulanova, Margot Fonteyn, and of course, Mrs. Mears. Everyone was in their prime and I had no right to be on stage with them, but there I was.

I most certainly was the rookie on a team full of all-stars, but on stage, they looked at me as their equal. I kept my eyes closed (in reality) to continue watching myself dance with my idols. We moved in unison as we danced one of my favorite routines. When it ended, we all looked at each other. We said nothing but we all smiled as sort of our silent congratulations on a job well done. My imaginary scene ended with a standing ovation from everyone in the crowd.

I opened my eyes and stared at myself in mirror in front of me. I was still holding the pose of the final move of the routine. I let myself relax. I thought about the audition that would be happening in a few days and how it would change my life. The questions born from fear were no longer there. Instead, I felt successful, I felt accomplished, and I felt like I had to (once again) thank God.

The floors of the studio were a bit too hard for me to kneel and pray on at the time, so I sat in a similar style to how we all did when we had to sit on our mats in elementary school. I hoped God would be okay with that.

"Father, thank you. Thank you for putting people in my life to help push me forward. Thank you for blessing me with parents who have always supported me and never tried to get me to stop dancing, no matter how expensive or time consuming it was. Thank you for giving me the right mindset and work ethic. And I continue to thank you for the life of my little sister. I'm so glad she was selfless enough to think about me and buy my 'fancy dancing dress.' I pray she feels her investment is paying off. Please take care of her until we see her again. In the name of Jesus, amen!"

When I stood up, I saw Mrs. Mears was standing nearby. I wasn't sure how long she had been there, but it was long enough for her to hear something that made her cry.

"I'm sorry for eavesdropping on your prayer. I came out here to ask you something, but when I heard you praying, I just got caught up in the words."

"It's totally fine, Mrs. Mears. What did you need to ask me, though?"

She looked as though she forgot what she was going to ask, at least for a few seconds.

"Oh yeah! I was going to ask, do you mind if we do a routine together? You'll be leaving soon and I don't know if I'll ever get the chance again when you do."

What she said reminded me of what my parents said earlier in the day, and just like when I thought about what they said, it was both sad and sweet at the same time.

"Of course, Mrs. Mears. What would you like to dance to?" I asked.

"I don't know. You can pick something out. Just surprise me. I just ask that you don't pick anything that moves too fast. I don't want you to embarrass me."

I had something in mind and started playing some music.

I selected one of the first routines I ever learned from her. Although I didn't tell her what it was, she jumped right in and nailed every move. It was like her muscle memory took over.

"That was nice," she said as we ended the dance.

"Yeah, I thought you might like that one." I replied.

"Yes, I did. It is obviously something I remember, at least the actual routine, but I can't say I recall exactly when it was originally put together."

"I didn't think you would, but that was one of the first routines I ever fully learned. It was from a performance we had."

She smiled and gave me a look similar to one my mother did when she had one of those "proud" moments.

"I can't believe you'd remember something from when you were a child. That's not something everyone can do," she said.

"Well, I think it's even more amazing you remembered."

"Why, because of my age?"

She laughed, but I could tell she hoped that wasn't the real reason I said what I did.

"No, ma'am. It's not that at all. I just know you've been teaching ballet for a long time and that means there has been a lot of choreography done over the years. For you to be able to remember the full choreography is just... well, it's pretty cool!"

I couldn't even stay in the moment because almost immediately after we finished dancing, I started to think about what was going to happen to the school once I left.

"Mrs. Mears, what's going to happen with the classes I teach?"

"I'm not really sure, but we'll figure it out."

I thought she was going to show confidence in her answer, which probably would have made me feel okay. When she didn't, it started to make me question things all over again.

"You're not sure? Well, I can just stay until we get everything worked out. Then hopefully I'll still be able to audition."

The instant I made my statement, she started to look upset.

"Elise, I thought we just moved past the doubt. The ticket you have shows this very real. If you just said what you did because of genuine concern for what's going to happen here, thank you. But if you said that because you want to be able to use this school as an excuse on why you're not going... don't do that! As a matter of fact, if you stay and I find out you used us to cover your fear, I don't even know if you'll be welcomed here any more. I love you as if you were my own daughter, Elise. So I will tell you just what I would tell my own kids: 'Fear is just another four-letter word that is not to be used around me.' So although you may not have used the word, you second-guessing yourself and concocting reasons to stay is showing that the fear is still in your head. I don't like that... I don't like that at all."

I had no idea she would react the way she did. I thought it was harsh, but at the same time, I wasn't offended by it. She said I was like a daughter to her, so she was just showing me some tough love. I can't really say that made her words any easier to take, though. I wanted to defend myself. I wanted to tell her I wasn't scared and I said what I did only because I cared about what was going to happen at the studio, but it wouldn't have been true. So, I couldn't do that. I just had to speak from my heart.

"I'm super excited about going, but when we danced one of my first routines, it made me think about when I first got there. That made me think about all of the beginners I teach. I'm concerned about them."

"I know you are, but like I said, we'll figure something out. You know what, Elise? You need to go. And I mean now."

"Are you serious? I'm so sorry!"

"I keep telling you, there's no need for you to apologize. You've never been kicked outta here, so I know this is weird, but it's not punishment."

"It's not? It sure seems like it is."

"You need to clear your mind, to relax... to find a way to get rid of some stress. I don't know how you're going to do that, but I don't believe it's gonna happen while you're here."

I tried to stall, perhaps even distract her long enough to make her forget she wanted me to leave, but she didn't let that happen. She was focused on making me clear my head and whether I wanted to or not. So, I didn't fight her long before I just gave in and left. When I walked in the studio that day, I was sure practicing was all I needed to help me mentally prepare for everything, but I was forced to find out I was wrong.

After I left, I couldn't stop laughing. I sat in the car for at least ten minutes, watching myself laugh so hard I was crying. I didn't even know why, but that didn't stop it from happening. If anybody passed by me, I'm sure they thought I had to be crazy. I know that was what I would have thought. Soon my face started to hurt from laughing, but it still didn't even make any sense why I was doing it. Then, it hit me. I had just been kicked out of the dance studio. I was working so hard that Mrs. Mears figured my work ethic lead to me overthinking, which in turn, could affect what I was working so hard on in the first place. I was laughing not because that was funny (in the traditional sense), but because it was so strangely ironic, I just had to.

Once the laughter died down, I needed to figure out what I was going to do for the rest of the day. I was terrible at finding things to take up my free time simply because I usually didn't have any. I drove around for a little while before I pulled into the parking lot of a nearby store. I looked at the clock on my car's radio to see how much time I had left before I needed to head back home so I could have dinner with my family.

When I saw I had a few hours to kill, some ideas started floating around in my head. Sadly, most of them were boring, normal, run-of-the-mill type ideas and that was not what I wanted to do. I wanted to do something fun, but not so far out of my character that it would make me feel uncomfortable. Out of nowhere, I decided to call Hamilton. We had a few minutes of small talk before I got to the point of the conversation. I asked him if he was okay with spending a little bit of time with me. I didn't know if he had anything planned for the day, so I could have been setting myself up for rejection, but it was okay.

Fortunately, he told me he didn't have much going on and he would love to spend some time with me. I didn't tell him what I had in mind, but I'm sure he thought we would just kinda hang out and get some lunch and that would be about it. If that were the case, I would have been cool with that, but that wasn't the plan for that day. I gave him the address to where I wanted to meet him and I had to keep my fingers crossed that he wouldn't look up what type of establishment he'd be coming to. I also had to let him know it would not be in his best interest to wear any of those "pretty boy" clothes that were a part of his signature look. I know that piqued his interest, but that was pretty much all the information I gave him.

Shortly after we talked, he showed up at the "secret location," the local paintball arena. I had never been there before and I had no idea it would look the way it did. I was expecting a little store where you could buy and rent stuff and then a tiny field, maybe about the size of someone's backyard to actually "play", but that was not how it was at all. The store was as large as any of those warehouse stores we all go to. As far as the "backyard" we'd be playing in, it turned out to be the size of a football field.

Since I had never done the whole paintball-thing before, I had to try to get myself ready. So, before Hamilton actually got there, I decided to treat myself to a little bit of paintball shopping spree. Well, let me rephrase that. Everything inside of that store was incredibly expensive, plus I didn't really know what any of it was. So, I looked at the paintball necessities chart they had hanging up all over the store and rented everything it said I needed.

I put on the vest I had to wear, the arm- and shin-guards I needed, an unattractive fanny pack of pellets, helmet (that unfortunately messed up my hair more than it already was), and then I grabbed the biggest paintball gun I could actually carry. I was a bit upset my gear didn't really match the way I wanted it to, but I still looked extremely cute. I rushed to get everything rented, not only so I could get dressed, but also so I could stand out in front of the building to see Hamilton's face when he pulled up and saw what we were about to do. I also wanted to see how scared he would be when he saw me in my gear.

So, after everything was on and my paintball gun was loaded, I just waited in front. I made sure my helmet was secure and I tried to stand perfectly still as a confused-looking Hamilton walked near the front entrance.

"Excuse me sir, do you need any help?" I said as I tried to disguise my voice the best I could.

"Elise? Elise, is that you?"

I was going to try and remain still and silent, but I couldn't hold back my laughter.

"Yes, it's me," I said as I tried to take my helmet off

"What in the world is going on?" he asked smiling.

"Well, we're out here because paintball is probably something you'd never expect me to do. Plus we needed to do something a little out of the ordinary to celebrate!"

"Celebrate what?"

"We're celebrating the fact my trip to LA has been finalized. So, it's official!"

"That's amazing, Elise!"

We talked for a few minutes about the details of the trip before I decided it was time to get down to business.

"Okay, that's enough talk, Hamilton. I need for you to go in there, get your equipment and prepare to get destroyed on the field."

"You think you're gonna beat me? I'm sorry, Elise, you can beat me in anything related to dance, but you will not beat me in paintball!"

"Hamilton, have you ever done this before?"

"Not exactly! I did see a commercial for it on TV, so I'm pretty sure I'll master everything within the first five minutes or so."

His false sense of confidence was entertaining and cute. I wanted to hurry up and take that confidence down a few notches. I helped him pick everything out so would could finally go out to the field. His initial reaction to the size of the field was very similar to mine.

"Are you ready?" I asked.

"Absolutely!" he responded.

"Okay, let's go!"

He put his hand on my shoulder.

"I don't really think it works like that," Hamilton said as he pointed at a sign that was posted in the ground.

I took a few minutes to read the rules that were posted on the sign. To my surprise, you couldn't just shoot people with all of the colors of your paint bullets whenever you wanted to. They didn't want you to have "free will" fun. They only allowed people to have regulated fun. According to the rules, a session wouldn't start until at least four players were ready. When enough players were available, an official would go over a few more rules and regulate the 30 minutes we'd be give to get as many points as possible. I didn't like it, not one bit.

I looked around to see if there were enough people to play, and of course, there were not. What was supposed to be fun was getting me more and more upset with each passing second.

"I don't like this at all!" I yelled.

"Babe, please don't pout. Don't be upset, we're here to have fun. I'm sure plenty of people will be here soon and when they get here, we'll forget all about the few minutes we had to wait."

He probably believed what he said, but I knew he was saying it mainly to try and keep me calm. I can't say it worked, but almost immediately after he talked, a huge group of people showed up seemingly out of nowhere.

"See, I told you," Hamilton said as he looked over at me and winked.

I didn't see the official at first, but soon he made his presence known.

"People, if you give me your attention for a few minutes, I promise we'll be out on the field collecting points very soon!"

He briefly went over the rules that were on the sign before going over the ones that weren't.

"I'll make this part quick. We're going to count off everyone who is going to participate. If there's an even number, we'll have teams. If there's an odd number, then it'll be every man for himself. Regardless of whether we have teams or not, we have a five-second re-spawn. That simply means when you're shot, you cannot get back to the game until you do a slow, 5-Mississippi count," he said.

"Will we have some type of devices to let everyone know that we're down, or when our time is up?" someone in the crowd asked.

"Not really. With that, we're kinda on an honor system. I will say, even though that's not really official, many times players will simply take a knee. It's like an unwritten rule that pretty much everybody respects. With that being said, let's count off so we can go ahead and get started!"

After a few minutes, we knew we had 30 people ready. We all decided to go with two large teams instead of multiple smaller teams. Each team was given either a blue ribbon or a red one, that way we'd all know who our enemies were. I still didn't understand how the point system worked, but I also didn't really care. I was just ready to go out there and have a great time.

"Before we go out there, I have one other thing I have to say," the official said.

"What?" members of the two teams asked.

"Well, to be honest, I've never really liked our 5-second policy. I'd like to try something different. How about we do a single-kill elimination?"

Some people, including myself, seemed to be a little confused at what he was saying, so I was really glad he decided to explain in more detail what he actually meant.

"By that, I just mean one direct hit and you're out! No kneeling down, no counting, none of that. If we do it that way, we'll probably be able to get more than one full game in. Is everyone okay with that?"

Almost in unison, we all loudly yelled out "yes!"

So, with that out of the way, we were finally ready. I looked over at everyone who had red ribbons. I silently let them know I personally planned to get each and every one of them. Some of them laughed it off, while other just ignored me completely.

"Okay people, in a minute I'll need the blue team to go on the north side, while the red goes to the south. In case you all hadn't noticed, there's plenty of open field to run around and plenty of items for you all to hide behind. Please use both of these because they will greatly enhance your paintball experience, but that's enough talk! Teams go ahead and take your positions. Do not start until you hear the whistle!"

We all took our positions. I made sure to stay close to Hamilton up to that point. When we reached our starting points, I looked over at him and asked what I thought was a very important question.

"Hamilton, you do realize being on teams just saved your paintball life, right?"

He laughed as he replied.

"Yeah, I'm very glad this team thing is happening."

"Don't worry: if they get you, I'll avenge your death," I told him.

"And the same goes for you" he replied.

"Cool! Now, let's go out there and show 'em what we're made of!"

Right then, the whistle blew and the excitement began. People were running in every direction and I thought it was so awesome!

Team members from each side were going down very rapidly. Fortunately, I wasn't one of them and neither was Hamilton. Everyone was hiding behind the trees, old vehicles, and everything else that was out in the field. It was truly exhilarating. Although Hamilton and I weren't really trying to stay close as we battled the other team, somehow we were. Every once and a while we would find ourselves looking at each other to make sure we hadn't been shot. Once we saw the other person was okay, we'd get back to our mission. It looked like we were going to be two of the last people standing, then everything changed.

  A member of the red team jumped out from behind one of the broken down trucks in the field. I thought for sure someone from our team would get them, but that didn't happen. He ended up getting clean shots and took down three members of our team. Once that was done, Hamilton had nobody close enough to him to actually help. I tried to shoot our enemy and yell out to warn Hamilton, but it was no use. My shot fell short and by the time I yelled, Hamilton was taking a yellow paintball bullet to the back.

  When he got shot, we both acted as though he had been shot with something far more serious than a paintball gun. It felt like we were in one of those action movies and we had reached a super dramatic slow-motion scene. I watched Hamilton fall to the ground and just lie there.

  "Noooooo!" I yelled out.
We promised each other if something happened to the other one on that paintball field, we would avenge their death. So I was given a chance to keep my promise.

  I only had the thought of revenge on my mind and everyone with the opposite-colored ribbon was my target. Actually, it was nowhere near being that serious, but I did have my competitive juices flowing. I wanted to win and both teams were down to only a few players. We had just as good of a chance to be victorious as they did. So I had to try my hardest to help us succeed.

  In my mind, I was ducking, dodging, rolling and shooting like they did in all of those video games. I'm pretty sure it probably didn't look as good in real life as it does in my memories, but I was still pretty effective, nonetheless. I remember looking over the field and seeing it had gone from thirty participants down to about five (and three were on the other team). The odds were stacked against us. I didn't even know the other member of my team, but if we wanted to win, we would have to find a way to work well with each other and we had to do it very quickly.

  The three members of the other team were moving closer to us, but we had to keep them all in our sights if we wanted to survive. The other guy on my team made some hand gestures to try and communicate what we needed to do. We both started laughing because neither of us had a clue what the other was trying to say. So both of us just shrugged at each other as we started to run towards our enemies.

My teammate and I soon found ourselves in the center of the field facing all three of our enemies. We knew it wasn't looking good for us at all. The odds were definitely stacked against us, but we were not going to surrender. How did we expect to get out of it? Well, to be honest, we didn't. So what do you do when you don't really know what to do? I'm not sure what anyone else would have done, but I decided to do what I was best at: dance.

Of course I know ballet logically had no place on the paintball battlefield. I also knew as I danced on the field, I had to look absolutely ridiculous doing pirouettes while wearing all of that gear, but because it looked so crazy, it was a distraction to the member of the other team. They were so stunned by my stupidity, they didn't move. They were frozen and this gave my partner a chance to try and eliminate them. It worked, but not as well as I hoped. I wanted him to get rid of everyone so we would win, but his reaction time wasn't quite quick enough.

Instead of him eliminating three people, he only was able to get rid of one. It was a little disappointing, but at least he evened the odds.

"That was cute, but you should've shot us all!" one of the other players said.

Immediately after that, they both began shooting at us. Fortunately, we were not hit. I tried to shoot back, but my paintball gun chose the perfect time to quit working. So, I did what I had to and I ran. I was sure I was going to get hit as I tried to get everything back in working order. Then, I heard my paintball gun click to let me know it was ready to go.

"Uh-oh! Elise is back in the game!" I said aloud.
Why did I say that? I really couldn't say for sure, but it probably had something to do with how much of an action hero I felt like the entire game.

I heard paintball pellets flying as I tried to find a good hiding spot. I still hadn't been hit yet, which was cool, even though I didn't understand how it was possible. Then, I heard a shot followed by the sound of a person with a lot of protective gear on, fall to the ground. I snuck a peak back to see if I was able to spot who it was. When I did, I saw it was my partner.

"Elise, it's all up to you!" I heard someone say from the other side of the field.
I'm pretty sure the voice I heard was Hamilton's, but i wasn't really able to verify it.

After what had to be about three minutes of very fast running, I made it to a large hill. I didn't hear any footsteps behind me, so I felt safe. Well, at least safe enough to get ready to get back into the game. I soon took a risk and stood up. To my surprise, there was somebody right in front of my face. With no time to think, I just reacted and shot. Admittedly, I didn't think the shot would do any good. It wasn't a head shot or anything, but a shot to the leg counted just the same!

I wanted to celebrate, but I couldn't. My team wasn't victorious yet, so I started looking for the last opposing team member. I didn't see him, so I immediately started to get nervous. I knew not seeing the opposition was a terrible thing, so I tried to scan everywhere. I saw nothing, but I soon heard the person I was searching for. The person who stood between a team win or a defeat decided he need to speak.

"Hey! Good game, but it's over now!"
Almost as soon as I heard that, I felt a blob of paint hit me on the right shoulder.

I knew it was just a game, but I was in shock at how it ended. I had convinced myself I was going to be the hero of it all, but that wasn't meant to be. While the whistle blew to signify the official end of the game, each ot the team members ran towards us. It was cool to see everybody gather together and show good sportsmanship, regardless of who won or lost. Surprisingly, I didn't see Hamilton.

I took my helmet off, hoping I'd be able to see a little more. Even though most of the people still had their helmets and other gear on, I still thought I'd be able to recognize Hamilton.

"There you are!"
I smiled as Hamilton finally started to head my way and take his helmet off.

"I was wondering where you were."

"Yeah, I saw you a few minutes ago and I was trying to run over here, but then everybody else obviously had the same idea. And when everybody got here, it got super confusing. I couldn't just run up and hug anybody. It would've been really awkward for everyone if I would've hugged someone who ended up not being you. Not only that, I'm sure you would have gotten kiiiiiinnnnnnddddaaaa upset with me and that wouldn't have been good."

"Good choice, sir. Good choice!"

We put our helmets back on. We held hands as we carried the paintball guns with us toward the building.

"Could I get everyone's attention for a moment?" the official asked.

We all stopped so we could hear what he had to say.

"I'd like to just thank everyone for coming out today. Hopefully everybody enjoyed their experience. I know we said we thought you had a chance to play multiple games, but unfortunately it won't happen. If any of you have a watch on, you'll be able to see we went waaaayyy over 30 minutes. According to the rules, I was supposed to stop you guys a long time ago, but the battle was far too epic to even think about trying to stop it before it actually ended."

Everyone cheered very loudly.

"I'm sorry we couldn't go again, but I'm pretty sure everyone feels like they got their money's worth."

We all agreed. I was so excited, I almost wanted to stay for another round, but I just didn't have it in me.

Hamilton and I returned our equipment inside the building and then we went and stood out in front to talk for a little bit.

"So, did you have fun?" Hamilton asked.

"Of course I did! How about you?"

"I had much more fun than I thought I would!"

"Yep! Me too! I thought it would be different, but in no way did I think I'd be so into it that I'd want to go right back to have another battle!" I said excitedly.

"You were pretty awesome out there and when you did that one dance move... it made everything so much better. Think about it, Elise, a person got shot because of that move. You had them hypnotized and I certainly know what that's like."

"Oh, you do?"

"Absolutely! I get hypnotized every time I see you walk or move. Sometimes just hearing your voice is enough to have me frozen. You are..."

"Stop! Stop! You're embarrassing me!" I said as I playfully put my hand up.

He stopped speaking for a moment and stared.

"Well, well, well. It seems like somebody doesn't know how to take a compliment. I won't say anymore of those cutesy little things you obviously don't like to hear."

"Okay."

I thought he was actually going to stop, but I was wrong.

"No, I won't keep talking about how beautiful you are or how brilliant of a dancer you are. Nope! I won't do that at all."

He seemed to get louder with almost every word. He made sure I knew he didn't care we were still around a large group of people who were still sporadically entering or exiting out the paintball store.

"I will not say how I fell in love with you the very first time I saw you and that when you said you'd actually be my girlfriend, that day was one of the greatest days of my life!"

I really did want him to be quiet— at least, at first I did. Sure, everything he said was really embarrassing, but it was honest and sweet. Plus, I realized he just wanted to express how he felt about me and what girl doesn't want to hear that kind of stuff?

"So, what do you want to do now, pretty lady?" Hamilton asked.

"I'm not really sure. I promised my folks I'd be home for dinner around 7."

"7:00? That's crazy because that seems like the exact same time I was hoping to be able to eat dinner."

"Hamilton, are you trying to invite yourself over to eat with my family?"

"Well, what I'm really trying to do is subconsciously persuade you to invite me over so I don't feel like a jerk for inviting myself."

"Oh, okay! Let me call my mom to make sure it's alright. I doubt she'll have any issues with it, though."

I called my mother, just like I said I would. For some reason she had a hard time believing I was trying to have someone over. Perhaps it was because it wasn't really something I had ever done, at least not with someone I was dating. My mother made a few kind-hearted jokes at my expense about it all, but I took them all in stride. Eventually she said it would be no problem to have him over.

"Congratulations, you can now officially go. You'll have a great home-cooked meal today. I do have a suggestion, though."

"Okay, what's up?"

"I just think before you make your way over to the house, you may want to go home and, well, you may want to freshen up."

"Soooo, are you saying I stink? Is that what you're telling me, Elise?"

"Umm, I'm not saying you stink, but I will say I know for sure you have seen much fresher days!"

"Daaaaang. I thought we were supposed to be cool, Elise. Is that how it is?"

"I'm only able to tell you because I care."

"Thank you, I guess. So, can I tell you something?"

"Sure!"

"I'm so glad we care about each other and can be honest and goofy with one another."

"Me, too!"

"Cool! So what I need to tell you...very seriously is... babe, I am not the only one who has seen fresher days!"

"What? How dare you, Hamilton!"

We both started laughing very hard. The people that passed by us going in and out of the store all seemed as though they wanted to join into our conversation. It was either that, or they thought we were both lunatics. This was especially true when I started to smell under my own arms to see if Hamilton was telling the truth or maybe just exaggerating a bit.

"Oh my goodness. That's terrible! Do I really smell like that?"

"I can do many things, Elise, but I could not ever create that, nor would I want to."

We laughed some more. I felt really great at that moment, not because I stunk, but because Hamilton and I were close enough that we could be ourselves and joke about each other's flaws without either of us getting offended. I tried not to ever think about finding "the one" or my "soulmate," especially at such a young age, but times like those made me feel like my search for my lifelong love were over. I didn't dare say anything about that aloud because of fear (not to mention I didn't want to inflate Hamilton's ego).

Anyway, after paintball, we spent a little while just walking around the nearby park. We talked about our lives as they were at that time, but we also spoke about us growing up. While I truly adored my upbringing, I should have known talking about it would have brought all of my painful memories to the forefront of my mind.

"Have you ever lost anyone close to you?" I asked as we found somewhere to sit.

"No, I can't really say that I have."

"Do you know how blessed you are to be able to say that?"

"I guess I never really thought about it."

I sighed very heavily.

"When I lost my aunt, I didn't think could get any worse. Then when the accident happened and we found out my father wouldn't ever walk again and I lost my sister... I literally dreamt about dying!"

I hadn't really discussed that aspect of my life in much depth with him (or anyone else) before. I didn't plan on doing it then, either, but it felt like I had to.

"Please don't tell me you meant that, Elise."

"Yes, I absolutely meant that. When Jazzy first died, I wished I was dead. My sister was everything to me. She inspired me, she pushed me, she was my friend, and all of that was taken away from me so quickly. For the most part, I try not to even talk about her, but sometimes she just becomes a part of the conversation.

"I may be totally out of line, but I think you should talk more about her and what she meant to you."

"Talk? For what? What good would that do?"

"Well, it'll be less like you're hiding her memory and more like you're honoring it."

I had never thought about it that way and once I did, I quickly realized he was right.

"What you're saying makes perfect sense, but it hurts very badly."

He already admitted he hadn't experienced loss the way I had, so he didn't pretend to understand my visible state of sadness. Instead of saying anything further, he just hugged me and waited to see if I would continue on with the conversation or not. Silently, we stood together for a few moments before I decided I had enough of the silence and the sadness.

"Are you ready to go?" I asked.

Hamilton probably found it be very awkward that I didn't actually end the conversation about my family; I just sort of moved on, but he didn't say anything about it. He just respected my decision and that was an incredibly wonderful thing.

Since we had finished talking and we both seemed like we had enough walking around, we both soon realized it was time to go. I was glad because it made the question I had just asked seem far less random and awkward. Neither of us wanted to be late, so we quickly got in our cars. We had different directions we were going to end up going, but we started off going the same way. As I was driving, thoughts of my sister kept entering my mind. At first, I just saw flashes of her. Then I heard her voice as she said, "I keep telling you I'm okay. I really am. You don't have to be sad when you think of me." I knew she wasn't actually around me saying that, but I heard it so clearly I had to pay attention to it. It was another one of the moments that I couldn't logically explain and didn't really want to believe it happened, but I felt in my spirit that it was real.

I felt myself starting to drive differently as I heard Jasmine over and over. One second I would be driving too fast and the next, I would drive so slow the car was barely moving. Things felt like they were out of my control. My eyes began to hold so much water, I could barely see the road in front of me. Every time I would wipe them, more tears would appear almost immediately. The closer we got to my house, the more I kept saying, "You can make it. You're almost home." Then, after going through a light about six blocks away from home, I found out how badly I was lying to myself.

I lost control of the car again and I was unable to regain it. The care was swerving, but it felt like my hands, arms, legs, and feet paid absolutely not attention to the signals my mind was trying to send to them. I saw myself going towards the ditch on the side of the road. All of a sudden, I felt like I was in the car with Jasmine and my dad. When the other car hit us, I was awakened to find myself alone in a car that was turned on its side. I thought for sure my stupidity, carelessness, and inability to control my emotions was going to cause my demise.

I started to hyperventilate. As I struggled to breathe, I saw Hamilton run to the car. He started pounding on the window and tried his best to pry the door open. He was yelling something to me, but I couldn't hear him. It was as though the world was on mute. It was getting harder and harder to breathe and to keep my eyes open. I soon faded out of consciousness.

"Get up! Don't you wanna live? You are not the same, Elise I knew. You can't be my sister! Who are you?"

What I heard the voice of my sister say as I was unconscious was very harsh, but it didn't seem like it was said to be cruel. It really seemed like it was said so I would actually fight for my own survival instead of accepting death.

"Elise! Elise!"

I heard Hamilton yelling before I was able to open my eyes to see him.

"Get up, babe! Please wake up!"

Hearing him and recalling what I heard my sister say shot a burst of energy all through my body. I couldn't let a car accident take my father's ability to walk, the life of my little sister, and take me out, too. That just wasn't going to happen. So, I fought. I tought to wake up, get out of my seatbelt, and help Hamilton get my door open.

I yelled loudly in pain as Hamilton tried to get me out of the car.

"Okay. Maybe you should just stay still until the ambulance gets here," he said, looking very concerned.

"I don't know... maybe... I..."

I tried very hard to get out an actual sentence, but the energy I had just gained quickly dissipated. It was a struggle to keep my eyes open, but I knew I had to do it.

I saw Hamilton use his phone to call 9-1-1. I don't know how long it took, but soon I heard the sirens of both a police car and an ambulance. My head started pounding, but I continuously tried to convince myself there was nothing wrong with me. Hamilton had stopped trying to pull me out of the car prior to the arrival of everyone, but he held onto my hand through the partially opened window until he was told he needed to move out of the way. As I struggled to keep my eyes open, I heard him constantly give me words of encouragement. He also tried his best to keep a smile on his face even though I knew he was very concerned.

Even though people's attention was on me, I didn't want it to be. I just wanted them to give me the go ahead to be able to leave so I could have dinner with my family. Maybe that was unrealistic, but outside of some soreness, scrapes, and a bit of a headache, I felt I was okay (for the most part).

"Can you please get me out?" I asked.

"We are trying our best. We just need to make sure we're extra careful. We don't want to take the risk of possibly causing any more damage."

Hamilton, who had sort of been pushed further back while everyone was trying to free me, felt he had to say something to keep me calm. I was feeling more and more pain as the minutes passed. As that happened, every question that was asked of me received increasingly rude and sarcastic responses. I didn't want to do that at all, but it felt like I was losing control.

"You're doing fine, babe. They almost have you out," Hamilton told me in a very calming tone.

They had been pulling on me while cutting and tearing parts of the car for a little while and then finally I had freedom! They got me out of my car and immediately put me on a stretcher. I felt it was totally unnecessary and a complete waste of time, but I also knew everyone was doing what was best for me, no matter what I thought or said about it.

When the EMT checked my vitals and made sure my neck was secure, I noticed each person on the road slowed down just enough to try and see what was going on with me. It upset me to see that out of the corner of my eye, but if the roles were reversed, I probably would have done the same thing.

"I know you're doing your job, but you don't have to....." Once again my mind presented more thoughts it wanted my mouth to get out, but my body wouldn't let that happen. The drowsiness finally made me close my eyes.

I woke up in a hospital room and that made me panic. I felt fine, for the most part, but just being there scared me. Was I fooling myself into believing I was okay? What was really going on?

"Where's Hamilton?" I asked anyone who could hear me.

"If you're speaking about that young man who showed up here with you, he just stepped out for a moment," a person who appeared to be a nurse, said.

"Okay. When can I go home?" I asked.

"Very soon! Your vitals and everything seem very good. We really just want to observe you for a few hours and then we think you will be able to leave."

I should've been happy to hear what was told to me, but I wasn't. I almost felt like I was being lied to. I wondered if someone told my sister she was only going to be in the hospital for a few hours and then released. Was she given a false sense of hope? Perhaps. Should I let a situation that may or may not have happened with Jasmine affect me? I wasn't sure what the "correct" answer to that question was, so I tried my best to stop thinking about it as quickly as I could.

I looked around the room and had an out-of-body experience. I not only saw myself in the hospital bed, but I saw my aunt, my dad, my sister, and my mom in hospital beds as well. Out of the five of us, two had passed away, one had his life changed with a disability which left only two of us. I didn't like those numbers. I didn't feel comfortable with that at all.

The few strangers in the room soon cleared out as Hamilton finally made his way back in. He had some mango juice, some roses, and a bag full of great smelling food.

"I'm glad you're awake." Hamilton said.

"Me, too. I'm ready to leave, though," I replied.

"They'll let you go soon. They just want to make sure everything is good."

His thoughtfulness, tone, and choice of words all made me feel better. That was something he had an uncanny ability to do, no matter what I was dealing with.

"I really hate that I'm gonna miss dinner with my parents, though. I was looking forward to it all day. I'm so stupid! I don't even really know why I crashed! I'm so.... I just am so mad right now!"

"Stop it, Elise! I won't allow you to blame yourself for what happened. Did you crash your car on purpose?"

At first, his question upset me and I didn't even want to dignify it with a response. I inhaled, made sure I maintained my composure, and gave him a response.

"No, of course I didn't crash the car on purpose. That would be stupid!"

"That's what I was hoping you'd say. If you know you didn't crash your car on purpose, then that would make it an accident. If it was an accident, then how in the world can you beat yourself up over it? How do you allow yourself to say bad things about your intelligence?"

His statements and questions made me think and they also humbled me very quickly.

"You're right. Dang! You're right."

There was nothing more I could say. He made his point and I realized what he was trying to say.

"I wasn't trying to be right, I just don't like you to get down on yourself. You're a wonderful person and you should always recognize that, no matter what type of mistakes you may make."

A little embarrassment tried to set in, but it had no place, so I had to force it to leave. I reached for my food, almost as a way to try and change the subject.

"Thanks for all of this. I really appreciate it. You know mango juice is my favorite and these flowers are beautiful. And what kind of food is this?" I asked as I started to open up the bad.

"Hold on! Before you do that... just hold on."

He ran out of the room very quickly without explaining why. A few seconds later, I heard my father's laughter as he, my mother, and Hamilton entered into the room.

"Are you okay?" my mom asked.

I was very shocked to see them.

"Yeah, I think so. Supposedly they're gonna let me leave in a few hours."

"We're so happy you're okay. When Hamilton first showed us the picture of the car, we expected much worse. Thank God!" my father said while keeping a huge smile on his face.

"Picture? What picture?"

"Oh, you haven't seen what your car looked like after the accident?"

"No, I haven't."

Hamilton walked over to me and showed me a picture he had taken with his phone. What I saw was devastatingly terrible and it made me very grateful I was still alive.

"I'm sorry, y'all. For whatever reason, when I was driving, I just kept thinking about everyone and I kept hearing Jazzy's voice. I just lost control."

My father moved over to me as Hamilton stepped back to give him room. He grabbed my hand and the smile that was on his face since he entered the room started to fade. He looked me directly in my eyes.

"Elise..."

"Yeah, dad?"

"I guess you just had to make sure you had your stay in the hospital just because the rest of us did. Well, now that you've done it, I hope they let you go soon. We end up in the hospital so much, they might start charging us rent or something!"

As soon he said that, the whole room was instantly filled with laughter. Only my father could find a way to make a joke about me being in the hospital after surviving a terrible accident. Strangely enough, it was kind of what we needed— well, it was what I needed. And as echoes of the laughter still floated around the air, I reached for my bag of food again. Then I realized all of us were supposed to be having dinner together at home. The guilt and sadness everyone had just helped me get rid of was returning very quickly.

"We were supposed to be eating at home. I'm sorry!"

My mom gave me a very serious look, while still managing to keep a bit of a smile.

"Girl, quit apologizing! It's not like you planned it. Plus we're all just glad you're okay."

"But what about having dinner together?"

"Go ahead and open that bag!" she said.

When I did, I saw it was way more food that I thought it would be. I should have realized how heavy it was, but for some reason I hadn't.

"You may be able to eat a lot, but I know you can't handle all of that. Your mom put all of that in there so we can still eat a meal together, even though we're not at home," dad said.

"Yeah, as soon as I called them, they told me what they were going to do. I'd like to publicly admit: your family is kinda awesome!"

He was right. Not everyone was blessed to have the type of family I had. Many people prayed for the type of love and closeness we had.

"Thank you everybody. I really appreciate everyone coming out here. Like Hamilton said, you guys are awesome. Now can we go ahead and eat?"

"Absolutely, but not before someone says grace," dad said as he looked around.

Surprisingly Hamilton was the person who volunteered to speak. It was a shock because, although he said he believed in God, some parts of his family didn't necessarily share his beliefs.

"Please forgive me if I don't totally do this correctly, but could everyone join hands?"

We put our food down and held each other's hands.

"Don't worry, Hamilton, there is no right or wrong way. Just talk to God honestly and from your heart."

He looked a little nervous, but he didn't back down as we all closed our eyes.

"God, I don't talk to you very often and I'm sorry. I pray that you don't give up on me. And God, I ask that you bless the Morgan family. They are great people and I hope the string of negativity doesn't continue to follow them. I pray Elise gets better soon. She deserves to get her shot at her dreams in Los Angeles. And lastly God, I'd like to thank you for this time together and for this meal. Thank you, God. In the name of Jesus we pray, amen."

As we opened our eyes and released each other's hands, Hamilton quickly moved over to me and kissed me on my forehead.

"Boy, you just finished praying and you're gonna disrespect me and my wife by kissing on our daughter right in front of us? What's wrong with you?"

I didn't know what to say or do. Hamilton looked as though his heart had just dropped to the ground.

"I'm sorry Mr. and Mrs. Morgan. I didn't mean any disrespect to Elise or either of you. I was just..."

"Stop, Hamilton. Just stop! You don't need to say another word. Plus... I was just playing with you, man! She's a beautiful young woman. I mean, look at her mother. How could she not be beautiful? You are supposed to show love to her and honor her. She will forever be our little girl, but right now, we recognize she is your woman. If she is your woman, that means you're her man. As such, it is your job to cherish her and protect her. You are a smart young man and I know you can handle it. Let me change that. I fully expect you to handle that job. Is that understood?"

"Yes, sir," Hamilton answered.

"Now, with all of that out of that way, let me say that was a good prayer, son. If y'all don't mind, could we go ahead and eat before all of this food gets cold?"

"Yep!" my mother and I both said at the same time.

While it may have been surprising and a little crazy to hear everything my father said to Hamilton, it was also cute to hear he still just wanted to protect me. Even though I was in pain, seeing my family interact with Hamilton as they all showed they cared about me cemented a smile on my face as we all passed around the food to make our plates. We all took our time eating, too. By the time I had all I could eat, a doctor walked into the room.

"Elise, I hate to interrupt your meal, but I have to give you some news."

"Okay…"

"You had a terrible accident. When anyone sees the condition of the car, they will automatically have assumptions about your condition. More than likely their assumptions will be very inaccurate because you are the personification of a miracle. None of the things that could have gone wrong actually did, and you surpassed even our greatest hopes. We tested for fractions, full breaks, internal bleeding, a concussion and many other things, but you have absolutely nothing wrong with you and you are free to go."

"Really?"

"Yes, really! Granted, you will be in pain and you will be sore, but it could be far worse than what it actually is."

I could do nothing but thank God for His mercy and favor. I understood from what my family had already gone through, I was very fortunate just to survive the accident. I had to praise and thank God over and over again. In about 15 minutes or so, I not only was done praising, but I found myself getting dressed as everyone else stood outside of the room and waited for me to finish.

"Okay everyone, let's hurry up and get out of here before they change their minds," I said, laughing as I exited out of the room.

Everyone wanted to leave just as quickly as I did. They helped me fill out my exit paperwork and carried the few things I had with me as we all headed outside. Even though I felt the pain that was present in every part of my body as I walked, for some reason, I didn't think about not having a car anymore.

"Where did I park?" I asked.

Mom looked at me and just shook her head.

"Elise, if you were driving, we wouldn't be here right now," she said.

They all had a laugh at my expense, but I wasn't joking. I had literally forgotten my car was totaled. It scared me. I prayed it was just a brief slip of my memory and nothing more serious. The fact the doctor said everything was okay didn't matter to me because I knew doctors were wrong all of the time. It was amazing how quickly I began to regret the decision to leave. I almost wanted to turn around and go back into the hospital, but I didn't. Instead, I just lied and pretended I was joking.

"Mom, you know I wasn't for real!"

I put a "fake" smile on my face and proceeded to make myself laugh as well.

As always, I hated to deceive my parents (especially for something so trivial), but I felt it was necessary. We started talking about who I was going to ride with before it was quickly decided Hamilton would be my best option. I agreed and we followed my parents home. During the drive, I wasn't really myself. I didn't initiate any conversations, or even turn on the radio. I just sat quietly in the passenger's seat as I recalled the day's activities.

The roads, buildings, people, and everything else I saw all seemed to move by very quickly. My life felt like it was doing the same thing. Everything was changing and I was the reason for it. I was feeling bad all over again, but I wouldn't allow myself to cry.

"I'm so glad you're okay, Elise," Hamilton said, breaking the silence that had endured since we left the hospital.
For about a minute or so, I didn't respond. It wasn't necessarily intentional, but it happened anyway.

"Have you ever thought about your purpose? Like, why are you here?"

"Those are good questions. I can't say I've ever thought about it a lot, but I guess those kind of thoughts and questions have crossed my mind."

"So what do you think?"

"Well, I think God gives us all talents. I think our purpose is to try to use those talents for the good of mankind."

"I like that! That's pretty good."

"Thank you. You know what? Not only are we supposed to do things for mankind, but I'm pretty sure our gifts are in us to help bring more people closer to God."

I loved to hear Hamilton speak about God. It didn't feel like he was being disingenuous with his responses, which was refreshing because sometimes even the people in the church were faking "The Spirit" just for the appearance of it all. It made me feel good to just hear him talk like that from his heart, but I still had more questions for him.

"But what if we sometimes question if we're good enough to handle our talents? What if you think... what if you..."
I felt my emotions pile up. I tried to continue, but it took me clearing my throat a few times and a few seconds before I actually could.

"... What if I don't think I should even still be here?"

He heard what I was asking, but he didn't really understand why I was asking it.

"What would make you ask those things?" Hamilton wondered.

"I think I have some talent, but I don't always know if my best is good enough and that scares me. I don't want to be a disappointment to anyone."

"Elise, there's no way you should ever feel like you're a disappointment to anyone.…ever! That's impossible! You work too hard to feel like that."

"But why am I here and my sister isn't? Why didn't I die in my car accident and she lived after hers?"

I didn't know if I expected him to answer me honestly, lie to me, or just ignore everything I asked.

"I don't have one of those perfect answers for you. What I can say is, I heard people say God doesn't make mistakes. So, as hard as it probably is to think about your sister, just think that God probably felt her job was done. You still have something you need to do here. So, it is not your time to go."
That was all I needed to hear.

"Thank you, Hamilton."

Saying thank you was all I could do, it was all I needed to do. I didn't have to create any more questions or force the conversation. For the remainder of the ride, I went back to just looking out of the window. We both said all we needed to say. I was happy Hamilton just allowed me to ponder over what he said while I looked at the outside world. He calmed me down when I was feeling overly emotional.

When we finally made it to my house, it was dark. The stars in the sky sparkled like diamonds and I just looked up and gazed in amazement once I got out of the car.

"They're beautiful, aren't they?" Hamilton asked as he leaned against his car.

"Yeah, they are. Nature's design is so perfect."
I briefly looked down to see my parents go inside while Hamilton grabbed my hand.

"I really admire your parents," he said.

"Really? Why?" I asked.

"They are just amazing people. They have so much love for each other, and as someone outside of your family, it seems like no matter what comes their way, they'll battle it together. These days, that's something you don't always see."

"That's true. They are very cool people and I'm glad I've been able to grow up around them. It has certainly given me a positive outlook on the possibilities of what love can be when you work at it."

"Very well said."

For the next five minutes or so, we quietly went back to just enjoying the stars while listening to only the sounds nature provided. Soon my aching body told me it was time to get some rest. As much as I would've liked to stay in the night air looking at the stars with Hamilton, I couldn't.

"I'm sorry, but I really need to get some rest."

"No worries. I completely understand."

He gave me a hug.

"I'm just really, really glad you're okay!" he said.

"Thank you!"

"You're welcome. Go get your rest and please just promise me we'll see each other again before you leave."

"Of course!"

"Do you mind if I walk you inside?"

"That would be great."

We walked to the door, only slightly slower than normal. I still had some pain, but it wasn't as bad as it was earlier in the day. I was very thankful for that. I was also grateful for the fact Hamilton was willing to move at my pace to make sure I was okay, even though I'm sure it had to be annoying to him.

"Here you go, Elise," he said when we reached the door.

"Thank you. Do you want to come inside for a few minutes?"

"That would be cool, but I know you really need your rest, so I'm gonna go."

"I appreciate you being so respectful and I'm sorry we had such a bad day."

"You sure do like to apologize when you have nothing to apologize for, don't you? We had some not-so-great moments today, but it wasn't all bad. Paintball was great and I ended up eating a wonderful meal with the Morgan family. Plus, you were a part of a miraculous act. So, I really don't have any complaints. I'm so thankful you're okay. Even if none of that other stuff had happened, it still would've been okay."

"You're a wonderful person, Hamilton."

"When you're right, you're right. I can't even disagree with you, but you're even more wonderful. Have a good night, Elise. I love you."

"I love you, too."

It was still somewhat strange to hear someone tell me that, but I was no longer hesitating to say it back.

With smiles on both of our faces, we ended our conversation and our day together. I went to bed that night with a lot of mixed emotions. I was happy about my relationship with Hamilton and my family, but I was still sad about my little sister not being around. I was beyond ecstatic I made it out of a terrible car accident with no major injuries, but my heart was weighed down heavily with guilt because the same thing couldn't be said for Jasmine (or my father, to a lesser extent). Those emotional conflicts caused me to toss and turn for a while before I was actually able to go to sleep. Because of that, I woke up a bit more restless than I would have hoped.

The next day, I didn't get up until around noon. Honestly I don't know if it would have happened then if I hadn't received a call from Little Jazzy.

"Hello Miss Elise, are you okay?"

"Yes, ma'am. I'm fine."

"That's good because I heard you were in a car accident and you went to the hospital and I got really sad. I mean really, really sad."

She always ran her words together when she was excited. She stayed true to form with that conversation. I knew, no matter how much pain I was in, I had to act as though I was okay. If I didn't, it would have caused her to worry even more than she already was.

"I was in an accident, but I'm okay. Don't worry about me, it's all good. I promise."

"Okay, that's good! Now do you think we can practice today?"

She had the uncanny ability to move on to the next subject, especially after she had some type of closure.

"I don't know if we should practice today. I don't know if I'm really up to it."

It wasn't very often that I questioned if I was going to ballet class or not. Of course I had a reasonable excuse. However, it did feel strange for me to say and by her response, she thought it was strange to hear.

"Huh? Are you sayin' you don't wanna practice? Are you sure you're okay? You know not wanting to dance is just weird!"

She was right. It was weird for me to not want to dance. The strange thing was, I couldn't tell if I was being hesitant to commit to going to the studio because I was in pain or because I was afraid to see how the accident really impacted my body and its ability to move properly.

"How about I make you a deal? We can go to the studio and I can help you with your movements and posture, but the focus will be on you today. I may or may not even dance at all. Is that okay?"

"That's okay, I guess."

She didn't sound very happy about what I said, but I couldn't really blame her. I could only imagine how I would have felt if Mrs. Mears ever said anything like that to me. Whether she admitted to it or not, I knew it had to be discouraging to her. I wanted to address it.

"How do you feel about that? Be honest and say what's on your mind."

It's always a strange thing when an adult gives a child permission to speak their mind. As a child, you get used to older people limiting what you can say. When someone goes against that, it almost feels like some sort of setup.

"Can I be honest, for real?"

Her question let me know how to set my expectations. She didn't have something simple to ask, at least that's how it seemed.

"Yes, you can be honest. Just make sure you don't use any bad language because I don't wanna hear that stuff."
I laughed a little to myself because I was sounding like a parent.

"Okay, Miss Elise. I look up to you. You work really hard and so I know if I ever want to be as good as you are, or even better, I have to work really hard, too. I have never, ever, ever heard you make an excuse for not being able to practice. No matter what, you just keep on working. Now you're saying you don't know if you're gonna dance today. That doesn't make any sense! You said you were okay. So, either you're not telling the truth about how hurt you are or....or... I don't even know! Something has to be wrong."

What she said made a lot of sense. Maybe I was lying to myself. Maybe I was a little bit more injured than I wanted to admit. Maybe fear was coming back into my mind. I didn't have the answers, so I needed to admit that to her.

"Thank you for saying all of that. I needed to hear it, but I have to let you know I don't know if any of what I said was a lie or not."

"What do you mean, Miss Elise? People know when they're lying. I don't even understand what you're saying."

"Most of the time we know when we are lying. Sometimes we're so confused we really have no idea. I think that's where I am right now."

"But you're really smart. What are you confused about?"

"I am confused about how I really feel. Not to mention the fact I have to leave everyone I know to tryout in Los Angeles. Who knows if I'm even gonna get it? I don't want to stop teaching! I don't want to fail!"

I had no idea why I was having a mini-breakdown. And the fact that I was expressing my innermost feelings and emotions to someone so young made everything about that situation even crazier.

"Miss Elise, you're better than this. You're just a human, so if you're hurt, just say you're hurt! And if you're scared of something, it's okay. If you tell someone, they may be able to help you. We all get scared sometimes. When I was a really little kid, I saw a movie about dinosaurs and it really scared me. I told my cousin about it and she helped me to not be scared anymore. You're really, really super cool and you'll be okay, I promise!"

You never can predict what a child will say, especially when you allow them to truly express themselves. They are usually not inhibited by the ways of the world. Their innocence normally lets their words come directly from their hearts. Many times what they say can hit you much harder than the words of other adults.

"Thank you for saying all of that, Little Jazzy. I needed to hear that."

"You're welcome! I don't like it when you're sad, Miss Elise. You're one of my favorite people on the face of the earth. When you're sad, it makes me sad, too!"

"I didn't want to make you sad, so I apologize for that."

"It's okay. I forgive you. So can we still practice for my recital? Our performance is in a few days."

With all I had going on, I almost forgot my students had a performance coming up. I wouldn't get to be there to see it, but I had to use the remaining time I had before I left preparing them to the best of my abilities.

"We will definitely go to the studio today, but do you also want to make sure everyone else is ready, too?"

Without hesitation she replied: "I want us all to be great, Miss Elise."

She was all about her team and you couldn't ask for any more than that.

"I was hoping you'd say something like that. That's a sign of a true leader! You want everyone to be at their best."

"Yep! If one of us looks bad, we all look bad!"

"That's a really mature way to look at things. And since you feel that way, I'd like to try to get as much of the class together as possible today. That way, we can go over the entire show. Does that sound good?"

"Yes, ma'am."

"Good. We need to see who's available, but first I need to ask if you've had anything to eat today."

"Yep! I had oatmeal with strawberries in it and then I had two huge glasses of chocolate milk."

"I'm glad you were able to eat. Now that we have that out of the way, is your mom at home?"

Since I first met Little Jazzy, she did a lot of things on her own. Most of the time when I asked about her mom, she would tell me she wasn't around. Every once and a while, Jazzy would shock me by telling me her mom was actually nearby. That conversation was one of those rare times.

"Yep! Momma's here. You wanna talk to her?"

"Only if she's willing to talk."

I was put on hold and I calmly waited.

When her mother finally got on the phone, she immediately sounded like she was ready to get off. It was normal for her to sound like that. It was always upsetting, but I tried to never let my anger come across in our conversation.

"Your daughter has a very important performance coming up very soon. She has been working very hard. She's shown more maturity, focus, and a greater work ethic than most adults. I understand you're very busy and she may not have even mentioned this to you, but it would mean the world to her if you could be there to see it."

"Look, I'm not about to explain my situation to you because I don't have to, but I don't have time to go see Jasmine fool around with this ballet stuff on stage. I have better things to do! It's enough that I allow her to keep dancing and be around and talk to you all the time. I'm getting mad just thinking about it because you almost act like she's your daughter, but she's not!"

The conversation escalated quickly and I felt it was completely unnecessary. It always felt as though she wanted everything to be about her. To me, it seemed like her daughter was the most mature member of that household. Her tone was disrespectful and I wanted to yell at her to let her know she wasn't the only one who could do it, but I knew that would be pointless. Instead I asked God to give me the strength to not speak back to her in the disrespectful manner I felt she had been speaking to me.

"I apologize for possibly overstepping my bounds, but I am begging you to try and find a way to be there. She can give you all of the details, but it would be a great thing for you to see her performance. She works really hard and she's an absolutely wonderful dancer."

"I'm not gonna make any promises, but when she tells me the date and time, I'll see what I can do."

"Thank you very much. I really appreciate that. Also, do you mind if I take your daughter to the studio today so we can practice?"

I tried to prepare for the worst because I didn't know how she'd respond.

"You know what? I don't think you'll need to take her practice."

I couldn't comprehend why she would say that, but I started to think of all of the possible reasons. Unfortunately, everything I thought of was negative. In my mind, I was getting defensive and even more upset about the reason for her statement even before I asked her about it. I knew that wasn't fair to anyone.

"Could I ask you why I don't need to take her to practice?" For a few seconds, she didn't say anything.

"Everything you just said made sense. And believe it or not, I know how people probably view me as a parent, even though none of you know the sacrifices I make for my child! But no matter what, I should be able to be there for my daughter. I'm not gonna act like I'll be able to show up for all of her practices or dances, but I'll be around a lot more. So you can't take Jasmine to practice today because I'm gonna do it."

I was pleasantly surprised by her response. It was good to hear a sense of remorse from her. That was something I didn't even think she was capable of. I was so glad I was wrong about that. I was so overjoyed by the fact she said she would be more involved in Jasmine's life, I almost yelled. It took a lot of self-control not to.

"I'm really glad you said that. Thank you."

"No disrespect to you, but I'm not doing it for you. I'm doing it for my daughter. You made me realize she deserves a lot more from me than I've provided."

The more pleasant, yet still very honest, tone she gave me in parts of that conversation allowed me to see a new side of her. It helped me a little with my perspective.

We ended the talk by simply agreeing on the time I wanted her to bring Jasmine to the studio. Once that was done, I immediately started calling the parents of the other girls in the class to see if any of them would be able to come to practice. I was hoping all of them would be able to make it, but that was not what happened. By the time I convinced my parents to let me use the car, get dressed, and get to the studio, only Jasmine and maybe about four other students were there with their parents. I was disappointed, but when I thought about it, I completely understood. The call to rehearsal was very last minute and it was during a time most of the parents were at work. So I had to change from being upset that not all of my students were able to show up, to happy that a few of them were.

    We got to work almost as soon as we entered into the main practice room. All of the kids had their bags, water bottles, and all of the proper attire. Most of them started stretching and warming up well before I said anything. All of them were very focused. I was wondering what was going on, then Little Jazzy walked over to me and pulled me over to the side.

    "Everybody's working hard, right?" she whispered.

    "Yeah, they are. What's going on?"

    "Umm... I called everybody and told them if they were coming to practice, they had to be serious because we didn't have much time left before the show and you would be leaving soon, so we can't waste your time."

    "Did you really tell them that?"

    "Uh-huh. We can't play around all of the time. You don't like that and Mrs. Mears doesn't like that, either."

    She was right and I appreciated the fact that she took it upon herself to speak to her peers. Sometimes hearing things from someone closer to you comes across better (and is more effective) than hearing the same thing from a teacher or someone in a leadership position. Her recognizing that was yet another confirmation she would soon be leading classes of her own. I was surprised she told them about me leaving, though. That was something I needed to address quickly.

    "Excuse me, ladies. Could I get everyone's attention, please?" Everyone moved to the center of the room, including Jasmine. All of their eyes were on me. I got nervous.

    "I know you all have heard about me leaving, is that right?" They all confirmed at the same time.

    "Does anyone know why, though?"
Jasmine said nothing and neither did anyone else in the class.

"Okay, let me explain. Since I was a little younger than all of you, I've practiced very hard and tried my best when it came to ballet. I've worked because I love it and I have always wanted to live up to my potential. Part of my goal was to show as many people as possible how beautiful the art of dance is.

"Over the years, some people outside of the friends and family of the studio have been paying attention to our performances. For whatever reason, they have decided I am good enough to try out for their dance company in Los Angeles."
One of my students raised her hand.

"What's up?"

"Why do they have to take you away from us? Why don't they just get people from there?"

"That's a good question. Can I ask you something?"

"Yes."

"What if you watched a TV show and everybody was the same? What if they all looked alike, sounded alike, and were all from the same place? Wouldn't that get boring?"

"Yeah, that would be dumb!"

"Exactly! It's the same with ballet. Nobody wants to go see a show where everyone is always the same. That's why they are trying to get new dancers. One of their main ballerinas was injured and they are trying to be more diverse with her replacement. I may not even be the best out there, but I owe it to myself and all of you to at least go and try. Does that make sense?"

"Yep! Well, most of it does. The only thing that didn't make sense to me was when you said you might not make it. Miss Elise, you're the best! If you don't make it, then they have to be crazy or something."
I smiled.

"Thank you for saying that. I love all of you so much!"

"We love you too, Miss Elise," they all said.

"I guess y'all must want to see me start crying, huh? Can we please get started before these tears start to roll?"

We got to work and we practiced that day like we had never collectively practiced before. I was in pain almost the entire time, but I couldn't let it stop me. My students were practicing more than what was required of them and I couldn't let any of them feel like I was wasting their effort. We worked until they couldn't move any more.

We rehydrated, rested for a little while, and then all of the kids let me know they wanted to get back to work. After another hour, the older kids started to walk in. Since they also had a performance the same night as my class, I expected them to try and rush us off the floor, but they didn't. They saw my kids were drenched in sweat and they appreciated the hard work all of them had put in. They asked if they could help us work on our routines to make sure we were ready. It was very nice of them and it was also very unexpected.

I spoke with their teacher briefly to make sure it was okay to spend about twenty more minutes on our closing number. She agreed, so we took full advantage of the extra time and having a few of the older kids partner up with my students. Once our allotted time was up, I was very confident we were ready for the show. I looked into the eyes of each one of the kids as we left the rehearsal room. There was so much joy in their eyes, I couldn't help but feel a bit of pride in their journey. Separately each of them told me they couldn't wait for the show. I was happy their excitement seemed to overshadow the sadness about me leaving they had expressed earlier. That's exactly what I hoped for.

I didn't really have a plan of how long we were going to practice, so I wasn't able to tell their parents when to come back. Since this was the case, I spent some of the time after practice calling the parents who weren't able to stay the entire time. As I finished making the last call in the office, Mrs. Mears allowed me to use since I started teaching, Jasmine quietly sat down in a chair next to me. She said nothing until she was sure I was finished with my task.

"Hey, pretty lady. How are you?"

"I'm good! Practice was really, really good."

"Yes, it was. It couldn't have happened without you, so I really thank you for being a leader. You wanted your team to be better and because of you, those girls out there are further along than they would have been without you."

When hearing someone basically tell you how great you are, most people would quickly eat that up. Their chest would fill with pride. They would take the positive words that were given to them and look at you as they silently ask you to give them more. Most of us have been guilty of this at one time or another, but that was not in Little Jazzy's character.

"Thank you, Miss Elise, but I didn't really do anything. They all want to make sure we have a good show. So, it wasn't me, it was us!"

In the midst of me throwing praise her way, she humbled herself and deflected the positive words enough for them to be spread equally amongst the team. Just another example of her showing she was a leader.

"I'd like to ask you something," I informed her.

"Okay."

"I remember how you reacted when I first told you I was leaving. How do you feel about everything now?"

She didn't say anything at first. She just looked around the office. It was almost like she was taking inventory of all of the decorations. The office wasn't completely mine, so not only did I have pictures on friends, family, and my students on the wall and desk, so did a lot of other people. Jazzy just seemed to be be making mental notes on each of them to help her with what she was about to say.

"There are a lot of people on that wall, Miss Elise."

It seemed like she was completely ignoring my question, but I went along with it.

"Yeah, there are."

"Do you think you're gonna miss all of them when you leave?" she asked.

I looked around at all the pictures for myself. It was something I hadn't really done in a while.

"Well, I don't quite know everyone in all of the pictures, but for everyone that I do know... yeah, I'll miss them."

"I'm pretty sure they'll miss you, too. I know I will."

She continued speaking as she started to put her head down.

"But I know when you go, you won't forget about us. I'll be sad every time I come to class and not see you there. And whenever I want to practice more and I remember that I can't call you to ask if we can come to the studio, that'll make me sad, too. I'm not upset

anymore, I'm just really sad. It's like my best friend is leaving and I don't know if you'll ever be back."
She tried very hard not to cry. Her battle with her emotions caused me to have one of my own.

"No matter what happens when I go to L.A., I will make sure I find a way to come back."

She seemed to be okay with my promise to her. We talked for a little while longer before the remaining parents began to show up. Once they did, I explained my situation to all of them. Some wished me well, a couple seemed to be legitimately upset, and the remaining few didn't seem to care at all. I wasn't offended by any of the responses, but they still all affected me.

With many of my kids gone, I was eventually left in the office alone. I looked around the office some more. I had a lot of memories of people associated with the studio and many memories that happened because of ballet. This made me sad, but for some reason, it made me feel like it was okay to move on. I had been going there since I was six and I loved everything I learned and everyone there; but at the same time, I realized it was okay to leave "home," even if it ended up being just for a little while.

I suddenly felt an increase in my confidence level. Although I was still experiencing some lingering pain from the accident and the tremendous workout I just went through, I stood up quickly and I left the office. I wanted to leave the studio, but I had to make sure all of my students were completely gone out of the building first. Not surprisingly, all of them were gone except for Jasmine. She had made her way to the corner of one of the smaller rehearsal rooms and looked as though she was about to start her own private rehearsal session. She had nothing to play her music, but she didn't let that stop her. She started to hum the music as she closed her eyes and started the routine we had just spent hours practicing.

She didn't even notice I was there, so I didn't say anything. I didn't want to be selfish and interrupt her, so even though I was initially ready to leave, I just sat there and watched. So many people compared the way she worked to me, but she worked harder than me. It was like she always had something to prove to someone. I wanted to find out what motivated her, so I patiently awaited the first moment when she decided to take a break. It took over fifteen minutes for that to happen, but when she stopped, she opened her eyes and was obviously very shocked to see me in the room with her.

"Hey Miss Elise, how long have you been here?"

"For a little while. Just long enough to see you go through the entire routine... again."

She giggled.

"That's funny! I didn't know you were there. That means you heard me singing and stuff, right?"

"I sure did!"

"Aww, man!"

"Don't worry, I won't tell anyone about it. I do have a question for you, though."

"Yes, ma'am."

Still trying to catch her breath. She waited for me to ask my question.

"What makes you work so hard?"

She seemed confused by the question. It was almost like she thought it was a trick.

"What do you mean?" she asked.

"Well, you're always practicing or wanting to practice. Most people, no matter what age they are, don't have that sort of dedication. So, I just want to know why do you work so hard? What keeps you motivated?"

I had asked something similar on multiple occasions, but I still found her answers to be very fascinating.

"I want to be good and I want people to be proud of me. And now I have another reason."

"What?" I asked.

"Well, since you're leaving, I want to keep working and get really good. That way, maybe one day they'll want me to come out to LA, too. That way, I'll be able to see you and that'll make me happy!"

Her words were very sincere and they just forced me to show how much I appreciated her by giving her a hug. I just held onto her until she remembered she had another reason why she was so dedicated.

"Do you wanna know my other reason?"

I released her from the hug and we both smiled.

"I'm sorry. Of course I want to know what the other reason is."

"Well, since you had that talk with my mom, she's been talkin' different. She told me she was sorry for not always watching me. She told me that she promised to do better. And because she made a promise to me, I made one to her. You know what I promised her, Miss Elise?"

"What did you promise her?"

"I promised her that I would always, always, always do my best when I dance. I think that will make her smile and if I can make her smile, that would be really cool!"

"You're right, that would be cool!"

Not only was she dedicated, but she was thoughtful as well. It was nice to see a young person behave like that.

I asked her if she wanted practice more. I expected her to say she did, but she told me she was ready to go home. We contacted her mother and she asked if I could wait until she got there. I obliged. Jasmine and I waited together until I got the call to let me know she had arrived.

"If it's okay, will you walk outside with me?" Jasmine asked when I told her mother was there.

I wasn't sure why she made the request, but I didn't ask for an explanation. I just grabbed her hand and we went outside. As soon as we made it outside, her mother was ready to talk to me. Even though we had a pleasant conversation earlier that day, I still prepared for the worse.

"Elise, believe it or not, I'm glad to see you."

It was still unusual to hear her say anything remotely positive, so I wasn't too quick to believe it wasn't just sarcasm. I made sure I didn't say anything that could've been perceived as negative.

"I'm glad to see you, too!"

Jasmine got in the car as her mother and I talked.

"I heard you always have things going on, so I'm not gonna hold you up for too long."

"It's no problem. What's up?"

"I know I said this earlier, but I need to say it in person. Thank you, Elise. Allow me to be honest with you for a minute."

"Okay."

"I haven't always been around for this dancing stuff because I haven't always seen the value of it, but I'm starting to. See, my daughter used to be shy and would hardly speak to people. When I first brought her to class, it started to change. She became more confident and more aware of her talents. Even as she started to show more interest in what she was doing and her desire to improve, I downplayed everything. I would show less interest, partially in hopes to make her show less interest in all of this. I know you may wonder why a mother would do this. Honestly I wondered, too. I had no answer until recently."

"What happened?"

"Well, one night after work, I came home and Jasmine was already in the bed. This isn't unusual because it happens whenever I have to pick up a late shift at work. That night was different, though. That night I looked at my baby in pajamas, all tucked into her bed, and I just broke down and started crying."

I don't know what made her open up to me, but I was thankful for it. I wanted to make sure the conversation continued.

"That's sad. Why did that happen?"

"At first, I thought it was just because I was seeing how independent she was becoming. Then I had a bit of an epiphany. Perhaps the reason I didn't show interest or was acting as though I was setting my daughter up for failure is because I saw her progress and it scared me. In a way, I didn't want her to succeed in life with her talents because I wasn't able to utilize my own. Most parents would want their kids to succeed where they have failed. Most would be overjoyed with their child embracing the talents God has given them, but I was being very idiotic and I needed to let go of my stubbornness to benefit my child. Speaking to you confirmed this."

"I don't know how I could have possibly said anything to make you feel like that, but that's good."

"Well it probably was more than what you have said to me directly. It was more than likely was a combination of our talks, your conversations with my daughter, and your willingness to take on the role of a mentor to her. I think the good Lord must be using you to help me learn things I may have not been able to learn on my own. I could go on for a while, but the main point I want to make sure I get across to you is in spite of how it may have seemed at different times, I appreciate your efforts. And as you go on to the next chapter of your life, I beg that you somehow keep that little girl a part of what you do," she said, pointing at Little Jazzy, who appeared to be falling asleep in the backseat of her mother's car.

"I promise I will do that."
She gave me a hug and thanked me again before she got back in the car and drove off.

I quickly recognized that whole exchange happened because of God. Over the years, there had been plenty of times when I hated that woman and how she was treating her child. I also understood there were plenty more times when I was positive that she also hated me. It wasn't right for either of us to feel that way, but we did. The crazy thing is, if I had to be hated (temporarily or permanently) for a parent to recognize what they were doing to negatively impact their kids, I would gladly take on that role.

I stood still just looking in the direction Jasmine's mother had driven off in for a while. The further they got into the distance, the more I started to miss Little Jazzy. I needed to distract my mind. I turned around, went inside of the building, got my bad and walked back outside. I just wanted to get in the car and leave, but for some reason, I couldn't. I ended up staring at the name of the dance studio as the sign started to light up in the evening sky. I remembered the first time I ever laid eyes on that sign.

When I was six, that simple sign was one of the greatest things I had ever seen. Even though I hadn't yet stepped foot in the studio, I felt like I was already on my way to being a dancer. I didn't say anything to my mother at that time because not only was I shy, but I was scared out of my mind. If my mom and Jasmine weren't there, I had no idea how things would have turned out.

Reflection, in that moment was beautiful. It gave me the chance to think about how far I had actually made it in my journey to become a professional. I left before I started crying again. I had to make sure I stayed focused on the road and keep my emotions in check. The pain that surged through my body was a reminder of what would happen if I was unable to do that.

As I drove, I got an unexpected phone call. My customized R&B ringtone let me know my friend Tracy was on the other line. It had been a little while since I talked to her and it hit me I hadn't even told her about everything I had going on in my life. I pulled over to the side of the road as I answered the phone.

"Hello."

"What's going on, Elise? Daaaanng, you can't call me anymore? I thought we were cool. What's up with that?"

I thought she was serious and that made me hesitate to respond. Then she put my mind at ease when she started to laugh.

"Girl, you had me not knowing what to expect. I thought you were upset for real!"

"Nah, I was just playing. How have you been?"

We exchanged some pleasantries and small talk before she asked me how my dancing was going.

"Everything is going pretty good. I actually have a huge opportunity coming up very soon!"

"Really? What?"

"Well, there's a dance academy in Los Angeles that's flying me out for an audition for them."

"Hold up! Are you really about to go to out to Hollywood?"

"Yeah. I'm a little scared, but I'm really going to go!"

"That is amazing! I'm happy for you, Elise. Can I go with you?" she said while laughing.

"I wish I could take everyone with me, but I can't. Anyway, what's been up with you?" I asked.

"Well, I just got some big news and that's why I called."

"Cool! What's up?"

"Well, earlier today, I found out... I found out I was pregnant!"

She was very excited about her news and I can't say that I really shared in her feelings. I had to try and hide my disappointment.

"Wow! Really?"

"Yep. It's really early in the pregnancy, so it'll be a while before I know if it's a boy or a girl."

"Which would you rather have?" I asked.

"I'll be happy with either as long as they're healthy, but I think I would rather have a boy."

"Cool! Why do you want a little boy, though?"

"I don't know really. I think part of it is that it would be cute to find his little outfits and get him a bunch of new shoes. I don't know, I just think having a boy would cool!"

"Yeah, it probably would, but can I ask you something?"

"Go for it!"

"Who's the father?"

It wasn't a smooth transition and I knew asking her about the father of her child wasn't exactly tactful, but I felt I had to do it.

"The father? You know, well, you remember TJ, right?"

"You mean your ex? You can't be talking about him because after he cheated on you, you swore you were done with him. That can't be who you're talking about."

She was silent for a little bit.

"Yeah. We hooked back up and he told me he wasn't gonna mess around on me anymore. He promised he would get it together for me and the baby."

"And you actually fell for that? How stupid can you be? You just messed your life up for that dude? I hope you realized you've messed up!"

I was sure what I said had to hurt her (at least a little), but I didn't really mean for it to come out the way it did.

"I'm sorry, Tracy," I said hoping she would actually forgive me.

"You ain't sorry! If that's what you said, that's what you meant! But it's all good. I'm grown! I don't need nobody's approval."

"You're right and for real, I apologize."

"You always thought you were better than everybody else. That's why I stopped messin' with you back in the day. I see 'Princess Ballerina' is still the same. It's cool, though. You don't have to worry about seeing me, TJ or our baby. You just do you!"

She was understandably upset. She didn't give me a chance to apologize again before she hung up the phone. I knew I was 100% wrong for passing judgement on her, who she chose to be with, or even the situation she had put herself in. I was a terrible friend to her (at that moment) and I immediately knew that would once again change the course of our friendship. I hoped, at some point, we would be able to at least be cordial to one another, but I knew that may not have been a realistic aspiration.

I took a little while to gather my thoughts and composure before I actually got back to driving. I watched all of the cars drive by. I looked inside of their cars and wondered who they were, what their story was, and what was going on in their lives. For many of them, I created stories in my head about them that explained why they were driving so fast (or so slow). I also created reasons for them having smiles or frowns on their faces. It was good to distract my mind from how I possibly ruined my friendship with Tracy permanently.

The plan to distract myself worked and I was finally able to get back on the road and head home. I took my time and drove slowly so I could enjoy all of my hometown roads. Memories were still floating around from every curve. I made sure to take them all in. When I finally pulled into the driveway at home, I felt refreshed. I got out and inhaled the crisp night air before going inside.

"Welcome home, Elise!" dad said almost as soon as I entered the house.

"Thank you. It's good to be back."

"Can I talk to you in the living room for a moment?" he asked.

"Yes, sir. What's up?"

"Nothing major. I just wanted to talk to you for a little bit. Actually did you want to get some food first. Your mother made some of her famous lasagna, while I made the best salad and homemade garlic knots you will ever eat in your life!"

He made a convincing case; I couldn't pass up the offer. My aching body allowed me to sprint to the kitchen to see exactly how much food was left. I wasn't sure when everything had been prepared, but the steam that was still rising from most of the food let me know it hadn't been out for very long.

"Did you make this for me?" I asked, yelling into the living room so my father could hear me.

"There's absolutely no way your mother and I spent so much time preparing your favorite meal just for you! That's crazy talk!" he replied as he made his way into the kitchen.

"Yeah, that wouldn't make any sense, dad."

"You know I'm just playing with you. Of course we made this for you. We tried to wait for you to get home, but I couldn't hold out. As soon as your mother took that stuff out of the oven, I started complaining about how hungry I was."

"And let me guess what happened next. Mom said 'Ian Morgan, quit complaining and eat!' Is that about right?" I asked jokingly.

"That's exactly right! Anyway I want you to enjoy your meal. Just come and talk to me once you get finished."

He left and went back into the living room. I took my time and enjoyed the meal that was prepared for me. Everything was absolutely delicious. Even though I was at home at that moment, I somehow felt as if I were already in Los Angeles and I started missing home cooked meals. It was strange, but at the same time, I understood it. My meal was good all the way to the last bite my body allowed me to take in. Once I was stuffed, I went to see what my father needed to say. As soon as I stepped in the room, my father started to smile.

"Have a seat, Elise." he said pointing to the chair closest to him.

"What's up, dad?"

"I just wanted to talk. So have you already packed?"

"Ummm... not really."

He let a hearty laugh.

"You do realize you'll be leaving soon, right?"

"Yeah. I don't know why I've been procrastinating."

"I think it's because you're a little afraid of the uncertainty that going to LA will bring. Packing just makes everything much more real. You've probably just been procrastinating to put that off a little."

I couldn't really dispute anything he was saying, so I said nothing. I just kept as quiet as I could to soak up as much knowledge as possible.

"You have to change that fear back into excitement. Those people in LA are lucky you're going out there! Trust me, you're ready."

He paused because he obviously wanted me to speak, so I did.

"Part of me agrees with you, but the other part wants me to believe I haven't worked hard enough."

"You have to be joking, right? How could you question how hard you've worked? Do you realize you've been practicing today even though you were just in an accident? While most people would have been in bed resting, you were working. Many people would have gotten down and stayed there. I know I don't always speak about God, but seeing what you've been able to do in your life shows me and everyone else that He has a purpose for us all. Some people are scared of their purpose. They run away from it because they know it comes with a lot of responsibility. You, on the other hand, have completely embraced your purpose and the responsibility that it comes with it, while asking what else you can do. Elise, you are a very special. I have no idea what I've done in life to make God bless me with my family, but it's very humbling. Even when I don't say anything, I know how blessed I am."

He stopped again, but I had nothing to say. My family always made me feel no dream was too large. That conversation was one example of that. We both sat and looked at each other for a little while. It looked as though we were both on the verge of crying, but we both tried to fight it.

"Elise, I guess the whole point I'm trying to make is that I love you and I'm very proud of you."

"Thank you, dad. That means the world to me and I love you too!" I said while moving closer to hug him.

As I let him go, he immediately left the room. He obviously felt he had to because he didn't want me to see him cry. It's a good thing he left because seeing him cry would have most certainly made me do the exact same thing.

Soon, I was sitting in that room with only my thoughts to keep me company. Everything my father said started to sink in. Internally, I was beaming with pride. I always considered myself a "Daddy's Girl", and whenever he told me something I was doing made him happy, it just made my day. So, I sat there for a little while, doing nothing more than smile and think. I would have stayed there a while longer, but in the midst of thinking, I felt it was necessary for me to at least go and clean up the kitchen.

Normally cleaning the kitchen was a chore I hated, but not that day. That day, I saw all of the work my parents did to create yet another wonderful meal. In turn, that made me think about everything they had done for me in general. Realizing how much someone has done for you can sometimes change your perspective. That's what happened then, so I just did what needed to be done.

While I was working, my mother walked into the kitchen.

"What are you doing, Elise?" my mother asked.

She looked like she had just woken up from a nap. She wiped her eyes as she awaited an answer from me.

"Nothing much, mom. I just wanted to go ahead and get the kitchen cleaned up."

She was shocked and she made that clear with the look on her face.

"Did you just say you actually wanted to clean the kitchen?"

"Yes, ma'am! I know it's unbelievable, but I didn't think it would be right for you or dad to have to clean. You've already done a lot."

She walked in and sat down at the table in the small "breakfast nook" portion of our kitchen.

"I appreciate it, but you can stop. I'll get the rest," she told me.

"Why?"

"I'm just thankful you got started, but I'm sure you haven't even packed for your trip yet."

"Dang, mom, you really do know me, don't you?"

"Yeah, I do. So, you just go ahead and get that taken care of. I don't want anything to hold you up when you have to leave."

I put everything down and went into my room. Never had I realized how many clothes I had. Every day I would say I had nothing to wear, but I'm sure if my closet were an actual person, it would have totally disagreed. I didn't know what I needed to pack. I didn't really know what the weather was going to be like in Los Angeles. Worse than that, I didn't even know how long I was going to be there. If it didn't go well, a few days worth of clothes would have been enough. On the other hand, if things did go well, I probably would be moving there.

I took my medium-sized rollaway suitcase down from the top of my closet and put it on my bed. When I opened it, I just looked at it.

"This is real," I said aloud to myself.

I put some clothes in the suitcase, then took them out. I put some more in and I quickly took them out as well. I was very indecisive, and after an hour the only thing I had packed was a pair of shoes and some socks. It was pretty terrible, but I soon found myself lying on top of a huge pile of clothes that I had rejected to bring with me on my trip. I started laughing at myself and I couldn't stop.

"Get it together, Elise!" I kept saying over and over in between the laughter.

If either of my parents could hear me, they probably thought I was going crazy. I was okay if that would have been their way of thinking because I felt like that myself. It was funny. While I was still laughing, I finally made myself get back up and get focused on what I needed to do. The suitcase was eventually filled up and I made sure to put all of my ballet gear on top. Getting that done gave me a light sense of accomplishment. Yet again, I became a bit anxious because of that, but I was also a bit refreshed.

I cleared the extra clothes off my bed, put my suitcase to the side, prepared for bed and called it a night. That night was another time I had a vivid and very memorable dream. In it, I was a dancer, but for most of the dream I wasn't dancing. Most of the time people (whom I was unfamiliar with) were speaking about me.

They were talking about how I was a positive role model, not only for their little girls, but for them also. They told me how their little girls didn't know black people could really be ballerinas. They thought only girls of other ethnicities could make it. They thought just because they looked a certain way, there were limitations attached to them from birth that they never would be able to get away from. They told me their kids may or may not pursue being ballerinas as they got older, but I helped them escape the lies of what they were told they couldn't do and embrace the truth of what they could. At the end of it all, the large crowd watched as I had a few minutes to perform and then I was given some time to speak to everyone.

I saw a future version of myself (maybe in my late 30s or 40s). I had a distinguished look. I saw some gray hairs scattered on my head and I loved them! They made me feel like the future Elise was a wise woman. I even remember some of what I said that night.

"Ladies, gentlemen, and all of the bright-eyed, ambitious kids here tonight, I truly would like to thank each and every one of you. Your words have done more for me than I have for you. I appreciate everything you have said because it lets me know my journey has not been in vain. You have inspired me to not give up on the plan and purpose God has given me. The light you said I have been able to shine into your world is now shining back on me ten times greater. Please remember to believe in God because I am just one example of how much He believes in us. Thank you and I love you all."

Light jazz music played as I walked off of the stage and the previously dimmed lights in the large auditorium slowly were brightened. I looked in the front row and saw my mother standing and clapping wildly while my father yelled loudly from his wheelchair. The dream felt so real I woke up smiling.

That day was pretty much a blur. For the most part, I just remember spending some more quality time with my family and trying to get in contact with everyone I needed to try to speak with before my trip. I spoke to Little Jazzy a few times throughout the day. She seemed excited and sad. I shared in those sentiments. I also spoke to Hamilton a few times. Whenever I spoke to him, I didn't hear sadness in his voice. He said he would miss me a lot, but he knew going to audition in Los Angeles was part of the bigger picture. He understood that trip could be a huge turning point in my life and he supported me. He was very encouraging. Things were not so good when I tried to speak to Tracy, though.

The first few calls went straight to voicemail; I knew she was ignoring my calls and it upset me. I wanted to just give up, but I didn't want to leave town with the cloud of uncertainty floating above our friendship. I either wanted to make up and get everything back on track or I wanted to know if our friendship had made it to the point of no return.

"What do you want?" she asked when she finally answered.

"I'm sorry, Tracy. I'm sorry for saying everything I did. I just thought things would be different."

"What do you mean?"

I wanted to be cautious with my words, but I also wanted to make sure I spoke honestly and said everything I needed to say.

"I don't mean any disrespect, Tracy. I just didn't think either one of us would be getting pregnant as soon as we got out of high school. I just didn't think that would be us."

"Us? Elise, everything doesn't involve you. This actually has nothing to do with you! This is about me and my child."

"You're right. It doesn't have anything to do with me, but believe it or not, I care about you. We've had our ups and downs, but we've been through a lot together. There have been many times we have almost thrown away our friendship over the years and I'm tired of that. We are officially grown now, so we both need to grow up. You've been like my sister, and if you think it's best to end our friendship, we can. Don't get me wrong, that is not what I want at all, but if you feel that would be best then..."
She exhaled.

"I don't want us to not be friends, Elise. I've dealt with that before and I don't like it at all. The truth of it all is you hurt my feelings. You told me about your great news and I was excited for you. I told you about my great news and you tell me you're disappointed in me. Don't you think I heard enough of that stuff from my family? When I told you, I just knew my friend— my sister would have my back, but you didn't! You treated me like everybody else. So yeah, me gettin' pregnant may have disappointed you, but you not being supporting of what I'm going through... that disappointed me."

Her words hit me like an unexpected punch to the back of the head. It hurt, and it was surprising, but I deserved it. I don't think I considered Tracy's feelings or tried to see things from her perspective when she initially told me.

"I truly apologize. When you told me, it was unexpected. I just blurted out what crossed my mind without thinking about it. You probably don't believe me, but I really didn't mean it to come across the way it did."

She was silent for a few seconds. At first, I thought the call had been disconnected, but every once and a while, I would just hear her breathing. I wanted to say something, but I wanted to make sure she had the time she needed without me interrupting her.

"Elise, it would be almost idiotic to think I want to be pregnant at 18. This is not what I expected, but I made a decision to do what I did and I am taking responsibility for it. I have literally beaten myself up every day since I found out. I wish I would've just waited like you, but sometimes I get so caught up in the moment, I end up making decisions that are not always good for me.

She allowed me to know how she really felt about everything without pretending she was 100% happy. When she opened up, it let me know she still valued our friendship.

"Tracy, we all do things that aren't planned. You may call it regrets, mistakes, lessons, or whatever, but it happens to all of us. So do you know what you need to stop doing?"

"What, Elise?"

"You need to stop beating yourself up and you need to stop that today! I can't have my nephew or niece's mom be upset everyday. That can't happen. So, you're going to find a way to accept the fact that you're having a baby."

"How can you say this positive stuff to me? Do you even believe what you're telling me? Will I be able to be a good mother?"

"Of course you'll be a good mother. Your child will be lucky to have you!"

By this time, there was no more anger in her words.

"Elise, how can you be nice to me right now? What is wrong with you?"

She was laughing and crying at the same time. I guess the crying was because we moved past being upset and things were back to normal. And I'm pretty sure she was laughing because she truly wanted to know what was wrong with me. And because of that, I laughed right along with her.

Our conversation went well after that. I was prepared to leave town with one fewer friend in my life, but I'm glad it didn't actually go down like that. After we finished talking, nothing memorable happened. I guess it was because the rest of the time was just checking over everything, making sure I was ready for my trip the next day. I thought my parents would be checking on me every hour, but they didn't. I'm sure they figured I had a lot on my mind and so, they just let me have the day to myself.

My body still hurt quite a bit, but it wasn't as bad as it was the previous days. Since I was feeling a little better, I wanted to see if scars were healing and would look a little better. The scrapes and bruises were never too pronounced, but every once and a while I would see the subtle reminders of the accident. When I stood in front of the mirror in my room, I saw how far I had come along in the healing process. Yes, my imperfections were still there and for a brief moment, I was discouraged, but then the reality of survival once again became dominant in my mind.

Looking at myself in the mirror made me want to practice. I smiled while going through my positions. It was crazy: I actually thought I would make it an entire day without practicing in some way even though that hadn't happened since my very first day of class.

After a while, I realized I had spent the majority of the day in (or around) my room, but I needed to step out so I could have a one-on-one conversation with my mother.

"Mom! Mom, are you busy?" I asked while searching the house.

"No, Elise, I'm not busy. I was just in the room reading this novel."

"Cool. What's the name of it? I pick up a book every once and a while, maybe I've read it."

"Well, it's a book called 'Gaby.' I'm about to put it down, though. I haven't even gotten that far in it and it's already making me cry. Anyway, what did you want to speak to me about?"

"Can we sit down?" I asked, standing in the doorway of my parents' room.

"Sure! Come on in!"

I sat on the end of the bed. It was something I hadn't done since I was a kid. Growing up, sometimes Jasmine and I would go to my parents room when we had something to talk to either of them about. I don't know why, but for some reason, we always felt comfortable there.

"Mom, I wanted to thank you for pushing me to take ballet. If you never would have done that, I don't think I would have had the courage to ever get started."

"I appreciate you saying that, Elise, but if I hadn't done it, Jasmine would have. We were not gonna let your fear stop you from pursuing your dreams. Nope! That was not an option."

"Well, I can never thank you enough. And I know I'm gonna miss everyone like crazy when I leave tomorrow, but I know it's gonna be life-changing. I feel that in my heart."

Just like when I was a kid, she playfully tackled me.

"I'm gonna miss you so much, Elise, but you're grown now. You were gonna end up leaving the house sooner or later anyway. If it weren't for ballet, it would have been for college. Either way, your father and I have been trying to emotionally prepare for the day you had to leave the nest. I can't say we're ready now, even after all of that preparation, but it's time for you to go out there and make your own way in this world."

"I promise I'm gonna try my best to make y'all proud of me, mom."

"We already are proud, Elise."

It made me feel good to hear my mom say something similar to what my father had. While my mother and I were still talking, my dad rolled past the room. Initially, he said nothing and just kept moving. Then, he couldn't resist joining in on our conversation, so he slowly rolled back to the room.

"So, y'all just want to have some happy, smile-creating conversation and not include me? That's so disrespectful!"

He could only pretend he was being serious for maybe two and a half seconds before he broke into laughter.

"Ian, get in here and talk with our little girl before she leaves tomorrow," mom said while laughing.

He moved slowly into the room.

"So, Elise, are you ready, now?" he asked.

"You know what? I think I am. I'm ready to try to go out there and start my next chapter. Like I was telling mom, I'm really going to miss everybody, but I have to do it."

"Yep, you certainly do! And we'll miss you, too, but when we see reports of all of the great things you're doing in all of the newspapers and magazines, and we start to see you on tv and we'll be able to tell everyone, "That's our daughter! That young lady who's changing the world of ballet is Elise Morgan!" We know what type of greatness is ahead. We're ready to see it all play out. Elise, we love you!"

I looked at my parents and thanked God for blessing me with the opportunity to be raised by such beautiful people. They had been through so much. Even during their lowest points, they still always tried their best to hold their heads up and keep dignity present in all of our lives.

"You two are the best parents anyone could ever have. God used you to teach me about strength, wisdom, persistence, and love. I thank you and I love you with all of my heart. There's no way I could be the woman I am, or get anywhere close to becoming the woman I want to be without you."

Saying that made us all emotional, but we all tried very hard to keep it together.

"Elise, have you called Mrs. Mears today? I'm sure you've talked to her before, but it would be good for you two to speak before you left," my mom asked.

The question was the perfect thing to keep our minds off the fact we were about to start crying like babies. I was sure she asked it to distract all of us, but I was glad she did. Even though Mrs. Mears was very important to me, somehow I had neglected to call and speak to her. I needed to change that as soon as possible.

"No, I haven't called her. I think I should go ahead and take care of that. Do you all mind?" I asked.

"Of course not. If you weren't going to call, we probably would have. That lady has been very good to us and an excellent mentor and teacher to you over the years," dad said.

"Okay, I love you. We'll talk more before we leave," I said as I exited their room and went back to my own.

As soon as I made it back to my sanctuary, I grabbed my phone and sat down in my corner. I knew she had the show to finish preparing for, so I hoped she would be at the studio. At the same time I hoped if there were any students there practicing, one of the other instructors was actually the one working with them. I dialed the direct number to her office. The phone rang about three times with no answer. I was just about to hang up and try another number when I finally got an answer.

"Mears Academy of Dance, how can I help you?"

Just by her answering like that, I knew she was either extremely focused on the show or she was stressed out. Normally when she saw my number on her caller ID, the conversation would start off in a more informal manner.

"Hello, Mrs. Mears. It's me, Elise."

"Hey, Elise. I wasn't paying attention to the phone number. What's going on?"

"Not much. I just wanted to make sure I spoke with you before I left town tomorrow."

"Wait a minute! Are you really leaving tomorrow?"

"Yes, ma'am. The time is here. I have to get up early to be there on time. Well, not really on time because you're supposed to be there like two hours before the actual flight leaves."

"Wow! That's crazy! It's been so long since I've had to take a flight anywhere, I didn't even know that. That's terrible!"

"Yeah, it's pretty bad, but they do it for security reasons. So, I guess it's better safe than sorry."

"You're right. Well, I would ask if you're ready to go, but I think you are," she said.

"Physically, even though I still have some pain left over from the accident, I've been ready. Plus, I have a routine in mind in case there's a portion of my audition that's freeform. The only problem I've been having was being mentally prepared for all of the changes that could possibly be about to happen in my life. Well, that was a problem I think that has passed," I said.

"That's good to hear, Elise. You know, I can't say I have any favorite students because I've always loved every one of you. However, over the years, I;ve been fortunate enough to teach some students whom I've known would make an impact. Some of the students weren't just learning ballet as a habit or something to pass the time because it meant more to them than that. For some people, dance is a part of who they are and I have always been able to recognize those who have that star factor. Elise, you're definitely one of those special students. Do you remember when you first started? We talked about your dreams and if you had to, you would dance professionally for free. Is that still true?

"Mrs. Mears, when I started, I just liked dance. It's different now. With each passing year, and the more work I've put into dance, the more I've learned to love it. So, just like we talked about way back then, if I had to dance for free, I still have to say I would."

"And because you would, I know you won't have to. Your skills as a dancer will impact a lot of people. When you go to LA, I know you will blow them away! You've been training for practically your entire life. Your hard work is about to pay off. Just promise to keep pushing the culture forward and every once and a while, please call and check on your students. They look up to you. Also, please keep the relationship you've built with Jasmine intact."

"I will. I promise you."

I was glad I was able to speak with her. She was actually the last person I spoke to on the phone before I left. Each of my "farewell" phone calls and in-person speeches stayed with me as I went to sleep that night. They helped me rest very easily. I woke up about thirty minutes before my alarm went off. I wanted to get all of the sleep I could, but my excitement wouldn't allow me to go back to sleep. I spent the extra time to speak with God again.

"Hello, God. Today is a big day for me. You allowed me to discover my gift early in life and I thank you. I pray I don't let the people down. I ask that you please look after everyone here and let them know I love them. Please give me grace as I go to California. I just want your will to be done. In the name of Jesus I pray, amen!"

The prayer filled me with calmness as I stood up, got dressed, and checked my bags to make sure I had everything I needed. I grabbed the red backpack that would serve as my carry-on and put it by the door. On my dresser was my cell phone which was immediately used to text Hamilton to make sure he'd be ready to pick me up. I was surprised at how quickly he responded and told me he'd be on the way.

As he traveled toward me, my mom knocked on my door to have a last-minute conversation with me. I was sure all of my moving around woke her up, so I apologized for waking her up. She told me she actually hadn't gone to sleep because of how excited she was. As she stood in my doorway wearing an oversized t-shirt with our favorite football team on it and some pajama pants that had bunnies all over them, she explained how happy she was for the opportunity and that she hoped I took full advantage of it.

She also opened up and told me that some of her friends didn't have the best of reactions to me leaving.

She went into details and said they asked her if she was upset that I was continuing with the "dance thing" instead of going to school. It was funny because she told me she responded to their questions by asking what their kids were doing in life. She said when she did that, they suddenly didn't have anything else to say.

We laughed, but our talk let me know how much she had my back. She then asked if I was sure I didn't need them to take me to the airport. I assured her Hamilton was on his way. I also told her part of the reason I didn't want them to take me because seeing them as I was about to go into the airport would make me have one of those sessions of the dreaded "ugly cry." She smiled and told me she understood. She turned around and went back to her room.

Since I had sent a text to Hamilton, I knew I only had about forty minutes before he'd be at the door. I used that time to double- and triple-check everything I was taking with me. I put a few books in my backpack and went through all of my clothes. When I felt I was good to go, I grabbed a snack and sat down in the living room. Almost as soon as I did that, the doorbell was ringing. My heart was pounding as I answered the door.

My mom stepped into the living room with a wallet in her hand as I let Hamilton in. She spoke to him as she politely pulled me over to the side. She pulled a few hundred dollars out of her wallet and gave it to me. I hadn't asked for anything, but she insisted I have it. As if that weren't enough, she reached back in the wallet and pulled out a picture. She didn't say what it was as she handed it to me with a smile on her face.

I started jumping up as soon as I saw it. Of course, Hamilton wanted to know what it was. I was going to keep him in suspense, but I decided we didn't really have time for that so I showed it to him. When he looked, it was easy for him to see why I got so excited about the picture. It was my sister and I after what seemed to be my first day of class. He commented on how beautiful she was and I agreed. My mother (and my dad who had just come into the room) talked about how my sister looked up to me and how much she knew I was going to be a ballerina. It was a beautiful moment that I was glad we all got to share. I told them I loved them, and then Hamilton and I were on our way.

    During the ride, we talked about what was going to happen with our relationship. He said he thought it would be difficult, but he didn't seem to have any questions about us being able to make it. He said, in his mind, he knew how well my audition was going to go. He said he had been mentally preparing for everything since he first learned about the trip. I was happy we started to talk more about how we were feeling, but I didn't think we made it to the best stopping point before we made it to my gate. He helped me get my bags before we said our goodbyes.

    We were both sad and tried to hold onto each other as long as possible, but eventually we knew it was necessary for me to leave so I wouldn't miss my flight. I went inside and the people and bright lights made me nervous, but I pretended it didn't. I went through security, and every once a while, I would look back to see Hamilton still standing there. When I got to the end, I looked back and he was still there. I started waving, but he didn't see me. So, I started jumping up and down as I waved. A bit of pain from the accident was still there every time I jumped, but it didn't matter. I continued doing it until I saw him wave back. That was when I knew it was really time for me to get moving.

    I quickly moved towards where I was supposed to be. I only had about thirty-five minutes and the more I moved, the more my stomach reminded me I needed to eat. Eventually, I was able to get an egg-white sandwich and an orange juice. It would have been nice to be able to sit down and enjoy my meal, but it didn't happen that way. I had to eat and drink while I walked. I reached my destination and I sat down to try and relax a little. I used my backpack as a pillow and I rested until I heard them call for us to start boarding.

    I just tried to keep to myself while we waited in the hall to get onto the plane, but this one lady would not allow that. She introduced herself to me and told me her name was Val. She asked me if I had been on a plane before and if I was going to Cali to visit or if I lived there. When I told her I was going to LA for an audition, she almost seemed upset, but she continued to talk until we reached her seat. When I found my own row, I kept looking at my ticket hoping I was in the wrong spot; sadly I wasn't. There was already someone sitting in the aisle seat and a rather large person sitting in the middle. I knew it was going to be an uncomfortable ride.

    I pointed to the window seat to let them know where I needed to go. They sighed heavily, as if they didn't want to allow me to sit down. I excused myself as I contorted my body to try and squeeze past them. Eventually, I made it. Once I sat down, I looked out of the window. The sun was finally starting to rise. The light that was coming from it turned the sky various hues of blue and yellow. It was a beautiful sight to see.

    I closed my eyes shortly after that. It seemed like I was going to be able to get some rest, then the guy next to me started moving around so much I had to see what was going on. When I opened my eyes, I saw Val standing near us. I wondered what she was doing there, but I soon found out she was talking to my "row mate" trying to get him to switch seats so she could sit next to me. He was not having it at first, but like a salesperson, she told him why he actually needed to switch spots. After a few minutes, he was moving to her seat in the aisle a few rows ahead.

    As Val was getting comfortable in her new seat, the pilot started speak. The "fasten your seat belts" icon was lit up as the flight attendants started to do their safety demonstration. A few minutes later, we were up in the air, ascending towards our "cruising altitude" of about 37,000 feet.

    "I'm not auditioning for a movie or anything," I said to Val, seemingly out of nowhere.

She had no idea what I was talking about. While we were waiting to board the plane, I mentioned I was going to LA to audition. She had a not so favorable reaction, so I explained I was a ballerina and I was going to audition for one of the most well-known schools in the country.

    She asked questions about dancing and if I ever wanted to quit. I explained the thought had crossed my mind when times got difficult, but I didn't think my love for dance would actually allow me to actually quit. She then told me whenever she saw ballerinas on TV or in the movies, it made her not like any of us. She said it always seemed like the dancers carried themselves in a way that made them seem like they thought they were better than everyone. I agreed and told her that we sometimes felt that way about each other, but it was all because we were taught we were supposed to carry ourselves in a certain manner.

"Ballet is an old form of expression and we're supposed to respect it and make sure all of our action showcases its beauty," I explained.

I started to feel selfish after a while. As much as I enjoyed talking about ballet, it was rude to just speak about what I did. I asked Val about her. Casually, she told me surfed for a living. I was amazed! She talked about her profession with as much passion as I talked about mine. She told me she had to travel a lot to to compete. It all seemed very exciting. She even offered to take me to the beach.

The more we laughed and talked, the more our neighbor seemed like she wanted to join in, but she seemed like she was scared. Val wouldn't allow anyone to be shy around her, though. She brought her into the conversation.

"Now, who are you and what do you do?" Val asked

"My name is Riley. I'm a game designer," she said humbly.

I "nerded out" when I heard that. While it was true I rarely had time to play video games, they were always something I was fascinated in. If nothing else, I respected the time and effort needed to actually bring them to life.

We had such a good time talking, it seemed like only a few minutes had passed before the pilot was telling us we were getting ready to land. Val thought it would be a good idea to exchange numbers in case we ever wanted to hang out. We agreed and we gave our numbers to each other. Although I thought it would be really cool, I didn't really think much would come out of it. I figured our conversation was just something to kill the time and we were simply crossing each other's path. If such was the case, it would have been okay.

When we got our bags from baggage claim, they both seemed concerned about me. They asked if had a ride to where I was going. I told them someone was supposed to be picking me up. They didn't want me to wait in the new city alone, so they both offered to stick around for a little bit to make sure I was able to leave. They didn't have to wait long, though. Soon, we all saw a girl who appeared to be a few years older than me. She had her hair in a bun. It was a little fizzy and it appeared it had been that way for a few days. She was wearing sweats, a plain shirt and some dreary-looking flats. The frown on her face looked like it was accustomed to being there. She didn't have a friendly demeanor, but I noticed she was holding a piece of cardboard that had my name on it.

I walked toward her first. Riley and Val walked behind me. I introduced myself and I attempted to shake her hand, but she left me hanging. I expected a smile to appear to let me know she was joking, but it didn't happen. Riley, Val, and I all looked at each other in amazement. She obviously didn't care about making a good first impression with me at all.

"Hello, Elise. I am Daria," she said with a very heavy accent as she threw away the cardboard with my name on it.
The girls saw I was with who was supposed to be taking me to my next stop, so they gave me a hug and said they'd see me later.

Once they were gone, things started to feel different. Daria hardly said anything to me until we got in her car and left the airport. Then, when she decided to talk again, I immediately wished she had remained silent.

"So, you are black," she said

For a moment, I thought maybe the combination of me still being in shock about the new city and her accent made me hear something she didn't really say.

"What did you say?"

"You, are black, yes?" she asked.

"Yes, obviously I am. Are we going to have problems because of that?" I asked angrily.
I knew my tone was bad and I didn't want it to be that way, but I didn't like how things started off with her.

"To be a famous ballerina, you must look like me. You cannot be famous looking like that!"

She was being judgmental, dismissive, arrogant, racist, and incredibly ignorant. I hadn't had such a strong desire to express myself by letting my fists meet with someone's face since I fought Tracy. I was a child back then, so I couldn't continue with childish actions as an adult. That wouldn't have made any sense. So, I just got on my phone to let my parents, Hamilton and Mrs. Mears know I had made it safely.

My conversations with everyone were pretty short. It seemed everyone was happy to hear I made it, but they all wanted me to enjoy Los Angeles and get settled in. Once I got done with my calls, I was less upset than I was before I made them. I didn't want to speak to Daria because I still had fear I would say or do something I shouldn't. So I just looked out at the unfamiliar city.

Los Angeles was very different than what I was accustomed to. Whether in cars or walking, people all seemed like they were in a hurry. It was very strange to me. The people who were walking ended up having their progress stopped by all the people on bikes and skateboards. People in cars had it much worse. There was so much traffic, everyone was basically in a hurry to stay in traffic and wait. Inside, I was questioning the intelligence of some of the people I was seeing just because they were all rushing. I didn't know any of the people I was judging and I didn't know their situations. I was wrong, and in that moment my way of thinking actually made me the dumb one.

It was so crazy how quickly the negativity of my new city was creeping into me even though I hadn't really been in the city yet. It was a little scary, so without thinking, I closed my eyes and prayed silently. I asked God to forgive me for the way I was feeling about others and for my thoughts of violence against Daria because of what she said. I asked that the negativity I was feeling be removed so my spirit would be renewed and I could have the righteous energy needed to do His will.

When I opened my eyes, the weight had once again been lifted. I felt as though I could try to speak to Daria without continuing to be upset with the comments she was making. I needed clarity.

"Let's get right to it, Daria. Why don't you like black people?"

"No, you have it wrong. I don't have problems with black people."

"If that's true, why you have been saying the things you have?"

"I don't have problems your people until you try to be dancers. I mean when you try to be a real dancer like with ballet. I think you should stay with your hip-hop and rap music. It is better for people like you."

"Look, if your objective is to get me to verbally or physically attack you, I'm sorry, but you won't succeed. See, I came out here to advance my career as a ballerina and that's what I'm going to do! I don't know why you are spewing such hateful words, but you're not going to get the results you want. What you have done during this car ride is made me fully aware of the type of people I may be dealing with while I'm here, but you've also done something that can impact you."

"What?"

"You have just let me know I need to focus more of my energy on my purpose and less on people. Daria, you better pray we are never compete directly for the same job because you will never defeat me. This is not arrogance, but a level of confidence that can only be given to me from the Lord. When you dance, yours may just come from you and the work that you've done. Not only do I have that, I also have God's favor!"

"What you say is cute, but it does not scare me."

"That's good! I don't want to scare you. I just need for you to be informed so after this day, you will never be able to claim ignorance and try to throw out limitations on what black women can do. If you haven't learned by what I've said, you will learn by my actions."

She didn't have any more snappy comebacks. In fact, she didn't have much to say at all. She was quiet the rest of the drive. When we finally made it to where we were going, she only opened her mouth to say we had made it. She didn't say anything else after that. She didn't offer to help me with my bags or anything. She taught me about racism that day. She taught me firsthand that a person can claim to not have a problem with you, but tell you what you can't accomplish because of your skin. I tried to dismiss everything she said as I entered into the house. I didn't want to carry that negative energy with me in case I had more roommates I had to speak with.

When I entered into the apartment, I was greeted by a preppy woman who appeared to be somewhere between 22 and 26 years old. She had fiery red hair and a shirt with a sparkly little animal on it. Her jeans were ripped and rolled up at the bottom. She asked me if I needed any help as she reached out for my bag.

She told me her name was Rachel and she heard a lot about me and she was happy I would be staying there during my time in LA. She also said she was grateful to have the opportunity to learn from me and that I shouldn't worry about anything Daria said because she was mean to everyone. We both shared a laugh and I felt a lot better.

She had me follow her as she guided me through the apartment. When she took me to one of the rooms, I stood in the doorway and just looked for a little while. It had a simple setup, but that made it beautiful. It had very nice hardwood floors and small- but very comfortable-looking sized beds. It also had two small desks in it. Of course, the desk I would be using was nearly empty, but Rachel's was not. Hers had a late model computer, some pencils, and what appeared to be a sketch pad. It had some headphones on it as well. She appeared to be ready for any situation. Her bed was neatly made and she had it decorated with very colorful pillows.

She graciously thanked me when I told her how nice her side was. Shortly after, she pointed out an envelope that was on my desk. I opened it and saw that it had the address and directions to the studio as well as the time and date of my audition. I got excited and was ready to do my audition right then. Rachel found it necessary to speak on how excited I obviously was.

"Elise, if that's your attempt at trying to hide your emotions, I would suggest you never play poker…like ever!"

I agreed and moments later we were talking about the plans I had for the day. Since I knew nothing about the city, I had no plans at all. She said she had some errands to run and she was going to rehearsal later. She asked me if I wanted to go with her. Of course I told her I did. She freshened up a little and we were just about to when I asked her if she knew why Daria treated me the way I did.

"I don't know, but I think she's very insecure. She's actually a great dancer, but I think she fears everyone new will take her place."

"Why is he like that?" I asked.

"I'm not sure, but ballet can have that sort of impact on people. It's a cutthroat world and people are always trying to take someone else's spot, but you can't control everything. As dancers, the main thing we can control is how we dance. If we practice and put in the work we're supposed to, then we've done our job"

I then said she probably never had to worry about losing her spot. She laughed at me as if I had just finished performing the greatest stand-up comedy routine she had ever heard. She proceeded to tell me how she had just lost her spot in something that she had been all but promised she had.

"When they told me, they didn't care what they had told me before or how hurt I was, especially since they decided to tell me in front of everyone, but I didn't let that stop me. I used that pain to make me work harder. So even though that one event didn't work out for me, I know my time will come."

The things she said not only gave me a better understanding of who she was, but a little more insight into Daria's behavior. We bonded a little right then. We talked some about our lives and what made us who were. When I first saw Rachel, I had pre-conceived notions about who I thought she was. Her red hair and perky personality made me think she grew up with a "perfect" family who had never dealt with any major issues. I was very wrong.

Throughout the day, I learned Rachel's upbringing was actually pretty rough. I found out her father left their family when she was three without any warning and he never had contact with them again. That would have been devastating to most people, so I asked her why she turned out the way she did. She told me her father caused her a lot of pain to her family for a long time, and when she turned eleven, she made a promise to herself and everyone around her that she was just going to try her best to be happy, no matter what.

Her story was sad but inspiring. It almost made me want to tell her more about what I had gone through, but I didn't. I felt if I had, it would have seemed like I was trying to compete over who grew up with the most difficult life. I didn't want that to happen. We had both been through a lot, yet dance remained a major component in both of our lives. It just so happened that as I made that decision, we had reached the dance studio.

I was nervous, not because we finally made it to the studio, but more because it wasn't "my" studio. It wasn't the place I had been going to exclusively since I was a little girl. It wasn't the place that helped me grow into a confident woman. It wasn't the place that Mrs. Mears taught me everything I knew. Instead, this was the place that would give some indication of if what I had learned would be enough to move forward in my profession.

    I told Rachel the studio looked different. She was confused and asked me if I had been there before.

    "Not in real life, but in my imagination, I've been here quite a few times."

She smiled without saying another word. We then moved towards the entrance.

    I asked if it would be okay for me to just observe once we went inside. She responded as if I had called her out of her name. She quickly informed me that the people there did a lot of research on everyone, and from what they knew about me, I was a bit of a workaholic. I agreed, but let her know I didn't have a change of clothes. She didn't believe I just wanted to watch and see how things worked in the studio. She also didn't believe I didn't have a change of clothes. She said I was just saying things to cover up my nervousness. I didn't want to admit it, but she was right. She wouldn't accept any of my excuses.

    "I know you're not tired because you wouldn't have agreed to come with me and as far as clothing, I always keep some extra clothes in my locker. Don't worry, they're clean and we look like we're about the same size, so you shouldn't have any problem fitting into them."

    Rachel had everything covered and I quickly realized, no matter what I would try to throw out, she would be able to dismiss it. So, I quit trying to make excuses and finally just agreed. We went inside and I was immediately impressed by what I saw. There was a long hallway that led to the receptionist's desk. The walls were filled with pictures of ballerinas I assumed had danced there at some point. Some photos were grainy and in black-and-white, while others appeared to be much more recent. All of the dancers were captured in very graceful poses. I loved looking at history, but I didn't like not seeing anyone who looked like me. Not only were there no African-American women, there didn't even appear to be any minorities represented at all. It was sad, but I kept my thoughts to myself. I didn't want to say anything that could have been mistaken for another excuse.

When we finally stepped foot into one of the rehearsal spaces, I was in awe. It was like I was in a different world. There were so many dancers in the room, it was almost intimidating. Rachel pointed to the locker room and asked me if I was going to change. My confidence suddenly re-emerged out of nowhere as I told her I was ready to change and get started. She lit up.

"That's the Elise I've been looking for! That's the one we've heard so much about!"

She yelled so loudly, everyone in the room turned around and gave us glaring looks that almost cut right through me. They stopped what they were doing and their eyes followed our every movement until we made it to the locker room. It was very intense, but Rachel explained that most of them were very strict with their routines, and if anyone disturbed them, they freaked out. She felt their inability to adjust to change may end up being their downfall.

"I hope they'll be able to work on that part of their personalities because I want everyone to be successful."

It was good to hear Rachel's positivity. As I got changed, hearing what she was saying almost made me forget I was in a new location. They key word was almost. Once I was finally in the borrowed clothing, the thought of going back in the room we briefly passed through crossed my mind. Again, I couldn't hide how I felt. Rachel could see I was no longer feeling comfortable. She quickly explained that room was for dancers who had an upcoming show; since that was neither one of us, we were able to go into one of the other rooms.

I was relieved. Walking into one of the smaller rehearsal halls set my mind at ease. Since neither of us had plans of what we were going to do, we improvised sort of a call and response. She would do a move, then I would respond. What made it more exciting was that we each had to remember the previous move and do that before we were able to do our next move. In essence, we were creating our own choreography on the spot. By the time it was all said and done, we had put together a twenty-five minute routine, and if I do say myself, it was a pretty awesome!

We decided to go over it again and we both had ideas on how it could improve. So, we worked on it until we felt it got better. Then Rachel had a brilliant idea of using our routine for the audition. She agreed to critique me as we tried to make sure I was doing everything perfectly while we continued to go over everything for about an hour. She told me she had a difficult time critiquing me because I was doing such a great job. That gave me a wonderful feeling.

Rachel had been nice to me since I stepped foot into the apartment, but at the studio is when I felt like we could actually become very good friends. She just seemed so genuine and we ended up staying in the studio a little while longer before we left to go see more of the city. With traffic being the way it was, we were only able to get some food and see only a few more locations, but it was still very enjoyable. Plus, I was very optimistic I was going to be in Los Angeles for a long time, so I wasn't in a hurry to see everything at one time.

When we headed home, we talked more about my audition. She recommended that I get as much sleep as possible so I could be fully prepared for my audition. I found out the auditions were normally held in two parts. One in the rehearsal hall and the other was normally in the auditorium. I found it very interesting that Rachel told me the "newbie" was normally taken to both parts of the audition by the same person who picked them up from the airport. That meant I would have to deal with Daria again. Rachel didn't feel that was a good idea, so she volunteered to take me to the first part of the audition, but she informed me she wouldn't be able to take me to the second because she had to work. She had mentioned the auditorium was in walking distance of the rehearsal halls, so I had no problem preparing myself for a walk the next day.

I went to sleep and it was very peaceful. I woke up before my alarm went off and I looked at the clock. As I stared, I once again felt the need to pray, so that's what I did. I thanked God for the day and the vision I had of being a ballerina. I thanked Him for the discipline to work towards what He showed me. I asked that I be given a chance to honor my family and His word with everything that I did. I asked for the strength needed to overcome any remaining nervousness or self-doubt I had trying to creep into my spirit. I ended the prayer by thanking Him for everything that was designed for me, good and bad.

I kept my eyes closed for a few seconds to make sure my prayer made its way to God's ears. I heard Rachel moving around in the room, but she didn't say anything until I finally opened my eyes and stood up. We talked for a little while before we left. Actually, Rachel did most of the talking. She wanted to make sure she provided all of the helpful hints she possibly could. I was happy to be quiet and listen to everything she said. She was still giving me information while I was getting out of the car. It was almost like she was trying to become the big sister I never had. It was pretty cool!

"I would say good luck to you, but I know you're prepared, so luck isn't something you need. Focus on what they say to you, not what you think they're trying to say."

I grabbed my bag and placed it on my shoulder before I made sure to get her phone number. Then, I walked through the front door.

I stopped at the front desk and gave the receptionist my name and waited for her to tell me where to go. She looked me up and down a few times before she gave me the information I was looking for. She told me I would be going to Room 104. After she finally gave me the directions, she said, "Good luck and don't worry about anything other than the dance."

She said some positive words, but it didn't seem like she meant them. It felt like it was more of an obligation than something she actually wanted to do, but I thanked her anyway. I made my way to Room 104. I sat down and waited patiently until someone came out to get me, just like I was instructed to do. I was soon told it was time for me to enter.

Once I walked inside, I saw three other people. The room seemed to be an area people held meetings in. It had a long oval-shaped table that was surrounded by very comfortable-looking leather chairs. I wanted to sit down but nobody offered me a seat, so sitting didn't seem to be an option for me. I told them the room wasn't large enough for me to dance in and they just laughed at me. It was the type of laughter that was intended to harm. It was the type of laughter that carried the "tone" to let me know they were laughing at me.

I put a huge smile on my face as if nothing was bothering me. Since I felt they were trying to take my confidence away, I decided to try and give them more confidence than I thought they would be able to handle. They proceeded to ask me question after question about who I was. They asked me when I started dancing, what I wanted to accomplish, and what made me unique. They even asked me about my family. I thought that was going to make me start crying, but thankfully I held it together. Then, they asked me something that caught me off guard, something I didn't have time to think about before I responded:

"Elise, what is your purpose?"

"My purpose is to obey and serve God."

It was amazing to see how their expressions changed from smug to confused.

They had a very difficult time getting the words together to ask me what I meant. I would have waited forever for them to be able to release a complete thought, but I wanted to make sure I would have a chance to perform the newly formed routine Rachel and I created.

"Let me clear up what I'm saying: Before we're born, we're given an assignment. Part of the assignment is to follow what you feel passionate about in your heart. You have to use the gifts you're given to bring people to God. And as you travel through life following your passion, you'll come across distractions. People will say and do things to try to halt your journey. Life will make you want to give up, but God has made promises to us all. We just have to obey what He has said and serve Him."

I stopped speaking. I learned if you come across as too "preachy", it can sometimes do more harm than good. Sometimes, just making your point will cause the people to yearn for more information. The Bible is clear about the importance of seeking out wisdom. So, I stood there for a moment awaiting a reply or any follow-up questions. They didn't say anything for a little while, either. Out of the people there, one seemed genuinely happy I said what I did. The others seemed to be a bit perturbed.

My statement caused them to immediately end the question and answer portion of my audition. They gave me the directions to where I needed to go next and they let me know I would have about twenty-five minutes to warm up. I took advantage of every minute I had. After changing, I ran to the next location which happened to be a large auditorium. It seated at least a few hundred people and there was nobody in there but me. I smiled as I faced all of the empty seats. I imagined how it would sound and feel during a sold-out performance. I wanted to experience that for real, so once again, I convinced myself the audition was going to go exceptionally well and the spot with the academy was mine for the taking.

A little more than twenty minutes had passed when I heard the doors open. I finished my movements as the people from the room, all armed with clipboards, sat in the center of the front row. As they sat, a few other people entered the room. A portly man who appeared to be in his forties headed to the back of the room. Two older women sat in the second row directly behind the people whom I had spoken with before. The male in the front stood and gave the "thumbs up" to the portly man, who seemed to be in some sort of tech room. When he did, the lights above the crowd became a lot dimmer and a spotlight, focused on me, appeared very suddenly.

I could no longer see anyone I was auditioning for.

"Are you ready, Miss Morgan?" someone asked.
I nodded my head.

"Before you get started, I'd like you to know this is when people give us their uninspired rendition of some scene from The Nutcracker. They think performing something we're familiar with will give them a better chance, but it's quite the opposite. Seeing something we've already seen countless times has made us almost jaded, so it takes a lot more to impress us with them. I wouldn't recommend dancing something well known, but that is up to you. Now do you have any questions or do you need any music?"

"No. I'm ready."

"Great! Let's get started then."

I moved to the center of the stage. I stretched my arms towards the heavens, silently thanked God once again, and closed my eyes. I wanted to play music that only I could hear, so in my mind, I started playing my favorite jazz song. I danced the routine Rachel and I created with energy and dramatic movements. The music of my mind had trumpet solos taking turns with saxophone harmonies. All the while, smooth rhythms of the percussion carried the overall feeling I wanted my dance to get across. I kept dancing, all the while I was expecting someone to tell me to stop. Even after I completed my routine and started to improvise additional moves, it still hadn't happened.

    I got to a point where I questioned if continuing to dance would be more detrimental than beneficial. I decided to keep going and give it my all until they stopped me, or until my body gave out from exhaustion. I danced my way all over the stage from the center, to all four corners and back again. My heart was pounding with excitement and while I danced, no pain from the accident appeared at all.

    "That's enough! Stop!" a lady yelled out.
I stopped in mid-movement. My heart was still moving rapidly as I stood still, waiting to see what was going on.

    The longer I had to wait, the more I started to question my movements. How did they view my brisés, my demi-ronds? How did they feel about the fluidity of the routine? What could I have done better? As I questioned myself internally, someone demanded that the lights be turned back on. They did and I saw non-expressive looks on everyone's faces. I wanted to ask some questions, but I impatiently waited on someone else to say something. Then, they started talking.

    Everything I did seemed to be getting ripped apart. When I told them I thought I did well, they replied by telling me nobody who did what I did actually did well. They told me it was dumb to dance across the entire stage because it made it difficult to focus on me. What they said hurt, but I took it. Then, they said something that wouldn't allow me to be quiet.

    "None of that was traditional. That was not what we are used to. That sort of thing is not what you think of when you hear the word ballet. You are not what people think of when they picture a ballerina."

    I was offended and needed things to be cleared up immediately.
"Do you plan on explaining what you meant by those last statements?" I asked angrily.

They looked at each other and they all tried to decide who was going to explain what had been said. Finally, someone became brave enough to speak.

"There's obviously an elephant in the room, so we need to go ahead and take care of that."

I moved towards the end of the stage and sat down. I wanted to be close enough to make sure I didn't miss anything that was being said.

"Ballet is about tradition. With that tradition comes certain things. People picture certain things when they think of ballet. It doesn't matter if you're watching a performance in person or if it's recorded, what you see is normally the same."

I didn't want to get more upset, but I did. I didn't want to be the first one to bring up race, but I was.

"Let's stop beating around the bush. I don't fit your picture of a ballerina because I'm black!"

Everyone acted like they were shocked that I actually had the guts to say what others had to be thinking.

"You're right. We need to quit wasting time and get to the point. Black ballerinas are not what you see all of the time. Most people say black people don't have the discipline or even the look it takes to be a ballerina."

The more they said, the more upset I got, but I listened because I was the one who asked for the conversation. So, even though I frowned, I sat quietly at the end of that stage until I felt it was necessary for me to say something again. The guy who was speaking continued.

"Honestly, at times I have agreed with that sort of thinking. Was my thinking caused by what I've seen or ignorance? Perhaps it was a little of both, but that has never stopped us from seeking out dancers of all colors. We just want the best of the best. Up until now, there just haven't been any black dancers who have met the requirements of what we're looking for. To be fair, there aren't a lot of white dancers who meet our requirements, either."

This was when one of the older ladies decided she needed to chime in.

"You are different. Your dancing literally moved me to tears and that hasn't happened in a long time. And I'm not just talking about individual dancers, either. No group from here or anywhere else I've seen has made me feel like they were truly conveying genuine emotions in their movements. Miss Morgan, you were able to tell a story while dancing without saying a single word. That was great!"

As soon as she expressed how she felt, she walked out. It made me feel great to hear she enjoyed what I did, but I wanted to know if the others shared her opinion. I couldn't thank her for her words because she was gone. So, I looked into the crowd so the others could finish their thoughts.

"Your routine was pretty good. There were moments that could have been improved, though. For example, your échappé left something to be desired. Also, near the end, your balance was a little off during the landing of your sissonne," one of the ladies said.

It was funny how the older lady had such positive words for me and the next person seemed like she said something just to humble me. She didn't say anything bad, but I could tell she didn't want me to have a problem with my ego, which I didn't. I also didn't have any issues with any other person who disliked what I did. I understood not everyone would feel the same.

I decided to keep all of the negative opinions in the forefront of my mind. If I ever developed an overly high opinion of myself, they would bring me back down. Also, if I ever needed something to help fuel my fire and make me dance with a bit of a chip on my shoulder, that would help with that, too.

I thought the judges would let me know my chances of actually becoming a member of the troupe, but they didn't. They told me they had other auditions and they would let me know later who would be able to stay. They didn't tell me when to expect a call. They didn't even give me any ideas of what to do with the rest of my day. Instead, they all just stared at me until I got the hint that I needed to leave. It was rude and unnecessarily mean, but it could have been worse.

When I left the performance hall, I quickly realized I needed to find something to do with the rest of my day. I couldn't go too far because I didn't have a car. Even if I did, I still probably would have wanted to stay close, just in case I had to go back for some reason. When I went outside, I looked around to see what was near me. I saw some food places near some shops that seemed interesting. So, I went back inside, got freshened up, changed clothes, and took my bag back outside with me as I started walking towards the shops. During my walk, it didn't take long to see how different the people were in LA than they were back home in Austin. Nobody said hello. Nobody even really looked in my direction as I walked past them. It was strange, but I tried not to let it even bother me.

    I stopped at a nearby Mexican restaurant and ordered some food. It was still early and I wasn't really hungry. More than anything, I think I ordered something to calm down the bit of nervousness that had stuck with me. About 5 minutes after ordering, I was eating the most delicious taco I had ever eaten and some nice vanilla-flavored rice drink to wash it down. I looked out of the window and reflected on the activities of the morning. I thought about my family and friends back home. I was going to call my parents, but I didn't want to do that until I actually knew if I would be staying or not.

    I went back to looking out of the window. The nearby palm trees were beautiful. They swayed lightly as the wind blew. The sun rested comfortably in the sky and there wasn't a single cloud in the sky. Although I was inside, I looked up.

    "Look at where we are, sister," I whispered to Jasmine.

    I smiled and went back to my food. As my plate became empty, my phone rang. It was from a number I didn't recognize. Normally, when that happened, I wouldn't have answered, but something told me I needed to pick up.

    "This is Anne Goldman from the Alkaev Academy of Classic Dance. How are you?"

    "I'm doing well."

    "That's good to hear. Hopefully you'll be feeling even better after this call. I'm not going to take up too much of your time, but you just finished your audition not too long ago, right?"

    "Yes, ma'am."

    "You'll be happy to know your skills were well received. Things went so well, we have decided to officially welcome you to the academy."

    I heard what she said, but I didn't believe it at first.

"But they said they were only selecting one person... and they still had more auditions to do... and they..."

I was rambling, throwing words together and not completing sentences, just like my sister did when she used to get excited about things when she was a little kid.

"Yes, they have additional auditions and they said only one of you would be selected, but the overall consensus was that you inspired them. They also felt it would be foolish not to welcome you with open arms. I don't know if they're still only selecting one person, but that isn't something you have to worry about. Congratulations, Elise. Save this number because you'll be hearing from us again later on."

The phone call ended there; for a little while, I barely moved. It was as though my mind had to process the conversation over and over again before I could fully process it. Then it finally hit me. I had been accepted into the Alkaev Academy of Classic Dance! Ballet had just officially moved me from Austin, TX to Los Angeles, CA. Suddenly, my excitement became public knowledge. I got up from the table and yelled!

"I can't believe it! Thank you, God! Thank you, mom and dad! Thank you, Jasmine! Thank you, Mrs. Mears! Thank you! We made it!"

I jumped up around my table in the small restaurant. The people in the restaurant at the time, including the people who worked there, looked at me like I was crazy and I completely understood that.

One of the waitresses came over and asked me if I was okay. I told her I just got some great news and I had just been accepted into the ballet school that was across the street from them.

"Oh! You're a ballet dancer?"

I laughed as she tried to do her best version of a simple tendue. She congratulated me and smiled as she walked away.

With my heart still pounding very heavily, I sat back down and pulled out my phone to make a few calls. Of course, I spoke to my parents first. When my mother answered the phone, I decided to speak in a tone that made her feel like things hadn't gone well. She started telling me that she could tell by how I was speaking that my audition hadn't gone as planned.

"Yeah, it's just that I worked so hard at this and to fly all the way out here just to audition and get accepted into the school of my dreams just makes me feel some kind of way."
I said everything very calmly and waited for what I said to hit her.

"Girl, did you just say you got in?"
Even though she couldn't see me, I stayed in acting mode by putting my head down as I told her in almost a whisper that I had gotten in.

She yelled so loudly I thought she was going to break the speakers on my phone. I smiled from ear to ear as I spoke to her and my father and gave them the full details about how my audition experience was. They expressed a high level of pride in what I was able to accomplish. I gave all glory to God and then told them it wouldn't have been possible without them. We all cried tears of joy together as we ended the call.

After my parents, there were a few more calls I had to make. I felt it was only right for Mrs. Mears to be the next person I tried to contact. Unfortunately, she was unavailable. I think that may have been better for me because I was able to leave a message that allowed me to express exactly what she meant to me over the years. I doubt I could have made it through everything I needed to say if I were actually speaking to her.

Once I left the voicemail, I reached out to Little Jazzy. Like Mrs. Mears, she was also unavailable. I knew she was at practice because I was able to have a long conversation with her mother. I asked her to tell Jazzy I had been accepted into the school and I wanted her to know how proud of her I was. I wanted her to know I thought she had the ability to go as far as she wanted to in ballet and I would do whatever I could to help her during her journey. I also felt it was necessary to let Laila, her mother, know how happy I was that she was doing more to show an interest in what Jasmine did. She asked me if I really thought I would be able to continue to help Jazzy out, even though I would be living in a different city. My confirmation of the dedication I had to help with her daughter was the main thing she needed from me. Once she had that, she congratulated me and ended the call.

With those calls out of the way, there was only one other call I needed to make: I had to call Hamilton. I was a little nervous about hearing how he would react. I knew he would be happy for me because he always supported my dreams, but I was more concerned with his honest reactions of how our relationship would be impacted. I dialed the number, but then I disconnected before the call actually went through. I started dialing the number again and just ended it before I even dialed all of the numbers.I put my phone on the table for a little while and just let it sit there.

"What are you doing, Elise?" I asked myself.

I let the phone sit a little while longer before I told myself to quit procrastinating and just make the call. Once I finally made the call, Hamilton answered very quickly. It had me off-guard for a moment, but I quickly got myself together. I was going to pretend things didn't go well again, but I decided not to. I started off by telling him about my experiences were with Daria and how Rachel made me feel much better about being out there. Then, he asked me when was the audition.

"It actually happened not too long ago," I said.

"Well, how'd it go?"

I told him things had gone much better than I could even hope they would.

"So when will they tell you their final decision? When will they tell you who got in?"

"Well, they liked what I did so much, they have already told me I'm in!"

He told me how amazing it was. Then it hit him that I was actually going to be moving to Los Angeles. That's when he realized we were officially in a long-distance relationship.

His tone changed a little, but he was still very happy for me. He told me living in LA was a part of my destiny and he knew I would be there for a long time. I wasn't really ready to hear that. I mean, all my life I had planned on being a ballerina, but I never really thought about leaving the only city I've ever known to accomplish that. I just thought I would travel when I needed to and go back home. Hamilton reminded me it probably wouldn't be that way. Our discussion from that point on was a bit more emotional than I wanted it to be. We discussed our future together, and although the majority of our conversation was happy and optimistic, we also had to deal the realistic negativity that could come our way because of the distance we would have between us. Then, he said something I didn't expect.

"Elise, I love you more than you can even imagine! If it ever seems like anything that's happening in my life will distract you from your goals, I will try my best to push you away."

"Why would you say something like that?" I asked.

"I never want to take away from anything you're trying to do. If anything were to happen, it would hurt me like crazy to push you away, but I'll sacrifice my happiness if it ensures you'll be able to reach your potential. I refuse to be a distraction to you."

It felt like we were breaking up, so I asked him if that's what was happening. He assured me he never wanted to actually break up with me; it was just very important to him that I was able to accomplish the things I was supposed to. He wanted to make sure I knew he would do anything in his power to not be an obstacle to where I was trying to go. When he explained it like that, I understood.

We talked for a while longer before we ended our talk. I had been in the restaurant for a while, so I decided it was time for me to go. I quickly drank a refill of my drink and paid my bill. It was for a little over $3. I reached in my pocket and grabbed the first bill I could. I thought it would be $5, but it ended up being a twenty. The people were so nice and I felt so good that I just let them keep the change. I hoped it would be enough for them to remember me because it seemed like the type of place I would visit again.

I grabbed my bag and went outside. The weather was cool enough to remind me I wasn't at home, but not cold enough to make me uncomfortable. It was symbolic of how my time in LA had been up to that point. The people were different enough to remind me I wasn't at home, and even though some of them made me uneasy, none of them made me uncomfortable enough to make me want to give up and go back home. I looked at the palm trees again and I was almost hypnotized.

I looked at the neighborhood. Then, I looked in the distance to see more of the city. I couldn't help but feel happy at the progress that had been made. I was very optimistic about what the future held.

"Welcome home, Elise. This is the start of your new life," I told myself.

That was the moment the expectations increased for me. I had conquered the audition, but that didn't mean it was time to slack off. That just meant it was time to get to work!

Part IV

After I made it to LA and got accepted into the dance academy, time seemed to move much quicker than it had at any previous point of my life. The remainder of my teenage years vanished quickly and before I knew it, I was twenty-two years old. It seemed like I went from being that young girl who had no idea how LA would treat her, to a fairly accomplished ballerina. I was actually starting to make a name for myself and it felt pretty good. The crazy thing was, my professional life was different, but so were some of my personal relationships were different as well.

I never really believed it when people said success changes the people around you until I moved. As I started to have more performances and gain a bit of attention around the city (and across the country), people started to treat me differently. When I first started noticing differences in people's actions, I tried to convince myself I was overreacting to something that didn't exist, but I kept seeing more examples that proved otherwise.

The academy once had a performance that I was fortunate enough to have Riley and Val show up. Now, we weren't best friends and we didn't talk everyday, but every now and again, we would check on one another and see how things were going. After the show, things seemed a little different with Riley, so I confronted her on it.

"What's up with you, Riley?"

"What's up with me? No, what's up with you?"

She had an inflection in her question that I really didn't like. My first thoughts were to go into attack mode, but I learned reacting based on your emotions could be very dangerous. I calmed myself down before reacting. I told her we were supposed to be friends and if I had done anything to upset her to please let me know.

"If you really want to talk about it, we can."

She made me feel like we were kids in high school about to argue over something incredibly stupid. We were both way too old to be childish, but I felt like we were about to disregard our age in an argument that would show a severe lack of maturity.

"Just because you've started to do better in your career, you've become more and more pretentious. When I first met you on that flight, you seemed like you were a cool person who was chasing a dream. Now you've become arrogant and you act like you're entitled to things. I don't like that at all," she told me.

"I'm not quite sure where any of that is coming from. I don't feel entitled to anything. In fact, I feel I have to outwork everyone to get better— not just for myself, but for the team."

"Yeah, I'm sure you work hard. You have to. You're a ballerina that doesn't... well, you really don't look like other dancers. Being black is probably a huge disadvantage for you, isn't it?"

I thought she was my friend, and for the past few years I had known her, she never brought up race. It would have been foolish for me to believe she didn't "see race" because we all did. Racist people generally just pre-judged others because of what they see; and because we hung out all the time, I never thought of her as being remotely racist. Her questions made me want to re-evaluate that.

"Let me tell you something, Riley. My race and appearance will not be what determines what I am able to do. And for further clarification, in spite of what you seem to think, you will never hear me say being black is a disadvantage! Black is what I am, but it doesn't define all that I am! You've really upset me. I didn't think you were like that, but I guess you are."

I understood the implications of what I said and I hoped she did, too. I absolutely despised racism and it upset me when people seemed to embrace that as part of who they were. I also knew racism was a form of hatred that could only be conquered by love. I didn't know if she was going to apologize for what she said or not, but I did know the way I was speaking was not actually helpful for the situation. It was probably making things worse because I had made myself act like an angry black stereotype and that was not what I wanted. That was not my character, but I allowed some misguided comments and questions temporarily make me be someone I wasn't. To make myself feel better, I needed to apologize.

"You upset me, Riley, but I shouldn't have reacted the way I did. I said I didn't want us to act like children, but that's exactly what I was doing. I apologize for my words and my tone."

It took a lot for me to apologize, but I felt better after I did it. It also changed the remainder of my talk with her.

"Thank you for apologizing, Elise. I'd like to apologize, too. I know the things I said sounded terrible, but I didn't really mean it like that. I was trying to say I know the world in general is not fair. It's even worse in ballet. Outside of you, I haven't really seen very many dancers of different races, but that's not it. My reactions have been building up for a while and seeing you perform almost made me hate you!"

I was so confused at what she was saying, but I wasn't going to allow myself to get upset again. I needed to hear her explain.

"Why is that?" I asked.

"When I see you dance, it's beautiful, but it got to me today. It got to me because I was literally watching you dance your dreams into reality. That got to me because I don't feel like I've been able to live my dreams. When I see you, it reminds me of how jealous I am. It reminds me of how little I have accomplished in my life. It made me so upset, I just couldn't contain it."

I told her why I admired her life and felt she had no reason to be jealous. She told me she was beyond blessed with her husband and her kids, but her job left her unfulfilled. She wanted to be happy with her job the way I was with mine. Her honesty cleared things up. I had no idea she felt the way she did. She generally spoke about her job in such a positive manner. I tried to ask her what she would do with her life if she could do anything she wanted to. Sadly, she was unable to answer. As her friend, I wanted to help, but it's incredibly difficult (if not impossible) to help someone who doesn't even know what they want.

By the time we stopped talking that night, I was a little confused at how I felt. I had some conflicting emotions that kept bothering me. I enjoyed the clarity of finding out why Riley was behaved the way she did, but I felt bad because she questioned her life because of how she viewed mine. I was happy she said I inspired her, but I was hurt to know seeing me dance evoked envy in someone I had grown close to.

That envious nature was what really caused a tremendous shift in our relationship. Even though we forgave each other, I understood with certain type of feelings in your heart, you can do things you may not know you're capable of. I had seen how jealousy could impact a person's heart and even though I tried my best not to bring up the negativity of that conversation, it seemed to stick around anyway. I didn't feel like I could trust her like I had before. That was the first relationship that began to change and fade away in LA, but it wasn't the last.

It's crazy that sometimes the more people you're around, the lonelier you feel. When I was growing up, I never had a whole lot of friends and that was partially because I didn't want to be around a lot of people. My family, Mrs. Mears, Hamilton, Tracy, and Little Jazzy were really the main people I was around. They were all I needed. For some reason, once I got to LA, I found myself trying to be around more people than I ever had before.

Perhaps it was because I wasn't living in the city I spent my first 18 years in, I felt it was necessary to surround myself with more people to feel comfortable. That was combined with the fact that the more responsibility ballet kept handing me, the more time I made for it, but the less time I spent with God. I was growing more and more unbalanced by the day, but I didn't even pay attention to it. The forced relationships were taking away from my spirit while I was actually sacrificing my relationship with the Lord. I felt the loneliness was a direct result of this, but I constantly made excuses for why I thought things were the way they were.

In the back of my mind, I knew things wouldn't turn out very well if I didn't change and get back to God, but I kept telling myself things like, "He understands what I'm going through", "He put me in this position so I would stay busy", and "I'm doing this for a reason." Yeah, they all sounded good and they were convincing reasons, but they were only partial truths. I was lying to myself and everyone around me. I kept a smile on my face in spite of the pressure I was feeling from everything that was happening in my life. I always asked God to help me become a professional dancer and I'm sure He was disappointed that as soon as He gave me what I prayed for, I started to pretend I was too busy for Him.

During the many times I felt bad, I could generally depend on Hamilton to help calm me down, but I called him one day and I quickly found out the relationship with him was changing as well. As soon as he answered the phone, it was as though he was just trying to see how quickly he could get me off of the phone. I wasn't used to that at all. We had promised ourselves we wouldn't become just another long distance relationship, but it seemed like we lied to ourselves. During the first few years of being in Cali, he used to visit all of the time, but that had all but stopped.

I remembered thinking he was going to see me for my birthday. I didn't hear him saying anything much about it, but I thought he was going to surprise me. That didn't happen. Instead, I got a card, a gift from my online wish list, and a call very late that night. It sounded like he was extremely tired when he called, too. Maybe he had been partying with other people. Whatever it was, I didn't ask and he certainly didn't volunteer to tell me. That day hurt me so much, but I tried not to think about it much because it would have just made me feel worse.

So, since I wasn't able to talk to him and I didn't want to call my parents about my problems, I felt like I didn't really have anyone. Even with that feeling like it was true, I couldn't let my issues defeat me. I never had and I hoped I never would. Common sense told me to just talk to God and it would get my life back in order, but I didn't. I chose to continue to try and deal with things on my own. It was not the best decision to make, and it seemed like because of that, things continued to get a little bit worse every day.

I remembered stuffing my face with red velvet ice cream one night while I stared at some show I really had no interest in watching. Rachel walked in and asked what was wrong with me. I insisted I had no problems, but she knew I wasn't telling her the truth.

Then she asked, "What happened to you?"

It was a great question I wished I had an answer for. Then, I thought back to my argument with Riley. It happened partially because she said I had changed. I vehemently denied it, but the truth of the matter was that I had changed. The Los Angeles version of me was different than the Austin version of me. It almost seemed like the older I got, the less I cared about other people. It wasn't like I was being mean to everyone because I knew I wasn't. However, it seemed like I was no longer putting forth my best effort to ensure the lives of the people around me were going as well as they could. I wouldn't say I wanted it to be like that, but it didn't necessarily bother me that I was, either.

I told Rachel the city and the work that came along with being a ballerina was getting to me.

"Maybe I was too ambitious and I took on more than I can actually handle."

She looked at me as if I had lost my mind. I could understand her shock because she had never heard me say anything like that. In fact, I don't know if I had ever questioned myself to that extent.

"I might just need to go back home for a little while."

She asked me if I was giving up. Right then, I was unable to find the words that would effectively express how I was feeling.

We started talking about how long I had been dancing. When I told her it had been about sixteen years, she simply asked me if I was ready to throw away all of the money, time, and effort that had been put into dancing.

"You want to quit after all of that? If you ask me, that sounds pretty stupid!" she said.

She stared at me glaringly for a few seconds before she stormed away and slammed the bedroom door. It was hard seeing her react like that, but it showed me she cared about what I was doing with my life. I appreciated it on one hand; but on the other, I almost wished she didn't care. That would have made it easier to continue to just slouch on the sofa. Instead, I got up and started to think about the people who were depending on me. I started to visualize everyone who made sacrifices for me throughout the years. I made a promise to try my best and not let anyone down, but there I was, ready to throw in the towel after a few years.

I had enough. I needed my mother to make me feel better. Even though I should have been able to make my way through my own problems, I couldn't and I prayed to God my mother would answer the phone. Sadly, she didn't. So, I stayed in the living room and poured my heart out to my mom through voicemail.

"Mom, I'm lost! I want to come home, but I know that's not the best thing to do. I'm tired, I'm stressed, and I don't even know what's going on! I feel alone and I just need to talk to. I love you!"

I wanted her to call me back immediately. Selfishly, I just needed her to use her "mommy magic" to make me feel better. I ended up carrying my pseudo-depression with me for a few more hours before she got back to me. When she did, I convinced myself the level of anxiousness I was feeling would be contagious and my mother would feel the same way. This was not the case.

She started off the conversation by apologizing for not being able to answer when I called. She said she and my father were at the hospital, which automatically made my mind go to a negative place. I really didn't want to hear any more bad news, but she assured me they were only there so he could get some necessary checkups. From there, she quickly transitioned back to me and what I was dealing with. I told her I was questioning everything in my life, including dancing. I told her many of the girls didn't respect me and that I had someone tell me I would be a better dancer if I was just able to "get the black off of me." I explained further how I'd been dealing with people speaking about my race as a disability since I got to LA.

"I thought I could deal with it because I already have been for so long, but I'm tired of this racist stuff on top of dealing with how demanding ballet is in the first place. Plus, it seems like people keep leaving my life. I want to give up, but I know I can't."

"There's something fundamentally wrong with what you're saying. You said 'I' and 'me' a lot. Your problem is, you got to LA and you started thinking you had to take on everything by yourself. I love you, but your way of thinking is wrong. Do you think this family would have been able to make it through all we did if we had to do it ourselves? All of our losses and failures would have stopped most people, but we made it through still having hope for better days because we talked to God."

She was right and it wasn't surprising she said what she did because she was always consistent with her beliefs. Then, she opened up and told me when we lost Jasmine and she thought about how difficult life was going to be having to take care of my father while raising me, she was ready to end her life.

"I wasn't thinking about the pain of you losing your little sister or watching your father lose his ability to walk. I wasn't thinking about that. I was selfishly just thinking about me. That's why I became so withdrawn. I was dealing with so many internal battles I couldn't even think straight. The only reason I was finally able to get it together was because your words helped me clear my head of my own ignorant thoughts. Once that was done, I had room for the word of God. As I thought more about Him, I became stronger. When that happened, I had confirmation that God was truly the source of my strength. Now, it seems like you have come to a fork in the road of your own life. You have to decide if you're going to continue down the road that takes you away from God, or the one that leads you towards Him."

I couldn't understand why I had almost turned my back on God. It was like I stopped trusting Him to continue to give me strength and pull me through things He had been pulling me through all of my life. He put a plan together for my life that brought me to Los Angeles and allowed me to dance almost on a daily basis, but I was acting as though He wasn't going to still be there for me. My mom was making me see the error in my thinking.

"Elise, you know your father and I love you and we can't watch you quit ballet. God has a spectacular life planned for you. To get to it, you will certainly go through more negativity. Life with God will be difficult, but life without God... Elise, that life is impossible. The choice is up to you."

"Thank you, mom. Tell dad I love him, and don't worry, God will get me back on track. I promise!"

Her "mommy magic" didn't come in the form I wanted it to, but it still worked, nonetheless. After our talk, I cleaned myself up and went for a quick walk. I wasn't concerned with how I looked, I just had to get outside and be in the sunshine. I didn't plan on going very far, but without even realizing it, I had walked a few miles away from the apartment. I soon found myself sitting on a bench in the middle of a park.

I sat silently while I watched all of the people pass by. I knew they all had their flaws and things they were dealing with, yet none of them were locking themselves in their homes and letting life pass them by. Many times the people of the city upset me because I wasn't in the area where folks looked like me; but at that moment, my perspective was different.

What normally caused me to be upset actually made me happy. The diversity of the people was inspiring. There still weren't people around that looked like me, but it made me embrace my role of bringing diversity to the area. Every once in a while, I would catch someone staring at me. For some, it may have been because I was young, for some it may have been because I was wearing less-than-flattering sweatpants and an old t-shirt with a dried-up ice cream stain on it. For others, though, I was all but certain they were looking at me because of my skin. The look I saw from some of them asked the question, "What are you doing here?" It was wonderful that speaking with my mother calmed me down because if I saw those people prior to that talk, I'm sure my reaction (and the smile I was able to keep on my face) would have been very different.

After I had been "people watching" for a while, I started to enjoy nature. The evening sky was beautifully painted by the Creator as the sun began to set. The hues of blue mixed together with the scattered clouds. The birds flew around the sky with the grace and confidence I hoped to have when I danced the stage. It was like they were the living definition of the term adagio.

As beautiful as everything was, I couldn't admire it for very long because I didn't want to be outside by myself once the sun had completely set. I quickly made my way back home. The journey drained me of all of my energy and I was about to call it a night when the talk I had with my mother came back into my head. I was reminded I needed to talk to who I had been avoiding; God.

I didn't care who was around me. I fell to my knees so I could pray. It had been a little while, so I felt very nervous.

"God, I'm sorry for not talking to you in a while. I honestly don't even know why I've been going away from you, but I'm begging for your forgiveness and asking that you get me back on track. Please help me. In the name of Jesus I pray, amen!"

That night, I rested well. I also felt very different when I woke up the next morning. I knew praying for one night wouldn't change everything I had been feeling, but it certainly wasn't going to hurt. My mother stressed the importance of re-establishing my connection with God and she had never led me astray, so I knew I had to work on maintaining my communication with the Lord. I had also learned over the years that when you show you trust God, your faith gets tested. Often times, what tests your faith ends up being a part of your testimony. I had to try and remember that because my test of faith came very quickly.

It was a Friday evening and I hadn't been at home long from ballet practice when I got an unexpected call from Hamilton. I greeted him happily, but he didn't respond the same.

"I don't know if you want us to pretend everything is okay, or if you want to keep the conversation honest and to the point." I was very surprised by his tone and rudeness. I tried not to be rude to him just because he was acting that way towards me. I don't like to speak to anyone for too long if they obviously have a problem with me, even Hamilton. I just wanted to find out what the problem was.

"Just say what you need to say. You don't need to waste any time," I told him.

"Okay, I'll do that. I don't think this relationship is working out for me anymore. This long-distance stuff is very irritating. I need someone who's here. I shouldn't have to fly out there to see you. I'm tired of it!"

We had gone through a lot, especially since I moved to LA, but I never expected to hear that. I didn't want to just give up on what we spent years trying to build.

The conversation continued to go downhill. When I asked about him moving to California to go to school, he told me he didn't feel he should have to change his entire life just so things could be more convenient for me. He was being a jerk and I really didn't understand why.

"Where is this coming from?" I asked

"I've been feeling different for a while. I've just finally made it to the point where I have to let you know how I'm feeling."

I just said okay and hung up the phone.

The talk with him gave me a horrible feeling. Of course I had been hurt before, but the pain of that moment was different than anything I had ever felt. All I could do was contemplate what I did over the years that took us to where we were. If a breakup was going to happen, why did it have to happen so soon after I tried to learn how to get my faith back? Was this the devil's doing? Did he want me to give up hope or was this God's first test in how I was going to react to even more diversity?

    I cried very intensely that night. I tried not to, but it seemed like every time I thought I had everything under control, the tears would start again. Out of frustration, I ended up yelling very loudly. I kept hearing God tell me, "Speak to your friend, she will help."

    I couldn't ignore what I was hearing, so I got up and knocked on her door. I knocked lightly at first because I was still a little conflicted on whether I should even bother her (especially at that time of night). After a few seconds, I realized part of the hesitation was because, for some reason, I felt ashamed that I needed help. As I continued to stand there knocking, trying not to walk away, Rachel finally opened the door. She wiped the sleep from her eyes before she stretched and let out a very long yawn.

    She asked me if I was okay. My emotions made me fall to the ground as my eyes began to overflow with tears. Rachel fell to the ground right along with me and gave me a hug. I started talking in incomplete sentences as I tried to ask her why he would do this to me.

    "Who are you talking about, Elise. Who did something to you?" she asked.

It took me a while to answer, but I finally told her Hamilton said we shouldn't be together anymore.

    She was upset and couldn't believe he did that. I assured her it happened and he sounded very strong in his conviction.

    "He said he wanted somebody close to him and I can't even blame him for that."

    "That dude is stupid! You are an amazing person, and if he doesn't realize that, he doesn't even deserve to be with you."

Her words seemed genuine, even if I wasn't completely sure she wasn't just saying them to make me feel better. Even if that were the case, it was a very nice thing to do and I appreciated it.

    "Thanks, Rachel."

    "Elise, you don't have to thank me for being a friend."

    And right then, out of nowhere, came a few seconds of happiness. That happiness stayed with me for the next few days. As

I went to my practices and performances, my breakup wasn't really on my mind, but then the thought of it appeared with a vengeance. It didn't make sense that Hamilton broke up with me, but it made even less sense that he completely cut off communication with me after it was done.

Had the feelings really gone from love to hatred that quickly? If so, why? Had I actually done anything, or were his feelings the outcome of something else he was going through? I had no idea, but I wanted to find out. So, I made the first move for us to talk again.

I decided to call him on a Sunday afternoon. Although it was football season, I knew his favorite team wasn't playing that day. I figured that would give me a better chance of being able to talk without being brushed off. I dialed the number very slowly. It was almost as if I was giving myself another chance to stop what I was doing with each number I dialed. Soon the full ten digits had been dialed and I was finding it hard to breathe as I awaited an answer. Then finally, it happened.

"Hello. Is this Elise?"

The voice on the other end was not Hamilton's. Instead, it was the voice of a woman. I was devastated.

"Yeah, this is Elise. Who is this? Where is Hamilton? Why are you answering his phone?"

Each question was something I honestly wanted an answer to, but at the same time, each question I asked immediately brought another one to my mind.

The woman tried to start talking as soon as I stopped to take a breath, but I couldn't stand to hear her voice, nor what she had to say. So, just like the last time I talked to Hamilton, the call ended with me abruptly hanging up the phone. I wanted to yell in agony. I wanted to throw my phone down and punch the wall or something, but I didn't do any of that. I ended up simply sitting on the end of my bed with my head buried in my hands. I didn't cry, not because I was being strong, but because I didn't have any more tears to give. At that moment, I was literally all cried out.

I was going to see if Rachel was available to talk again, but I didn't. I didn't want to feel like I was abusing our friendship. So I prayed a simple prayer asking for strength and peace. I also made sure to stress the fact that I wanted a true understanding of why things had gone the way they did in my relationship. Of course, I wanted to feel better as soon as the prayer left my lips, but I didn't.

Instead, I had to live with my pain. I had to co-exist with it. It was unrealistic for me to think I would be able to forget about the breakup, the years spent together with Hamilton or even the voice of the woman who answered his phone, but that was still what I wanted. Again, I wanted my prayer to be answered immediately, but because it wasn't, it felt like it had just fallen on deaf ears.

I had always been told it was never about our own personal timing, but about God's. Did I like that? I'd be lying if I said I did. Generally, we want the things that make us feel bad to end. God doesn't work like that. He will allow those negative moments to happen sometimes so we will be forced to learn things we may not have learned otherwise.

Unlike people, God won't just be with you during the good times. Many times, it's actually during those times He will take steps back to allow you to celebrate those victorious moments. This can be very dangerous because people tend to think they are the reasons good things happen. We don't praise Him, yet we'll call out for Him as soon as things look like they may go in a negative direction. We're all guilty of it, even when we don't want to admit it.

I wasn't able to hide what I was going through, nor did I have the energy to pretend I was happy. The hurt that resided in my heart was showing itself in my facial expressions, my body language, and in everything I said and did. I had quickly fallen back into a state of depression and I didn't see a light at the end of the emotional tunnel. Then, one day things started to change when I got a simple text message from Little Jazzy.

"Hi, Miss Elise. How are u? I miss u!"
It was so sweet and innocent and it showed she cared about me. I was going to reply via text, but I decided to call her instead.

It was still strange that I was calling the little girl I met when she was five years old on her very own cell phone, but that was exactly what was happening. Her voice made me happy and I couldn't help but smile when she told me how things were going for her. She then told me Mrs. Mears sometimes had her up front of the class with her when she was teaching the beginning classes with the four-year-olds.

"Do you mean to tell me you're teaching classes now?" I asked.

I imagined her smiling and putting her head down as she talked. She always got embarrassed when we were having a conversation mainly about her. She had been doing it since she was a little girl and I didn't expect her to be any other way. It was cute. She never wanted a conversation to be focused on her, even when it needed to be.

We talked for a couple of hours and she made me forget I was even upset. All of the negative emotions, for that moment, were gone. When I was at home, talking to Jazzy always made me feel better. It was good to see her happiness still reached me even when I wasn't close. I was also glad she was able to help my emotional rollercoaster get back on the upward trend.

Although she made me happy that night, as the days progressed, I found I still had some of that "breakup pain" with me. I dealt with it daily and I was ready for something outside of my everyday routine to distract me a little. I temporarily got my wish in the form of a party to celebrate a performance we had. None of us really hung out together outside of the 3 Ps; practices, performances, and parties.

While there, we were all having a great time as all kinds of music was being played. All of us were either ready to get on the dance floor or trying to stay away from it. I was definitely a part of the group staying away from it.

Then, everything changed when I got a call form Hamilton. I wasn't going to answer it at first, but I decided I needed to give him a piece of my mind. As soon as I heard someone on the other line, I started to yell. Everyone started to stare at me, but I didn't care. I was able to say everything I wanted to say and I wanted him to respond, but he wasn't doing that.

"You called me to talk, so talk!"

I started to hear crying on the other end, but it didn't sound like Hamilton. I wanted to keep yelling, but I didn't because it wasn't doing me any good. I told myself to be quiet in hopes of actually finding out what the purpose of the phone call was.

"Elise?"

As I suspected, it wasn't Hamilton. It sounded like the voice of the lady I heard before. I went back to yelling. I needed answers.

"Who are you and what do you want from me?"

"I'm sorry to have to call you, but my name is Jean and I'm Hamilton's mother."

I instantly felt like an idiot. During both of the times I had been on the phone with her, I hadn't really been very nice to her. Now she was on the phone crying and I didn't know why.

I apologized. She told me she understood why I had the tone that I did. She said she could only imagine the type of thoughts I had going through my mind and who I thought she was. She forgave me very quickly and I hoped she would tell me the actual purpose of her calling. She kept crying, but she also continued speaking. She told me Hamilton spoke very highly of me. I didn't understand that and wondered if he thought so highly of me, then he wouldn't have broken up and stopped communication with me.

"He had other things he was dealing with," she told me.

She was his mother, so of course she was going to make it seem like her son was innocent and there was a reason that he had been such a jerk to me.

"Can you just tell me what's going on?"

I tried to ask respectfully, but I don't know if it came across that way. She took a few very deep breaths.

"I called...to... I called to let you know Hamilton has passed."

I heard what she said, but I had a very difficult time processing it. It took a few minutes to respond. I begged her to tell me she wasn't serious. I pleaded with her to tell me it was a horrible nightmare, but it was real. I screamed out in pain. It felt like someone had ripped out my heart and stepped on it repeatedly. Not since my sister died had I felt so much pain.

I stumbled around for a little bit before I fell to the ground. I paid no mind to the people at the party who were once again staring at me. I expected there to be some level of human decency to be shown to a person who was obviously hurting, but I was expecting too much. Everyone there was far too self-absorbed to be concerned with my well-being. They made it obvious since day one they didn't want me to be a part of their dance group, which meant they did care if I was in pain.

I needed to know what happened. So, I asked. His mother responded with some questions.

"Did it seem like Hamilton had a lot of mood swings? Was he being mean with you recently?"

"Yeah, he was. He made me call out his name a few times because of it."

"Don't feel bad about that. Trust me, his attitude made me call him a few things too!"

I was able to wipe the tears from my eyes as we shared a laugh. That moment allowed me to smile. It also helped me take a breath and gather myself enough to walk away from the crowd. The people watched me almost every step of the way, but nobody seemed to think about if I was okay. I should've expected that.

I continued to talk to Jean, and although we were able to make each other laugh a little, I still needed to know what caused Hamilton's death. I knew it had to be difficult for her to explain, so I waited patently.

"He had been telling me he was having severe headaches. He soon told me he couldn't take the pain and needed to go to the doctor. That's when I knew it was bad. When the doctors did all of their tests, they discovered he had an inoperable brain tumor. So, in addition to the headaches and mood swings, he also had to deal with nausea, vomiting, and a tremendous amount of pain.

"He was going through all of that and I wasn't there for him! What kind of person am I?" I asked.

Jean reminded me I had no way of knowing because he didn't want me to.

"He wanted you to just be able to focus on ballet. He told me you are going to travel the world because of your talent and he didn't want to stand in your way."

"Is that why he pushed me away?"

"Yes, it is. Hamilton loved you more than you know. When you two first met, he told me he found the last girl he was ever going to date. You were his world, Elise. He only wanted what was best for you."

I couldn't even move as I thought about the love of my life living his final days in pain without me just because he wanted me to stay focused. I started to blame myself, but Jean wouldn't allow it. She told me she just needed to call so I could learn what really happened.

"I know it's hard, but could you tell me what happened on the last day?"

I almost regretted asking as soon as the words left my mouth. I didn't know if it was insensitive or not, but she answered.

"Yeah. Basically he was visiting our house and he suddenly had a seizure. We didn't really know what to do, so we just called the ambulance. They were able to get him to the hospital, but he wasn't able to open his eyes or respond to any of us. We were at the hospital every hour of the day. The doctors told us he would never open his eyes again, but we didn't believe it until God time confirmed it. Once we heard that, we let him go. We told the doctors to disconnect him from anything that was keeping him alive. A few minutes later, he took his last breath. It was almost like we could see his spirit leave his body... and while we knew he was going to glory, it was still very sad to come to the realization we would never hear him speak to us in this world again."

Hamilton's story reminded me of Jasmine's. After she told me how her son made his transition, she pushed through to tell me about the funeral arrangements. She really wanted me to be there and say a few words. Of course it was not something I wanted to do, but I agreed to it simply because it was not about me. She also told me that their family was going to pay for my flight. Even though I needed the help, I didn't want to accept it. I heard the voice of God tell me to accept the blessing, so that was what I did.

When I hung up the phone, I still thought everything was a part of a nightmare I was going to wake up from. I was there physically, but mentally I had left almost as soon as Jean told me what happened. My body felt weak and I didn't know if I would be able to make it home by myself. I had driven to the party in a car I was able to get a few months before, but I didn't think it would have been a smart idea to drive home in the condition I was in.

I hadn't seen Rachel all night and I wasn't sure if she made it to the party, but I called her in hopes that she had. The phone rang a few times and when it did, I became less hopeful that she would pick up, but eventually she did. I told her I had just gotten some bad news and asked if she could take me home. Within a matter of minutes, she was in front of me. She reached for my keys as she hugged me and let me cry on her shoulder. I leaned on her for support as we walked through the parking lot to find my car. We headed home and I saw she had one of her friends follow us so she could get back to the party.

There was very little talking in the car until I just blurted out what was wrong.

"Hamilton's dead! A brain tumor killed him! He's gone!" She said she was sorry for my loss, but what else could she really do? Hearing her say she was sorry reminded me of all the people I had lost. I leaned back in the seat and I thought about how life would be if Jasmine was still around. I pictured an adult version of her saying whatever she felt like to Hamilton as he tried to push through the shock of whatever it was she had to say. I pictured my aunt sitting at the dinner table during family gatherings as my dad walked around and joked non-stop with my mother about something only he thought was funny. That life would have been awesome, but it was not the one I had.

The vision of everyone soon faded and once again I felt like I was alone. That's when I heard God speak.

"Why do you always want to make yourself believe you're alone? Are the people around you not good enough? Is your family not there for you? Do you not believe I am here for you? Do you say you have faith in me and what I will do for you in public and continue to act like life is hopeless in private? Are you lying to yourself or do you think I'm lying to you?"

The more He talked, the more intense the conversation got. I had plenty of opportunities to speak, but honestly I was a little afraid.

We soon made it home. Rachel parked my car and asked me if it was cool for her to go back to the party. I didn't want to ruin her fun, so I told her it was. The rest of the night I cried, prayed, and tried to go to sleep. My attempts at sleep failed and before I knew it, the sunlight was bursting though every window in the apartment. For a few minutes, the beauty almost made forget how terrible I was feeling. I had practice scheduled for the day, but I had no desire to go. I felt spiritually low and I knew that could impact my physical movements, but I didn't want to let my team down, so I tried to keep going.

I moved slowly. Rachel soon came out and asked me how I was doing. I told her life was terrible and I started naming all sorts of questions I had for her and God.

"Elise, I'm sorry for your losses, but I'm even more sorry for your obvious loss of faith. I thought you were a believer."

I hated that she said that and I responded horribly. She tried to stay calm with me, but when I told her she didn't understand how painful my life was, she stood up and vented in frustration.

"You're really misguided. You don't get it. You don't have the exclusive rights to misery! There's a reason people say misery loves company. At some point, it tries to become best friends with all of us. So, just because you see me smiling, don't you dare think I haven't experienced pain! Don't make assumptions about my life!"

She was right, I did make a lot of assumptions about her her life, and throughout much of the day, we continued to speak about it, even while we were in practice. I was thinking about what she was saying more than I should have and this became evident when one of the instructors called me out in front of everyone and said I lacked focus.

"What do you call yourself doing? If you are going to be here, then you need to be here physically and mentally. You're not here right now and we can all see that."

I apologized. He told me my half-heated attempt may have worked in Texas, but I was a long way from home and it wouldn't work there. I was sure his rant was intended to motivate me enough to get back to being my best, but it didn't have that effect at all. For the first time, he made me not care about dance. I didn't know how long that feeling would last, but right then, nothing in that studio mattered. I grabbed my things and headed towards the door.

"Feel free to leave, just know you're risking everything you worked for. Remember, even the great ones need to be coached. If they can't play within the rules, they will soon find themselves without a team to play with," he told me.

I ran out of the door. As I moved toward my car, I soon heard Rachel running behind me, trying to get me to turn around.

She tried to convince me to go back into the studio by telling me all of the people who wanted to see me succeed, all of the people who had sacrificed for me.

"I love dancing, but I have missed out on so much because of it. I can't do it anymore. Ballet has defeated me. It won and I don't think I have any more fight left in me."

My attitude was like a leech, sucking away her positive energy. As hard as she tried, she knew there was no convincing me, so she turned around and went back inside. She was disappointed in me, but so was I.

I made my way back home, but I didn't do anything once I got there. I just sat in my sorrow and wallowed in my pain. While at home, I got a call from Jean letting me know my flight was the next day. It all seemed rushed, but I had no control over it. I made myself pack my clothes and get ready for my trip. As I packed, I regretted my decision to leave the studio and how I talked to Rachel.

For my entire time in LA, she had done nothing but be a friend to me. She didn't deserve how I had spoken to her, so I decided to write down an apology.

"Rachel, I was acting like a brat and I'm sorry. You know everything I'm going through, but that didn't give me the right to act so poorly. I appreciate you being such a good friend to me even when I didn't deserve it. Hamilton's death is very painful and I don't know what will happen after this, but I pray you'll continue to stick around. Good friends are very hard to find, and even if you decide you no longer want to deal with me, I'm still grateful I got a chance to know you! Keep smiling and keep dancing!"

The next morning, as I was getting ready to go, I put the short letter on the kitchen counter where I knew she would see it. Surprisingly, she soon woke up and looked at the letter. I didn't want her to read it then, but she did. She smiled when she finished.

"I forgive you and I understand," she said as she hugged me.

After that, she offered me a ride to the airport and I couldn't turn it down. Soon, we were at the departure gates and I was saying goodbye to my friend. It was more emotional than I thought it would be. I guess it was because I didn't know if I was coming back, and if that were the case, I didn't know if I would ever see her again.

A few hours after saying goodbye to her, I was hearing the captain on the plane tell us we had reached our destination. We were all anxious to get off the plane, but we knew we were at the mercy of the staff to let us go. As we waited, we were told information about baggage claim and connecting flights. With that information in mind, I sent a text to my parents to let them know where I was going to be.

When we were given the go-ahead to exit, everyone rushed out of the plane— well, everyone except me. While I was happy to be back home, I had to remember I was there for a funeral. That thought made me reluctant to move. I wanted to sit there for a while longer, but I was forced to get up. I was literally the last passenger on the plane. Slowly, I walked to get my bag from baggage claim. I waited about twenty minutes outside before my parents saw me.

My mother got out of the car and greeted me while helping me put my things in the car. When we got in, my father started talking. He told me he understood the feelings I had, even if I didn't really understand them. He also told me one of the simplest, but still some of the greatest advice I could hear at that time: he told me it was okay to release my emotions. He said sometimes you have to not worry about other people's feelings and thoughts so you can actually deal with your own.

With those words in the atmosphere, my father didn't really say much else for the rest of the ride. In fact, nobody did. So, I had time to reflect and look out at the city I was from. Just as I had grown, my city had done the same. There were houses, hotels, and apartment complexes in places that were open fields when I left. There were new entrances and exits to highways that I wasn't familiar with. Roads that I had never heard of took us home by routes I didn't know existed. I know it's stupid, but I was almost upset the city grew without me. Like a broken relationship, it was like Austin had moved on and it didn't feel good at all.

When we made it to the house, my parents asked me if I needed some time alone. I nodded in silence. With that, my mother helped my dad out and they went inside so I could have some time to myself. I looked at everything around, but I wasn't really focused on anything. I stared at our house and I thought about the past. I saw Jasmine and I playing a game of "tag" outside after we had both finished our homework. I felt like I was really re-living those moments. I smiled as I tried my best not to let my little sister catch me. Those were much different times and the simplicity of it all was something I truly missed.

  I went in the house and I realized even that had changed. My parents had new, modern furniture. My mom said they had been having the same furniture in the house since I was a little girl and they just had to change it up a little. Them speaking of change made me to talk about how much I had changed and that I questioned who I was and what I actually wanted to. I didn't know exactly how they'd respond, but I expected them to say something to make me feel better. This time, they said nothing. My mom hugged me while my dad held my hand. I don't know how long we sat there, but I felt a lot better.

  "Thank you," I told them.
They were the only words that seemed appropriate. I excused myself into my room after that.

  I soon called Jean and asked her if she needed any help with any of the last-minute stuff. She told me everting was taken care of. Once I was off the phone, something made me go to my text messages and look at the thread of conversations I had had with Hamilton. The most recent messages were ones of anger. They were the ones where Hamilton was saying things to make me upset so I would want to end our relationship. They were the ones where I was telling him how stupid he was being and how much he was making me hate him.

  "Why didn't you just tell me, Hamilton?" I yelled out.

  We really believed we were going to grow old together. We talked about how our relationship wouldn't become a casualty of distance and that we'd eventually end up in the same city again. Well, we did end up back in the city (sort of), but neither of us would have ever thought this would be how it all ended. It was sad and the more I thought about it, the worse I felt. I needed a distraction, so I asked my parents if I could use the car to drive around for a bit. They made sure I was okay before they said yes.

  I didn't know where I was driving to, but God guided me on the new roads until I ended up in very familiar territory. I was right in front of the dance studio where everything got started. Joy made an instant and unexpected return to my heart. I had absolutely no intention of going there, but God showed me He knew what I needed, even when I didn't.

I got out of the car and walked into the building. Before speaking to anyone, I felt like I was at home. I never had that feeling when I was dancing in LA. Maybe that was because I never got used to being there and never felt like I was accepted.

"Wait a minute! Is that Little Miss Elise Morgan?"
The voice was coming from behind me, so I wasn't sure who it was. When I turned around, I was beyond excited to see it was Mrs. Mears.

I started to jump up and down like a little kid. We conversed about the studio. She tried to ask me why I was in town, but I skipped over that and talked more about the studio. Mrs. Mears immediately tried to get me to get back in front of a class to teach, but my energy level was not at a place where I would have done anybody any good. I asked if Jasmine was there. She told me she was in a class, so we went and observed.

We stayed until the end of the class, but I hadn't seen her. I looked everyone in their eyes as they headed out of the building. Every once and a while I would randomly ask a young lady if she was Jasmine. They respectfully told me "no" as they kept moving. I didn't mind, though. I just kept asking until I reached the last girl in the studio.

I tapped her on her shoulder and asked her the question I had asking everybody else. The young lady turned around.

"It's me, Miss Elise! It's me!"
I heard what she said, but I couldn't believe it. There was no way the young lady I was seeing was my Little Jazzy. There's no way she had grown that much in such a short amount of time. I talked in disbelief. I was dumbfounded and so happy to see "my little girl."

Mrs. Mears didn't want to intrude on our moment, so she patted us both on the back and left us alone. When I finally stopped hugging Little Jazzy, I just stared at her. I told her how proud I was. I held her hand and took her to some of the nearby seats. I told her sticking with ballet over the years was a major accomplishment and I was so happy she was still doing it. She told me she never thought she would be able to quit because she loved it so much. Her words reminded me of how I used to feel. I could remember a time when I wouldn't have considered giving up dancing, no matter what the circumstance was. Things were different for me at that point, though. When you're young, you're optimistic about life, but as you grow older, you realize life will continuously throw things at you that you never thought about.

    We talked for a while longer before she started to wonder what I was doing in town. To try to avoid more pain, I was going to lie, but I decided to just speak the truth. When I did, that little girl held onto me like a parent would to her child. She was silent, just in case I needed to vent. Like my sister, she was very nurturing and I didn't understand how they were able to be that way, but I wasn't able to ask.

    Thirty minutes passed before we went outside. I saw her mother in the parking lot.

"Elise, is that you?"

"Yes, ma'am."

She got out of her car. With a huge grin, she gave me a giant hug. Like her daughter, one of the first things she asked me was what I was doing there. I looked over at Little Jazzy. I knew she was wondering if I was going to tell her the real reason I was there.

    I couldn't do it. Instead, I told her I couldn't go too long without checking on Little Jazzy in person. She told me she was very happy I was staying true to my word.

"She's very important to both of us."

"Yes, she is," her mother said.

    She went on to explain to Jasmine part of the reason she didn't like me at first was because my words about her seemed too good to be true and she was protecting her. She also let Jazzy know she was jealous of our relationship. The two of them talked amongst each other while I remained quiet. Just as Mrs. Mears had let Jasmine and I have our moment, I had to do the same for her and her mother.

    "I wasn't trying to make you jealous, mom. It's just that she's a really good dancer and a nice person and she just inspires me to be a better dancer," Little Jazzy told her mom.

    I was trying not to interject, but I had to at that point.

"I appreciate that, but I believe with all my heart there is nothing that I have done in ballet that you won't be able to surpass," I told her.

She told me I was putting a lot of pressure on her, which I was, but I still believed everything I was telling her.

"If someone told you that you would be the best dancer ever, you'd work really hard, right?"

"Yeah, I'd have to. I mean, the people would be depending on me, so I wouldn't want them to be wrong."

"So, don't you already work really hard because people are depending on you?"

She stood silently for a few minutes before she put her head down and replied.

"Yes, I do."

"And that's my point. You already do what's necessary to be the greatest. You are putting in the work because that's how great you are. There's no larger amount of pressure anyone could put on you than you already put on yourself. You set your own standard, and no matter how high anyone tries to set the bar for you, you will undoubtedly already have it set higher for yourself."

She raised her head and her stance changed to one of extreme confidence.

"You're right, Miss Elise," she replied.

Her mother smiled.

"You see the confidence she has? This is why you can't leave our lives. This talk is more important than you may ever know. Thank you so much!"

"You're very welcome!"

She went back to making me the subject of the conversation.

"So, Elise, how long do you think you'll be in town?"

It was a very difficult question. I had thought about it before I left LA and since I made it back into town. At various times, I was sure I was only going to stay for a few days. Other times, I felt like I never wanted to leave.

"I don't really know yet. I'm kinda playing it all by ear," I finally said.

"I can certainly understand that, but I hope you'll be in town long enough to see them in the show they have coming up next week."

"Yeah, that's a definite possibility," I said.

Jasmine hadn't mentioned a date or time. In fact, she didn't even mention the performance, so saying I would possibly stay long enough to see it was subconsciously done just to end the conversation. The plan was successful and the soon hugged me again before they decided to leave.

"What are you doing, Elise? Did you just lie to them?" I asked myself as soon as I was alone.

I couldn't provide myself with any answers. I couldn't even understand why I asked myself the questions in the first place. I didn't spend very much time thinking about it, though. Even if I wanted to continue to ponder the reasoning behind my actions, I couldn't because Mrs. Mears came outside to see if I was still there.

We stood outside for a while and talked. I was sure we were just going to talk about ballet, but that wasn't what happened. For some reason, I felt the urge to ask her how dance affected her life.

"Were there ever moments when you thought all of the work that goes into this was just way too much?" I asked.

"Do you mean running this school, or just dance in general?"

"Just dance. Have you ever started to second-guess yourself about what you were doing?"

"I have absolutely questioned what I was doing a countless amount of times."

"So what made you stay with it?"

"Elise, that's a good question. In order for me to answer that, I have to tell you a little more about me and my story. Is that okay?"

"Yes, ma'am!"

In my mind, I knew what she was going to say. She was going to tell me how the work was hard, but she wouldn't have it any other way. That was the sort of thing she always told us in class, but I found out this was a different sort of conversation. It included far more transparency than I ever before.

"I don't know if I've told you this before, but this whole ballet journey of mine started before I was even born."

"How is that even possible?" I asked.

She smiled and sort of patted me on my shoulder before she continued with her story.

"My mother wanted to be a ballerina. I remember her telling us stories about how she had to beg her mother to even consider allowing her to try dancing. Eventually, she said, she wore her mother down and she was able to get started. She finally told my sisters and I that she actually loved ballet, but she messed up her chances with it because she had me at the age of sixteen."

That part of her story made me think of Tracy. I wondered how she felt at that point about the decisions she had made. I hadn't talked to her specifically about that sort of thing in a while and I didn't know if it was something I would take the time to do while I was in town. I had to force myself to think about that at a later time because I really wanted to focus on what Mrs. Mears was telling me.

"How did that make you feel?" I asked.

"What?"

"You said your mom told you she messed up everything when she had you. How did that impact everything?"

"It impacted me a lot. It caused me to constantly have to deal with a lot of emotions. I felt guilty about ruining her life. I was sad because my birth ultimately put a stop to her dreams. There were just so many things I had to deal with, but eventually I was able to forgive her for telling me it was my fault she wasn't a professional. Even though I forgave her, I still have thoughts in the back of my mind that force me to still deal with that. I brought her up as a part of this story for a reason, though. Her dreams, although they stopped for her because of me, also continued because of it.

"From as far back as I could remember, I've wanted to do nothing but dance. I never saw her dance, but ballet is in my blood. I started taking classes when I was three. Can you imagine a three year old being so set on what she wanted to do that she would literally beg her mother to allow her to dance?"

"Your mom had to be excited you wanted to dance, right?"

"No, no, no! It was actually the opposite. She hated the idea!"

"But why? That doesn't make sense to me. Why wouldn't she want you to do something she had so much passion for?"

"I wondered the same thing, but I never had the nerve to ask her. When she passed away, I thought a lot about that. I came to the conclusion she didn't want me to do it for two main reasons: firstly, she wanted to protect me and secondly, I honestly believe she didn't want me to pursue ballet because she didn't want me to be able to get further than she did, but I'll never know for sure. Either way, it's okay. None of that answers your question, though. I'm sorry."

"It's okay. I enjoy hearing you speak about your life."

"You wanted to know if ballet has been worth it. My mom was brought up because I said I felt she wanted to protect me. I had to gain a lot of life experience to fully understand what she was trying to protect me from."

"What do you mean? Do you think she was trying to make sure you didn't work too hard? Is that what she was trying to protect you from?"

"I wish it were that simple, but that's not it. I grew up in Mobile, Alabama. It's not really the first place you think of when it comes to ballet. So, even with perfect conditions, things would have been difficult, but we didn't have perfect conditions. When you grow up in the south, your approach to life has to be different than it would be in different parts of the world."

"Yeah, I kinda get what you mean. People can be kinda... well, they aren't always the most accepting to diversity," I said.

"Exactly! And you're young. We live in an age where people are far more accepting than they used to be. Imagine me as a young black girl in Alabama, trying to work my way into the ultra-exclusive world of ballet."

I knew my struggles of people not wanting to include me were difficult, but I had never really considered anyone else's journey, especially Mrs. Mears or anyone else her age.

"If you don't mind, can you tell me a little more about the kind of stuff you had to deal with?"

"It's painful, but I will because it's necessary to fully answer what you want to know."
She stopped only briefly to wipe tears from her eyes.

"I remember when I was about five. I had my favorite pink backpack on and I was fresh out of dance class. I was so excited about class, I didn't even want to change clothes. I knew I would be walking a few streets over to stay with my mom's friend until my mom got off of work, so I wanted everyone to see me in my ballet

attire. So, with a gigantic smile on my face, I proudly walked towards my destination. Everything was good until I saw an older man on the opposite side of the street. "Hey" he yelled at me. He waited for a moment before he said, "Don't you hear me talking to you, little girl? Don't be disrespectful!"
I had to interrupt to express how things were sounding.

"That's strange," I said.

"Yeah, and it really scared me. He had to be at least thirty or forty years old, and even at that age I knew it wasn't right for him to talk to me. I tried to ignore him, but he wouldn't leave me alone. My heart started beating very quickly and the fear kept growing as the speed of my walk increased to a run. The crazy thing was, the faster I ended up going, the closer he seemed to get. Before I knew it, he was right in front of me."

I was hanging on to every word. Her words were creating a visual movie. I had to know how it was all going to play out.

"What happened, then?"

"Well, he stood there for a minute. Whenever I tried to move, he stepped in front of me. I looked around, hoping I would see someone who could help me, but there was nobody there. He looked me up and down. "Why are you wearing that?" he asked. I told him I was a ballerina and he just started laughing at me. What he said after that... it was... well... he told me ugly little colored girls can't do ballet because it was made for beautiful white girls. He told me I was stupid and was wasting time and taking up space that should be going to a qualified white girl. If that weren't bad enough, he then threw my backpack to the ground. I knew it wouldn't do any good to say anything, so I didn't. I just reached down and tried to pick up the bag that he made sure was covered in dirt. As I was putting it back on my shoulders, he stuck his leg out. Of course, I didn't notice it out there, so I ended up tripping over him and falling to the ground. My leg started to bleed and I tried to hold in my tears, but I couldn't. I just sat on the ground bleeding and crying, just hoping this adult, who obviously hated me because I was black, would apologize or something. He stuck his hand out to help me up. I didn't trust him, but I stuck my hand out anyway. He grabbed ahold of it long enough for me to start to gain my balance. I almost got back on my feet when he let me go, causing me to fall back to the ground even harder than I had the first time. He just laughed again and then walked away."

"What? What was the point of that? Why would anyone do something like that to a child?"

"Elise, it's because of hatred."

"Didn't that make you mad?" I asked.

"Of course it did. That was just the intro to what I've had to deal with. I've been scrutinized, ridiculed, laughed at, and talked down to. I was told I would never amount to anything and that it was dumb for me to even try. I've been beaten by people my age and by those older than me. I've dealt with such sever cases of racism, I can't even go into detail about them. All that has brought me here. Has my journey been difficult? Absolutely, but because of that journey I've been blessed to teach and work with brilliant young people like you. When I see you and Jasmine, I not only see me, but I see hope and progress. I see you breaking down doors that I've never even been able to reach...and I love that! Have I been hurt along the way? Yes. Have I had to make sacrifices? Yeah, I have. Ballet has caused me so much physical and emotional pain that I have spent nights alone crying, feeling lost and alone. Family members have left me because of ballet and I lost relationships because of it, I've literally lost track. Was it all worth it? Elise, I've been able to make a living from ballet. I've been able to travel the world and God has used me to inspire a lot of people, so when you look at the pros and cons of it all, the pros outweigh the cons by quite a bit. So, yes, it has all been worth it. Without hesitation, I would do everything all over again if I knew it would lead me back here."

The story she told was heartbreaking, but it was incredibly motivational. I could relate to many things she spoke about and it gave me a different perspective on my own life.

"Again, I'm sorry I was so long-winded, Elise, but it was necessary to fully answer your question. I hope you can understand how I really feel about ballet."

"Yes, ma'am, I understand and I appreciate you. Thank you for taking the time to tell me your story."

"You're welcome! As great as it was talking to you about all of this, I need to go back inside. You know we have a performance coming up soon, right?"

"Yes, ma'am. I just learned about it."

"Cool. Maybe you'll get to see it."

I couldn't lie to her, so I didn't say anything at all. She patted me on the shoulder once again before she left me alone with my thoughts.

Mrs. Mears' story caused me to do a lot of reflecting. I leaned against a nearby wall and I thought about everything I had gone through because of ballet. And although I was inspired by the story I had just been told, I still didn't know if I wanted to continue with it. It was worth it for her, but I wasn't sure if it was still right for me. I turned and faced the wall and banged my balled-up fists against it. I'm not sure why, but it was a reaction my body felt was necessary.

Once again, tears made an appearance. I cried for a while as I prayed. Unlike other times when I prayed, I can't recall exactly what I prayed for. I just remember after the prayer was complete, I felt a bit uneasy. In spite of how I felt right then, I still made sure to thank God for my breakthrough. In the the blink of an eye, I was back at home in a deep slumber.

The night seemed to pass by very quickly and I soon found myself preparing to go to the funeral. It was terribly surreal. I hated the fact the day had actually arrived, but at the same time, I was ready to get it over with. I put on a black dress, but I added a few accessories. Hamilton's favorite color was green, so I added a few splashes of it to my ensemble just for him. I looked at myself in the mirror and tried to give myself a pep talk before I left, but it didn't really seem to help at all.

After I had the conversation with myself, I left my room to see if anyone else was up. Of course, both of my parents were.

"Good morning, Elise," my father said.

He didn't have his normal joking tone. He knew I wouldn't be able to handle that and he was respectful of my mood.

"Morning," I replied.

I couldn't even get myself to say the word "good" at the beginning of the sentence. There was nothing good about it at all.

"Would you like some breakfast, Elise?" my mother asked.

She always wanted to make sure everyone around her was okay; that day was no exception.

"Yes, ma'am, I'll try to eat something."

"Good. Go ahead and sit down so I can fix you a plate."

I did what she suggested. She soon placed my food down in front of me. She then sat, said grace, and began to enjoy the plate she prepared for herself.

Even though I wasn't quite sure what type of appetite I had, everything looked great! My mom, in my mind, was the best cook ever. She made me a veggie omelet with mushrooms, tomatoes, onions, mozzarella, and a small amount of goat cheese. I had oatmeal with some fresh berries and pancakes. I grabbed my fork and was about to start eating when I had to do a double-take.

"Mom, did you really just...."

I couldn't even finish my question before a huge smile appeared. My mother had taken the time to shape my pancakes like one of the many cartoon characters I enjoyed watching when I was a kid. She smiled back at me.

"I just wanted to do something to bring you at least a brief moment of happiness today," she said.

"Thanks, mom. I really appreciate it."

And with that gesture from my mom and the greeting from my dad, I was able to get myself together. When I finished eating, my parents asked if I needed them to go. I didn't think I would. I just wanted to try to make it through the day alone, but as I looked at them, I knew I needed them more than I had in a long time.

"So, is that a yes or a no? It's okay, either way."

"Yes, ma'am. I think I need you both to go with me," I said. I had my head down when I answered them. I guess for some reason, I was both humbled and embarrassed.

"Pick your head up, Elise. We'll make it through this together," my father told me.

I nodded to acknowledge my agreement.

Twenty-five minutes after eating, we were all in the car and heading towards the church. It was an expectedly quiet ride. My mother drove, my father sat in the back seat, and I sat in the passenger's seat. When we finally made it to the church, I had a better understanding of how many people Hamilton's life had impacted. The parking lot was full of cars and everywhere I looked, there were crowds of people who were all in a great deal of pain.

"Well, we can go in," I said, holding my emotions back.

My parents said nothing. My mom got out of the car and she and I helped my dad get situated in his chair outside of the car. I took in a few breaths while I pushed my father's wheelchair and my mom walked beside me. I moved slowly, as if it were actually going to prolong anything.

When we walked in, the building was dimly lit. Soft music was being played by someone on the piano at the front and a preacher stood as everyone got situated. My family and I went towards the first available seats we saw. Before we were able to sit, we were each handed a program with Hamilton's picture on it.

"Well, no denying this is really happening, huh?" I asked as we tried to get comfortable

"No, baby. I'm sorry," my mom said while hugging me.

I looked at the program. I stared at the picture on the front and remembered the conversations I had with Hamilton and how much he made me laugh. When I opened up the program, I was able to read about Hamilton's family and aspects of his life I never got to learn about. It was cool to discover things about his family. Surprisingly, it actually made me smile.

I looked around again at all of the people. That was when I realized even though we were sad, we weren't there for Hamilton's death; we were there for his life. That made me feel a lot better.

"Ladies and gentlemen, could we please take our seats so the family may enter?" the preacher asked.

The music started to get played much softer and at a slower pace as Hamilton's mom, dad and the rest of the family entered. I could only imagine the emotions his family was dealing with. Then, I looked over at my mom. Even though the scenario was completely different, seeing a mother who had lost her child had to take my mother back to when we lost Jasmine. She was trying to fight her emotions. Just like with Jasmine, it was like she was trying to be strong to make sure I was alright. I reached out and grabbed her hand.

"It's okay, mom," I whispered to her.

She pulled out some tissue from her purse and wiped the tears that managed to sneak out. I continued to hold her hand as we listened to the preacher, Hamilton's friends and his family speak about how much he meant to them. Then, his mother spoke.

"Wow! Hammy was a pretty popular dude, wasn't he?" We all laughed out loud as she continued.

"Ever since he was four, he used to tell us how many friends he had. I would always tell him to quit exaggerating, but looking out at everyone here, I guess he was telling the truth. I thank you all from the bottom of my heart for being here. Hamilton loved each one of you. He would always tell me stories about the crazy things you all would do! Trust me, I know so many secrets about everyone, I could write a book. Don't worry, I'll keep them to myself, though."

The people all seemed to breathe a collective sigh of relief as they laughed again.

"I'm only partially joking, but honestly, he truly loved you all. However, there was one person he loved just a little bit more. He used to tell me he had found 'the one.' As a mother, it's difficult to hear your son say that because it makes you realize you have to share his love. I'll say this: I've had a chance to speak with this young lady, and no matter what, she will always be a part of our family. Elise, could you please say a few words about our baby?"

I stood up and my heart started pounding. I let go of my mother's hand and made my way to the front. I was already nervous, but seeing the people watch my every step increased that feeling.

When I finally made it to the front, his mother hugged me. She held onto me very tightly and even though she didn't cry, I felt her pain. She didn't want to let go, but eventually she did. She went back down to her seat, which meant I had to start speaking.

"Hello, everyone," I said very nervously.

The crowd responded. Their greeting, while a bit loud, was filled with love and that made me much more comfortable.

"Hamilton was very important to me. From day one, he always accepted me for who I was. I can be a little quirky and he never talked bad about me because of it. He helped build me up when I was feeling low. He was so supportive of everything I wanted to do, too. When I told him I had to move to Los Angeles to further my career in ballet, he encouraged me to do it, even though the distance would make our relationship much more difficult. Now, I don't want to get up here and lie about the love of my life. He was one of the greatest people I have ever been able to meet, but he was not perfect. Like every couple, we would argue. When we did, it usually was about something very stupid, but Hamilton never wanted to admit defeat and he never wanted to give in. Dang! He could be so stubborn sometimes! When he had an opinion about something, he was not afraid to speak his mind and try to convince you to switch to his way of thinking. It was so annoying, but at the same time, it showed he didn't want to give up on what he believed in. That kind of perseverance was what helped me fall in love. We weren't from the same part of town. We didn't have the same group of friends. At first, we didn't have the same interests. To be honest, when we first met, I had a pre-conceived notion of who we was going to be and I didn't want to deal with him. Again, that was at first. We all know that Hamilton is... I'm sorry... was… a different kind of guy. Once he roped you into a conversation, you had to listen to what he had to say. Ultimately, you may not have agreed with him, but you will gain a new perspective. He was a blessing. He had the ability to show me love, no matter what. When some people around him thought he was crazy for talking to me, he didn't care. When I was down about something and I didn't seem to love myself, he was there for me. He helped me see my worth when I couldn't and that's something I'm really going to miss because... who do I talk to now, Hamilton? Who? Why God? Why him? Why now? You may not be here anymore, babe, but your impact will be here forever. I love you."

  I held it together much longer than I thought I could, but in the end, after I told him I loved him, I fell to my knees and cried. At that moment, it felt like there was nobody in the room except for me and the body that used to hold Hamilton's spirit. It was a feeling I'll never forget, and after a few minutes, I felt a hand on my shoulder. By that time I had closed my eyes and before I opened them, I saw Hamilton again. He wasn't in the casket. It was the Hamilton I knew. He had a bright light around him, and as he moved closer to me, I almost had to turn away because it was so blinding. He said nothing as he smiled, kissed me on my forehead, and then waved goodbye. He soon faded away. When he did, I opened my eyes. I saw it was his mother who had her hand on my shoulder. She helped me stand up and face the audience again. They were crying, but they were silent.

"Thank you, Elise. I know that was difficult for you."

I couldn't even respond vocally, so I nodded my head as I hugged her again and left the stage.

"Ladies and gentlemen, that was love. Her words expressed how she really felt about my son. Just to make sure she knows: Elise, Hamilton loved you. We love you and we are forever linked. You are family!"

She spoke a while longer, but nothing else was directed at me. When she finished, a few people sang Hamilton's favorite songs. Then, there was a very emotional jazz tribute by a few people who went to school with him. It was beautiful. When they were done, the preacher read a few scriptures and asked us all to pray.

"Father, we know from the first day you allow us to see this world, it's only a matter of time before you call us home. We understand that time has come for brother Hamilton Toler. Father, we thank you for his life. We thank you for all of the things he was able to do and for the sea of people he was able to impact. Help comfort the family, God, as they deal with the fact their beloved Hamilton has made his transition. Give them the strength to move on with their lives. May they, and everyone who knew Hamilton, be able to keep his memory tucked away in their minds and their hearts. Let this incredibly difficult moment be encouraging enough for someone else to give their life to you. God, there is someone here who is struggling and they feel they are doing alone simply because they don't know you. Please, Father, change that. Give their spirits the strength to push the fear out and move them up here. Father, we thank you. As difficult as this day is, we thank you for it. We thank you for sharing Hamilton with us as you prepared him to get his wings. Knowing what kind of young man he had turned out to be, we know those wings will fit him nicely! We know that since he is now with you, we can see him again if we move towards you, too. All praises and honor to you. In the name of Jesus we pray, amen, amen, and amen!"

When I opened my eyes, there had to be at least six or seven people who had been inspired enough to give their lives to Christ.

Like Jasmine, Hamilton was positively affecting people's lives in death and that was beyond amazing.

After the service was over, we went to the cemetery where Hamilton's body was being put to rest. My parents spoke a lot more during that trip, especially my father.

"You did a great job up there, Elise. You're a strong woman, just like your mother. I am so proud of you!"

"Thanks, Dad."

I appreciated the statement, but I wasn't quite sure I agreed with it. How could he say I was strong when I had just cried my eyes out in front of everybody? Maybe we had different opinions on what strength was. Whatever the case, I just rolled with it.

"Are you okay?" my mother asked as we made it to our destination

"I think so," I said, obviously lacking confidence.

We got out of the car and stood where the large group of people had gathered. I wanted to stand in the back, but Jean wouldn't allow it. When she saw me, she beckoned for my family to move up to where she was. So that's what we did.

As if we all were really a part of their family, we stood up in front as everyone else said their final words. The time went by quickly and after about thirty minutes, they were lowering the casket into the ground and covering it up. His mother and I lost control of our emotions at nearly the same moment. It was a good thing my mother was there because she really helped us out. Even though she had yet to be formally introduced to Jean, she comforted her as if they knew each other all of their lives.

"In time, you'll be okay, trust me. It won't be easy and I'm not going to lie to you, you're going to miss your son every day. You'll feel weak, and as a mother, you're so used to being strong for everyone else. Being vulnerable is abnormal, but you can't get stronger without dealing with the pain. And please, pray!"
She hugged Jean, she hugged me, then she stepped back. Other people wanted to talk to Jean about their experiences with Hamilton and my mother didn't want to be in the way. Jean appreciated that.

When the day wound down, Jean and my mother exchanged information. It made me smile because it let me know Jean would not be left to deal with her pain by herself. My mom was willing to possibly relive the pain of losing her child to help out another mother who had just lost hers.

"Mrs. Morgan, I hate that we met under these circumstances, but I'm glad we had the opportunity. God certainly works in mysterious ways, doesn't He?"

"Yes, He does."

While my father spoke with some of the other people, we all said our goodbyes to each other. We vowed to keep in contact, but I didn't know if we were just saying that to be nice.

When we left, I kept looking back at the cemetery. We weren't the first to leave, but with tons of cars behind us, we knew we weren't the last ones, either.

"This kind of day saddens me. This was another reminder of how fragile life is. We can literally be here one day and....."

My father couldn't finish the statement. Just like when similar conversations happened when we lost Jasmine, finishing the statement was not necessary to understand what he was saying.

"I don't say it enough, but I love y'all. I know I smile most of the time, but I have so much pain that I carry with me. Elise, one time I heard you say you felt guilty because you weren't able to protect Jasmine. I know you felt that way because you're the oldest, but there was nothing you could've done to change what happened. Have I ever told you that?"

"I'm not really sure, Dad."

"And I apologize for that. You being unsure if I've said that or not is a failure on my part and I take full responsibility for that. So, again, I apologize to both you and your mother."

My mother seemed very confused that my father felt the urge to apologize to her.

"Babe, you haven't done anything that needs an apology," she said.

"I have to disagree with you. I never meant to hurt you, but I took your daughter away from you. I did that and I'm sorry!"

He wasn't really a crier, but at the at moment, he was. His body language made it seem like he felt alone. It also let us know how he really felt about the accident and I don't think he had ever really done that before. There was no reason he needed to feel like that and that helped me realize I didn't need to feel guilty, either. We both needed to let go of the unwarranted guilt.

"Ian, that accident was not your fault and you didn't take our daughter away from us! Is that how you've always felt?"

"Yeah, it is."

Every word he said was filled with so much pain. I wanted to take it all away from him, but I was in no position to be much help.

"What was done was an accident and it was not caused by anything you did. You're the best father anyone could ever hope to have. You are a great protector! You are a wonderful husband and an awesome father! I cannot allow you to doubt who you are and I will not allow you to think about taking responsibility for Jazz not being here. That's not something that's going to happen. I love you. Do you hear me, Ian? I love you!"

"I love you. That goes for you, too, Elise. See, this is why I need you two to know how important you are to me. There's no way I would have been able to make it if you were not here."

The dialog continued even after we made it back home. What started off as a day to mourn the loss of Hamilton, ended up being a day that allowed us all to release some emotional baggage we had been carrying around with us for far too long. The release helped us all make it through the night; but for me, once the sun rose to start the new day, I felt even worse than I had the day before.

I started the next day by pacing back and forth with my phone in my hand. I went into my contacts and stopped on Hamilton's info. The hardwood floor in my room began to squeak the more I walked. I was trying to decide if I was going to call his number so I could hear his voice on the voicemail. Soon, I went ahead and did it. I hoped his mom hadn't canceled his phone service or the call would've been pointless.

It rang over and over. Each second felt like a million hours and my anticipation kept growing. I prepared to apologize to the person who picked up if the number had already been reassigned to someone. Then, it stopped ringing.

"Hello," I said nervously.

"Hey everybody! You've reached Hamilton and unfortunately I'm unavailable to accept your call. Let me know who this is and I promise I'll try to get back to you as soon as I can. Have a good one!"

The message played in its entirety. The beep even went off for me to start my message. For about a second, I considered leaving a message, but I just couldn't bring myself to do it. Hearing his voice just broke me down because I kept having visions of him in that casket in the church and I kept reliving the moment they put him into the ground.

Out of sadness, I threw my phone down on the ground and I went to the ground right along with it. I ended up sitting with my back to the door. I sobbed silently. The more I cried, the more I put my head down. Soon, I was looking directly at the ground and that was when I saw an envelope. I hadn't seen it before, but I was curious to find out about its contents. I wiped my eyes as I opened it up. Immediately, I saw it was something written by Hamilton. The tears I had just cleared from my face quickly came back with a vengeance.

"Hey, Elise. If you're reading this, it means our 'forever' was cut short. Babe, I'm really sorry I was a jerk, but I couldn't make myself break up with you. I didn't want to tell you about anything because as I write this, I'm not really sure what's wrong. All I know is from the first time I saw the doctor, it felt like I may not have much time left. I just had the feeling, and in case you're wondering, I was praying all the time. I know the few family members who knew about me going to the hospital started praying that I would have a quick recovery, but I begged that God's will be done. Elise, I pictured us getting married and getting really, really, really, really old together. I wanted us to have kids together, maybe a few little boys and a little girl. That way they could have all looked after their sister, but I guess it wasn't meant to be. Look, with or without me, I know you're going to continue taking the ballet world by storm. Whenever I saw you in practice or during one of your performances, it was like watching an angel. Believe it or not, when it first started to feel like I didn't have long, I pictured you dancing and it calmed me down. It may seem stupid, but it was almost like God let me be in a relationship with an angel to help with my transition. Who knows? Anyway, I asked my mom to get this letter to you only after I passed. Hopefully she actually listened to me.

You know how mothers can be! Lol! Elise, just know I loved every hour we were together, every minute we were able to talk and every second I was fortunate enough to cross your mind. Somehow, God used you to cram a lifetime of the greatest relationship ever into a few years of time. He is cool like that, so I guess it's not really surprising. Elise, I could sit here and write until my fingers hurt, but I still wouldn't be able to express how important you are to me. I just have to make some requests: please, never give up on ballet! You're awesome at it and it would be a shame if you ever wasted your gift. Never forget that I love you. I didn't say it in past tense, because even if I have been called "home" by the time you read this, my love is still there. And finally, I beg you to enjoy your life. Live every day to the fullest and don't stop yourself from moving on. You deserve to be happy. I love you and may God continue to bless you, now and forever." – Hamilton

 I pulled the letter close to my heart. I felt his presence in each of the handwritten sentence that filled the page. I heard his voice in every word. He made sure we had the last conversation in a way that would be best for both of us. He expressed himself in that letter like very few people could. He calmly mentioned death as he talked about life. These were his last words to me and I cherished them. I wiped my face again, but it was no use. The tears were flowing and I couldn't stop them, so I stopped trying.

 I stood up. I almost found it unbelievable that Hamilton took the time to write that to me. Who knew how much pain he was in as he did it? He never mentioned any of that pain, though. He made sure he said he wanted me to keep dancing. If nothing else, Hamilton was very consistent because he always told me how important it was that I continued to dance. In between my tears, that actually made me smile. I looked in the mirror that was on my dresser. There was a slight reminder of the smile, but for the most part, the tears had drowned it out. Around my eyes were red, so there was no denying my pain.

 It didn't take long for me to get tired of me looking at the face of the sad woman's face who stared back at me in the mirror. I moved around my room again. This time I wasn't pacing. With my letter tightly gripped in my hand, I started searching for clothes as if I had plans to go somewhere. I soon stumbled upon one of the outfits I had to wear for a recital when I was about sixteen. I wasn't quite the same size I was then, but for some reason, I wanted to try it on.

I put the letter down gently on my bed, then I tried to get into the outfit. My expectations were very low, but to my surprise, it was almost a perfect fit. That made me feel good. I turned on some music and pretended I was dancing a pas de deux with Hamilton as my partner. I smiled again as I danced across the room, but then I made it back to the mirror and I saw myself. For some reason, part of me didn't want the other part to be happy.

"What are you doing?" I asked myself.
I stopped and stared at my reflection again.

"Take that off! You're not a dancer anymore! You don't have the heart for it. That Elise with ambition and passion for dance is a distant memory. I don't know who you are anymore! I guess when Hamilton died, he took the strong version of Elise with him. You're weak and disgusting! You're an embarrassment to who you used to be and anyone who has ever believed in you."

I was so confused. I didn't know if the words I was hearing were true. Was the devil using my own reflection against me or was it just me hearing what I really thought about myself? How could I go from happily dancing around the room to verbally abusing myself in a matter of minutes?

"Stop it! Stop it! Stop it!" I yelled as I continued to stare at myself

"You're pitiful!" I seemed to hear the reflections say.

I couldn't take it anymore. Like a madwoman, I ripped the mirror away from the dresser it was attached to and threw it on the ground with no regard to my own safety. As I looked down, many large pieces of glass still remained. That meant I was still able to see my reflection, and I wanted no part of that at all. So, what did I do? I picked it up and threw it down on the ground again.

It was dangerous! Glass flew everywhere and I thanked God that I escaped that moment of stupidity without any serious injuries, at least not any physical ones. I did, however, give myself a ton of emotional scars when I looked back down at the smaller pieces of glass I had just "created". I said something to myself right then that I'll never forget:

"Congratulations, Elise, that's you! Without question, you are completely broken! So what are you gonna do about it?"

Part V

  A few years have passed since Hamilton's death. I am now into my 25th year of life, I still feel lost and alone. The day I read Hamilton's letter, I felt good for a little while, but it didn't last long. Throwing down that mirror and yelling the way I did scared everyone in the house. I remember my mother rushing into the room as I stood over that broken mirror. My tears flowed consistently on the shattered glass. She felt bad just because I did. For some reason, I yelled at her as soon as she walked through the door.

  "What are you doing in here? Who said I needed you in here?"

  She didn't respond verbally. She hugged me in spite of my my tone and words. I stood still for a few seconds before that unnecessary anger came back. I pushed her away as I picked up the letter from Hamilton I had placed on the bed and I held it in front of my mother.

  "How did I even get this? Did you have something to do with this?"

  She didn't understand why I was speaking to her like that. Honestly, I didn't know why either.

  "Elise, I know you're upset, and you should be. You've lost someone very important to you, but that doesn't give you the right to disrespect me. As for that letter, yeah I had something to do with it. Jean gave it to me at the funeral. She made me promise to give it to you after the burial. Why are you so upset, though? She told me Hamilton wrote some words to remember him by. Isn't that what this is?" she asked.

"Yeah, Mom, he wrote the nicest letter. And that was the last one I'll ever get from him! He's gone! God took him away from me way too young! I don't understand why this keeps happening to me!"

Looking back, I see how terrible my viewpoint was. The love of my life died, my little sister died, and my aunt died (which ended up killing the relationship with my favorite cousin). My mom was robbed and beaten and my father was paralyzed. All of this happened around me, but none of it happened to me. My mom tried to explain this, but I was being too stubborn to pay attention. I just continued to disrespect her simply because I was hurt.

"Elise, I love you too much to speak to you the way you're speaking to me, so I'm going to leave. Hopefully, you'll get back to being yourself soon because you won't speak to me like that again without some serious repercussions."

Once she said that, she left. Mentally, I was in such a terrible place I acted as though I didn't care about what she told me. Over the years, she never gave me any indication she would break her word, but for some idiotic reason, I needed to find out for myself. During the days that followed the incident, my sadness grew into what I assumed was another case of depression. With that, my "I don't care" attitude got a lot worse. The way I spoke to my parents was deplorable and totally uncalled for. It didn't take long for me to reach the end of the rope.

They gave me chance after chance to stop moping around the house and yelling. All they wanted me to do was get myself together, but I didn't. I couldn't decide if I wanted to go back to Los Angeles, but worse than that, I didn't know if I was going to keep dancing. All I wanted to do was sit at their home and do nothing. At first, I would get a call from Rachel every few days. She would ask me when I was coming back. I just dismissed her question. Soon, she quit calling. Around the same time she did, my parents had a conversation with me I never thought they would.

"Lord knows we love you, Elise, but this is not who we raised. Where is your ambition? Where is your drive?" Mom asked.

"I don't know!" I responded

"And that's the problem. You're better than this. You knew more about what you wanted to do as a child than you do as an adult. We can't be your enablers any more," dad told me.

Neither of them said anything for a few seconds. Then my dad spoke again:

"You have to go, Elise. You can't be here. We won't allow you to waste your life. We can't be a part of that."

"You're kicking me out, for real? Where am I supposed to go? What am I supposed to do?"

"You had an apartment in LA. If you talk to your roommate, she may let you come back. Or you can stay in town— it just won't be here! You really need to fix your life and we wouldn't be doing this if we didn't think you could."

And just like that, they gave me two weeks to leave their house. It wasn't enough time, but that didn't matter to them. They gave me a suitcase to put my stuff in and they sent me on my way. Days before my "eviction day", I had been calling around to see if anyone was willing to help. There were some people I was too embarrassed to ask (like Mrs. Mears and Jean), but pretty much everyone else just told me no. It was devastating, but I deserved it. See, after Hamilton's death, I was mean to a lot of people and many of them decided to distance themselves from me. Surprisingly, the person who gave me a chance was Tracy.

She was raising her child on her own, so her living conditions weren't what I was accustomed to, but I was in no position to be picky. I didn't even have my own room. Instead, I had to make myself comfortable on the couch. Again, I started to hate my life so much I wanted to end it all. Almost every night after Tracy and her son, Morris (who we called Mo) went to sleep, I would just cry until my eyes couldn't stay open any longer. The sad thing was, as bad as I felt, I still didn't have the desire to do anything to change my situation.

Life was in a terrible circle of mediocrity and uneventful circumstances and I just let it continue like that. My twenty-third and twenty-fourth years of life wasted away as I felt sorry for myself. During that time, I ended up getting several jobs, but I lost them all because of my lack of effort. Tracy was struggling to take care of her bills and part of why she let me stay with her was because she thought I would be able to help out. Every time I lost a job and couldn't help with the rent, she got closer to kicking me out. I'm pretty sure one of the main reasons she didn't was because she had become very spiritual and kicking me out didn't seem like the Christian thing for her to do.

As my relationship with God was once again fading, hers was growing stronger. It didn't make sense to me. Not too long ago, she invited me to church and I could no longer keep my questions to myself.

"What's up with you, Tracy?" I asked.
"Why is this church thing so important to you?"
"Elise, are you, of all people, really asking me that question? You've always been the one trying to get other people to go to church."
"Yeah, you're right. That's how I was, but you see where that got me? I'm living with you and your son."
She shook her head at me like a disappointed parent.
"When did you stop walking in faith, Elise?"
She probably didn't expect me to answer, but I did.
"Probably right when Hamilton died."
She stop for a few seconds before she moved towards me. She grabbed my hand and started pulling me up. When Mo saw she needed help, he started pulling me up, too.
"Like it or not, you're coming to church with us today," she said.

It was easy to see they weren't going to give up, so as much as I really didn't want to go, I told them I would.
"Look, I'll go today, but only if you promise to leave me alone about it afterwards. Is that a deal?"

Tracy and Mo looked at each other. Tracy was trying to process my proposal, but Mo was a different story.
"It's a deal!" he said as he shook my hand frantically.
"Let me at least go get dressed," I said.
"Okay, but we don't have all day. Please try to hurry."
I resented saying I would go almost immediately, but I did what I said I was going to do. I got dressed as quickly as I could and then we headed to church.

During the ride, I kept thinking about how long it had been since I stepped inside a church. I wondered if the people would be able to sense that. I wondered if they would judge me. Out of everything I wondered, the most pressing thing was if God was willing to accept me, even though I couldn't except myself.

"Are you okay?" Tracy asked as we made it to the church.

"Yeah, I'm just a little nervous."

"Don't be scared, auntie, it'll be okay."

Mo started calling me auntie as soon as I moved in with them. It made me smile almost every time I heard it because it reminded me of when my little sister and I used to talk to Aunt Katie. Jasmine called her "auntie" when she was trying to get extra cookies or something. Of course, Aunt Katie knew what she was doing, but she never was able to resist. Those thoughts helped ease my mind as I slowly got out of Tracy's small, early model car.

"I'm good," I said.

That wasn't really true, though. The site of the church made me nervous and going inside almost made me unable to breathe. My nerves were getting the best of me, but I had to pretend they weren't. When the service started, I looked around to make sure my actions were similar to what other people were doing.

They soon began to sing songs I somehow knew. I didn't dare sing anything aloud, but in my head I was singing as though I were supposed to be singing a solo in front of everyone. A few minutes later everyone started clapping when the preacher came out and took his place in the pulpit. I don't know why, but this made me feel even more uneasy. It seemed many of the people were there more for him than to actually hear the word of God. I didn't want to judge them, though.

"Thank you, God! We are here for you. We give you praise, we honor you!"

When he started talking, I closed my eyes and remained standing. I don't know why I did it, but it felt like I was supposed to. The longer he talked, the more I felt people around me sitting down (including Tracy and Mo). I put my hands together tightly as if I were praying and the uneasy feeling soon gave way to comfort.

"If you don't mind, I want to talk to y'all about life when you follow Christ. Is that okay?"

The people cheered loudly.

"See, the problem with this Christianity thing, the thing that people get confused, is that they think this is supposed to be easy. Why is that?"

He pointed his microphone towards the crowd as people shouted out answers to his questions.

"What we do, or at least what we are supposed to do, is follow the path of Jesus. It is through Him we're able to receive the blessing that is made for us. He is who we follow. And if we follow Him, then He is our leader. Let me circle back to the confusion. We want things to be easy. We have convinced ourselves that just because we believe, we shouldn't have to deal with any obstacles. We feel like we won't run into setbacks. No, no, no. See, we have it twisted. Following Jesus doesn't mean we won't have a difficult journey. In fact, those who follow him, at times, may have it more difficult than others. This is why we must rely on faith. When we have faith, we won't avoid the difficulties, we will just be able to push through and be much stronger afterwords. Christ went through more than we can imagine, and to follow Him is to mentally, physically, and spiritually be prepared to go through some of the same things. Let me say it again: you will not have it easy! Your journey will not be complete if you're not broken to a point where only God can put you back together. You have to be broken so He can mend your heart with his word."

The word "broken" was being repeated and that stuck out to me. It made me think back to when my mother told me I had to make sure I was able to dance when I was broken, but I wasn't doing that. Hamilton's death brought me to my worst point. I was at my lowest. I was the most "broken" I had ever been because everything had been building up inside of me for so long. At the time when I needed to do it most, I was unable to dance— literally or spiritually.

I was still standing and I still had my eyes closed. For the first time since the preacher really started speaking, I opened my eyes and looked around at everyone. Seeing how the people were reacting to what was being said let me know regardless of what a person looked like, no matter how old or young they were, no matter how poor or rich they seemed to be, we all could relate to being broken. That helped me out a lot.

I finally sat down. I listened to the rest of the service in tears because I felt more and more weight being lifted off my shoulders.

"Are you okay, auntie?" Mo asked.

"Yeah, Mo, I'm great. This is something I really needed."
I glanced over at Tracy. We didn't say anything to each other, but she could tell how the service was helping me. She allowed me to just observe and listen without interrupting.

After the sermon was done, the preacher did the altar call. This was when he asked if anyone was ready to give their life to Christ. I felt like he was talking to me, but I was so scared I couldn't even walk. My legs shook nervously and I just stared up front.

"I can see you want to go up there. Let's get rid of the fear. We'll go up there with you if you want us to."
I nodded my head and seconds later, Tracy and Mo were both grabbing my hands and taking me to meet the preacher.

I was more fearful then than I ever was for any performance. I thought I was used to people focusing on me, but this was something different. It felt like some people were judging me, while others were happy for me. There also seemed to be some who just wanted to get things over with so they could go home. All of their energy fed into how I was feeling.

When I made it to the front, not only were Mo and Tracy with me, but there was a large group of other people who also heard God speak to them during the service. That helped me feel even more comfortable.

"Are you all perfect?" the preacher asked.
The question was confusing to all of us. It was obvious because we all looked at each other, but none of us knew what to say.

"I take it by your silence that none of you feel you are and I'm glad. This walk with Christ is not about being perfect because that's a goal we'll never accomplish. It's about following the only perfect person to walk this earth, and that is Jesus!"

He talked more about the journey we we'd be going through after reconnecting with Christ.

"If you think it's about to get easy, if that's what you're up here for, you might want to turn around because it's not. It's about to get even more difficult because the enemy now knows you want to connect with God. He knows how much God will bless you if you remain faithful, so he will try his best to make you lose faith. He doesn't want you to succeed, but God will test you, too. So I need for y'all to be prepare for this. Can we pray?"

I closed my eyes, just as I had for most of the service. Tracy and Mo continued to hold my hand as I was "reborn". When the preacher was finished, he looked at all of us.

"Now the hard work begins. Life will be different for you as soon as you turn around. Are you ready?"

We all had tears on our faces as we nodded and headed back to our seats. I felt much different going back to my seat than I did going away from it. There was no more nervousness. People congratulated me and welcomed me to the Kingdom. I felt good, but at the same time I wondered if the feeling I had was going to lead me back to feeling more depressed. Even though I wasn't sure about that, I knew questioning the outcome after I had literally just committed my life to Christ was not the best way to show I was walking in faith. So, I immediately stopped myself from thinking that way. I felt it was necessary for God to truly enter my heart.

After service was over and we were walking back to the car, Tracy stopped walking. Not knowing why, I stopped as well.

"How do you feel?" she asked.

"I actually feel pretty good."

"I'm glad to hear that! Maybe that means we'll get the old Elise back. She's been gone for a long time!"

I hadn't really thought about who I had become until she said that. The "old" Elise was a focused young woman who was determined to meet every goal she set for herself. The person I had become was far from that. I had become a woman who was satisfied with doing just enough to make it. That change also took me away from being happy Elise to being someone who alienated and disrespected people. It was sad, but I hardly even checked on Little Jazzy and my relationship with my parents had gotten so bad, we hardly ever spoke. When we did, I usually said some sly remarks that almost forced them to end the conversation with me. What made it even worse was I didn't feel guilty at all. In fact, I hadn't even really thought about it until Tracy made her statement.

"Tracy, I don't think the old me is ever going to return. She is gone."

Her disappointment was evident.

"Why not?" she asked.

"The old Elise can't make a return because that means the new and improved me wouldn't be able to exist."

The look she had vanished. It was replaced by the biggest smile I had seen directed towards me in a long time.

"That's awesome!" she said.

With that, we got back in the car and went home.

When we got there, I had a heavy heart. I felt I couldn't waste any more time in trying to make amends to everyone I had offended. I walked out of the apartment and made a call to my parents. After I dialed, the phone just rang and rang. It wouldn't have surprised me if they didn't answer me because I didn't really deserve it. As their child, my acts of disobedience and disrespect were uncalled for, and if it took me years of begging to try to get our relationship back on track, then I was more than willing to do that.

"Hello," my father said when he finally answered the phone.

"Hey dad! How are you?"

"I'm okay. How are you?"

He had almost no emotion attached to his words.

"I'm good, dad. It's been a while since I've talked to you. I just wanted to apologize to you and mom for how I've been over the last few years. Mentally, I have not been in a very good space. I have lashed out on you and most of the people in my life who care for me. I just didn't know how to deal with life anymore."

"Elise, I appreciate you saying that and it sounds good, but I don't know if I believe you just changed out of the blue."

That was the first time in my life I poured my heart out to my father and he didn't believe me. It hurt, but I knew he wasn't actually saying anything to intentionally make me feel bad. I could tell his words came from an honest place. Yes, it hurt me to hear what he was saying, but I was sure I had hurt him and my mother. I had to deal with their pain just as I hoped they would be willing to do. I wanted us to all heal.

"I know it may sound crazy, but I finally smartened up and cleared a path for God to make a way back into my life."

When I said that, his tone changed.

"Really? How?"

I explained that I had gone to church and the message felt like it was directed at me. He was happy to hear that and when I told him I got saved, he was absolutely ecstatic.

"Elise, that's great! When it's all said and done, your mother and I just want our Lisey-poo back!"

"She's making a comeback," I said, laughing.

And that was how that conversation ended, but it was only the first call in my "apology tour." The next call was with Little Jazzy, which was far more difficult than I thought it would be.

When I called, she answered the phone, but she didn't say anything at first. Her silence made me almost want to hang up.

"Hey, Jazz! How are you?"

"I'm okay, Miss Elise. How are you?"

The excitement she normally had when I spoke to her was nowhere to be found. She was not disrespectful, but it seemed like she was just tolerating me long enough for the phone call to be over with.

"I'm good. I'm calling because I want to apologize. I haven't been the friend or mentor you've deserved. I haven't kept my promise to you or your mother. I haven't helped nurture your career over the past few years. My focus on life and the lives of those I love was compromised. I was in so much pain I lacked clarity. I'm sorry! I know I've hurt you, but I'd like to ask for your forgiveness."

"Miss Elise, I don't know if hurt is even the right word for me. Over the years, you've built up a level of trust with me that, at times, was even greater than it was with my mother. It was never a question how much I looked up to you and you just acted like none of that mattered. How could you do that to me?"

She really wasn't the little girl I used to know. She was speaking to me more like an adult, than like the child I expected. The statements she made, and the questions she asked, made things more difficult. I wanted to avoid responding to it, but that would have defeated the purpose of me calling.

"Jazz, to be honest with you, I didn't know things I did got to you like that. I never meant to hurt you. I just kept losing people who I cared for and I wasn't strong enough to handle it by myself."

"I can understand that, but Miss Elise, why did you feel you have to handling by yourself? You didn't. I know your parents were there for you. I used to envy your relationship with them because my life wasn't like that. And you know Mrs. Mears would've done anything in the world for you. She loves you and she always made that clear. Even while you were in LA, she talked about you being one of her favorites. On top of that, I know you have friends, so how in the world could you feel like you were alone?"

"I was lost, Jazz. That's it. I wasn't talking to God and because of that, the devil was able to easily influence me. He told me that in my darkest moments, nobody would be able to help me. I tried to fight it off, but eventually I started to believe the lies that were being told to me."

"So how is it different now?" she asked.

"God was given his proper position back. So, now things are going to get back to how they are supposed to be. Today, I recommitted my life to God and I know things are going to change."

"That's good and I hope things stay that way. Let me ask you something: how has dance played a role in everything? Do you still care about that, or was it something you let go of, too?"

"That's a good question. I wouldn't say I let it go, but it is something I really haven't dealt with in a few years. I still love it, but just like the people I love, the last few years have caused me to distance myself."

I could tell she got a little upset about my answer and what she said made it clear.

"That's a great answer for someone who doesn't know you, but I don't really want to hear one of those perfect little answers. What's up with you? I know who you were, but who are you now?"

I had a very difficult time speaking to her. Unlike my father, she didn't hold anything back. She also didn't seem ready to say she forgave me. I understood and I was prepared to prove myself to everyone I had let down. She wanted to know who I was. I had to be honest with her and tell her that I didn't really know. All I knew was that I needed to completely get rid of the version of myself that I had been for the past few years. That's what I expressed to her.

"As for ballet, the past few years were different. I don't even know how much I thought about dancing. I left LA without giving notice to anyone. I didn't go to any recitals or performances. I didn't even make myself practice. I just left it alone."

It was necessary for me to share that with her. She seemed to appreciate that as much (if not more) than anything else I said during our talk. When we were done, I felt better because I had expressed myself honestly. I also appreciated the talk because her approach made me reflect even more on how my actions impacted everyone. I've always heard the phrase "hurt people hurt people". I thought I understood what it meant, but speaking with Jasmine really opened my eyes to see how much truth was in that statement.

After Jasmine, I spoke to others I had hurt. I was open to all of the reactions that came my way. Some people reacted harshly or rejected me, while others were very accepting of my apology and they were very forgiving. Every response and reaction was genuine. Everything, good or bad, was earned by my actions.

I spent the next few days thinking. I thought about my life, my family, and my friends. I thought about everyone I lost and what they meant to me. I also thought about how much it hurt me that I hadn't even talked to my favorite cousin since I lost my aunt. I thought about my sister and how she cared so much about everyone even though she was so young. She would forever be in my heart and I knew she would love me forever, but I also knew she had to be disappointed in who I was for almost three years.

That thought let me know I had more apologies to do. So, one day, I went to the park and sat in an area away from everyone. I aimed my head towards the sky and I apologized to my sister, Hamilton, and to God. I spoke to them for two hours and I felt infinitely better. Even though there wasn't really anyone physically in my presence, I felt like they were sitting on that bench. Talking to them also made me think more about ballet.

I had very clearly heard God, Jasmine, and Hamilton each say something to me about dance. Hamilton told me he wanted me to live up to my potential and quit using him as an excuse. Jasmine wondered when I got so weak and became a quitter. She reminded me that we were not raised that way. If that weren't enough, God asked me a simple question that really made me re-evaluate things:

"What's the point of me giving you talent if you've decided you're not going to use it?"

Hearing those things from them made me finally want to work my way back into dancing, but it took me a few more days to think of what I was going to do to work off the "dance rust." Then, one day I felt obligated to dance. Strangely enough, it was on a day when ballet was not on the forefront of my mind.

It was a rainy day and I woke up thinking it was like any other day. I found out I was wrong when Tracy told me one of my favorite artists, Prince, had passed.

"You can't be serious! That doesn't even seem possible. What happened?" I asked.

"They don't have the details yet, but they found his body..."

I didn't need more information. The fact of the matter was, one of the people I grew up listening to would never be heard from again. He was a musical genius and people knew him all over the world. I didn't know him personally, but it felt like I did. The crazy thing is, we sometimes forget celebrities are just humans because of the lives they live. It is only in death we're reminded about their mortality and how similar we all really are.

Tracy and I spoke about his music and what our favorite songs were. We were smiling like crazy as we had a very friendly debate over his top five songs. As we were doing that, Mo came into the room.

"Who is this Prince y'all are talking about? I've never heard of him."

I looked at Tracy as she put her hands on her head and acted as though she was fainting.

"I have totally failed you as a mother, Mo. We have to change this immediately!"

She went to the music store on her phone and bought a collection of Prince's greatest hits. Once it had downloaded, she connected the phone to a small pair of speakers she had nearby.

"Are you listening, Mo?"

"Yes, ma'am."

As soon as she turned on the music, Tracy and I look at each other again and reacted like old people did when they heard something they haven't heard in a while.

"That… is… my song!" we both said in unison.

We started dancing. I went over to Mo and made him dance with us. There was no way we were going to leave him out.

At first he acted like he didn't want to join us, but right after hearing those crazy guitar riffs for a few seconds, the rhythm grabbed ahold of him as well. Even though I wasn't being serious, it was the first time (in a long time) I had danced. Even though I was dealing with yet another death, I felt happy. The music was forcing us to celebrate life and that was what I should have been doing with all of the other people I lost over the years.

"Keep the music playing, Tracy! I have to find something," I told her as I started digging through my bags.

I wasn't exactly sure what I was looking for, but when I stumbled upon my purple bandanna, I knew my search was over. I wrapped the bandanna around my head. The color purple was almost owned by Prince, so it made me feel closer to him. As the music played, I opened the door and stood in the doorway. It was still raining, but for some reason, I wanted to go outside and dance.

"I have to do it, Tracy," I said as I pointed outside.

Without fully explaining what I meant, she already knew. She turned up the music and then, I tied my bandanna and went outside. I don't know why, but my body made me do ballet moves I hadn't done in years. Was I rusty? A little, but it still felt great!

The more I danced, the more of an audience I started to get. It felt just like old times and it inspired me to keep going. The rain continued to pour down, but it felt like it was washing away my troubles. It felt like it was cleansing me of my pain. I kept dancing until the music quit playing.

"Thank you, Tracy. I really needed that," I said as I remained outside. She could tell I needed to be alone for a moment. So, she gave me a thumbs-up salute and more time to myself.

I closed the door to the apartment that had remained open, mainly so I could hear the music. Once the door was closed, I stared at all the other apartments in the complex. I thought about the residents and the things they had gone through in their own lives. I was sure I wasn't the only one who had dealt with tragedies, but I wondered if everyone else let the negative aspects consume them the way I had. As I thought, once again I heard God talk to me:

"It's time to snap out of it! It's time to get back to work!"

And that was it. That was all I needed to hear.

During my dance, I cried tears of sadness and joy. They mixed in with the rain and it really made me feel good. I wiped my face before I cautiously walked back inside. When I did, I saw Tracy had put some towels by the door for me to dry off. Once I was dry, I sat on the couch and contacted Mrs. Mears. God told me it was time to get back to work and I didn't want to waste any time doing so.

When she answered the phone, I got right to the point and asked if it would be possible for me to return. As I asked, I almost expected her to tell me no, but she didn't. She told me I hurt a lot of people with my actions, including her, but she said she was not in a position to be unforgiving. She said she was willing to give me a chance to get back into dancing, but things wouldn't be like they were for me before I let everyone down.

I apologized to her as well. Although her response wasn't quite what I was expecting, I was okay with it. I was back to being the Elise who was willing to put in work to get what she wanted and I made that very clear to Mrs. Mears. She sounded happy I seemed to be getting closer to whom she knew. When she was about to hang up the phone, she didn't even say goodbye. Instead, she told me, "Welcome back." It did my heart well to hear that.

The next day, after I got off of my shift at a local store (that I had just recently gotten), I headed right over to the studio. I didn't know who would be there, or if I would even be allowed to go in and practice, but I had to try. When I entered, I saw a lot of instructors and students I had never seen before. I also was surprised that I didn't see Natalie, Mrs. Mears' longtime assistant. I didn't really think about it much, though. When someone asked me what I was doing there, I told them I was hoping to practice.

"Who are you?" they asked, very aggressively.

"My name is Elise Morgan."

They stopped in their tracks and they looked me up and down.

"Oh, so you're the big shot?"

"No, I'm definitely not a big shot. I'm just someone who desperately needs to practice," I told her.

She looked at me as if she didn't believe a word I was saying, but she pointed to a nearby room and told me I could practice in there.

It was certainly not like the main rehearsal hall I was used to, but I didn't complain. Over the next few weeks, that room became my best friend. I ended up quitting my job and spending more time with that room than I did with anybody else. Every day I was able to go there, I practiced harder than I had the time before. I practiced as if I were going to perform the most important show of my life. In reality, I wasn't was specifically working on anything. I was just trying my best to make up for the time I had squandered away.

As my relationship with ballet improved, so did my relationships with the people I had treated improperly. It was a very welcome change, especially when I saw how things were improving with my parents. During my most recent visit with them, my mother asked me a few questions that really made me think.

"Elise, how are you feeling about life these days?" she asked.

"Life is still hard, but I feel good about it."

"What about ballet? Do you hate it, like it, or love it?"

"As much as I used to love ballet, I can honestly say I love it more than I ever have before. I think I can appreciate it more."

"That's good to hear. In fact, that's what I was hoping you would say. I've noticed how you've been recently. It seems like you're actually a much stronger person than you were before, and that's saying a lot. I've been thinking about something."

"What's up, mom?"

"This may seem like a stupid question, but do you feel like you've gone through a lot in your life?"

She was right, it did seem like a stupid question, but I knew there had to be a reason she asked. Instead of a disrespectful answer, I simply answered truthfully.

"Yes, ma'am. I've been through a lot."

She stood near me with her hand on my shoulder as I sat down trying to figure out where this talk was going.

"Off the top of your head, what are some of the things you've had to deal with?" she asked.

"Low self-esteem, death, racism, hatred, wanting to quit ballet, and moments where I didn't even want to live anymore."

She knew about some the things, but hearing there were times when I wanted to die may have been something she was unaware of. She seemed to be fighting back tears and she continued:

"Through all of that, you're still here! I've learned something, though. Life isn't just about when we can make it through, but what we can help others make it through. I think your experiences can really help someone else. Somewhere there are little girls who need to learn about you and your story. They probably think nobody understands them. You can help them see they can persevere through the most terrible times they can ever imagine."

I listened as my mother spoke. At first, it seemed like she wanted me to write a book or something. I did not want to do that at all, but I still didn't say anything. She continued to talk and she told me she thought it would be a wonderful testimony to the power of God if I told my life story through dance. Immediately, I got excited. Having a ballet tell my story could definitely help someone out, especially other dancers who have had to deal with any of the things I had to.

We talked for a long time, not about if I wanted to move forward, but how and when we were going to move forward. That day, we discussed every possibility of how we could get things done. Finally, we decided we needed to stop overthinking the situation and go after the most simplistic solution. What was that? Well, we decided to ask Mrs. Mears if she and the rest of the school would help me tell my story.

A few days later, I approached Mrs. Mears about it and she absolutely loved the idea. She told me to write a basic outline of the story and she would be able to take it from there. That's exactly what I did. About three days later, I was handing over an outline of how I thought the ballet of my life should go. She looked it over in great detail. She was there for most of the times I had written about, but she said actually seeing everything gave her a greater appreciation that I was able to keep moving forward (in spite of some major setbacks).

I wasn't sure how things were really going to play out, but I totally trusted whatever vision Mrs. Mears would have for the project. It didn't take long for my mentor to justify the high level of trust I had for her. From a simple five-page outline, she created an entire performance. She already had very detailed notes about choreography and who was going to play certain roles. A few main characters were missing, though.

"What you've created is amazing, Mrs. Mears, but I don't see who will be playing you. You have to be a part of this!"
She smiled.

"I was hoping you'd notice that. I didn't have anything written down because I wanted to ask you about that in person."

"Okay, what's up?"

"I wanted to know if you would be willing to play me."

"Are you serious? I would be honored to play you, but I'm just now getting back into this and I'm not really sure I'll be able to do a good enough job."

"Just as you have trusted me to get this together, I trust you to be Mrs. Mears," she said very confidently.

I wanted to make more excuses why I couldn't do it, but she obviously believed in me and I didn't want to let her down (again).

"Okay! If you think I can do it, I'll do it!"

"That's great news! Now you may have noticed there's nobody here to play you."

"Yeah... I kinda noticed that," I said somewhat smugly as we both started laughing.

"Well, I was thinking, and the best choice became so obvious, I almost felt dumb for not thinking of her sooner."

"Okay, now I'm really intrigued. Who do you have in mind?"
She didn't hesitate at all before she answered me.

"Jasmine!"

Just like Mrs. Mears, I got upset at myself for not thinking about her at first, but once I did, I got excited about the potential of how great the performance could be. I always thought Jasmine was a better dancer than I was at her age. So, to have her be a part of the ballet based on what I had gone through in my life would be a wonderful thing, but we weren't the same as we were before.

"Do you think she'll even do it? I asked humbly.

"Why wouldn't she? Do you think because you two had a falling out, she wouldn't want to do this?"

"Actually... yeah."

"That girl loves you like you were actually a member of her family. If you sit down and talk to her, I'm sure she'll want to participate."

Even though I wasn't one hundred percent sold on Jasmine going along with it, I put the fear of rejection aside so I could ask her to participate. It was not an easy conversation at all. She questioned why I wanted to do a story of my life in ballet form. I explained that I wanted little girls to see you should never give up on your goals. I told her, no matter how many times you fall, you have to find a way to get back up. I told her there's power in ambition and there's power in faith.

"That sounds good, but do you actually mean it, or is it just talk?" she asked.

The level of trust I had established with her over the years still was nowhere near where it once was. Every time I talked to her, her words were reminders of how badly I really damaged what had been built over the years. Her mother told me she had been hurt by many people in her life who she cared about. I had to deal with the fact I had become one of those people. If I have to be on "damage control" with her for the rest of my life, I would be willing to do that with her and everybody else.

"I really mean it, Jazzy. I had some good moments, but I have also had plenty of bad ones. Some of the things that happened were absolutely my fault, but not everything was. I'm at the point now where I need to share my life experiences because I know they can help others.

"Somewhere out there there's a little girl who wants to be a ballerina. She's afraid to try because somebody has convinced her she's not pretty enough, or too short, or too skinny, or maybe they told her she can't do it because she's the wrong color. Don't you think we owe it to her to show her she has no reason to be afraid to follow her dreams?"

She sighed heavily as if she hated that I made some valid points.

"Yeah, we owe it to her. They told me I couldn't dance because I was poor and because I'm black and I cried so much because of it. How can people intentionally be so hurtful to a kid?"

"Maybe when they were a child, someone told them they couldn't reach their dreams and they just decided to spread that negativity to everyone they could. At some point, someone has to break the cycle."

"You know what? You're right! I need to be a part of this. Please tell me all you can. I need to make this the best performance of my life! You never know who this may end up inspiring."

And just like that, she was on-board. She did everything very seriously, too. Every free moment she had, she was practicing. She watched the way I moved so she could perform the way I would, but she took it even further than that. She read over the outline several times. She had questions about everything, but she mainly wanted to know how things actually made me feel. She asked what thoughts went through my head when I had to deal with racism. I responded honestly and openly even though it didn't feel very good to relive those moments. Then, she asked me something I wasn't quite prepared for:

"How did everything change when your sister died? How was it different than when you lost Hamilton?"

It took me a while to gather my thoughts after that. Those questions literally left me speechless for a few minutes.

"My sister meant the world to me. When she died, it felt like the world ended. I miss her smile and hearing her giggle every day. And when I found out Hamilton was gone, I thought the ability to love was gone, too. His death caused me to hit my lowest point. That's when I really didn't care about anything anymore."

I put my head down. Soon after, I fell to the floor. I didn't cry because at that moment, I didn't even have the energy to.

"I'm sorry, Miss Elise. Maybe I went too far. I can't even pretend like I asked that stuff just to learn how you were feeling. I think I may have done it to hurt you. I'm sorry. I shouldn't have done that."

I pulled myself together just enough to sit up.

"Maybe I deserved it, Jazzy. It's okay. Could you come here, though?" I requested.

She sat down on the floor with me. When she did, I put my arms around her and hugged her. For moment, it was like nothing had ever gone wrong and I had my friend Little Jazzy back.

"Are we even now? Can you finally forgive me for real?"

"Yes, ma'am. We're even and I forgive you, Miss Elise." That moment changed things for us in a very positive way. We worked together like a well-oiled machine over the next few weeks as I prepared to portray my mentor and Jasmine prepared to play hers. It felt like old times again and I was incredibly grateful for it all. Sometimes when we practiced, Mrs. Mears would be there to oversee how things were going. When that happened, it made me very emotional because it was almost like three generations of dancers coming together for a common goal.

As time went by, I talked more to my mother about the project she basically was responsible for. She had a great sense of pride about it, but it wasn't because she initiated it. She said she was incredibly happy because I was finally getting back to using the skills God gave me.

"Elise, I've been waiting a long time to see you make your comeback to ballet. I'm so happy for you!"

"Thanks, mom. I didn't know if I was ready, but it feels really good to be dancing again. I have to admit something, though. Working on this project about my life is a bit surreal. I mean, who am I to have an entire ballet? I'm not a rich celebrity or anything. I'm just a regular twenty-five year old."

"You may not be a rich celebrity, but you are anything but regular. I guarantee when people learn about you, you will inspire them in ways you can't even imagine."

"Thank you, mom."

We talked for a while and it felt good. She reminded me of how shy I was the first day I went to class. She said she was very proud of how far I had come, but she said I still had a long way to go to meet my potential.

"Can you imagine how different things would've been if your sister would've never bought you that tutu for your birthday?" she asked.

That question was asked often by mother or me over the years.

"No! I can't imagine that! I still think it's crazy that she even knew I wanted to dance. I didn't even talk about it."

"You didn't talk about it, but you didn't have to. Your sister was very observant. She paid attention to all of us, but she always wanted to make sure her big sister was happy. I'm not sure if you're aware or not, but she practically begged every day to get that tutu. She always used to say her sister wanted one of those pretty 'dancing dresses.' If you didn't get that tutu, we would've never heard the end of it."

"Yeah, you're probably right about that. She was very persistent."

"She learned about persistence from you, Elise. I mean, look at you. Those who don't know just see another pretty exterior and they'll think that's all you are. It takes way more than a pretty face to endure everything you have. You didn't really tell us but I've learned how racist the world of ballet can be. I know the so-called purists don't want to see people of color being involved. They want to keep their traditions the way they are and the majority of the people won't embrace change. You have dealt with that while following your passion. I don't know if I would've been able to handle that. Outside of everything else, do you realize that just because you have stuck with ballet, you're helping to blaze the trail for other little girls? See, if people my age wanted to be dancers, we didn't have many people out there to try to be like. If we would've heard we couldn't be dancers based on how we look, we would've believed it. Many of us would have given up. Your persistence shows everybody what's possible."

It was a lot of responsibility, but my mother just reminded me of what I had been carrying for years. It made the upcoming performance even more important than it already was. Speaking with her let me know we had to get everything right. Not only would everyone involved need to dance like they had never danced before, but I would have to do everything in my power to make sure all of the behind-the-scenes stuff was taken care of. I would have to make sure the auditorium would be set up properly and I had to make sure the entire city knew about. That meant I would have to do a lot of promoting. When I discussed that with my mother, she agreed with me, but she asked me a very important question.

"I know you're already thinking about how you're going to market this, but do you even know what you're going to call it?"

Talk about feeling like an idiot! I was thinking about everything, but somehow I forgot to even think about a fitting title. I couldn't just attach some random name to it because it meant far too much to me for that. Whatever this performance would be called, hopefully it would stick in the minds of everyone who would see it. Hopefully, the name would be good enough to help a little girl who would one day be looking adversity right in the eyes know she can not only stand with confidence, but walk forward in victory. That was the type of name I wanted.

"I don't know what to call it, but I promise when I hear it, there will be no doubt!"

My mother could tell by my words and my tone how serious the title was to me.

"Okay, let's conquer this now, Elise. Let's find this title," my mother told me.

So we started to brainstorm right then and there. We were both determined to complete our goal that day. We sat at the kitchen table and started throwing out any suggestion, question, and name we thought may help us out, but nothing felt right. I was starting to get frustrated and I really didn't want to give up, but the names we were coming up with were not very good. We had titles like "Elise's Journey," "The Austin Ballerina", and several others that just didn't fit what we were searching for.

"Elise, what is one of the main points you want to get across with this ballet?" my mother asked, hoping to stir something inside my mind.

"They just have to keep going! My worst years were when I stopped doing what I loved to do."

"Okay, we need a title to convey that message."

That was when it finally hit me.

"Mom, when Jazzy and daddy were in the hospital, I asked you how I can be spiritually strong like you. Do you remember what you told me?"

I gave her a moment to think, but her smirk let me know I had stumped her.

"I think you may have to tell me what I said to you."

"Well, you told me we all have to dance while we're broken. That's it, mom!"

"I'm still confused. You're gonna have to explain it a little more, Elise."

"Okay, no problem! Life has knocked me down and stepped on me, but God let me keep going. Over the years, especially the last few years, I've been broken, but guess what? In spite of that, I am mentally, spiritually, and literally dancing again. This performance is about a broken woman who is still able to dance. That's why it has to be called 'Dance of the Broken'."

My mother stood up and gave me a round of applause as tears fell from her eyes.

"That's brilliant! You hit the nail right on the head."

Hearing her say that was like giving me the green light to tell everybody about it. After that, everywhere I went I was talking about the upcoming performance. When talking wasn't enough, I even handed out flyers; and even though I'm not into social media, I made a Twitter account using the name @danceOTbroken. Sadly, I had to put "OT" instead of having the words "of the" because the name would have been too long. It was the minor setback, but I was still able to get the word out to even more people about the ballet.

Every day, every spare moment I had went to "Dance of the Broken." I was getting more and more excited, which made me feel like I had to continue working harder than I even thought was possible.

Even though I didn't have a major role in the performance, I had to make sure I did all I could to make it be the best it could be. I was also able to start working with Jasmine on a consistent basis, which made the whole experience even greater. One day while we were practicing, Jasmine stopped in the middle of her warm-up to ask me a question.

"Miss Elise, I know we've talked about before, but can you tell me why you and Mrs. Mears are really doing this performance?"

I wanted to tell her everything I had already told her and everybody else, but I didn't think it was needed. Instead, I just gave her a simple answer.

"Little girls need to know they can be anything they want to be. They need to see women in a positive light, instead of what they see most of the time. And…I want them to see life won't be easy, but they have the strength to push through."

She nodded her head.

"Okay, let's get back to work," she said.

That's exactly what we did. Surprisingly, after we'd been practicing for about an hour, Mrs. Mears entered the small room we were in.

"'I know you two are very busy, but can I have a few minutes of your time?" She asked.

It was amazing how different she had become over the years. When I first started taking classes, she had a larger-than-life personality. She was boisterous, in-your-face, and very demanding. Back then, she would tell you what she wanted from you, whether you liked it or not. She was no longer that person. She was a much kinder instructor who showed her love for her students much more openly than she did when I was younger. Even with the changing personality, the respect level we had for her never changed. When she wanted to talk to you, you pretty much stopped everything you were doing to hear whatever it was she had to say.

"Of course, Mrs. Mears. What's up?" I asked.

She motioned for us to have a seat in the chairs that were in the back of the room. Jasmine and I looked at each other as we did so because we knew it had to be something serious.

"How's the show preparation going?"

"It's going well. I'm so ready for the show to happen!"

"That's good because we only have a week left."

"Yup! We'll be ready!" Jasmine chimed in.

"Do you two realize how important this show is? Your story is relatable, Elise, that's why it's going to inspire so many people. And with Miss Jasmine playing the younger version of you, this show has no choice but to be a hit!"

"I agree!"

"Well, let me go ahead and get to the point. Ballet has always been a part of my life and in some way or another, it always will be. With that being said, things are about to change around here."

I couldn't tell what she was trying to tell us, but it didn't feel good. I remained quiet, though. I didn't want to miss any part of what she was trying to say.

"As much as I hate to admit it, after decades of dancing, my body isn't able to do what it once could. I can't move the way I'd like and my energy isn't where I want it to be, either," she said.

"So what are you saying, Mrs. Mears?" Jasmine asked.

It was the same question I had in my mind, so I eagerly awaited her answer. She took a deep breath. She started to talk, but she stopped herself almost immediately. She took another deep breath before she finally continued.

"I'm saying... well... after this performance, I'm officially going to retire. This show will be it for me."

I heard what she said, but it was incredibly difficult for me to fully process it. I sat very still for a moment.

"This has to be some kind of joke, right?" I asked.

"No, Elise, it's not. There comes a time in everyone's life when we have to end one chapter so we can go to the next. It's time for me to move on."

"But… what are we supposed to do? What's gonna happen to the school?" Jasmine asked.

"That's a good question, but it has a fairly simple answer. It's time for me to pass the baton so someone else can run it. If she'll accept it, I'd like to offer the job of director to you, Elise."

My first thought was to tell her I couldn't do it. It was a lot of responsibility and I really wasn't sure if I was ready for that, but obviously Mrs. Mears was. Plus, I would almost be a fraud if I was about to put on a show to inspire girls to press on in spite of obstacles and fear the challenge of being a leader.

"Yes, ma'am, I would be honored to take on that role!"

"That's what I was hoping for. Don't worry about that now, though. We'll talk more about that later. For now, just get back to work and make show the best thing we've ever had anything to do with. Is that understood, ladies?"

"Yes, ma'am!" we said together.

As soon as that was done, Mrs. Mears left the room without saying another word. When she was gone, Jasmine walked over and gave me a hug.

"I knew it was only a matter of time. You have earned it and I'm very, very happy for you."

"I really appreciate it. I'm still in shock, though."

"Don't be shocked, Miss Elise. You've worked hard to get to this position!"

We celebrated for a few seconds more before we went back to work.

After Mrs. Mears gave us the news, we only had a small amount of time left to get ready. We didn't waste any of that time. Not only were Jasmine and I focused, but so was everyone else involved. I couldn't help but be happy. We always had practices with everybody, but the closer the show got, the more we all practiced together. We all were extremely excited and that showed more each day. I heard about each of them getting their friends and families to buy tickets and it made me very proud, but it also made me feel like I hadn't quite done enough.

Each night when I got home, I searched through my phone to find contacts of those people I may not have spoken to in a while, or those who I had just neglected to tell about the show. One night, I saw Rachel's name and I just stared at her info. I had spoken to her on more than one occasion since I left LA, but for some reason I was debating if I needed to call her about the show or not. Finally, I stopped battling and just made the call.

In the beginning of the call, we dealt with a lot of awkward moments, but after about five minutes, we were speaking (and laughing) like best friends. I told her about the show and she genuinely sounded happy for me. She asked me about the details of when and where it was. She told me she would love to attend, but didn't really think it was possible for her to be able to pay for the flight. I wasn't expecting her to be able to attend; I just wanted her to know that I was finally making progress again. I needed her to know I finally made it out of the state of sadness I was in.

We talked for a while and exchanged updates on our lives. I was glad to hear she was still doing ballet, but I was surprised when she told me she was leaving LA.

"Why? Is everything okay?" I asked.

"It's more than okay, Elise. I don't know how it happened, but I have an opportunity to dance with a wonderful new troupe in New York!"

"Are you serious?"

"Yep! It was founded by some of the best dancers from all over the world. Somehow they found me and asked if I wanted to be on the ground floor of something wonderful. I couldn't turn it down. I think it's gonna be great!"

"Of course it will! I'm so happy for you, Rachel!"

"Thank you, Elise. I'm happy for you, too. Elise, it made me feel bad when you decided not to come back here, but I understood the reasons. When I heard you were no longer dancing, that actually hurt. You have too much talent to ever give up ballet."

"I appreciate that and trust me, I don't see myself ever stepping away from dance again. Plus, I just got the job as director of the school I've been going to all of my life."

I didn't anticipate me telling her about the job because I hadn't even told my parents. Other than me, the only people who knew about it were Mrs. Mears, Jasmine, and God. I planned on keeping it to myself for a while, but for some reason I felt I needed to tell her.

"Elise, that is amazing! Only you could leave one of the top troupes in Los Angeles, go back to Austin, quit ballet altogether for like three years— return, get a show about your life, and be named director of the dance school you learned in, all by the age of twenty-five! Only you can do that, Elise!"

"Dang, Rachel! When you say it like that, it really seems like I've done a lot"

"Well, duh! It seems like you've done a lot because you have!"

I was doing what most of us end up doing; I was downplaying my own accomplishments. I couldn't even say I wasn't doing it on purpose because I was. I laughed as we talked about the things I had done, but truthfully, I was ashamed. There were so many people who had given their entire lives to ballet, taken no time off, and were still struggling to find an entry into a decent dance troupe. I disrespected those people by taking all of those years off and then coming back as if I had never left. I didn't deserve any of the stuff I was getting, so why was I getting it?

The longer the conversation went on, the more I was questioning everything. When it ended, I went to God to get some clarification. Since I was still living with Tracy and Mo and didn't have my own space, having personal conversations with God was a little difficult at times. So, like I had many times before, I found it necessary to leave the apartment. I walked to the end of the street and closed my eyes.

"God, I'm grateful for everything you're doing for me, but I don't deserve these opportunities, so why am I getting them?"

Whenever I spoke to God, He would either give me so many signs that I would be almost forced to understand what He was saying, or He would answer me so clearly I would no longer have any questions. During that talk, He certainly spoke very clearly.

"You are getting these opportunities because I said you're supposed to have them!"

When I heard that, everything was crystal clear. When God has something planned for us, we can't even stop it.

With a better understanding of why things were happening, I was able to focus on everything I needed to do. As the countdown to the show continued to move towards zero, the nervous energy I thought I would have was non-existent. My days were spent perfecting the show while also learning about all of the duties I would be taking on with my new job. The show would officially be the start of the next phase of my life and I was ready to get to it.

I was literally spending all of my time either at the school, my parent's house, Tracy's house, or at church. I didn't want to be any place that wouldn't help me prepare. Sundays and Wednesdays were spent at church. It was necessary for me to start off my week by hearing the word and to get a refresher course during the middle of the week. I was pretty much only at Tracy's house to sleep and I was at my parent's house when I wanted (and needed) to be around them. The night before the show, I was with them and it was so comforting just to talk.

"Elise, Elise, Elise. I'm so proud of you, baby!" my father said.

"Yeah, the show tomorrow has been in the making since you were six. Your passion and pain will be on display and we can't wait," my mother added.

"Mom, dad... all my life I just wanted to make you proud. During the past few years, I know I wasn't doing that. I was just so ready to give up. I'm sorry!"

"We appreciate the apology, but it's no longer necessary. We have already forgiven you, but let me ask you something."

"Yeah, dad. What do you want to ask?"

"Do you know why we decided to kick you out when you were seemingly at your lowest point?"

"You did it because I wasn't doing anything. You did it because I was content with sitting around doing nothing."

"That's part of it, but that's not it. See, we knew the strength that was in you. It may have seemed like we were punishing you because you were weak, but if we would have continued to enable that weakness, you wouldn't have been able to find your strength again. We couldn't have that."

"But didn't you fear things might not go well?"

"Do you remember when you wondered how I was able to be strong spiritually and always seem to have faith?" mom asked.

"Yeah, I remember."

"In order to have strong faith, you have to put it into practice. When we put you out, that's what we were doing. We had faith God would bring you back better than ever. We just had to be obedient and follow His commands."

My mother's explanation removed some pain I probably would have never admitted existed. Being around them made me feel so secure and so happy.

"I know we just finished talking about when you kicked me out, but would you two mind if I spent the night here?"
We all started laughing.

"You can stay, but only for the night, okay?" dad replied.

"Yes, dad, it'll only be for tonight. I promise."

The laughter and great conversation continued, but not for much longer. Soon, their eyelids started to get heavy and they began to have trouble staying awake. They tried their best, though. It was like watching little kids who didn't want to go to sleep because they would miss their favorite cartoon. It was so cute!

I convinced them to get their rest and when they finally went to bed, I did the same thing. That night, as I stayed in my childhood bed again, I had the best sleep I had in a long time. When I got up the next day, I jumped out of the bed. The day I had been waiting on had finally arrived. I planned on spending the entire day practicing, but as I moved about the house that morning, I found out things weren't quite going to go as planned.

My mother was up early as usual, making a great breakfast. When she finished, she called my father to the table as I sat down. I heard my father rumbling around in the room. I had no idea how he was getting himself into his chair, but when I got up to go help, my mother motioned for me to sit down. She told me he could do it. Sure enough, he could and we were soon eating breakfast like a family again. It was cool to sit, talk, and eat with the people who raised me. The moment was made even cooler when I realized my mother made my pancakes in the shape of a ballerina. She loved to make special pancakes and I loved the fact that she did!

"This is awesome, mom!"

"Thanks, Elise. You deserve it!"

"Whoa! Your mother may have made them, but the idea came from this guy!" he said, smiling and pointing at himself.

"Well, that's true," mom said.

"Thank you, too, dad," I said as I got up and gave them both a kiss on their cheeks.

"I know you have an important event later on, but do you think you can spend the day with us, just hanging out?" mom asked.

It was unexpected, but it was certainly one of those offers I couldn't refuse. So, after breakfast, we spent a large portion of the day just being together. We went to see a movie, went shopping, and had some lunch. Everything we did as a family just relaxed me and made me even more ready for the show. As it grew closer to time for our group to have a final walkthrough, I thanked my parents for everything they had done for me and I told them I loved them. We went back home just long enough for me to get my car so I could go to the auditorium where the show would take place.

When I got there, cars were already in the parking lot. It was good to see the parents had already brought their kids. Before I went around the side doors where all of the performers entered, I was stopped in my tracks by what I saw at the front. I knew we were going to have signs, but I didn't expect to see a huge banner with "Dance of the Broken" on it. Sure, in reality, it was just a simple sign with a few words on it, but it meant so much to me. Those four words represented being triumphant when situations seemed like they would remain tragic. In a way, the show was going to be about my story. In other ways, it was the universal story of all little girls who have had to prove themselves by overcoming adversity.

I stared at the sign some more, then I turned and looked at all of the cars in the parking lot again. All of those cars represented at least one person who believed in the project we were about to put on. A lot of thoughts went through my head as I looked around and the collection of them made me cry (again). These tears were different, though. Normally my tears evoked some level of embarrassment, which made me quickly wipe them away and pretend they never were there. The tears I cried then were like medals of honor. They carried a certain level of pride. Their existence meant I had gone through something, but I was still standing and that was something I wanted everyone to see.

By the time I entered the building, I almost had that "ugly cry" going, but I was able to maintain my composure (at least a little bit). All of the parents and students saw me crying. Without even knowing why I had tears coming out of my eyes, many of them started to cry right along with me.

"Can I have everyone's attention, please?" I asked.

The people all gathered together, anticipating what I had to say.

"Today is important for us and I just want to thank everyone for the sacrifices that have been made to make this happen. There are two people I have to bring the spotlight on: Mrs. Mears, Jasmine... are you two here?"

We all looked around and finally, from two different sides of the room, they walked over towards me.

"Everyone in here is important to me, but these two ladies have pretty much been around for most of what will be portrayed in the ballet tonight. They had a lot to do with the woman I am, and in front of everyone, I just want to tell you I appreciate everything you've done for me. I couldn't have made it here without you and I love you from the bottom of my heart!"

I wanted them to speak to the people, but neither of them wanted to do that. Instead, they both whispered that they loved me too and then they blended back into the crowd.

"Last thing I want to say is I am proud of all of us. Society says this can't happen. Many other ballerinas don't believe we can do what they can do. What they will see tonight is that, not only can we do it, but we can do it better! No longer will we doubt ourselves! We are more than capable of accomplishing our goals! Now let's do this last walkthrough so we can put on a great show!"

Many tears still remained, but a lot more smiles became present. It was wonderful to see those girls start to walk around full of pride and hope. We went through our final "practice" right before a member of the security staff from the auditorium told us we had about forty-five minutes before the show and they would soon be opening the doors for the public to enter. Once we found this out, we started to move a little more frantically to make sure we all had our costumes on and that we were ready to be in our spots.

Within a matter of moments, I started to hear the crowd come into the building. There was no turning back. This was really about to happen. It seemed like every second that passed brought more and more people. Hearing the growing crowd made my adrenaline rush. I ran back to the center of the backstage area. In the loudest possible whisper I could do, I asked if anyone wanted to lead us in a quick prayer.

All of the students looked at each other, but it seemed like nobody was going to volunteer, so I prepared to do it myself when Jasmine finally spoke up.

"Can I say something, Miss Elise?"

"Absolutely!" I said as I stepped back so she could have the floor.

"God, you put us here together for a purpose and we pray that we fulfill that purpose. Yes, we have worked hard to get here, but the honor and praises go to you. God, please bless Mrs. Mears and Miss Elise for showing the rest of us how to be leaders. We pray we make them proud. We also pray that this show goes well, not just so we can feel good, but also so we can give little girls in the crowd hope that they can do this, too! We thank you God for blessing us with ballet. Our hearts would feel almost empty without it. We will continue to follow you, God and in Jesus' name we pray, amen."

We clapped and hugged each other. Jazzy prayed that they made Mrs. Mears and I proud. I couldn't speak for her, but if she felt anything like what I was feeling, she was already proud.

"Five minutes until showtime," a staff member told us.

"Well, that means it's time for me to go take my seat out there for the first time," Mrs. Mears said.

For the first time since she started taking ballet as a child, she was actually going to be able to sit down and enjoy the show along with the rest of the audience. I gave her a long hug as she left the backstage area. I walked over to Jasmine.

"Well, young lady, it is your time to shine. Are you ready?"

"Yes, ma'am. I promise I won't let you down."

"I know you won't."

I let her have a few seconds alone before she had to take center stage.

I moved over to the curtain and pulled it back just far enough for me to see the faces of the people who were supporting us. It was great to see there were no empty seats. Tracy and Mo were in the crowd. I saw Jasmine's mother near the center and I even noticed Jean there. Seeing them was great, but I got super excited when I saw my parents sitting next to Mrs. Mears in the front. It was like my first show again, except my sister wasn't there. I knew she was still watching me, though. I took solace in that.

My heart was pounding, but I knew we were ready. I smiled because, seemingly out of nowhere, I heard lines from an Eminem song in my head. As if I were actually listening to the radio I heard, "Lose yourself in the moment, you own it, you gotta never let it go... this opportunity comes once in a lifetime..."

And it was true. This type of opportunity was a once-in-a-lifetime thing and we were going to make the most of it. All of the people in the crowd were there to see us, the little girls of color who weren't supposed to be here— at least according to the doubters. Yet here we were. All of the tragedies and hardships had led me to that moment, on that night, in that building with those young women.

My life hadn't been easy by any stretch of the imagination, but I was here. People wanted to see me fall and they did, but they didn't see me stay down. Some people did all they could to stop me. Did they succeed? Well, they had temporary victories, but I won the war.

I once asked Mrs. Mears if she felt all of her struggles and the sacrifices she made for ballet were worth it. She said they were because they helped her to be able to inspire people like me. Now, after my own struggles, I not only understand it, but I agree with it 100%. Without life breaking me down, God really wouldn't have been able to make me dance while I was broken!

"It's showtime!" they said.

Indeed, it is. It's time for all of us to show the world what we are capable of. It's time for every one of us to show the nay-sayers how wrong they are— not by our words, but by our actions. We have been the ones holding ourselves back for too long; it's time to change right now! I know it can be done because this life that God has allowed me to live is proof. Now, if you don't mind... Jasmine, my students and I all have a show to put on!

My name is Elise Morgan. You now know my story, so what's yours?

Thank You

I truly believe I didn't create "Dance of the Broken" because God sent it to me. With that being said, I'd like to keep this very simple.

I thank God for giving me the vision and the ability to complete this project.

I thank my family for believing in me.
I thank my friends for encouraging me.
And I thank you, the reader, for supporting this story.

I truly appreciate everyone because you all have helped me tremendously.

CPSIA information can be obtained
at www.ICGtesting.com
Printed in the USA
BVHW040957290119
538860BV00022B/112/P